KU-215-205

Nora Roberts is the Number One *New York Times* bestselling author of more than 190 novels. With more than 300 million copies of her books in print, and over 150 *New York Times* bestsellers to date, Nora Roberts is indisputably the most celebrated women's fiction writer today.

Visit her website at www.nora-roberts.co.uk

By Nora Roberts

Homeport
The Reef
River's End
Carolina Moon
The Villa
Midnight Bayou
Three Fates
Birthright
Northern Lights
Blue Smoke
Montana Sky
Angels Fall
High Noon
Divine Evil
Tribute
Sanctuary
Black Hills
The Search

Three Sisters Island Trilogy:
Dance Upon the Air
Heaven and Earth
Face the Fire

Chesapeake Bay Quartet:
Sea Swept
Rising Tides
Inner Harbour
Chesapeake Blue

The Key Trilogy:
Key of Light
Key of Knowledge
Key of Valour

In the Garden Trilogy:
Blue Dahlia
Black Rose
Red Lily

The Irish Trilogy:
Jewels of the Sun
Tears of the Moon
Heart of the Sea

The Circle Trilogy:
Morrigan's Cross
Dance of the Gods
Valley of Silence

The Dream Trilogy:
Daring to Dream
Holding the Dream
Finding the Dream

The Sign of Seven Trilogy:
Blood Brothers
The Hollow
The Pagan Stone

As J. D. Robb:

Naked in Death
Glory in Death
Immortal in Death
Rapture in Death
Ceremony in Death
Vengeance in Death
Holiday in Death
Conspiracy in Death
Loyalty in Death
Witness in Death
Judgement in Death
Betrayal in Death
Seduction in Death
Reunion in Death
Purity in Death
Portrait in Death
Imitation in Death
Divided in Death
Visions in Death
Survivor in Death
Origin in Death
Memory in Death
Born in Death
Innocent in Death
Creation in Death
Strangers in Death
Salvation in Death
Promises in Death
Kindred in Death
Fantasy in Death
Indulgence in Death

By Nora Roberts and J. D. Robb

Remember When

Carolina Moon

Nora Roberts

piatkus

PIATKUS

First published in the US in 2000 by G. P. Putnam's Sons
This edition published in Great Britain in 2000 by Piatkus
Reprinted 2000, 2001 (twice), 2002 (twice), 2003, 2004, 2005 (twice),
2006 (twice), 2007, 2009, 2010

A CIP catalogue record for this book
is available from the British Library.

ISBN 978-0-7499-3215-2

Printed in the UK by CPI Mackays, Chatham ME5 8TD

Papers used by Piatkus are natural, renewable and
recyclable products sourced from well-managed forests and certified
in accordance with the rules of the Forest Stewardship Council.

Mixed Sources
Product group from well-managed
forests and other controlled sources
www.fsc.org   Cert no. SGS-COC-004081
© 1996 Forest Stewardship Council

Piatkus
An imprint of
Little, Brown Book Group
100 Victoria Embankment
London EC4Y 0DY

An Hachette UK Company
www.hachette.co.uk

www.piatkus.co.uk

To Ruth Langan and Marianne Willman,
For the past, the present, and the future

*To the friends of my childhood,
blood sisters and confidantes who
helped turn backyards into magic forests*

Tory

To me, fair friend, you never can be old,
For as you were when first your eye I eyed,
Such seems your beauty still.

—William Shakespeare

Chapter One

She woke in the body of a dead friend. She was eight, tall for her age, fragile of bone, delicate of feature. Her hair was the color of corn silk, and slid prettily down her narrow back. Her mother loved to brush it every night, one hundred strokes with the soft-bristled, silver-backed brush that sat on the graceful cherrywood vanity.

The child's body remembered this, felt this, each long, sustained beat with the brush and how it made her imagine herself a cat being petted. How the light slanted over the pin boxes and the bottles of crystal and cobalt, and struck the silver back of the brush as it flashed over her hair.

She remembered the scent of the room, smelled it even now. Gardenia. Always gardenia for Mama.

And in the mirror, by lamplight, she could see the pale oval of her face, so young, so pretty, with those thoughtful blue eyes and smooth skin. So alive.

Her name was Hope.

The windows and French doors were closed because it was high summer. Heat pressed its damp fingers against the glass, but inside the house the air was cool, and her cotton nightgown stayed so crisp it crackled when she moved.

It was the heat she wanted, and the adventure, but she kept those thoughts inside as she kissed Mama good night. A dainty peck against a perfumed cheek.

Mama had the hall runners taken up and rolled into the attic every June. Now the loblolly pine floors with their coating of paste wax felt slick and smooth under the young girl's bare feet as she wandered out, down the hall with its panels of bald cypress and paintings in thick frames of dull gold. Up the sharp, winding curves of the stairs to her father's study.

There her father's scent. Smoke, leather, Old Spice, and bourbon.

She loved this room, with its rounded walls and big, heavy chairs with leather the color of the port her papa sometimes drank after supper. Here the circling shelves were jammed full with books and treasures. She loved the man who sat behind the enormous desk with his cigar and his shot glass and his ledgers.

The love was an ache of the heart in the woman inside the child, a shaft of longing and of envy for that uncomplicated and complete love.

His voice boomed, his arms were strong and his stomach soft as he enveloped her in a hug that was so different from the gentle and restrained good-night kiss from Mama.

There's my princess, going off to the kingdom of dreams.

What will I dream about, Papa?

Knights and white chargers and adventures over the sea.

She giggled, but rested her head on his shoulder a bit longer than usual, humming a little in her throat like a purring kitten.

Did she know? Somehow did she know she would never sit safe on his lap again?

Back down the stairs, past Cade's room. Not his bedtime, not yet, because he was four years older and a boy and could stay up late on summer nights watching TV or reading books as long as he was up and ready for his chores in the morning.

One day Cade would be the master of Beaux Reves, and sit at the big desk in the tower study with the ledgers. He would do the hiring and firing and oversee the planting and the harvest and smoke cigars at meetings and complain about the government and the price of cotton.

Because he was the son.

That was fine with Hope. She didn't want to have to sit at a desk and add up figures.

She stopped in front of her sister's door, hesitated. It wasn't fine with Faith. Nothing ever seemed to be all right with Faith. Lilah, the housekeeper, said Miss Faith would argue with God Almighty just to irritate Him.

Hope supposed that was true, and even though Faith was her twin, she didn't understand what made her sister so prickly all the

4

time. Just tonight she'd been sent straight to her room for sassing. Now the door was shut tight and there was no light under it. Hope imagined Faith was staring up at the ceiling with that sulky look on her face and her fists clenched tight as if she waited to box with the shadows.

Hope touched the doorknob. Most times she could coax Faith out of those black moods. She could huddle in bed with her in the dark and make up stories until Faith laughed and the spit in her eyes dried up again.

But tonight was for other things. Tonight was for adventures.

It was all planned, but Hope didn't let the excitement come until she was in her own room with the door shut. She left the light off, moving quietly in the dark that was silvered by moonlight. She changed her cotton gown for shorts and a T-shirt. Her heart drummed pleasantly in her chest as she arranged the pillows on the bed in a shape that to her naive and childish eyes resembled a sleeping form.

From under the bed, she took her adventure kit. The old dome-topped lunch box held a bottle of Coca-Cola gone warm, a bag of cookies sneaked carefully from the kitchen jar, a small, rusted penknife, matches, a compass, a water pistol – fully loaded – and a red plastic flash-light.

For a moment she sat on the floor. She could smell her crayons, and the talc that clung to her own skin from after her bath. She could hear, just barely hear, the music drifting out from her mother's sitting room.

When she slid her window open, quietly took out the screen, she was smiling.

Young, agile, and bright with anticipation, she swung her leg over the sill, found a toehold in the trellis mad with vining wisteria.

The air was like syrup, and the hot, sweet flavor of it filled her lungs as she climbed down. A splinter stabbed into her finger, causing her to hiss in a breath. But she kept moving, keeping her eyes on the lighted windows of the first floor. She was a shadow, she thought, and no one would see her.

She was Hope Lavelle, girl spy, and had a meeting with her contact and partner at precisely ten thirty-five.

She had to stifle a giggle, and was breathless from the laughter that wanted to bubble out as she hit the ground.

5

To add to her own excitement, she darted and dashed behind the thick trunks of the grand old trees that shaded the house, then peeked around them toward the faint blue light that pulsed against the window in the room where her brother watched TV, up to the clearer yellow glow where each of her parents spent their evening.

Discovery now would mean disaster for the mission, she thought, crouching as she raced through the gardens and the sweet scent of roses and night-blooming jasmine. She must avoid capture at all costs, as the fate of the world rested on her shoulders and those of her stalwart partner.

The woman inside the child screamed out. *Go back, oh please, go back.* But the child didn't hear.

She wheeled her pink bike out from behind the camellias, where she'd stashed it that afternoon, snuggled her kit into the white basket, then pushed it over the cushion of grass alongside the long gravel drive until the house, and the lights, were dim with distance.

When she rode, she rode like the wind, imagining the pretty little bike was a souped-up motorcycle, complete with nerve gas dispenser and oil slick shooter. The white plastic streamers danced from the ends of the handlebars and slapped each other gaily.

She flew through the thick air, and the chorus of peepers and cicadas became the panther roar of her speeding machine.

At the fork in the road, she bore left, then jumped nimbly off her bike to wheel it off the road, down into the narrow gully where it would be hidden by brush. Though the moon was bright enough, she took the flashlight out of her kit. The smiling Princess Leia on her watch told her she was fifteen minutes early. Without fear, without thought, she turned onto the narrow path into the marsh.

Into the end of summer, of childhood. Of life.

There the world was alive with sound, water and insects and small night creatures. The light came in thinning ribbons through the canopy of tupelo and cypress with its dripping moss. Here magnolia blossoms grew fat with a perfume high and sweet. The way to the clearing was second nature to her. This meeting place, this *secret* place, was well tended, guarded, and loved.

As the first to arrive, she took old twigs and stubby branches from the stockpile of wood and set to making a fire. The smoke discouraged mosquitoes, but she scratched idly at bites already dotting her legs and arms.

6

She settled down to wait with a cookie and her Coke.

As time passed her eyes drooped, and the music of the marsh lulled her. The fire ate through the thin scraps of wood, then settled down to a simmer. Drifting, she rested her cheek on her updrawn knees.

At first the rustling was just part of her dream of dodging down twisting Paris streets to evade the wicked Russian spy. But the snap of a twig underfoot had her head jerking up and the sleep clearing from her eyes. The wide grin came first, but she quickly shifted into the stern professional expression of a top secret agent.

Password!

There was silence in the marsh but for the monotonous buzz of insects and the faint crackle of a fire dying.

She scrambled to her feet, the flashlight cocked in her hand like a gun. *Password!* she called again and aimed the short beam of light.

But now the rustle came from behind her, so she whirled, heart leaping, beam dancing in nervous jerks. Fear, something so rarely tasted in eight short years, slicked hot and burning in her throat.

Come on, cut it out. You're not scaring me.

A sound from the left, deliberate, taunting. As the next snake of fear curled in her gut she took a step in retreat.

And heard the laughter, soft, panting, close.

Running now, running through thick shadows and jumping light. Terror so sharp in the throat that it slices screams before they can escape. Footsteps pounding behind her. Fast, too fast; and too close. Something hits her from behind. Bright pain in her back that vibrates down to the soles of her feet. The jolt of bone and breath as she falls hard to the ground. Air rushes out of her lungs in a sob as the weight of him pins her down. She smells sweat and whiskey.

She screams now, one long cry of desperation, and calls out for her friend.

Tory! Tory, help me!

And the woman trapped inside the dead child weeps.

When Tory came back to herself she was lying on the flag-stones of her patio, wearing only a nightshirt already soaked through from the thin spring rain. Her face was wet, and she tasted the salt of her own tears.

7

Screams echoed in her head, but she didn't know if they were her own or those of the child she couldn't forget.

Shivering, she rolled onto her back so the rain could cool her cheeks and wash the tears away. The episodes – spells, her mother always called them – often left her weak and queasy. There had been a time she'd been able to fight them off before they swamped her. It had either been that or the shocking sting of her father's belt.

I'll whip the devil out of you, girl.

To Hannibal Bodeen, the devil was everywhere; in every fear and temptation lurked the hand of Satan. And he'd done his best to drive that wickedness out of his only child.

At the moment, with the sickness circling in her belly, Tory wished he'd managed it.

It amazed her that for a space of years she'd actually embraced what was in her, had explored it, used it, even celebrated it. A legacy, her grandmother had told her. The sight. The shining. A gift of the blood through the blood.

But there was Hope. More and more there was Hope, and those flashes of her childhood friend's memories hurt her heart. And frightened her.

Nothing she'd experienced, either blocking or embracing this gift, had *taken* her like this. Taken her away, taken her over. It made her helpless, when she'd promised herself she would never be helpless again.

Yet here she was, sprawled on her own patio in the rain without any memory of how she got outside. She'd been in the kitchen brewing tea, standing at the counter, the lights and the music on, reading a letter from her grandmother.

That was the trigger, Tory realized, as she slowly got to her feet. Her grandmother was her link to her childhood. To Hope.

Into Hope, she thought, as she closed the patio door. Into the pain and fear and horror of that terrible night. And still she didn't know the who or the why.

Still shivering, Tory went into the bath, stripped and, turning the shower hot, stepped under the spray.

'I can't help you,' she murmured, closing her eyes. 'I couldn't help you then, I can't help you now.'

Her best friend, her sister of the heart, had died that night in the swamp while she'd been locked in her room, sobbing over the latest beating.

And she had known. She had seen. She had been helpless.

Guilt, as fresh as it had been eighteen years before, swarmed through her. 'I can't help you,' she said again. 'But I'm coming back.'

We were eight years old that summer. That long-ago summer when it seemed those thick, hot days would last forever. It was a summer of innocence and foolishness and friendship, the kind that combines to form a pretty glass globe around your world. One night changed all of that. Nothing's been the same for me since. How could it be?

Most of my life I've avoided speaking of it. That didn't stop the memories, or the images. But for a time I tried to bury it, as Hope was buried. To face it now, to record this out loud, if only for myself, is a relief. Like pulling a splinter out of the heart. The ache will linger awhile.

She was my best friend. Our bond had the deep and immediate intensity only children are capable of forging. I suppose we were an odd pair, bright and privileged Hope Lavelle and dark, shy Tory Bodeen. My daddy leased a small patch of land, a little corner of the grand plantation hers owned. Sometimes when her mama gave a big society dinner or one of her lavish parties, mine would help out with the cleaning and serving.

But those gaps of social standing and class never touched the friendship. Indeed, they never occurred to us.

She lived in a grand house, one her reputedly eccentric ancestor had built to resemble a castle rather than the Georgian style so popular during its era. It was stone, with towers and turrets and what you would call battlements, I suppose. But there was nothing of the princess about Hope.

She lived for adventures. And when I was with her, so did I. With her, I escaped from the miseries and turmoils of my own house, my own life, and became her partner. We were spies, detectives, knights on quests, pirates, or space marauders. We were brave and true, bold and daring.

In the spring before that summer, we used her pocketknife to cut a narrow slice in our wrists. Solemnly, we mixed our blood. We were lucky, I suppose, we didn't end up with lockjaw. Instead we became blood sisters.

9

She had a sister, a twin. But Faith rarely joined in our games. They were too silly for her, or too rough, too dirty. They were always too something for Faith. We didn't miss her temper or complaints. That summer, Hope and I were the twins.

If someone had asked me if I loved her, I would have been embarrassed. I wouldn't have understood. But every day since that terrible time that August, I have missed her as I have missed that part of me that died with her.

We were to meet at the swamp, in our secret place. I don't suppose it was really much of a secret, but it was ours. We often played there, in that damp green air, having our adventures among the birdsong and moss and wild azalea.

It was against the rules to go in after sunset, but at eight, rules are an exciting thing to break.

I was to bring marshmallows, and lemonade. Part of that was pride. My parents were poor and I was poorer, but I needed to contribute, and had counted out the money from the mason jar I hid under my bed. I had two dollars and eighty-six cents on that August night – after having bought the supplies at Hanson's – the sum account of my financial worth rested in a glass canning jar and consisted of pennies and nickels and some hard-won quarters.

We had chicken and rice for supper. The house was so hot, even with the fans going on high, that eating was a chore. But if there was a grain of rice on your plate, Daddy expected you to eat it and be grateful. Before supper there was grace. Depending on Daddy's mood it would last anywhere from five minutes to twenty, while the food sat going cold and your belly grumbled and the sweat ran down your back in nasty rivers.

My grandma used to say that when Hannibal Bodeen found God, even God tried to find another place to hide.

He was a big man, my father, and grew thick in the chest and arms. I've heard that he was once considered handsome. Years carve a man in different ways, and my father's years had carved him bitter. Bitter and stern with a meanness under it all. He wore his dark hair slicked back, and his face seemed to rise out of that dome like sharp-edged rocks out of a mountain. Rocks that would flay the skin off your bones at

10

one careless misstep. His eyes were dark, too, a burning kind of dark I recognize now in the eyes of some television preachers and street people.

My mother feared him. I try to forgive her for that, for fearing him so much she never came to my side when he used his belt to whip his vengeful god into me.

That night I was quiet at supper. Chances were he'd take no notice of me if I was quiet and cleaned my plate. Inside me, the anticipation of the night was like a living thing, jittery and joyful. I kept my eyes down, trying to pace my eating so he wouldn't accuse me of dawdling over the food, or of bolting it. It was always a fine line to balance with Daddy.

I remember the sound of the fans whirling, and of forks scraping against plates. I remember the silence, the silence of souls hiding in fear that lived in my father's house.

When my mother offered him more chicken, he thanked her politely and took a second helping. The room seemed to breathe easier. It was a good sign. My mother, encouraged by this, made some mention of the tomatoes and corn coming in fine, and how she'd be canning for the next weeks. They'd be canning over at Beaux Reves, too, and did he think it was a good idea for her to help out there as she'd been asked.

She didn't mention the wage she'd earn. Even when Daddy's mood was mild, you were wise not to bring up the coin that the Lavelles would dole out for a service. He was the breadwinner in his house, and we were not permitted to forget this all-important point.

The room held its breath again. There were times just the mention of the Lavelles put the thunder in Daddy's dark eyes. But that night he allowed as that would be a sensible thing. As long as she didn't neglect any of her chores under the roof he was putting over her head.

This relatively pleasant response made her smile. I remember how her face softened up, and how it made her almost pretty again. Now and again, if I think very hard, I can remember Mama being pretty.

Han, she called him when she was smiling. Tory and I'll keep things going around here, don't you worry. I'll go on over and talk to Miss Lilah tomorrow and see about getting

11

it all done. With the berries coming in, I'll be making jelly, too. I know I've got some paraffin around here, but I can't think where it's got to.

And that, just that casual remark about jelly and wax and absent-mindedness changed everything. I suppose my mind had drifted off during their conversation, that I was thinking of the adventure to come. I spoke without thought, without knowledge of the consequences. So I said the words that damned me.

The box of paraffin's in the top shelf of the cabinet over the stove, up there behind the molasses and the cornstarch.

I simply said what I saw in my head, the square box of block wax behind the dark bottle of blackstrap, and reached for my cold sweet tea to wash down the starchy grains of rice.

Before I took the first sip, I heard the silence come back, the mute wave that swamped even the monotonous hum of fans. My heart started to pound inside that vacuum, one hard hammer strike after the next, with a ringing that was only inside my own head and was the sudden and vicious pulse of blood. The pulse of fear.

He spoke softly then, as he did, always did, just before the rage. *How do you know where the wax is, Victoria? How do you know it's up there, where you can't see it? Where you can't reach it?*

I lied. It was foolish, because I was already doomed, but the lie tumbled out, a desperate defense. I told him I guess I saw Mama put it there. I just remember seeing her put it there, is all.

He tore that lie to shreds. He had a way of seeing through lies and ripping them to uneven pieces and sticky parts. *When did I see that? Why didn't I do better in school if my memory was so keen I could remember where the paraffin was a year after the last canning season? And how was it I knew it was behind the molasses and cornstarch and not in front of them, or beside them?*

Oh, he was a clever man, my father, and never missed the smallest of details.

Mama said nothing while he spoke in that soft voice, punching the words at me like fists wrapped in silk. She *folded her hands, and her hands shook. Did she tremble for me? I suppose I like to think so. But she said nothing as his voice grew louder, nothing as he shoved back from the table. Nothing as the glass slipped from my hand and crashed to the floor. A shard of it nicked my ankle, and through the rising terror I felt that little pain.*

He checked first, of course. He would tell himself that was the fair thing, the right thing to do. When he opened the cabinet, pushed aside the bottles, slowly took that square blue box of canning wax out from behind the dark molasses, I cried. I still had tears in me then, I still had hope. Even as he yanked me to my feet, I had the hope that the punishment would only be prayers, hours of prayer until my knees went numb. Sometimes, at least sometimes that summer, that was enough for him.

Hadn't he warned me not to let the devil in? But still, I brought wickedness into his house, shamed him before God. I said I was sorry, that I didn't mean to. Please, Daddy, please, I won't do it again. I'll be good.

I begged him, he shouted scripture and with his big, hard hands dragged me toward my room, but still I begged him. It was the last time I did so.

There was no fighting back. It was worse if you fought him. The Fourth Commandment was a sacred thing, and you would honor your father in his house, even when he beat you bloody.

His face was deep red with his righteousness, big and blinding as the sun. He only slapped me once. That was all it took to stop my pleading, and my excuses. And to kill my hope.

I lay across the bed on my stomach, passive now as any sacrificial lamb. The sound his belt made when he slid it out of the loops on his work pants was a snake hissing, then a crack, sharp, slick, as he snapped it.

He always snapped it three times. A holy trinity of cruelty.

The first whip is always the worst. No matter how many times there's been a first, the shock and pain is stunning and rips a scream from your belly. Your body jerks in protest. No, in disbelief, then the second slap bites into you, and the third. Soon your cries are more animal than human. Your humanity has been compromised, buried under an avalanche of pain and humiliation.

He would preach as he beat me, and his voice would become a great roar. And under that roar was a hideous excitement, a vile sort of pleasure I didn't understand and recognize. No child should know that slippery undercoating, and from that, for a time, I was spared.

The first time he beat me, I was five. My mother tried to stop him, and he blackened her eye for it. She never tried again. I don't know what she did that night while he whaled away, beating at the devil that gave me visions. I couldn't see, not with eyes nor with mind, anything but a blood-red haze.

The haze was hate, but I didn't recognize that either.

He left me weeping and locked the door from the outside. After a while, the pain sent me to sleep.

When I awoke, it was dark and it seemed a fire burned in me. I can't say the pain was unbearable, because you bear it. What choice is there? I prayed, too, prayed that whatever was inside of me had finally been driven out. I didn't want to be wicked.

Yet even as I prayed, the pressure built in my belly, and the tingling came, like sharp little fingers dancing over the back of my neck. It was the first time it came into me this way, and I thought I was sick, feverish.

Then I saw Hope, as vividly as if I were sitting beside her in our clearing in the swamp. I smelled the night, the water, heard the whine of mosquitoes, the buzz of insects. And, like Hope, I heard the rustling in the brush.

Like Hope, I felt the fear. Fresh, hot gushes of it. When she ran, I ran, my breath sobbing out so that my chest hurt from it. I saw her fall under the weight of whatever leaped out at her. A shadow, a shape I couldn't see clearly, though I could see her.

She called for me. Screamed for me.

Then I saw nothing but black. When I woke, the sun was up, and I was on the floor. And Hope was gone.

Chapter Two

She'd chosen to lose herself in Charleston, and for nearly four years had managed it. The city had been like a lovely and generous woman to her, more than willing to press her against its soft bosom and soothe the nerves that had shattered on the unforgiving streets of New York City.

In Charleston the voices were slower, and in their warm, fluid stream she could blend. She could hide, as she'd once believed she could hide in the thick, rushing crowds of the North.

Money wasn't a problem. She knew how to live frugally, and was willing to work. She guarded her saving like a hawk, and when that nest egg began to grow, allowed herself to dream of owning her own business, working for herself and living the quiet and settled life that always eluded her.

She kept to herself. Real friendships meant real connections. She hadn't been willing, or strong enough, to open herself to that again. People asked questions. They wanted to know things about you, or pretended they did.

Tory had no answers to give, and nothing to tell.

She found the little house – old, run-down, perfect – and had bargained fiercely to buy it.

People often underestimated Victoria Bodeen. They saw a young woman, small and slight of build. They saw the soft skin and delicate features, a serious mouth, and clear gray eyes they often mistook for guileless. A small nose, just a little crooked, added a touch of sweetness to a face framed by quiet brown hair. They saw fragility, heard it in the gentle southern flow of her voice. And never saw the steel inside. Steel forged by countless strikes with a Sam Browne belt.

What she wanted she worked for, fought for, with all the focus and determination of a frontline soldier taking a beach. She'd wanted the old house with its overgrown yard and peeling paint, and she'd wheeled and dealed, badgered and pushed, until it was hers. Apartments brought back memories of New York, and the disaster that had ended her life there. There would be no more apartments for Tory.

She'd nurtured that investment as well, using her own time and labor and skill to rehabilitate the house, one room at a time. It had taken her three full years and now the sale of it, added to her savings, was going to make her dream come true.

All she had to do was go back to Progress.

At her kitchen table, Tory read over the rental agreement for the storefront on Market Street a third time. She wondered if Mr. Harlowe at the realtor's office remembered her.

She'd been barely ten when they'd moved away from Progress to Raleigh so her parents could find steady work. Better work, her father had claimed, than scratching out a living on a played-out plot of land leased from the almighty Lavelles.

Of course they'd been just as poor in Raleigh as they'd been in Progress. They'd just been more crowded.

Didn't matter, Tory reminded herself. She wasn't going back poor. She wasn't the scared and skinny girl she'd been, but a businesswoman starting a new enterprise in her hometown.

Then why, her therapist would ask, *are your hands trembling?*

Anticipation, Tory decided. Excitement. And nerves. All right, there were nerves. Nerves were human. She was entitled to them. She was normal. She was whatever she wanted to be.

'Damn it.'

Teeth gritted, she snatched up the pen and signed the agreement.

It was only for a year. One year. If it didn't work out, she could move on. She'd moved on before. It seemed she was always moving on.

But before she moved on this time, there was a great deal to be done. The lease agreement was only one thin layer of a mountain of paperwork. Most – the licenses and permits for the shop she intended to open – were signed and sealed. She considered the state of South Carolina little better than a mugger, but she'd paid the fees. Next up was the settlement on the house, and dealing with the lawyers, who she'd decided gave muggers a bad name.

16

But by end of day, she'd have the check in her hand, and be on her way.

The packing was nearly finished. Not that much to it, she thought now, as she'd sold nearly everything she'd acquired since her move to Charleston. Traveling light simplified things, and she'd learned early never, never to become attached to anything that could be taken from her.

Rising, she washed out her cup, dried it, then wrapped it in newspaper to store in the small box of kitchen utensils she thought most practical to take with her. From the window over the sink, she looked out at her tiny backyard.

The little patio was scrubbed and swept. She would leave the clay pots of verbena and white petunias for the new owners. She hoped they would tend the garden, but if they plowed it under, well, it was theirs to do as they liked.

She'd left her mark here. They might paint and paper, carpet and tile, but what she had done would have come first. It would always be under the rest.

You couldn't erase the past, or kill it, or wish it out of existence. Nor could you will away the present or change what was coming. We were all trapped in that cycle of time, just circling around the core of yesterdays. Sometimes those yesterdays were strong enough, willful enough, to suck you back no matter how hard you struggled.

And how much more depressing could she be? Tory thought with a sigh.

She sealed the box, hefted it to take out to her car, and walked out of the kitchen without looking back.

Three hours later, the check from the sale of her house was deposited. She shook hands with the new owners, listened politely to their giddy enthusiasm over buying their first home, and eased her way outside.

The house, and the people who would now live in it, were no longer part of her world.

'Tory, hold on a minute.'

Tory turned, one hand on the car door and her mind already on the road. But she waited until her lawyer crossed the bank parking lot. *Meandered* was more the word, Tory corrected. Abigail Lawrence didn't hurry anything, especially herself. Which

17

probably explained why she always looked as though she'd just stepped graciously from the pages of *Vogue*.

For today's settlement, she'd chosen a pale blue suit, pearls that had likely been handed down from her great-grandmother, and thinly spiked heels that made Tory's toes cramp just looking at them.

'Whew.' Abigail waved a hand in front of her face as if she'd just run two miles rather than strolled ten yards. 'All this heat and it's barely April.' She glanced past Tory to the station wagon, scanned the boxes. 'So that's it?'

'Seems to be. Thank you, Abigail, for handling everything.'

'You handled most of it. Don't know when I've had a client who understood what I was talking about half the time, much less one who could give me lessons.'

She took a peek into the back of the station wagon, vaguely surprised that one woman's life took up so little room. 'I didn't think you were serious about heading straight out this afternoon. I should've known.' She shifted her gaze back to Tory's face. 'You're a serious woman, Victoria.'

'No reason to stay.'

Abigail opened her mouth, then shook her head. 'I was going to say I envy you. Packing it up, taking what fits in the back of your car, and going off to a new place, a new life, a new start. But the fact is, I don't. Not one little bit. God almighty, the energy it takes, and the guts. Then again, you're young enough to have plenty of both.'

'Maybe a new start, but it's back to my beginnings. I still have family in Progress, such as it is.'

'You ask me, it takes more guts to go back to the beginning than just about anyplace else. I hope you're happy, Tory.'

'I'll be fine.'

'Fine's one thing.' To Tory's surprise, Abigail took her hand, then leaned over and brushed her cheek in a light kiss. 'Happy's another. Be happy.'

'I intend to.' Tory drew back. There was something in the hand-to-hand connection, something in the concern in Abigail's eyes. 'You knew,' Tory murmured.

'Of course I did.' Abigail gave Tory's fingers a light squeeze before releasing them. 'News from New York winds its way down here, and some of us even pay attention to it now and again. You

18

changed your hair, your name, but I recognized you. I'm good with faces.'

'Why didn't you say anything? Ask me?'

'You hired me to see to your business, not to pry into it. The way I figured it is if you'd wanted people to know you were the Victoria Mooney who made news out of New York City a few years back, you'd have said so.'

'Thank you for that.'

The formality, and the caution, had Abigail grinning. 'For heaven's sake, honey, do you think I'm going to ask you if my son's ever going to get married, or where the hell I lost my mama's diamond engagement ring? All I'm saying is I know you've been through some rough times, and I hope you find better. Now, if you have any problems up there in Progress, you just give a holler.'

Simple kindness never failed to fluster her. Tory fumbled with the door handle. 'Thank you. Really. I'd better get started. I have several stops to make.' But she held out her hand once more. 'I appreciate everything.'

'Drive safe.'

Tory slid inside, hesitated, then opened the window as she started the engine. 'In the middle file cabinet drawer of your home office, between the D's and E's.'

'What's that?'

'Your mother's ring. It's a little too big for you, and it slipped off, fell in the files. You should have it sized.' Tory reversed quickly, swung the car around while Abigail blinked after her.

She headed west out of Charleston, then dipped south to begin her planned circle of the state before landing in Progress. The list of artists and craftsmen she intended to visit was neatly typed and in her new briefcase. Directions for each were included, and it meant taking a number of back roads. Time-consuming, but necessary.

She'd already made arrangements with several southern artists to display and sell their work in the shop she would open on Market Street, but she needed more. Starting small didn't mean not starting well.

Start-up costs, buying stock, finding an acceptable place to live were going to take nearly every penny she'd saved. She intended to make it worthwhile, and she intended to make more.

In a week, if everything went as planned, she would begin setting up shop. By the end of May, she would open the doors. Then they would see.

As for the rest, she would deal with what came when it came. When the time was right, she would drive down the long, shady lane to Beaux Reves and face the Lavelles.

She would face Hope.

At the end of a week, Tory was exhausted, several hundred dollars poorer thanks to a cracked radiator, and ready to call an end to her travels. The replacement radiator meant she had to postpone her arrival in Florence until the following morning, and make do for a night with the dubious comfort of a motel off Route 9 outside of Chester.

The room stank of stale smoke, and its amenities included a sliver of soap and pay movies designed to stimulate the sexual appetites of the rent-by-the-hour clientele that kept the establishment out of bankruptcy. There were stains on the carpet, the origin of which she decided it best not to contemplate.

She'd paid cash for one night because she didn't like the idea of handing over her credit card to a sly-eyed clerk who smelled like the gin he cleverly disguised in a coffee mug.

The room was as unappealing as the idea of climbing back behind the wheel for another hour, but it was there. Tory carried the single flimsy chair to the door and hooked its spindly top under the knob. She decided it was every bit as security-proof as the thin and rusted chain. Still, using both gave her the illusion of safety.

It was a mistake, she knew, to allow herself to become so fatigued. Resistance went down. But everything had conspired against her. The potter she'd seen in Greenville had been temperamental and difficult to pin down. If he hadn't also been brilliant, Tory would have walked out of his studio after twenty minutes instead of spending two hours praising, placating, and persuading.

The car had taken another four hours, between getting towed, negotiating for a reconditioned radiator at the junkyard, browbeating the mechanic to do the repair on the spot.

Add to that, she admitted it was her own stupidity that had landed her in the By the Way Inn. If she'd simply booked a room back in Greenville, or stopped at one of the perfectly respectable motor lodges on the interstate, she wouldn't be stumbling with exhaustion around a smelly room.

Only one night, she reminded herself, as she eyed the dingy green cover on the bed. For pocket change, it offered the questionable delights of Magic Fingers.

She decided to pass.

Just a few hours' sleep, then she'd be on her way to Florence, where her grandmother would have the guest room – clean sheets, a hot bath – ready. She just had to get through the night.

Without even taking off her shoes, she lay down on the spread and closed her eyes.

Bodies in motion, slicked with sweat.

Baby, yeah, baby. Give it to me. Harder!

A woman weeping, pain rolling through her hot as lava.

Oh God, God, what am I going to do? Where can I go? Any place but back. Please don't let him find me.

Scattered thoughts and fumbling hands, all panicked excitement and raging guilt.

What if I get pregnant? My mother will kill me. Is it going to hurt? Does he really love me?

Images, thoughts, voices washed over her in waves of shapes and sounds.

Leave me alone, she demanded. Just leave me alone. With her eyes still shut, Tory imagined a wall, thick and high and white. She built it brick by brick until it stood between her and all the memories left hanging in the room like smoke. Behind the wall was all cool, clear blue. Water to float in, to sink in. And finally, to sleep in.

And high above that pale blue pool the sun was white and warm. She could hear birdsong, and the lap of water as she trailed her hands through it. Her body was weightless here, her mind quiet. At the edges of the pool she could see the grand live oaks and their lacing of moss, and a willow bowing like a courtier to dip its fronds in the glassy surface.

Smiling to herself she closed her eyes and drifted.

The sound of laughter was high and bright, a girl's careless joy. Lazily, Tory opened her eyes.

There, by the willow, Hope stood waving.

Hey, Tory! Hey, I was looking for you.

21

Joy struck first, a bright arrow. Turning in the water, Tory waved back. Come on in. The water's great.

We get caught skinny-dipping, we're both going to get it. But giggling, Hope shucked off her shoes, her shorts, then her shirt. *I thought you went away.*

Don't be dopey. Where would I go?

I've been looking a long time. Slowly, Hope eased into the water. Willow slim and marble white. Her hair spread out to float on the surface. Gold against blue. *Forever and ever.*

The water darkened, began to stir. The graceful fronds of the willow snapped up like whips. And the water was cold, suddenly so cold Tory began to shiver.

Storm's coming up. We'd better go in.

It's over my head. I can't reach the bottom. You have to help me. As the water churned, Hope flailed out, her thin young arms beating, spewing up curtains of water that had gone the murky brown of a marsh.

Tory struck out, strong strokes, frantic speed, but every arm span took her farther away from where the young girl struggled. The water burned her lungs, dragged at her feet. She felt herself going under, felt herself drowning with Hope's voice inside her head.

You have to come. You have to hurry.

She awoke in the dark, her mouth full of the taste of the swamp. Without the heart or energy to build her wall again, Tory rolled out of bed. In the bathroom, she splashed rusty water on her face, then raised it, dripping, to the mirror.

Eyes shadowed and still glazed from the dream stared back at her. Too late to turn back, she thought. It always was.

She grabbed her purse and the unused travel kit she'd brought in with her.

The dark was soothing now, and the candy bar and soft drink she'd bought from the rumbling vending machine outside her room kept her system wired. She turned on the radio to distract her mind. She wanted to think of nothing but the road.

When she hit the heart of the state the sun was up, and the traffic thick. She stopped to refuel the gas-guzzling station wagon before heading east. When she passed the exit that led to where her parents had once again relocated, her stomach clenched and stayed tight for another thirty miles.

She thought of her grandmother, of the stock loaded in the back of the car or being shipped to Progress. She thought of her budget for the next six months and the work involved in having her store up and running by Memorial Day.

She thought of anything but the real reason driving her back to Progress.

Just outside of Florence she stopped again and used the rest room of a Shell station to brush her hair, apply some makeup. The artifice wouldn't fool her grandmother, but at least she'd have made an effort.

She stopped again, on impulse, at a florist. Her grandmother's gardens were always a showplace, but the dozen pink tulips were another kind of effort. She lived – had lived, Tory reminded herself – just under two hours from her grandmother and hadn't made the trip, the effort of it, since Christmas.

When she turned down the pretty street with its blooming dogwoods and redbuds she wondered why. It was a good place, the kind of neighborhood where children played in the yards and dogs napped in the shade. A gossip-over-the-backyard-fence-kind of place where people noticed strange cars and kept their eye on their neighbor's house as much out of consideration as curiosity.

Iris Mooney's house sat in the middle of the block, bandbox neat with old and enormous azaleas guarding the foundation. The blooms were past their peak, but the faded pinks and purples added a delicate color to the strong blue paint her grandmother had chosen. As expected, her front garden was lush and lovely, the gentle slope of the yard well trimmed and the stoop scrubbed and swept.

A pickup truck with the sign ANYTIME PLUMBING was parked in the drive behind her grandmother's aging compact. Tory pulled to the curb. The tension she'd ignored along the drive began to ease as she walked toward the house.

She didn't knock. She'd never had to knock on this door, and had always known it would open in welcome to her. There had been times when that alone had kept her from crumbling.

It surprised her to find the house quiet. It was nearly ten, she noted, as she stepped inside. She'd expected to find her grandmother in her garden, or fussing around inside the house.

The living room was cluttered, as always, with furniture, knickknacks, books. And, Tory noted, a vase holding a dozen red roses

23

that made her tulips look like poor relations. She set aside her suit-case, her purse, then turning toward the hallway called out.

'Gran? Are you home?' Carrying the flowers, she started back toward the bedrooms, then lifted her eyebrows when she heard the movement behind her grandmother's closed door.

'Tory? Honey-pot, I'll be right out. Go on back and . . . get yourself some iced tea.'

With a shrug, Tory kept walking toward the kitchen, glancing back once when she heard what sounded like a muffled giggle.

She laid the flowers on the counter, then opened the refriger-ator. The pitcher of tea was waiting, made as she enjoyed it most, with slices of lemon and sprigs of mint. Gran never forgot anything, Tory thought, and felt tears of sentiment and fatigue sting her eyes.

She blinked them back when she heard Gran's quick steps. 'Goodness, you're early! I didn't expect you until after noon, if that.' Small, slim and agile, Iris Mooney swept into the room and caught Tory in a hard hug.

'I got an early start, and just kept going. Did I wake you? Aren't you feeling well?'

'What?'

'You're still in your robe.'

'Oh. Ha.' After one last squeeze, Iris drew back. 'I'm just as fine as rain. Let me look at you. Aw, honey, you're wore out.'

'Just a little tired. But you. You look wonderful.'

It was inevitably true. Sixty-seven years of living had lined her face, but it hadn't dulled the magnolia skin or dimmed the deep gray of her eyes. Her hair had been red in her youth, and she saw that it remained that way. If God had meant a woman to be gray, Iris liked to say, he wouldn't have invented Miss Clairol. She took care of herself, and pampered her looks.

Which, she thought now, was more than she could say about her granddaughter.

'You sit down right here. I'm going to fix you some breakfast.'

'Don't trouble, Gran.'

'You know better than to argue with me, don't you? Now, sit.' She pointed to a chair at the little ice cream parlor table. 'Oh, look at these. Aren't they pretty!' She swept up the tulips, her delight in them sparkling in her eyes. 'You're the sweetest thing, my Tory.'

'I've missed you, Gran. I'm sorry I haven't visited.'

24

'You've got your own life, which is what I always wanted for you. Now, you just relax and when you've got your feet back under you, you can tell me all about your trip.'

'It was worth every mile. I found some wonderful pieces.'

'Got my eye for pretty things.' She winked, turning just in time to see her granddaughter gape at the man who had stepped into the kitchen doorway.

He was tall as an oak with a chest wide as a Buick. His grizzled hank of hair was the color and texture of steel wool. His eyes were the burnished brown of acorns and drooped like a basset hound's. His leathered face was tanned to match. He cleared his throat with an exaggerated flourish, then nodded at Tory.

'Morning,' he began in an upcountry drawl. 'Ah . . . Miz Mooney, I got that drain cleared for you.'

'Cecil, stop being a moron, you don't even have your toolbox with you.' Iris set aside a carton of eggs. 'No need to blush,' she told him. 'My granddaughter's not going to faint at the notion her grandma's got herself a beau. Tory, this is Cecil Axton, the reason I'm not dressed at ten this morning.'

'Iris.' The blush rose up to his cheeks like fire under cordwood. 'I'm pleased to meet you, Tory. Your gran's been looking forward to seeing you.'

'How do you do,' Tory said, for lack of something more clever. She offered a hand, and because she was still dazed, and Cecil's feelings were so close to the surface, she had a quick and blurred image of just what had made her grandmother giggle behind the bedroom door.

She shut it off fast as her eyes met Cecil's with mutual mortification. 'You're . . . you're a plumber, Mr. Axton?'

'He came to fix my water heater,' Iris put in, 'and's been keeping me warm ever since.'

'Iris.' Cecil ducked his head, hunched the twin mountains of his shoulders, but couldn't quite hide the grin. 'I gotta get on. Hope you enjoy your visit, Tory.'

'Don't you think about running off without kissing me good-bye.' To solve the matter, Iris crossed to him, took his weathered face between her hands to pull it down to her level, and kissed him firm on the mouth. 'There now, lightning did not strike, thunder did not roll, and the child here did not collapse in shock.' She kissed him again, then patted his cheek. 'You go on, handsome, and have a good day.'

25

'I guess I'll, um, see you later on.'

'You'd better. We decided on this, Cecil. Now, you scat. I'll talk to Tory.'

'I'm going.' With a hesitant smile, he turned to Tory. 'You can argue with this woman, but it just gives you a headache.' He took a faded blue gimme cap from a kitchen peg, set it on his wiry hair, and hurried out.

'Isn't he the cutest thing? I got some nice lean bacon here. How do you want your eggs?'

'In chocolate chip cookies. Gran.' Tory drew a careful breath and rose. 'It's absolutely none of my business, but . . .'

'Of course it's not your business, unless I invite you into it, which I have.' Iris laid bacon in the old black spider skillet to sizzle. 'I'm going to be very disappointed in you, Tory, if you're shocked and appalled by the idea of your grandmother having a sex life.'

Tory winced, but managed to compose her face when Iris turned toward her. 'Not shocked, not appalled, but certainly a little disconcerted. The idea of coming here this morning and nearly walking in on . . . hmmm.'

'Well, you were early, honey-pot. I'm going to fry these eggs, and we're both going to indulge in a nice, greasy midmorning breakfast.'

'I guess you worked up an appetite.'

Iris blinked, then threw back her head and laughed. 'Now, that's my girl. You worry me, sugar plum, when you don't smile.'

'What have I got to smile about? You're the one having sex.'

Amused, Iris cocked her head. 'And whose fault is that?'

'Yours. You saw Cecil first.' Tory got down two glasses, poured the tea. How many women, she wondered, could claim a grandmother who had hot affairs with the plumber? She wasn't sure whether she should be proud or amused, and decided the combination of both suited the situation. 'He seems like a very nice man.'

'He is. Better, he's a very good man.' Iris poked at the bacon and decided to get it done all at once. 'Tory, he's living here.'

'Living? You're living with him?'

'He wants to get married, but I'm not sure that's what I want. So I'm taking him for what you might call a test drive.'

'I think I'll just sit down after all. Jesus, Gran. Have you told Mama?'

'No, and I don't intend to as I can live without the lecture on living in sin and perdition and God's almighty plan. Your mama is the biggest pain in the butt since self-service gas stations. How any daughter of mine turned out to be such a mouse of a woman is beyond me.'

'Survival,' Tory murmured, but Iris only snarled.

'She'd've survived just fine if she'd walked out on that son of a bitch she married twenty-five years ago, or any day since. That's her choice, Tory. If she had any gumption, she'd have made a different one. You did.'

'Did I? I don't know what choices I made or which were made for me. I don't know which were right and which were wrong. And here I am, Gran, circling right back to where I started. I tell myself I'm in charge now. That it's all my decision. But under it all, I know I just can't stop it.'

'Do you want to?'

'I don't know the answer.'

'Then you'll keep going until you find it. You've got such a strong light in you, Tory. You'll find your way.'

'So you always said. But the one thing that's always scared me the most is being lost.'

'I should have helped you more. I should have been there for you.'

'Gran.' Tory rose, crossed the room to wrap her arms around Iris's waist, to press cheek to cheek while the bacon snapped and sizzled. 'You've always been the one steady hand in my life. I wouldn't be here without you.'

'Yes, you would.' Iris patted Tory's hand, then briskly lifted out bacon to drain. 'You're stronger than the lot of us put together. And that, if you ask me, is what scared Hannibal Bodeen. He wanted to break you, out of his own fear. In the end, well, he forged you, didn't he? Ignorant s.o.b.' She cracked an egg on the side of the skillet, let it slide into the bubbling grease. 'Make us some toast, honey-pot.'

'She's nothing like you. Mama,' Tory said as she dropped bread into the toaster. 'She's nothing like you at all.'

'I don't know what Sarabeth's like. I lost her years ago. Same time I lost your granddaddy, I suppose. She was only twelve when

27

he died. Hell, I was hardly more than thirty myself, and found myself a widow with two children to raise on my own. That was the worst year of my life. Nothing's ever come close to matching it. Sweet Jesus, I loved that man.'

She let out a sigh, flipped the eggs onto plates. 'He was my world, my Jimmy. One minute, the world was steady, and the next it was just gone. And there's Sarabeth twelve years old, and J.R. barely sixteen. She went wild on me. Maybe I could've reined her in. God knows I should have.'

'You can't blame yourself.'

'I don't. But you see things when you look back. See how if one thing was done different the whole picture of a life changes. If I'd moved away from Progress back then, if I'd used Jimmy's insurance instead of taking a job at the bank. If I hadn't been so hell-bent to save so my children could have a college education.'

'You wanted the best for them.'

'I did.' Iris set the plates on the table, turned to get butter and jelly from the refrigerator. 'J.R. got his college education, and he used it. Sarabeth got Hannibal Bodeen. That's the way it was meant to be. That's why my granddaughter and I are going to sit here and eat a couple of heart attacks on a plate. If I could go back and do that one thing different, I wouldn't. Because I wouldn't have you.'

'I'm going back, Gran, knowing I can't do anything different.' Tory put the toast on a little plate, carried it to the table. 'It scares me that I need to go back so much. I don't know those people anymore. I'm afraid I won't know myself once I'm there.'

'You won't settle yourself until you do this thing, Tory. Until you take hold of it, you can't let go of it. You've been heading back to Progress since you left it.'

'I know.' And having someone else understand that helped. Smiling a little, Tory lifted a slice of bacon. 'So, tell me about your plumber.'

'Oh, that sweetie pie.' Delighted with the topic, Iris dug into her breakfast. 'Looks like a big old bear, doesn't he? You wouldn't guess looking at him how smart he is. Started that company on his own over forty years back. Lost his wife, I knew her slightly, about five years ago. He's mostly retired now. Two of his sons do most of the running of the business. Got six grandsons.'

'Six?'

'Yes, indeed. Fact is, one of them's a doctor. Good-looking young man. I was thinking—'

'Stop right there.' Eyes narrowed, Tory slathered jelly on toast. 'I'm not interested.'

'How do you know? You haven't even met the boy.'

'I'm not interested in boys. Or men.'

'Tory, you haven't been involved with a man since . . .'

'Jack,' Tory finished. 'That's right, and I don't intend to be involved again. Once was enough.' Since it still left a bitter taste in her mouth, she picked up her tea. 'Not all of us are made to be half of a couple, Gran. I'm happy on my own.'

At Iris's lifted eyebrows, Tory shrugged. 'Okay, let's say I intend to be happy on my own. I'm going to work my ass off to make sure of it.'

Chapter Three

It had been too long, Tory thought, since she'd sat on a porch swing watching the stars come out and hearing the crickets chirp. A long time since she'd been relaxed enough to simply sit and smell the breeze.

Even as she thought it, she realized it was likely to be a long time before she did so again.

Tomorrow she'd travel the last miles to Progress. There she would pick up the pieces of her life and finally lay a dead friend to rest.

But tonight was for soft breezes and quiet thoughts.

She glanced up at the squeak of the screen door and offered Cecil a smile. Her grandmother was right, she decided. He did look like a big old bear. And, at the moment, a very nervous one.

'Iris kicked me out of the kitchen.' He had a dark brown bottle of beer in one hand and shifted uneasily from foot to foot on size fourteen boots. 'She said how I should come on out here and sit a spell, keep you company.'

'She wants us to be friends. Why don't you sit a spell? I'd like the company.'

'Feels a little funny.' He eased his bulk down on the swing, darted a look at Tory out of the corner of his eye. 'I know what you young people think. An old coot like me courting a woman like Iris.'

He still smelled of the Lava soap he'd used to wash up before dinner. Lava soap, Tory mused, and Coors. It was a pleasantly male combination. 'Your family doesn't approve?'

'Oh, they're all right with it now. Iris's charmed the socks off my boys. She's got that way about her. One son, Jerry, he got a mite huffy about it, but she brought him around. The thing is . . .'

He trailed off, cleared his throat twice. Tory folded her hands and bit back a grin as he launched into what was surely a prepared speech.

'You're mighty important to her, Tory. I guess you're about the most important thing there is to Iris. She's proud of you, and she worries about you, and she brags on you. I know there's a rift between her and your mama. Guess you could say that makes you even more special to her.'

'The feeling's mutual.'

'I know it. I could see how it is over dinner. The thing is,' he said again, then lifted his beer and gulped deeply. 'Oh hell. I love her.' He blurted it out and color sprang into his cheeks. 'I guess that sounds foolish to you coming from a man who won't see sixty-five again, but—'

'Why would it?' She wasn't comfortable with casual touching, but since he seemed to need it she patted his knee. 'And what does age have to do with it? Gran cares for you. That's good enough for me.'

Relief slid through him. Tory could hear it in his sigh. 'Never thought I'd have these feelings again. I was married forty-six years to a wonderful woman. We grew up together, raised a family together, started a business together. When I lost her I figured that was the end of that part of my life. Then I met Iris and, Christ Jesus, she makes me feel twenty years old again.'

'You put stars in her eyes.'

He blushed deeper at that but his lips twitched into a shy and delighted smile. 'Yeah? I'm good with my hands.' At Tory's uncontrollable snort of laughter, his eyes went huge. 'I mean to say I'm handy around the house. Fixing stuff.'

'I know what you meant.'

'And Stella, that was my wife, I guess you could say she trained me pretty good. I know better than to track in mud on a clean floor, to toss dirty towels on the floor. I can cook a little if you're not too particular, and I've got a decent living.'

Gran was right, Tory decided. The man was a sweetie pie. 'Cecil, are you asking for my blessing?'

He huffed out a breath. 'I mean to marry her. She won't hear of it just now. Mule stubborn, that woman. But I got a hard head of my own. Just want you to know that I'm not taking advantage, that my intentions . . .'

'Are honorable,' Tory finished, wonderfully moved. 'I'm pulling for you.'

'Yeah?' He sat back again, making the swing groan. 'That's a relief to me, Tory. That's a relief, all right. God almighty, I'm glad that's over.' With a shake of his head, he drank more beer. 'My tongue gets all tangled up.'

'You did fine. Cecil, you keep her happy.'

'I aim to.' At ease again, he draped his arm over the back of the swing and looked out over Iris's back garden. 'Nice night.'

'Yeah. A very nice night.'

She slept deep and dreamless in her grandmother's house.

'I wish you'd stay, just another day or two.'

'I have to get started.'

Iris nodded, struggling not to fuss as Tory carried her suitcase toward the car. 'You'll call, once you settle in a bit.'

'Of course I will.'

'And you'll go see J.R. right off, so he and Boots can help you along.'

'I'll go see him, and Aunt Boots and Wade.' She kissed both her grandmother's cheeks. 'Now, stop worrying.'

'I'm just missing you already. Give me your hands.' When Tory hesitated, Iris simply took them. 'Indulge me, honey-pot.' She held firm, her eyes blurring a bit as she focused.

She didn't have the brilliance of light her granddaughter had been gifted with. She saw in colors and shapes. The smudgy gray of worry, the shimmering pink of excitement, the dull blue of grief. And through it all was the dark, deep red of love.

'You'll be all right.' Iris gave her hands a last squeeze. 'I'll be right here if you need me.'

'I've always known that.' Tory climbed in the car, took a deep breath. 'Don't tell them where I am, Gran.'

Iris shook her head, knowing Tory meant her parents. 'I won't.'

'I love you.' She kept her eyes straight ahead as she drove away.

The fields began to roll, gentle ripples on the earth covered with the tender green of growing things. She recognized the row crops.

Soybeans, tobacco, cotton; the delicate shoots hazed the brown soil.

She'd missed planting time.

The land had never called to her as it did to some. She enjoyed puttering in a flower garden now and then, but had no driving need to feel earth under her hands, to tend and harvest, to put by what she'd grown.

Still, she appreciated the cycle, the continuity. She enjoyed the look of it. The neat and practical fields men plowed and nurtured rode side by side with the tangled lushness of the live oaks and moss, the ubiquitous sumac, the ribbons of dark water that could never, would never, be truly tamed.

The smell of it was rich and again dark. Fertilizer and swamp water. More, she thought, the perfume of the South than any magnolia. This was its true heart, after all. Beyond the formal gardens and lavish lawns, the South beat on crops and sweat and the secret shadows of its rivers.

She'd taken the back roads for solitude, and with every mile felt herself drawn closer to that heart.

On the west edge of Progress some of the farms and fields had given way to homes. Tidy developments with yards kept green and lush with underground sprinklers. There were late-model sedans and minivans in the drives, and sidewalks running wide and even. Here were the young marrieds, she mused, most with double incomes, who wanted a nice home in the suburbs for raising a family.

These were her target customers, and the primary reason she'd been able to justify the move. Successful home owners with disposable income enjoyed decorating their space. With the right advertising and clever displays she would draw them into her shop.

And they would buy.

Were there any living well in those quiet homes she'd known as a child? Any who might remember the thin young girl who'd come to school with bruises? Would they remember she'd sometimes known things she wasn't supposed to know?

Memories were short, Tory reminded herself. And even if some remembered, she would find a way to use it to promote her store.

The houses elbowed closer together as she approached the town line, as if they were anxious for company. Into her mind flashed an image of the far side, where the narrow whip of the river was the border of Progress. In her youth, the houses that slipped and slithered down into the holler had been small and dark, with leaky roofs and rusted trucks that most often stood on chipped cinder blocks. A place were dogs snarled and leaped viciously at the ends of their chains. Where the women hung out dingy laundry while children sat on patchy grass that was mostly dirt.

Some of the men farmed to eke out a living, and some of them simply lived on beer and mead. As a child she'd been one shaky step above that fate. And even as a child she'd feared losing the balance and tumbling into the holler, where daily bread was served with exhaustion.

She saw the church steeple first. The town boasted four, or had. Still, nearly everyone she'd known had belonged to the Baptist church. She'd sat, countless hours, on one of the hard pews listening, listening desperately to the sermon because her father would quiz her on the content that night before supper.

If she didn't respond well, the punishment was hard and it was quick.

She hadn't been inside a church of any kind in eight years.

Don't think about it, she ordered herself. Think about now. But now, she saw, was very much like then. It seemed to her very little had changed inside the edges of Progress.

Deliberately, she turned onto Live Oak Drive to cruise through the oldest residential section of town. The homes here were large and gracious, the trees old and leafy. Her uncle had moved here a few years before she'd left Progress. On his wife's money, her father had said brittlely.

Tory hadn't been allowed to visit there, and even now felt a twinge of guilty panic just driving by the lovely old white brick home with its flowering shrubs and sparkling windows.

Her uncle would be at work now, managing the bank as he'd managed it nearly as long as she could remember. And though she had a great deal of affection for her aunt, Tory wasn't in the mood for Boots Mooney's fluttering hands and whispery voice.

She wove through the streets, past smaller homes and a small apartment complex that hadn't existed sixteen years before. She lifted her eyebrows at a corner convenience store that had sprung up in bright reds and yellows out of the old Progress Drive-In.

The high school had an addition, and there was a charming little park just off the square where there'd once been a line of crumbling row houses. There were new young trees planted among the old soldiers and graceful flowers spilling out of concrete pots.

It all seemed prettier, cleaner, fresher than she remembered. She wondered how much would turn out to be the same under that new coat of varnish.

As she turned onto Market, she was ridiculously pleased to see Hanson's was still standing, still wore the same battered old sign, and its front window remained patchworked with flyers and billboards.

The sweet childhood taste of Grape Nehi immediately filled her mouth, her throat, and made her smile.

The beauty salon had changed hands, she noted. Lou's Beauty Shoppe was now called Hair Today. But the Market Street Diner stood where it had always stood, and it seemed to her the same old men wearing the same overalls were loitering outside to gossip.

Midway down the block, tucked between Rollins Paint and Hardware and The Flower Basket was the old dry-goods store. That, Tory thought, as she pulled to the curb, would be her change.

She climbed out of the car and stepped into the thick midday heat. The outside of the building was exactly as she remembered. The old clinker bricks cobbled together with the mortar gray as smoke between. The window was high and wide and just now coated with dust and street grime. But she would fix that.

The door was glass as well, and cracked. The landlord, she determined, taking out her notebook, would fix that.

She'd put a bench outside, the narrow one with the black wrought-iron back she was having shipped. And beside it pots filled with purple and white petunias. Friendly flowers.

High on the window above the bench, she'd have the store name printed.

SOUTHERN COMFORT

That would be what she offered her clientele. Comfortable surroundings where the stock was stylishly displayed and discreetly tagged.

In her mind she was already inside, filling shelves, arranging tables and lamps. She didn't hear her name called until she was scooped off her feet.

The blood rushed to her head, ringing there while her pulse went into panic trip.

'Tory! I thought that was you. I've been keeping an eye out for you the last couple days.'

'Wade.' His name came out in a whoosh.

'I scared you.' Immediately contrite, he set her back on her feet. 'Sorry. I'm just so glad to see you.'

'Let me catch my breath.'

'You catch it while I look at you. Damn, has it really been two years? You look wonderful.'

'Do I?' It was nice to hear, even if she didn't believe it for a minute. She pushed back her hair while her pulse leveled.

Though he was a couple of inches shy of six feet, she had to tip her head back to study his face. He'd always been pretty, she remembered, but she imagined he was relieved that the angelic face of his youth had weathered a bit. His eyes were a deep, slumberous chocolate. His face had fined down from childhood, but he still boasted dimples. His hair, shades lighter than her own, was well cut to tame the tendency to curl.

He was dressed in jeans and a plain cotton shirt of faded blue. As she took his measure his lips quirked.

He looked, she decided, young, handsome, and quietly prosperous.

'If I look wonderful, I don't have words for how you look. You got all the handsome in the family, Cousin Wade.'

He flashed a grin at that, quick and boyish, but resisted hugging her again. Tory, he knew, had always been skittish about hugs and strokes. He settled for giving her hair a little tug.

'I'm glad you're back.'

'I couldn't have picked a better welcoming committee.' She gestured widely. 'The town looks good. The same in a lot of ways, but better. Tidier, I suppose.'

'Progress in Progress,' he said. 'We owe a lot of it to the Lavelles, the town council, and particularly the mayor of the last five years. You remember Dwight? Dwight Frazier?'

'Dwight the Dweeb, one of the Mighty Three formed by you, him, and Cade Lavelle.'

'The Dweeb hit his stride in high school, became a track star, married the homecoming queen, went into his daddy's construction business, and helped turn Progress around. We're all goddamn solid citizens these days.'

Standing there with the light traffic cruising the street behind him, hearing the familiar rhythm of his voice, she remembered why he'd always held her affection. 'Miss hell-raising, do you, Wade?'

'Some. Listen, I'm between appointments. I have to get back and convince a Great Dane named Igor he needs his rabies shot.'

'Better you than me, Dr. Mooney.'

'My office is across the street, end of the block. Walk up with me, and I'll buy you an iced tea.'

'I'd like that, but I need to go by the realtor, see what they've got lined up for me.' She caught the flicker in his eyes, tilted her head. 'What?'

'I don't know how you'll feel about it, but your old place? It's vacant.'

'The house?' Instinctively she crossed her arms, hugged her elbows. Fate, she thought, had such a long and sneaky reach. 'I don't know how I feel about it, either. I guess I should find out.'

In a town of less than six thousand it was hard to walk two blocks without running into someone you knew. It didn't matter if you'd been away sixteen years or sixty. When she stepped into the realtor's office there was only one person manning a desk.

The woman was pretty, petite, and polished. Her long blond hair was swept back from a heart-shaped face dominated by big baby-blue eyes.

'Afternoon.' The woman fluttered her lashes and set aside a paperback novel with a bare-chested pirate on the cover. 'Can I help you?'

Tory had a quick image of the playground at Progress Elementary. A group of little girls shrieking in fear and disgust and running away. And the smug, satisfied look in the big blue eyes of the leader as she tossed a sneer over her shoulder while her long blond hair flew behind her.

'Lissy Harlowe.'

Lissy cocked her head. 'Do I know you? Why, I'm so sorry, I just don't . . .' Those blue eyes widened. 'Tory? Tory Bodeen? For heaven's sake.' She gave a little squeal and hauled herself to her feet. She looked to be about six months pregnant from the bulge under the pale pink shirt. 'Daddy said how you'd be coming by sometime this week.'

Despite Tory's automatic step in retreat, Lissy scurried around the desk to embrace her like a long-lost friend. 'This is so exciting.' She pulled back to beam cheer and welcome. 'Tory Bodeen come back to Progress after all this time. And don't you look pretty.'

'Thank you.' Tory watched Lissy's eyes scan, measure, then glint with satisfaction. There was no doubt here who'd grown up better. 'You look so much the same. But you were always the prettiest girl in Progress.'

'Oh, what foolishness.' Lissy waved a hand but couldn't stop herself from preening a bit. 'Now, you just sit right down and let me get you something cold to drink.'

'No, don't bother. I'm fine. Did your father get the lease agreement?'

'Seems like he mentioned he did. The whole town's talking about your shop. I can't wait till you're open. You just can't find pretty things in Progress.' She walked behind the desk again as she spoke. 'Lord knows you can't be driving down to Charleston every time you want something with a bit of style.'

'That's good to know.' Tory sat, and found herself eye level with the sign that identified Lissy Frazier. 'Frazier? Dwight? You married Dwight?'

'Five happy years. We have a son. My Luke's the cutest thing.' She turned a framed photo around to show off a bright-eyed, towheaded toddler. 'And we're expecting his brother or sister by end of summer.'

She gave the mound of her belly a satisfied pat, and wiggled her fingers so her wedding and engagement rings caught the light and flashed fire from the diamonds.

'You never married, honey?'

There was just enough bite in the question to let Tory know Lissy still liked being the best. 'No.'

'I just admire you career women more than I can say. You're all so brave and smart. Y'all put us homebodies to shame.' When Tory lifted a brow at the desk and the name plate, Lissy laughed and waved her hand again. 'Oh, I just come in a couple times a week to help Daddy out. Once the baby's born, I'm sure I won't have the time or energy.'

And would, Lissy thought, go quickly and not so quietly mad at home with two children. But she'd deal with that, and Dwight, when the time came.

'Now, you just tell me everything you've been up to.'

'I'd love to chat, Lissy.' If you yanked my tongue out and wrapped it around my neck. 'But I need to get settled.'

'Oh, how silly of me. You must be just worn out and ready to drop.' The thin smile told Tory that if she wasn't, Lissy certainly thought she looked it. 'We'll have ourselves a nice, long catch-up once you're rested.'

'I'll look forward to it.' Remember, Tory told herself, this is just the type of customers you need. 'I ran into Wade just a few minutes ago. He mentioned the house – my old house – might be available to rent.'

'Why, it sure is. The Lavelle tenants moved on just a couple weeks back. But, honey, you don't want to live way out there, now, do you? We've got some nice apartments right here in town. River Terrace has everything a single girl could want, including single men,' she added with a sly wink. 'Modern fixtures, wall-to-wall carpet. We've got us a garden unit available that's just lovely.'

'I'm not interested in an apartment. I'd enjoy being out in the country a ways. What's the rent?'

'I'll just look that up for you.' She knew it, of course. Lissy's mind was much sharper than people expected. She preferred it that way. She shifted her chair, fumbled with the keyboard of her computer a bit for form. 'I swear, I'll never get the hang of these things. You know that's a two-bedroom, one-bath frame construction.'

'Yes, I know.'

Scanning the screen, Lissy tossed off the monthly rent. 'Now, that's a good fifteen-, twenty-minute drive from town. This sweet little apartment I was telling you about's no more'n a ten-minute walk on a pretty day.'

'I'll take the house.'

Lissy glanced up, blinked. 'Take it? Don't you want to run out and see it first?'

'I have seen it. I'll write out a check. First and last month's rent?'

'Yes.' Lissy shrugged. 'Just let me print out the rental agreement.'

Less than thirty seconds after the deal was signed and sealed and Tory walked out with the keys, Lissy was on the phone spreading the word.

This, too, had changed. The house stood as it had always stood, back from a narrow dirt lane a short spit from the swamp. Fields spread on its west side, the tender shoots of cotton already sprung up out of the earth, their rows neat as docile schoolchildren. But someone had planted azaleas in pink and white, and a young magnolia tree near the bedroom window.

She remembered the screens going rusty, and the white paint going gray. But someone had taken care here. The windows sparkled, and the paint was a fresh and soft blue. A front porch had been added, wide enough for the rocking chair that stood alongside the door.

It was almost welcoming.

Her pulse beat dull and thick as she walked toward it. There would be ghosts, but ghosts were why she'd come back. Wasn't it better to face them all?

The keys rattled in her hand.

The screen door squeaked. She told herself it was a homey sound. A friendly screen door should squeak, and it should slam.

Bracing it open, she fit the key in the lock, turned it. She took one deep breath before stepping inside.

She saw the ragged couch with its faded roses, the old console TV, the frayed braided rug. Dull yellow walls with no pictures to brighten the space. The smell of overcooked greens and Lysol.

Tory! You get in here and clean yourself up this minute. Didn't I tell you I wanted this table set for supper before your daddy gets home?

Then the image winked away, and she stood in an empty room. The walls were painted cream, a plain but serviceable color. The floors were bare but clean. The air carried the faint scent of paint and polish, more efficient than offensive.

She stepped through to the kitchen.

The counters had been redone in a neutral stone gray, and the cabinets painted white. The stove was new – or newer than the one her mother had sweated over. The window over the sink looked out to the swamp, as it always had. Lush and green and secret.

Gathering her courage, she turned and headed toward her old bedroom.

Had it always been so small? She wondered. Barely big enough to swing a cat in, she decided, though it had been large enough for her needs. Her bed had been close to the window. She'd liked looking out into the night, or into the morning. She'd had a little dresser, and its drawers had swelled and stuck every summer. She'd hidden books in the bottom drawer because Daddy didn't approve of her reading anything but the Bible.

There were good memories mixed with the bad in this room. Of reading late into the night in secret, of dreaming private dreams, of planning adventures with Hope.

And, of course, of the beatings.

No one would ever lay hands on her again.

It would make a reasonable office, she decided. A desk, a file cabinet, perhaps a reading chair and lamp. It would do.

She would sleep in her parents' old room. Yes, she would sleep there, and she would make it her own.

She started to go out, but couldn't resist. Quietly, she opened the closet door. There, the ghost of herself huddled in the dark, face streaked with tears. She'd shed tears of a lifetime before she was eight.

Crouching, she ran her fingers along the baseboard, and they trembled over the shallow carving. With her eyes closed, she read the letters with fingertips, the way the blind read braille.

I AM TORY

'That's right. That's right. I am Tory. You couldn't take that from me, couldn't beat that out of me. I'm Tory. And I'm back.'

Unsteadily she got to her feet. Air, she thought. She needed air. There was never any air in the closet, never any light. Sweat sprang to her palms as she backed up.

She turned to dash from the room, would have run from the house. But a shadow wavered outside the screen door. The afternoon sun poured in behind it, outlined it into the shape of a man.

As the door squeaked open, she was eight years old again. Alone, helpless. Terrified.

41

Chapter Four

The shadow said her name. The whole of it, *Victoria*, so that it flowed out like something rich poured from a warmed bottle.

She might have run, and it shamed and surprised her to find there was still that much rabbit inside her that wanted to careen away, plunge into a bolt-hole at the first snap of a twig. The ghosts of the house circled around her, whispering taunts in her ear.

She'd run before. More than once. It had never saved her.

She stood where she was, frozen. Panic swam up sickly from gut to throat as the door creaked open.

'I've frightened you. I'm sorry.' His voice was quiet, the tone a man uses to soothe the injured, or complete a seduction. 'I wanted to stop by, see if you needed anything.'

He stood just inside the door so the sun beamed behind him, blurred his features. In her mind, thoughts tumbled, going soft so they spilled over each other. 'How did you know I was here?'

'Have you been away so long you don't know how quick the grapevine climbs in Progress?'

There was a smile in his voice, calculated, she thought, to put her at ease. It meant the fear showed, and made her too easy a target. That, at least that, she could stop. She folded her hands. 'No, I haven't forgotten anything. Who are you?'

'That sound you hear's my ego crumbling. Even after all these years, I could've picked you out in a crowd. It's Cade,' he said, and stepped closer. 'Kincade Lavelle.'

He stepped out of the harsh light, until it fell behind him into sun and shadow. The keenest edge of fear ebbed with the glare, and she saw him clearly.

Kincade Lavelle, Hope's brother. Would she have recognized

him? No, she didn't think so. The boy she remembered had been thin of body and soft of face. This man's build was rangy, hinted of tough in the muscles of the forearms showing under the rolled-up sleeves of his work shirt. And though he smiled easily enough, there was nothing soft in the sharp bones and high planes of his face.

His hair was darker than it had been, the color of walnuts, with the curling tips bleached out by the sun. He'd always been one for the out-of-doors. She remembered that. Remembered she'd some-times see him walking the fields with his father in a kind of swagger that came from owning the land your feet landed on.

The eyes, she thought. She might have placed the eyes. That deep summer blue, like Hope's. The sun had left its mark there as well with faint lines etched into the corners. The kind, she thought, that brought men character and women despair.

Those eyes watched her now, with a kind of lazy patience that might have embarrassed her if her pulse had been level.

'It's been a long time,' was the best she could do.

'About half my life.' He didn't offer his hand. Instinct told him she'd only jolt and embarrass both of them. She looked ready to jump, or collapse. Neither would suit him. Instead he tucked his thumbs casually in the front pockets of his jeans.

'Why don't you come on out on the front porch and sit down? It appears that old rocker's the only chair we've got right now.'

'I'm fine. I'm all right.'

White as death was what she was, with those soft gray eyes that had always fascinated him still wide and bright. Growing up in a household largely dominated by women had taught him how to get around female pride and sulks with the least fuss and energy. He simply turned back, pushed open the screen.

'Stuffy in here,' he said, and stepped out, keeping the door wide and banking on manners, nudging her to follow.

Left with little choice, she crossed the room, walked out onto the porch. He caught the faintest drift of her scent and thought of the jasmine that preferred to bloom at night, almost in secret his mother's garden.

'Must be an experience.' He touched her now, ligh her to the chair. 'Coming back here.'

She didn't jump, but she did edge away i motion. 'I needed a place to live, and

Her stomach muscles refused to loosen up again. She didn't like talking to men this way. You never knew, not for certain, what was under the easy words and easy smiles.

'You've been living in Charleston awhile. Life's a lot quieter here.'

'I want quiet.'

He leaned back against the rail. There was an edge here, he mused. However delicate she looked, there was an edge, like a raw nerve ready to scream. Odd, he realized, it was just what he remembered most about her.

Her delicacy, like the business end of a scalpel.

'There's a lot of talk about your store.'

'That's good.' She smiled, just the faintest curve of lips, but her eyes remained serious and watchful. 'Talk means curiosity, and curiosity will bring people through the door.'

'Did you run a store in Charleston?'

'I managed one. Owning's different.'

'So it is.' Beaux Reves was his now, and owning was indeed different. He glanced behind him, out to the fields where seedlings and sprouts reached for the sun. 'How does it look to you, Tory? After all this time and distance?'

'The same.' She didn't look at the fields, but at him. 'And not at all the same.'

'I was thinking that about you. You grew up.' He looked back at her, watched her fingers curl on the arms of the chair as if to steady herself. 'Grew into your eyes. You always had a woman's eyes. When I was twelve, they spooked me.'

It took the will, and the pride she'd carved into herself, to keep her gaze level. 'When you were twelve, you were too busy running wild with my cousin Wade and Dwight the — Dwight Frazier, to pay any notice of me.'

'You're wrong about that. When I was twelve,' he said slowly, 'here was a space of time I noticed everything about you. I still that picture of you inside my head. Why don't we stop of a she's not standing right here between us?'

The w a jerk, walked to the far end of the porch and stood, help you.' her chest, to stare out at the fields.

' Cade said. 'We both lost her. And neither

chest, like hands pushing. 'I can't

'I'm not asking you for help.'

'For what, then?'

Puzzled, he shifted, then settled back again to study her profile. She'd closed up, he realized. Whatever small opening there'd been was shuttered down again. 'I'm not asking for anything, Tory. Is that what you expect from everyone?'

She felt stronger now, on her feet, and turned to give him a steady stare. 'Yes.'

A bird darted behind him, a quick gray flash that swept by and found a perch in one of the tupelos edging the swamp. And there, it seemed to her, it sang its heart out for hours before Cade spoke again.

Had she forgotten this? she wondered. The long, easy pauses, the patient rhythm of country conversations?

'That's a pity,' he said, as her blood began to beat in the silence. 'But I don't want anything from you, except maybe a friendly word now and then. The fact is, Hope meant something to both of us. Losing her had an effect on my life. I hesitate to call a lady a liar, but if you were to stand there, eye to eye with me, and tell me it didn't affect yours, that's what I'd have to do.'

'What difference does it make to you how I feel?' She wanted to rub the chill from her arms, but resisted. 'We don't know each other. We never really did.'

'We knew her. Maybe your coming back stirs things to the surface again. That's no fault of yours, it just is.'

'Is this visit a welcome back, or a warning for me to keep my distance?'

He said nothing for a moment, then shook his head. The humor slid back into his eyes, a glint so much speedier than his voice. 'You sure grew up prickly. First, I don't make a habit of asking beautiful women to keep their distance. I'd be the one to suffer, wouldn't I?'

She didn't smile, but he did, and this time deliberately took a step closer. Perhaps the motion, perhaps the sound of work boots on wood, sent the bird deeper into the swamp and silenced the song.

'You could always tell me to keep mine, but I'm unlikely to listen. I came by to welcome you back, Tory, and to get a look at you. I got a right to my own curiosity. And seeing you brings some of that summer back. That's a natural thing. It's going to

45

bring it back for others, too. You had to know that before you decided to come.'

'I came for me.'

Is that why you look sick and scared and tired? he wondered. 'Then welcome home.'

He held out his hand. She hesitated, but it seemed as much a dare as an offering. When she placed hers in it, she found his warm, and harder than she'd expected. Just as she felt the connection, a kind of quiet internal click, unexpected. And unwelcome.

'I'm sorry if it seems unfriendly.' She slid her hand free. 'But I've got a lot of work to do. I need to get started.'

'You just let me know if there's anything I can do for you.'

'I appreciate that. Ah . . . you fixed the house up nice.'

'It's a good house.' But he looked at her as he said it. 'It's a good spot. I'll let you get doing,' he added, and started down the steps. He stopped beside a tough-looking pickup that desperately needed washing. 'Tory? You know that picture of you I carried in my head?' He opened the truck door, and a quick little breeze ruffled through his sun-streaked hair. 'I got a better one now.'

He drove off, keeping her framed in the rearview mirror until he made the turn from hard-packed dirt to asphalt.

He hadn't meant to bring up Hope, not right off. As the owner of Beaux Reves, as her landlord, as a childhood acquaintance, he'd told himself it was a straight duty call. But he hadn't fooled himself, and he obviously hadn't fooled Tory, either.

Curiosity had sent him straight out to what people hereabouts still called the Marsh House, when he'd had a dozen pressing matters demanding his attention. He'd been raised to run the farm, but he ran it his own way. That way didn't please everyone.

He'd learned to play politician and diplomat. He'd learned to play whatever role was required, as long as he got what he wanted.

He wondered just what role he'd need to play with Tory.

Whether she was ready to admit it or not, her coming back shifted all manner of balances. She was the pebble in the pond, and the ripples were going to run long and wide.

He wasn't sure what to do about her, what he wanted to do about her. But he was a man of the land, and men who made their living from earth and seed and weather knew how to bide time.

On impulse he pulled the truck to the side of the road. He had no business making this stop when all his responsibilities were gathered at Beaux Reves. The new crops were coming up, and when the crops grew, so did the weeds. He had cultivating to oversee. This was a pivotal year for the plans he'd implemented. He wanted his finger on every step and stage.

Still, he got out of the cab, walked across the little wooden bridge, and stepped into the swamp.

Here the world was green and rich and alive. Paths had been cleared and alongside them, neat as a park, grew azaleas in staggering, stubborn bloom. Among the magnolia and tupelo were swaths of wildflowers, tidy hills and spears of evergreens. It was no longer the exciting, slightly dangerous world of his youth.

Now it was a shrine to a lost child.

His father had done this. In grief, in pride, perhaps even in the fury he'd never shown. But it had lived inside him, Cade knew, like a cancer. Growing and spreading in secret and silence, those tumors of rage and despair.

Grief had been treated like a disease inside the walls of Beaux Reves. And here, he thought, it had been turned to flowers.

Lilies would dance in the summer, a colorful parade, and the delicate yellow irises that liked their feet wet were already blooming in the spring shadows like tiny sunbeams. Brush had been cleared for them. Though it grew back quickly, as long as his father had lived there had been hands to hack it down again. Now that responsibility lay on Cade as well.

There was a small stone bench in the clearing where Hope had built her fire that last night of her life. There was another arched bridge over the tobacco-brown water haunted by cypress trees, bordered by thickly curling ferns and rhododendrons flowering in sheer white. Camellias and pansies that would bring flower and scent over the winter when they thrived.

And between the bench and the bridge, in the midst of a pool of pink and blue blossoms, stood a marble statue carved in the likeness of a laughing young girl who would be forever eight.

They had buried her eighteen years before, on a hill in the sunlight. But here, in the green shadows and wild scents, was where Hope's spirit lay.

Cade sat on the bench, let his hands dangle between his knees. He didn't come here often. Since his father's death eight years before no one did, at least no one in the family.

As far as his mother was concerned, this place ceased to exist from the moment Hope had been found. Raped, strangled, then tossed aside like a used-up doll.

Just how much, Cade asked himself, as he had countless times over that long sea of years, just how much of what had been done to her was on his head?

He sat back, closed his eyes. He'd lied to Tory, he admitted now. He did want something from her. He wanted answers. Answers he'd waited for more than half his life.

He took five precious minutes to steady himself. Strange he hadn't realized until now how much it had unnerved him to see her again. She'd been right that he'd paid scant attention to her when they were children. She'd been the little Bodeen girl his sister had run with, and beneath the notice of a twelve-year-old boy.

Until that morning, that horrible morning in August when she'd come to the door with her cheek raw and bruised and her wide eyes terrified. From that moment, there'd been nothing about her he hadn't noticed. Nothing about her he'd forgotten.

He'd made it his business to know all there was to know about where she'd gone, what she'd done, who she'd been long after she left Progress.

He'd known, nearly to the hour, when she'd begun making her plans to come back.

And still he hadn't been prepared to see her standing in that empty room, the color leached out of her face so that her eyes stood out like pools of smoke.

They'd both take time to settle, Cade decided as he got to his feet. And then they'd deal with each other. Then they'd deal with Hope.

He walked back to his truck, drove out to check his crops and his crew.

He was hot, sweaty, and dirty by the time he turned between the stone pillars that guarded the long, shady lane to Beaux Reves. Twenty oaks, ten on either side, flanked the drive and arched over it to make a green and gold tunnel. In between their thick trunks he could see the flowering shrubs in bloom, the wide sweep of lawn, the ribbon of a bricked path that led to the garden and outbuildings.

When he was tired, as he was now, this last stretch never failed to reach out to him, to stroke at his fatigue like a loving hand. Through drought and war, through the ripping apart of one way of life and the making of another, Beaux Reves stood.

More than two hundred years the land had been in Lavelle hands. They had tended it, nurtured it, abused it, and cursed it, but it survived. It had buried them, and it had birthed them.

And now it was his.

Perhaps the house was one huge eccentricity in the center of elegance, more fortress than house, more defiant than graceful. The stone caught sparks from the dying sun, and glinted. The towers lanced arrogantly into a sky going the color of a fresh bruise.

There was a huge pool of flowers in the oval centering the circular drive. Some long-ago ancestor's attempt to soften the arrogantly masculine lines, Cade had always thought. Instead, the sea of flowers and shrubs served as a sharp contrast to the massive front doors of deeply carved oak and the straight spears of windows.

He left the truck at the far curve of the drive and walked up the six stone steps. The veranda had been added on by his great-grandfather. A bit of civility, Cade mused, with its shading roof and twining vines of clematis. He could sit, if he chose, as those of his blood had sat for generations, and look out over grass and tree and flower without smudging the view with the vicious and sweat-soaked work of the fields.

Which was why he rarely sat there.

He scraped the soil off his boots. Inside those doors was his mother's domain, and though she would say nothing, her disapproving silence, her cool-eyed stare at any trace of the fields on her floors, would be worse than a blistering lecture.

Spring had been kind, so the windows were open to the evening. The scents from the gardens spilled in to mingle with the perfumes of the flowers that had been selected and arranged indoors.

The entrance hall was massive, the floor marbled in sea green so it felt as though his feet would simply sink into cool water.

He thought of a shower, a beer, and a good hot meal before he tackled the evening's paperwork. He moved quietly, listening, and felt no guilt at the hope he could avoid any contact with his family until he was clean and refueled.

He'd gotten as far as the bar in the main parlor, had just popped the top on a Beck's, when he heard the feminine click of heels. He winced, but his face was composed and relaxed when Faith swirled into the room.

'Pour me a white wine, darling, I got some rough edges need smoothing.'

She stretched herself out on the sofa as she spoke, with a fussy little sigh and a finger brush of her short bob of blond hair. She was back to blond. There were those who said Faith Lavelle changed her hair color nearly as often as she changed men.

There were those who relished saying it.

She'd been divorced twice in her twenty-six years, and had gathered and discarded more lovers than most cared to count. Particularly Faith. Yet she managed to project the image of the delicate southern flower with camellia-white skin and the Lavelle blue eyes. Moody blue eyes that could well up with tears on command, and were skilled at making promises she might or might not intend to keep.

Her first husband had been a wild and handsome boy of eighteen with whom she'd eloped two months before she graduated from high school. She'd loved him with all the passion and capriciousness of youth and had been devastated when he'd left her flat, and broke, less than a year later.

Not that she let anyone know that. As far as the world was concerned, she'd dumped Bobby Lee Matthews and had come back to Beaux Reves because she'd grown bored playing house.

Three years later, she'd married an aspiring country-western singer she'd met in a bar. That she had done out of boredom, but she'd stuck it out for two years before she realized Clive had also aspired to live the cheating, beating lyrics of the songs he scribbled in a haze of Budweiser and Marlboros.

So once again, she was back at Beaux Reves, edgy, dissatisfied, and secretly disgusted with herself.

She sent Cade a sweet and melting smile when he brought her a glass of wine. 'Honey, you look worn out. Why don't you sit down and put your feet up for a while?' She grabbed his hand, gave it a little tug. 'You work too hard.'

'Anytime you want to pitch in . . .'

Her smile sharpened, a blade turned to the keen edge. 'Beaux Reves is yours. Papa made that clear all our lives.'

'Papa's not here anymore.'

Faith merely moved one careless shoulder. 'Doesn't change the facts.' She lifted her wine, sipped. She was a lovely woman who took great pains to exploit her beauty. Even now, for an evening at home, she'd added soft color to her cheeks, painted her sensuously wide mouth a poppy pink and had draped herself in a silk blouse and slacks in soft rose.

'You can change anything you want to change.'

'I've been raised to be decorative, and useless.' She tossed her head, then stretched like a cat. 'And I'm so good at it.'

'You irritate me, Faith.'

'I'm good at that, too.' Amused, she nudged his leg with her bare foot. 'Don't be cross, Cade. Arguing's going to spoil my taste for this wine. I've already had words with Mama today.'

'A day doesn't go by you don't have words with Mama.'

'I wouldn't if she wasn't so critical of every damn thing. She's been in a mood most of the day.' Faith's eyes glittered. 'Since Lissy called from town, anyhow.'

'No point in it. She knew Tory was coming back.'

'Coming's different from being. I don't think she likes the idea of renting the Marsh House to her.'

'If she doesn't live there, she'll just live somewhere else.' Since he was tired, he lay his head back and tried to will the tension of the day out of his neck and shoulders. 'She's back, and it appears she means to stay.'

'So you did go see her.' Faith drummed her fingers against her thigh. 'I thought you would. Duty first for our Cade. Well . . . What's she like?'

'Polite, reserved. Nervous, I think, about being back.' He took a sip of beer. 'Attractive.'

'Attractive? I remember tree-bark hair and knobby knees. Skinny and spooky.'

He let it pass. Faith tended to pout if a man, even her brother, commented on another woman's good looks. He wasn't in the mood for her sulks. 'You could make the effort to be nice to her, Faith. Tory wasn't responsible for what happened to Hope. What's the point of making her feel as though she were?'

'Did I say I wasn't going to be nice to her?' Faith ran her fingers around the rim of her glass, she couldn't seem to keep them still.

'I imagine she could use a friend.'

Faith dropped her hand, and her silky voice went flat. 'She was Hope's friend, never mine.'

'Maybe not, but Hope's not here anymore, either. And you could use a friend yourself.'

'Honey, I've got plenty of friends. It's just that none of them happens to be a woman. Fact is, things are so dull around here, I might go into town tonight after all. See if I can find me a friend for a few hours.'

'Suit yourself.' He pushed her foot aside and rose. 'I need a shower.'

'Cade,' she said before he got to the door. She'd seen that flare of derision in his eyes, and it stung. 'I got a right to live my life as I choose.'

'You've got a right to waste your life as you choose.'

'All right,' she said evenly. 'And so do you. But I'm saying maybe for once I agree with Mama on one thing. We'd all be better off if Victoria Bodeen went back to Charleston and stayed there. You'd sure as hell be better off keeping your distance from whatever trouble she's carrying with her.'

'What are you afraid of, Faith?'

Everything, she thought, as he walked away. Just everything.

Restless now, she uncurled herself and paced to the tall front windows. Gone now was the languorous southern belle. Her movements were quick, almost jittering with nervous energy.

Maybe she would go into town, she thought. Go somewhere. Maybe she'd just leave altogether.

And go where?

Nothing was what she thought it would be when she left Beaux Reves. No one was how she thought they would be. Including herself.

Every time she left she told herself it was for good. But she always came back. Every time she left she told herself it would be different. That she would be different.

But she never was.

How could she expect anyone to understand that everything that had happened before, everything that had happened since, all hinged on that one night when she – when Hope – had been eight?

Now the person who connected the night with all the others was back.

Standing, looking out over the lawn and gardens going silver with dusk, Faith wished Tory Bodeen to hell.

It was nearly eight when Wade finished with his last patient, an elderly mixed breed with failing kidneys and a heart murmur. His equally elderly owner couldn't bring herself to put the poor old dog down, so Wade had once again treated the dog and gently soothed the human.

He was too tired for the diner and thought he'd just slap together a sandwich or open a can.

The small apartment above his office suited him. It was efficient, convenient, and cheap. He could have afforded better, and so both of his parents continually reminded him, but he preferred to live simply and shovel the profits of his practice back into it.

He had no pets of his own at the moment, though he'd had quite a menagerie as a child. Dogs and cats, of course, and with them the prerequisite wounded birds, the frogs, the turtles, the rabbits, and once a runt pig he'd called Buster. His indulgent mother hadn't drawn the line until he'd wanted to bring home a black snake he'd found stretched across the road.

He'd been sure he could talk her into it, but when he'd come to the kitchen door with a plea in his eyes and four feet of wiggling snake in his hands, his mother had screamed loud enough to bring Mr. Pritchett from next door leaping over their shared fence.

Pritchett had sprained his hamstring, Wade's mother had dropped her beloved milk glass pitcher on the kitchen tiles, and the snake had been banished to the river outside of town.

But bless her, Wade thought, she'd tolerated everything else he'd dragged in with hardly a word of complaint.

Eventually he'd have a house and yard and the time to indulge himself. But until he could afford a larger staff, most of his workdays ran ten hours minimum, and that didn't count the emergencies. People who didn't have the time to devote to pets shouldn't have them. He felt the same way about children.

He headed into the kitchen first, grabbed an apple. Dinner, such as it was, would wait until he'd washed the dog off him.

Crunching into the apple, he flipped through the mail he'd carried up with him as he walked to the bedroom.

He smelled her before he saw her. That hot wave of woman hit his senses, scattered his thoughts. She stirred on the bed, a rustle of silky skin against the sheets.

She wore nothing but an invitational smile.

'Hello, lover. You worked late.'

'You said you'd be busy tonight.'

Faith crooked a finger. 'I intend to be. Why don't you come over here and occupy me.'

Wade tossed the mail and the apple aside. 'Why don't I?'

Chapter Five

It was a pitiful thing, Wade supposed, for a man to be hung up on one woman all of his life. More than pitiful when that woman insisted on flitting in and out of that life like a careless butterfly. And the man let her.

Each time she came back, he told himself he wouldn't play the game. And each time she hooked him in until he was too deep into the pot to fold his hand and walk away.

He'd been the first man to have her. He had no hope of being the last.

He was no more able to resist her now than he'd been over ten years before. That bright summer night she'd climbed in his window, and into his bed while he slept. He could still remember what it had been like, to wake with that sleek, hot body sliding over his, that hungry mouth smothering him, devouring him, clamping over him until he was rock hard and randy.

She was fifteen years old, he thought now, and she'd taken him with the quick, heartless efficiency of a fifty-dollar whore. And she'd been a virgin.

That, she'd told him, had been the point. She didn't want to be a virgin, and she'd decided to get rid of the burden with as little fuss as possible, and with someone she knew, liked, and trusted.

Simple as that.

For Faith it had always been simple. But for Wade, that summer night, weeks before he'd gone back to college, had layered on the first of many complicated tiers that made up his relationship with Faith Lavelle.

They'd had sex as often as they could manage that summer. In the backseat of his car, late at night when his parents slept down the hall, in the middle of the day when his mother sat on the veranda gossiping with friends. Faith was always willing, eager, ready. She'd been a young man's wet dream sprung to life.

And had become Wade's obsession.

He'd been sure she'd wait for him.

In less than two years, while he'd been studying fiercely and planning for the future, their future, she'd run off with Bobby Lee. Wade had gotten drunk and stayed drunk for a week.

She'd come back, of course. To Progress, and eventually to him. With no apology, no tearful plea for forgiveness.

That was the pattern of their relationship. He detested her for it, nearly as much as he detested himself.

'So . . .' Faith climbed over him, tugged a cigarette from the pack on the nightstand, and straddling him, lighted it. 'Tell me about Tory.'

'When did you start smoking again?'

'Today.' She smiled, leaning down to give him a little nip on the chin. 'Don't give me grief on it, Wade. Everyone's entitled to a vice.'

'Which one have you missed?'

She laughed, but there was an edge to it, an edge in her eyes. 'If you don't try them out, how do you know which ones fit? Now, come on, baby, tell me about Tory. I'm just dying to know everything.'

'There's nothing to know. She's back.'

Faith let out a huge sigh. 'Men are such irritating creatures. What does she look like? How does she act? What's she up to?'

'She looks grown-up, and acts very much the same. She's up to opening a gift shop on Market Street.' At Faith's cool stare, he shrugged. 'Tired. She looks tired, maybe a little too thin, like someone who hasn't been altogether well just lately. But there's a sheen on her, the kind you get from city living. As for what she's up to, I can't say. Why don't you ask her?'

She trailed her hand over his shoulder. He had such wonderful shoulders. 'She's not likely to tell me. Never liked me.'

'That's not true, Faith.'

'I oughta know.' Impatient, she rolled off him, off the bed, graceful and contrary as a cat, drawing deep on her cigarette while she paced. The moonlight shimmered over her white skin, lending

56

it a faint and exotic blue cast. He could see fading smudges on her, the shadows of bruises.

She'd wanted it rough.

'Always staring at me with those spooky eyes, hardly saying boo, except to Hope. She always had plenty to say to Hope. The two of them were all the time whispering together. What's she want to move back into the old Marsh House for? What's she thinking?'

'I imagine she's thinking it'd be nice to have a familiar roof over her head.' He rose, quietly closing the curtains before one of the neighbors saw her.

'You know what went on under that roof as well as I do.' Faith turned back, her eyes glittering when Wade switched the bedside light on low. 'What kind of person goes back to a place where they were trapped? Maybe she's as crazy as people used to say.'

'She's not crazy.' Weary now, Wade tugged on his jeans. 'She's lonely. Sometimes lonely people come back home, because there's no place else.'

That hit a little too close to the heart. She turned her eyes away from his, tapped out her cigarette. 'Sometimes home's the loneliest place of all.'

He touched her hair, just a light stroke. It made her yearn to burrow in, cling tight. Deliberately she lifted her head, smiled brilliantly. 'Why are we talking about Tory Bodeen, anyway? Let's fix ourselves some supper, and eat in bed.' Slowly, her eyes on his, she drew down the zipper of his jeans. 'I always have such an appetite when I'm with you.'

Later, he woke in the dark. She was gone. She never stayed, never slept with him in the most simple way. There were times Wade wondered if she slept at all, or if that internal engine of hers forever ran, fueled on nerves, and on needs that were never quite met.

It was his curse, he supposed, to love a woman who seemed incapable of returning genuine feelings. He should cut her out of his life. It was the sane thing to do. She'd only slice him open again, and every time she did, it took longer to heal. Sooner or later there'd be nothing left of his heart but scar tissue, and he'd have no one but himself to blame.

He felt the anger building, a black heat that bubbled in the blood. Leaving the lights off, he dressed in the dark. His fury needed a target before it turned inward and imploded.

It would have been smarter, more comfortable, God knew more sensible, to have booked a room in a hotel for the night. It would have been a simple matter to have accepted her uncle's hospitality and slept in one of the overly fussy, decorated-to-death bedrooms Boots kept ready in the big house.

As a child she'd often dreamed of sleeping in that perfect house on that perfect street where she'd imagined everything smelled of perfume and polish.

Instead, Tory spread a blanket on the bare floor and lay awake in the dark.

Pride, stubbornness, a need to prove herself? She wasn't sure of her own motives for spending her first night in Progress in the empty house of her childhood. But she'd made her bed, so to speak, and was determined to lie in it.

In the morning there would be a great deal to do. Already that evening she'd gone over her lists and made a dozen more. She needed to buy a bed, and a phone. New towels, a shower curtain. She needed a lamp and a table to put it on.

Camping out wasn't quite the adventure it used to be, and having simple tastes and needs didn't mean she didn't require basic comforts.

Lying there in the dark she used her lists, in much the same way she had used the sheer white wall. Each item mentally ticked off was another brick set in place to block out images and keep herself centered in the now.

She'd go to the market and stock the kitchen. If she let that go too long she'd fall back into the habit of skipping meals again. When she neglected her body, it was more difficult to control her mind.

She'd go to the bank, open accounts, personal and business. A trip to the *Progress Weekly* was in order. She'd already designed her ad.

Most of all, while she set up the store in the next weeks, she needed to be visible. She'd work on being friendly, personable. Normal.

It would take time to weather the expected whispers, the questions, the stares. She was prepared for it. By the time she opened for business, people would be used to seeing her again. More, much more important, they would become used to seeing her as she wanted to be seen.

Gradually, she'd become a fixture in town. And then she would begin to explore. *She* would ask questions. She'd begin to look for the answers.

When she had them, she could say good-bye to Hope.

Closing her eyes, she listened to the night sounds, the chorus of peepers, so cheerfully monotonous, the sharp and jarring screech of an owl on the hunt, the soft groans of old wood settling, the occasional sly riveting of mice making themselves at home behind the wall.

She'd have to set traps, she thought sleepily. She was sorry for it, but she didn't care to share her space with rodents. She'd put mothballs under the porches to discourage snakes.

It was mothballs, wasn't it? It has been so long since she'd lived in the country. You put out mothballs for snakes and hung soap for deer and protected what was yours, even though it had been theirs first.

And if the rabbits came to nibble at the kitchen garden, you laid out pieces of hose so they thought it was the snakes you shooed away with the mothballs. Else Daddy'd come home and shoot them with his .22. You'd have to eat them for supper, even though you got sick after because you could see how cute they were twitching their long ears. You had to eat what God provided or pay the price. Getting sick was better than getting a beating.

No, don't think about that, she ordered herself, and shifted on the hard floor. No one was going to make her eat what she didn't want to eat, not ever again. No one was going to raise a strap to her or a fist.

She was in charge now.

She dreamed of sitting on the soft ground by a fire that snapped and smoked and burned the marshmallow she held into the flame on a stick. She liked it burnt so that the outside was black and crackled over the gooey white center. Lifting it out, she blew on the fire that came with it.

She singed the roof of her mouth, but that was all part of the ritual. The quick pain, then the contrast of crisp and sweet sugar.

'Might as well eat charcoal,' Hope said, turning her own candy so that it bubbled gold. 'Now, this is a perfectly toasted marsh-mallow.'

'I like them my way.' To prove it, Tory got another from the bag and stabbed it onto the pointy end of her stick.

'Like Lilah says, "To each his own, said the lady as she kissed the cow." Grinning, Hope nibbled delicately on her marshmallow. 'I'm glad you came back, Tory.'

'I always wanted to. I guess maybe I was afraid. I guess I still am.'

'But you're here. You came, just like you were supposed to.'

'I didn't come that night.' Tory looked away from the fire, into the eyes of childhood.

'I guess you weren't supposed to.'

'I promised I would. Ten thirty-five. Then I didn't. I didn't even try.'

'You have to try now, 'cause there were more. And there'll still be more until you stop it.'

The weight was lowering again so that her eight-year-old chest strained under it. 'What do you mean, more?'

'More like me. Just like me.' Solemn blue eyes, deep as pools, looked through the smoke and into Tory's. 'You have to do what you're supposed to do, Tory. You have to be careful and you have to be smart. Victoria Bodeen, girl spy.'

'Hope, I'm not a girl anymore.'

'That's why it's time.' The fire climbed higher, grew brighter. The deep blue eyes captured glints of it, specks of wild light. 'You have to stop it.'

'How?'

But Hope shook her head and whispered, 'Something's in the dark.'

Tory's eyes shot open. Her heart was thundering in her chest, and in her mouth was the taste of fear and burnt candy.

Something's in the dark. She heard it, the echo of Hope's voice, and the rustle, like a tail of the wind through the leaves, just outside her window.

She saw it, the faint shifting of the light as someone stepped into the path of the moon.

The child inside her wanted to curl up, to cover her face with her hands, to will herself invisible. She was alone. Defenseless.

Whoever was outside was watching, waiting. Even through the fear she could feel that. She struggled to blank her mind, to bring the face, the form, the name into it. But there was only the sheer glass wall of terror.

Not all the terror was hers.

They're afraid, too, she realized. Afraid of me. Why?

Her hand trembled as she slowly reached out for the flashlight beside the blanket. The solid weight of it helped her beat back the worst of the fear. She would not lie helpless. She would defend herself, she would confront, she would take charge.

The child had been a victim. The woman wouldn't be.

She swung up to her knees, flicked at the switch, fumbled, nearly screamed when the beam flashed on. She aimed it at the window like a weapon.

And there was nothing there but shadows and moon.

Her breath came in pants, but she got to her feet. She rushed to the door, slapped on the overhead lights. Whoever was outside could see her now. Let them look, she thought. Let them see she wouldn't cower in the dark.

The beam of light bobbed as she hurried from the bedroom into the kitchen. Again, she switched on the overheads. Let them look, she thought again, and grabbed a carving knife out of the wooden block she'd unpacked. Let them look and see I'm not defenseless.

She'd locked the doors, a habit she'd developed in the city. But she was well aware how useless such a precaution was here. One good kick would spring the locks.

She stepped out of the light, into the shadows of the living room. With her back to the wall, she willed herself to regulate her breathing, until it began to come slow and quiet. She couldn't see if her thoughts were tumbling, couldn't concentrate if her blood was screaming.

For the first time in over four years she prepared to open herself to the gift she'd been cursed with at birth.

But lights stabbed through the front window and washed across the room. Her thoughts scattered wild as blown petals at the sound of a car driving fast up her lane.

Tires sent the thin layer of gravel spitting, an impatient, demanding sound. Her breath came harsh again as she forced herself to the door. She jabbed the flashlight in the pocket of the

61

sweats she'd slept in, gripped the knife firmly in one hand and turned the lock.

The car lights clicked off as the driver yanked open the door. 'What do you want?' Snatching the flashlight again, Tory shoved at the switch. 'What are you doing here?'

'Just visiting an old friend.'

Tory aimed the beam at the figure that stepped out of the car. Her knees went weak, her skin clammy. 'Hope.' She choked out the name as the knife slipped from her fingers and clattered to the floor. 'Oh God.'

Another dream. Another episode. Or maybe it was just madness. Maybe it always had been.

She stepped up to the porch. Moonlight shimmered onto her hair, into her eyes. The screen door creaked as she opened it. 'You look like you've seen a ghost, or were expecting one.' She bent down, picked up the knife. With one elegant finger she tapped the tip of the blade.

'But I'm real enough.' So saying she held up the finger, and the tiny drop of blood gleamed. 'It's Faith,' she added, and simply walked in. 'I saw your light as I was driving by.'

'Faith?' There was a rush like the sea in her head. The joy in it, that frantic leap of it, ebbed as she said the name again. 'Faith.'

'That's right. Got anything to drink around here?' She wandered into the kitchen.

As if she owned the place, Tory thought, then reminded herself that the Lavelles did indeed own the place. She ran a hand over her face, into her hair. Then bracing herself, followed Faith into the kitchen.

'I have some iced tea.'

'I meant something with a little more punch.'

'No, I'm sorry. I don't. I'm not exactly set up for company as yet.'

'So I see.' Intrigued, Faith did a turn around the kitchen, laying the knife on the counter as she passed. 'A little more spartan than I expected. Even for you.'

This was how Hope would have looked if she'd lived. Tory couldn't get the thought out of her head. She would have looked just like this, deep blue eyes against clear white skin, hair the color of corn silk. Slim and beautiful. And alive.

'I don't need much.'

'That was always the difference, one of them, anyway, between us. You didn't need much. I needed everything.'

'Did you ever get it?'

Faith arched a brow, then only smiled and leaned back on the counter. 'Oh, I'm still collecting. How does it feel to be back?'

'I haven't been back long enough to know.'

'Long enough to come to the door with a kitchen knife in your hand when someone pays a call.'

'I'm not used to calls at three in the morning.'

'I had a late date. I'm between husbands at the moment. You never did marry, did you?'

'No.'

'I swear I heard something about you being engaged at one time. I guess it didn't work out.'

The sense of failure, despair, betrayal wanted to come. 'No, it didn't work out. I take it your marriages – two of them, weren't there? – didn't work out, either.'

Faith smiled, and this time meant it. She preferred an even match. 'Grew into your teeth, I see.'

'I don't want to take a bite out of you, Faith. And it seems pointless for you to take one out of me after all this time. I lost her, too.'

'She was my sister. You never could remember that.'

'She was your sister. She was my only friend.'

Something tried to stir inside her, but Faith blocked it off. 'You could have made new friends.'

'You're right. There's nothing I can say to make up for it, to change things, to bring her back. Nothing I can say, nothing I can do.'

'Then why come back?'

'They never let me say good-bye.'

'It's too late for good-byes. You believe in fresh starts and second chances, Tory?'

'Yes, I do.'

'I don't. And I'll tell you why.' She took a cigarette out of her purse, lighted it. After taking a drag she waved it. 'Nobody wants to start over. Those who say they do are liars or delusional, but mostly liars. People just want to pick up where they left off, wherever things went wrong, and start off in a new direction without any of the baggage. Those who manage it are the lucky ones

63

because somehow they're able to shrug off all those pesky weights like guilt and consequences.'

She took another drag, giving Tory a contemplative stare. 'You don't look all that lucky to me.'

'You know what, neither do you. And that's a surprise.'

Faith's mouth trembled open, then she shut it again and smiled thinly. 'Oh, I travel light and travel often. You just ask anyone.'

'Looks like we've landed in the same place. Why don't we make the best of it?'

'Long as you remember who got here first, we won't have a problem.'

'You've never let me forget it. But right now this is my house, and I'm tired.'

'Then I'll see you around.' She started out, trailing smoke. 'You sleep tight, Tory. Oh, and if staying out here all alone gives you the willies, I'd trade that knife in for a gun.'

She stopped, opened her purse, and lifted out a trim, pearl-handled pistol. 'A woman just can't be too careful, can she?' With a light laugh, she dropped the gun back into her bag, snapped it closed, then let the screen door slap behind her.

Tory made herself stand in the doorway, even when the head-lights blinded her. She stood there until the car reversed out of the lane, swung onto the road, and sped away.

She locked the door, then went back in the kitchen for the flash-light, and the knife. Part of her wanted to get into the car, drive into town, and knock on her uncle's door. But if she couldn't spend this first night in the house, it would be that much easier to avoid the next, and the next.

She lay with her back to the wall, her eyes on the window until the dark softened and the first birds of morning woke.

He had been afraid. When he'd crept so quietly to the window, he'd felt what he felt so rarely. A fist of fear squeezing at his gut.

Tory Bodeen, back where it had all started.

She was sleeping, curled on the floor like a gypsy, and he could see the curve of her cheek, the shape of her lips in the slant of moonlight.

Something would have to be done. He'd known that, had begun to plan for it in his quiet and steady way. But what a jolt to see her here, to remember it all so vividly just by seeing her here.

He'd been startled when she'd woken, coming out of sleep as fast and straight as an arrow from a bow. Even in the dark he'd seen visions in her eyes. It had brought sweat to his face, to the palms of his hands. But there were plenty of shadows, plenty of shelter to slide into. Cracks in the wall.

He'd folded himself into one of the cracks and watched Faith arrive. The bright hair gleaming in the moonlight in such an interesting contrast to Tory's dark. Tory who seemed to absorb the light rather than reflect it.

He'd known, of course, in that instant when they'd stood together, when their voices had mixed, where they would take him. Where he would take them.

It would be as it had been the first time, so long ago. It would be what he'd been trying to recapture for eighteen long years.

It would be perfect.

She'd planned to be up early. When the knock at the front door woke her at eight, Tory wasn't certain if she was more irritated with herself or the new visitor. Rubbing the sleep from her eyes, she stumbled out of the bedroom, blinked at the sunlight, and fumbled with the lock.

She gave Cade one bleary stare through the screen. 'Maybe I shouldn't be paying rent if the Lavelles have decided to make this their home away from home.'

'Sorry?'

'Nothing.' She gave the screen one halfhearted push that wasn't entirely an invitation, then turned away. 'I need coffee.'

'I woke you.' He stepped in to follow her into the kitchen. 'Farmers tend to think everyone's up at dawn. I—' He stopped by the open door of the bedroom, swore. 'For Christ's sake, Tory, you don't even have a bed.'

'I'm getting one today.'

'Why didn't you stay with J.R. and Boots?'

'Because I didn't want to.'

'You prefer sleeping on the floor? What's this?' He walked into the room, taking over, Tory thought, much as his sister had the night before, then came out holding the knife.

'It's my crochet hook. I've got a hell of an afghan going.' When he only stared at her, she hissed out a breath and stomped into the kitchen. 'I had a late night, and I'm surly, so watch your step.'

Saying nothing, he slid the knife back into its slot in the block. While she measured out coffee and water, he set the plate he carried on the counter.

'What's that?'

'Lilah sent it over, she knew I was coming this way this morning.' Cade peeled up a corner of the foil. 'Coffee cake. She said you had a taste for her sour cream coffee cake.'

Tory merely stared at it, shocking them both when her eyes filled. Before he could move, she held up a hand, kept it aloft like a shield as she turned away.

Unable to resist, he ran a hand over her hair, then let it drop when she stepped quickly, deliberately out of reach.

'You tell her I appreciate it very much. She's well, is she?'

'Why don't you come by and see for yourself?'

'No, not for a while yet. I don't think for a little while yet.' Steadier, she opened a cupboard and took down a cup.

'You gonna share?'

She glanced back over her shoulder. Her eyes were dry now, and clear. He didn't look like a damn farmer, she thought. Oh, he was tanned and lean, and his hair streaked from the sun. His jeans were old and his shirt faded blue. There were sunglasses hooked carelessly by one earpiece in the breast pocket.

What he looked like, she decided, was some Hollywood director's image of a young, prosperous southern farmer who could ooze charm and sex appeal with one easy smile.

She didn't trust images.

'I suppose I have to be polite.'

'You could be rude and greedy,' he said, 'but you'd feel terrible about it later.'

She had four cups, he noted, four saucers, all in solid, sensible white. She had an automatic coffeemaker, and no bed. Her shelves were already tidily lined, again in white. There wasn't a single chair in the house.

Just what, he wondered, did such matters say about Tory Bodeen?

She took out another knife, then lifted her eyebrows at him as she measured a slice. He wagged his fingers until she widened it. 'Got an appetite this morning?' she asked as she cut through.

'I've been smelling that all the way over here.' He picked up the plates. 'Why don't we have this out on the front porch? I take my coffee black,' he added, then walked out.

Tory only sighed and poured two cups.

He was sitting on the steps when she came out, resting his back against the top riser. She sat beside him, sipping her coffee and looking out over his fields.

She'd missed this. The realization came in a backward slap of surprise that was more shock than pain. She'd missed mornings here, when the heat of the day had yet to smother the air, when the birds sang like miracles, and the fields lay green and growing.

She'd had precious mornings like that even as a child, when she had sat on what had been a cracked concrete stoop, studied the coming day, and dreamed foolish dreams.

'It's a nice smile,' he commented. 'Is it the cake or the company that tugged it out of you?'

It vanished like a ghost. 'Why were you coming this way this morning, Cade?'

'I got fields to look after, crews to check.' He broke off a corner of coffee cake. 'And I wanted another look at you.'

'Why?'

'To see if you were as pretty as I thought you were yesterday.'

She shook her head, took a bite of cake, and went straight back to Miss Lilah's wonderful kitchen. It cheered her so much she smiled again, took another bite. 'Why, really?'

'You did look a sight better yesterday,' he said conversationally. 'But I have to take into account you didn't get much sleep on that floor. You make a fine cup of coffee, Miz Bodeen.'

'There's no reason you have to feel you need to check up on me. I'm fine here. I just need a couple of days to settle in. I'm not going to be here half the time anyway. Setting up the store's going to take most of my time.'

'I imagine so. Have dinner with me tonight.'

'What for?' When he didn't answer, she turned her head. His eyes were amused, his lips faintly curved. And in that mild and friendly expression she saw something she'd successfully avoided for years. Frank male interest.

'No, no. Oh no.' She lifted her cup, gulped down coffee.

'That was pretty definite. Let's make it tomorrow night.'

'No, Cade, I'm sure that's very flattering, but I don't have the time or the inclination for any sort of a . . . of a thing.'

He stretched out his long legs, crossed them at the ankles. 'We don't know what sort of a thing either of us has in mind at this stage. Me, I enjoy a meal now and again, and find I enjoy one more in good company.'

'I don't date.'

'Is that a religious obligation or a societal preference?'

'It's a personal choice. Now ...' Because he looked to be settling in, entirely too comfortably, she got to her feet. 'I'm sorry, but I have to get started on my day. I'm already behind schedule.'

He rose, watched her eyes go wide and watchful when he shifted just an inch closer. 'Somebody roughed you up plenty, didn't they?'

'Don't.'

'That's just the point, Tory.' Because he didn't care to have her flinch away from him, he eased back. 'I wouldn't. Thanks for the coffee.'

He walked to his truck, pausing to turn back when he'd opened the door. He gave her a good long stare, figuring it would do them both good for her to get used to it. 'I was wrong,' he called out as he climbed in the cab. 'You're just as pretty today.'

She smiled before she could help herself, watched him grin before he backed out of the lane.

Alone, she sat back down. 'Oh hell,' she muttered, and stuffed more cake into her mouth.

Chapter Six

Independent small-town banks were a dying breed. Tory knew this because her uncle, who'd managed Progress Bank and Trust for twelve years, rarely failed to mention it. Even without the family connection, she would have chosen it for her business. It was just good politics.

It sat on the east side of Market, two blocks down from her shop. That added convenience. The old redbrick building had been carefully and lovingly preserved. That added charm. The Lavelles had established it in 1853, and maintained a proprietary interest.

There, she thought, as she turned toward the front door, was the politics. If you wanted to do business successfully in Progress, South Carolina, you did business with the Lavelles.

It was a rare pie their fingers weren't dipped in.

The interior of the bank had changed. She could remember visiting her grandmother and thinking the tellers worked in cages, like exotic animals in the zoo. Now the lobby area was open, almost airy, and four tellers manned a long, high counter.

They'd added a drive-through window in the back, and behind a waist-high wooden rail and gate two employees sat at lovely old desks topped with sharp and efficient-looking computers. There were several nicely executed paintings of South Carolinian land and seascapes adorning the walls.

Someone, she mused, had figured out how to modernize without deleting the soul. She wondered if she could gently nudge her uncle into one of the paintings or wall hangings she'd soon have for sale.

'Tory Bodeen, is that you?'

With a little jolt, Tory turned her attention to the woman behind the rail. She worked up a smile as she tried to place the face, and came up blank.

'Yes, hello.'

'Well, it's just so nice to see you again, and all grown-up, too.' The woman was tiny, could barely have topped five feet. She came through the gate, held out both hands. 'Always knew you'd be a pretty thing. You won't remember me.'

It felt so rude not to in the face of such sincere delight. For a moment, Tory was tempted to use the connection, grab on to a name. But she couldn't break a vow over something so trivial. 'I'm sorry.'

'Now, there's no need for that. You were just a bit of a thing last I saw you. I'm Betsy Gluck. Your grandma trained me when I was just out of high school. I remember how you used to come in now and again and sit quiet as a mouse.'

'You gave me lollipops.' It was such a relief to remember, to have that quick, sweet taste of cherry on her tongue.

'Why, imagine you remembering that after all this time.' Betsy's green eyes sparkled as she gave Tory's hands a squeeze. 'Now, you're here to see J.R.'

'If he's busy, I can just—'

'Don't be silly. I've got instructions to take you straight into his office.' She wrapped an arm around Tory's waist as she led her through the gate.

She'd have to get used to this, Tory reminded herself. To being touched. Handled. She couldn't be a stranger here.

'It must be so exciting, opening a store all your own. I just can't wait to come shopping. I bet Miz Mooney's just so proud she could pop.' Betsy rapped on a door at the end of a short hall. 'J.R., your niece is here to see you.'

The door swung open, and J.R. Mooney filled it. The size of him always astonished Tory. How this big, brawny man had come from her grandmother was one of life's mysteries.

'There she is!' His voice was as big as the rest of him and boomed out as he made his grab.

Tory was braced for it, and still lost her breath when he scooped her off her feet into his wild grizzly hug. And as always, the surprise came as her toes left the ground that the rib-cracking embrace made her laugh.

'Uncle Jimmy.' Tory pressed her face into his bull's neck, and finally, finally, felt home.

'J.R., you're going to snap that girl like a twig.'

'She's little.' J.R. winked at Betsy. 'But she's wiry. You make sure we got us a few minutes' quiet in here, won't you, Betsy?'

'Don't you worry. Welcome home, Tory,' Betsy added, and closed the door.

'Here, now, you sit down. Want anything? Coca-Cola?'

'No, nothing. I'm fine.' She didn't sit, but lifted her hands, then dropped them. 'I should have come to see you yesterday.'

'Don't you fret about that. You're here now.' He leaned back on his desk, a man of six-two and a muscled two-fifty. His ginger-colored hair hadn't faded with age, but there were thin wires of silver woven through the mass of it. The brush mustache that added a bit of dash to his round face had grown in pure silver, as had his woolly caterpillar eye-brows. His eyes were more blue than gray, and had always seemed so kind to Tory.

Abruptly, he grinned, big as the moon. 'Girl, you look like city. Just as pretty and polished as a TV star. Boots is gonna love showing you off.' He laughed at Tory's automatic wince. 'Oh now, you'll indulge her a bit, won't you? She never did have that daughter she pined for, and Wade just won't cooperate and get married to give her little granddaughters to dress up.'

'She tries to put a lace pinafore on me, we're going to have trouble. I'll go see her, Uncle Jimmy. I need to get settled first, get into the shop and roll up my sleeves. I've got stock and supplies coming in over the next few days.'

'Ready to work, are you?'

'Eager. I've wanted to take this step a long time. I hope the Progress Bank and Trust has room for another account.'

'We've always got room for more money. I'll set you up myself, and we'll get to that in just a minute. Honey, I heard you rented the old house.'

'Does Lissy Frazier hold the record for biggest mouth in Progress these days?'

'She runs neck and neck with a few others. Now, I don't mean to crowd you or anything like that, but Cade Lavelle wouldn't hold you to that lease if you wanted to change your mind. Boots and I wish you'd come stay with us. We got room, God knows.'

'I appreciate that, Uncle Jimmy—'

'No, hold on. Don't say 'but' just yet. You're a grown woman. I got eyes, I can see that. You've been on your own some years now. But I can't say as I like the idea of you living out there, not in that house. I don't see how it can be good for you.'

'Good or not, it feels necessary. He beat me in that house.' When J.R. closed his eyes, Tory stepped closer. 'Uncle Jimmy, I don't say that to hurt you.'

'I should've done something about it. I should've got you out of there. Away from him. Should've got you both out.'

'Mama wouldn't go.' She spoke gently now, because he seemed to need it. 'You know that.'

'I didn't know how bad it was, not then. I didn't look hard enough. But I know now, and I don't like to think about you being out there, remembering all that.'

'I remember it wherever I am. Staying there, well, that proves to me I can face it. I can live with it. I'm not afraid of him anymore. I won't let myself be.'

'Why don't you come on to the house, just for a few days then. See how you settle?' He only sighed when she shook her head. 'It's my plight to be surrounded by stubborn women. Well, sit down so I can do this paperwork and take your money.'

At noon the bells of the Baptist church chimed the hour. Tory stepped back, wiped the sweat off her face. Her display window sparkled like a diamond. She'd carted boxes in from her car and stacked them in the storeroom. She'd measured for shelving, for counters, and made a list of demands and requirements she intended to take down to the realtor.

She was working on the second list, one she would take to the hardware store, when someone tapped on the cracked glass of the shop door.

She studied the spare man in workman's clothes as she approached. Dark hair, well cut, a smooth, handsome face with an easy, crooked smile. Sunglasses hid his eyes.

'I'm sorry. I'm not open,' she said as she opened the door.

'Looks like you could use a carpenter.' He tapped his finger at the crack again. 'And a glass man. How's it going, Tory?' He took off his sunglasses, revealing dark, intense eyes, and a tiny hook-shaped scar just under the right one. 'Dwight Frazier.'

'I didn't recognize you.'

72

'Few inches taller, several pounds lighter than the last time you saw me. Thought I should come by, welcome you as mayor, and shift hats to see if there's anything Frazier Construction can do for you. Mind if I come in a minute?'

'Oh, sure.' She stepped back. 'Nothing much to see just now.'

'It's a good space.'

He moved well, she noted. Not at all like the awkward, chubby boy he'd been. The braces were gone, and so was the ruthless buzz cut his father had insisted on.

He looked fit, and he looked prosperous. No, she thought. She wouldn't have recognized him.

'It's a solid building,' he continued, 'with a strong foundation. And the roof's sound.' He turned back, flashing the smile that had helped his orthodontist buy a cabin cruiser. 'I should know, we put it on two years back.'

'Then I'll know who to come after if it leaks.'

He laughed and hooked his sunglasses in the collar of his T-shirt. 'Frazier builds to last. You're going to want counters, shelves, displays.'

'Yes, I was just measuring.'

'I can send you a good carpenter, at a fair rate.'

It was smart, and again political, to use local labor. If, she thought, local labor met her budget. 'Well, your idea of a fair rate and mine might not connect.'

His grin was lightning and full of charm. 'Tell you what. Let me get some things out of my truck. You can tell me what you've got in mind, and I'll give you an estimate. We'll see if we can make them connect.'

He was aware she was measuring him, even as he measured her walls. He was used to it. As a boy, his father had measured him, and had forever found him just short of the mark.

Dwight Frazier, ex-marine, avid hunter, town councilman, and founder of Frazier Construction, had high standards for the fruit of his loins. His disappointment when that fruit had turned out undersized and soft had been keen.

Young Dwight Junior had never been allowed to forget it.

The truth was, Dwight mused, as he scribbled numbers on his clipboard, he *had* been short of the mark. Short, fat, clumsy, he'd been a prime candidate for jokes and sneers, and his father's tight-lipped disappointment.

Worse, he'd had a brain. As a boy, there was no more deadly combination than a pudgy body, clumsy feet, and a sharp brain. He'd been the darling of his teachers, which meant he might as well have painted a kick-my-ass sign on his back.

His mother had struggled to make up for it the best way she knew how. By shoving food in his face. There was nothing like a box of Ho Ho's, in his dear mama's thinking, to make all right with the world again.

His salvation had been Cade and Wade. Why they'd befriended him had never made full sense to Dwight. Class had been part of it. They had come from three of the town's most prominent families. For that he had been, and continued to be, grateful.

Perhaps there was, still, a tiny splinter of resentment in his gut over the whims of fate that had made those two tall, handsome, and agile, while he'd been plump, plain, and awkward. But he'd made up for it. In spades.

'I started running when I was fourteen.' He said it casually as he drew out his measuring tape again.

'Excuse me?'

'You're wondering.' He crouched, noted on his pad again. 'Got sick of being the fat kid and decided to do something about it. Took off twelve pounds of blubber in a couple of months. First few times I ran, I did it at night when no one could see me. I got sick as three dogs. Stopped eating the cupcakes and candy bars and chips my mother packed in my lunch every day. Thought I'd starve to death.'

He rose, flashed his grin again. 'First year of high school I started going out to the track at night, running there. I was still overweight, still slow, but I didn't puke up dinner anymore. Seems that Coach Heister used to come out there at night, too, in his Chevy sedan in the company of another man's wife. I won't mention who, as the lady remains married and is the proud grand-mother of three now. Hold this end for me, sugar.'

Fascinated, Tory took the end of the measuring tape as Dwight walked backward to span the projected counter area.

'Now, it so happened that on one of our mutual visits to the Progress High School track, I got an eyeful of the coach and the future grandmother of three. It was, you can imagine, a rather awkward moment for all parties involved.'

74

'To say the least.'

'And the least said, the better, which is what Coach suggested to me as he clamped his hands around my throat. I had to agree. However, being a fair man, or perhaps just a suspicious one, he offered me a token in return. If I continued to train, and could take off another ten pounds, he'd give me a place on the track team come spring. This was our tacit agreement, that I would forget the incident and that he would refrain from killing me and burying my body in a shallow grave.'

'Seemed to work for everyone.'

'Sure worked for me. I took off the weight, and shocked everyone, including myself, by not only making the team but blowing the competition to hell in the fifty- and hundred-yard dash. I was a hell of a sprinter, it turned out. I won the All Star trophy three years running, and the love of pretty Lissy Harlowe.'

She warmed to him, one outsider to another. 'That's a nice story.'

'Happy endings. I think I can help you get your own here in your shop. Why don't I buy you lunch and we'll talk about it.'

'I don't—' She broke off as the door opened behind her.

'Don't tell me you're hiring this two-bit hustler.' Wade strolled in, swung an arm around Tory's shoulder. 'Thank God I got here in time.'

'This puppy doctor here doesn't know a damn thing about building. Go give a poodle an enema, Wade. I'm about to take your pretty cousin, and my potential client, to lunch.'

'Then I'll just have to come along and protect her interests.'

'I need shelves more than I need a sandwich.'

'I'll see you get both.' Dwight winked at her. 'Come on, sugar, and bring this dead weight along with you.'

She took thirty minutes, and enjoyed herself more than she'd expected. It was a pleasure to see the adult friendship between Dwight and Wade that had its roots in the boys she remembered.

It made her miss Hope.

It was easy enough for a woman who was rarely comfortable around men to relax when one was her cousin and the other tidily married. So tidily, Dwight was showing off pictures of his son before the sandwiches were served. Tory would have made the appropriate and expected noises in any case, but the truth was the little boy was seriously adorable, with Lissy's pretty face and Dwight's snapping eyes.

And, she decided, as she headed off to do errands, it had been constructive as well as easy. Not only did Dwight understand what she wanted, but he improved on her basic layout, and the estimate slipped comfortably into her budget. Or did after she wheedled, refused, questioned, and pushed. And, wiping imaginary sweat from his brow, he promised the work would be done before the middle of May.

Satisfied, she went out and bought a bed.

She really meant to pick up just the mattress and box spring. Years of frugality had never permitted her to impulse buy. And it was rare, very rare, for her to experience the deep-seated desire to own something.

The minute she saw it, she was hooked.

She walked away from it twice, and back again. The price wasn't out of line, but she didn't need a lovely, classic iron bed with slim, smooth posts to frame both head and foot of the mattress. Yes, it was practical, but it wasn't necessary.

A sturdy bed frame, and a good solid mattress set, that was all she required. All she was going to do was sleep in it, for goodness sake.

She argued with herself even as she pulled out her credit card, as she drove to the loading dock, as she drove home. Then she was too busy hauling and cursing and tugging to waste time arguing.

Standing between rows of newly cultivated cotton, Cade watched her struggle for ten minutes. Then he did some cursing of his own, marched to his truck, and drove down to her lane.

He didn't slam the door after he climbed out, but he wanted to.

'You forgot your magic bracelets.'

She was out of breath, some stray wisps of hair had escaped her braid and were plastered to her face, but she had the huge and heavy box halfway up the porch steps. She straightened, tried not to pant. 'What?'

'You can't be Wonder Woman without your magic bracelets. I'll get this end.'

'I don't need any help.'

'Stop being an ass, and get the door.'

She stomped over, yanked the door open. 'Are you always here?'

He took off his sunglasses, tossed them aside. It was a habit that cost him a pair on the average of two a month. 'You see that field over there? It's mine. Now, move aside while I get this up there. What the hell kind of bed is this?'

'Iron,' she said with some satisfaction, when she noted he had to put his back into it.

'Figures. We need to angle it up through the door.'

'I knew that.' She planted her feet, crouched, and took the weight of her end. There was a lot of muttering, a great deal of finessing, and a scraped knuckle on her end, but they got it through. She continued to walk backward, forced to trust him as he directed her right or left, until they muscled it into the bedroom.

'Thank you.' Her arms felt like rubber. 'I can manage from here.'

'Got any tools?'

'Of course I have tools.'

'Good. Get them. It'll save me from going for mine. Might as well set this up before we bring the rest in.'

In one irritable gesture, she pushed her sweaty hair back. 'I can do it.'

'And you're almost contrary enough for me to let you. I am trapped by my superior breeding.' He took her hand, examined the broken skin, and kissed it lightly before she could snatch it free. 'You can put something on that while I do this.'

She considered insulting him, ordering him out, even kicking him out, and decided every option was a waste of time. She got the tools.

He admired the seriously efficient black toolbox. 'Aren't you just prepared for everything?'

'You probably don't know pliers from a wrench.'

Obviously amused, he pulled out a pair of needle-nose pliers. 'Scissors, right?'

When the breath she huffed out ended on a laugh, he got to work on the heavy-duty staples plugged into the box. 'Go put something on that knuckle.'

'It's all right.'

He didn't bother to look at her, or change the tone of his voice, but there was the light and tempered steel of command. 'Put something on it. Then why don't you go fix us something cold to drink?'

'Look, Cade, I'm not the little woman.'

He glanced up now, measured her with one cool look. 'You're little, and you're a woman. And I've got the scissors.'

'I don't suppose my suggesting just where you might shove those pliers would wipe that smile off your face.'

'I don't suppose telling you you're sexy when you're frazzled would convince you to christen this bed with me once we set it up?'

'Jesus,' was all she said as she strode out of the room.

She left him alone. She could hear the clatter, and the occasional oath, as she hauled in groceries, put them away, brewed tea. He had long hands, she mused. Elegant pianist's fingers that contrasted with the hard, calloused palms. She was sure he knew how to plant and tend and harvest. He'd been raised to do so. But everyday chores? No, that was a different matter.

Since she didn't expect he'd put together a single bed frame in his own privileged life, she imagined she'd walk in on complete chaos. And she was determined to give him plenty of time to make a mess of things.

She hooked up her new kitchen phone, put away her new dishcloths, and lazily sliced lemons for the tea. Satisfied he'd had enough time to mortify himself, she poured two glasses over ice and strolled into the bedroom with them.

He was just turning the last bolt.

Her eyes lit up, and the quick little sound she made was one of sheer, feminine delight. 'Oh! It's wonderful. It's really wonderful. I knew it would be.' Without thinking, she shoved the glasses into his hands so she could run hers over the iron.

His first reaction was amusement, then a cool satisfaction. Just as he started to sip the tea, she stepped into the center of the frame, and ran her fingertips up the iron rungs.

And his reaction turned to sheet lust, so basic, so strong, he took one deliberate step in retreat. He could imagine, perfectly, wrapping her fingers around those posts, holding them there as he thrust into her. One hard, long stroke after another while those long-lidded witch eyes of hers went to smoke.

'It's sturdy.' She gave the headboard a little shake, and his stomach pitched and knotted.

'Damn well better be.'

'You did a good job, and I was rude. Thank you, and I'm sorry.'

'You're welcome and forget it.' He handed her the glass, then reached up to tug the chain of the ceiling fan. 'It's warm in here.' He wanted to bite that spot just under her left ear where her jaw began its curve.

Because his voice was clipped, she suffered another pang of guilt. 'I really was rude, Cade. I'm not very good with people.'

'Not good with people? And you're going to open a shop where you'll deal with them every day?'

'That's customers,' she said. 'I'm very good with customers. I'm positively gracious with customers.'

'So . . .' He moved in until he stood just on the other side of the frame. 'If I buy something from you, you'll be friendly.'

She didn't have to read his thoughts when she could read his eyes. 'Not that friendly.' Nimbly, she sidestepped him and moved out of the room.

'I could be a very good customer.'

'You're trying to frazzle me again.'

'I am frazzling you again. Tory.' He laid a hand on her shoulder. 'Stop that,' he said mildly when she stiffened. He set his glass on the floor, then turned her to face him. 'There, that didn't hurt a bit, did it?'

He had gentle hands. It had been a long time, a very long time, since she'd felt a gentle touch from a man. 'I'm not interested in flirtations.'

'I am, but we can compromise for now. Let's try to be friends.'

'I'm not a good friend.'

'I am. Now, why don't we get the rest of your bed in here so you can get a decent night's sleep tonight.'

She let him get nearly to the door. She'd told herself she wouldn't speak of it. Not to him. Not to anyone, until she was ready. Until she was strong and she was sure. But it was bubbling up inside her.

'Cade. You never asked. Not then, not now. You've never once asked how I knew.' Her palms went damp as he turned, so she clutched them to her elbows. 'You've never asked how I knew where to find her. How I knew what had happened.'

'I didn't have to ask.'

Her words rushed out now, popping like overwound springs.

'Some people think I was with her, even though I said I wasn't. That I ran away and left her. That I just left her—'

'That's not what I think.'

'And the ones who believed me, believed that I saw the way I said I did, they stepped back from me, kept their children away from me. They stopped looking me in the eye.'

'I looked you in the eye, Tory. Then and now.'

She had to take a breath to settle herself. 'Why? If you can believe I have that inside me, why didn't you step back? Why are you coming around here now? Do you expect me to tell you the future? Because I can't. Or give you some stock tips? Because I won't.'

Her face was flushed, he noted, her eyes dark and alive with ripe and ready emotions. One of those emotions, one that prickled through the surface of all the others, was anger.

He wouldn't play to it, or to what he believed were her expectations. 'I prefer living each day as it comes, thanks all the same. And I've got a broker to take care of my portfolio. Did it ever occur to you that I'm coming around here now because I like the look of you?'

'No.'

'Then you are the first and only female without vanity I've had occasion to meet. Wouldn't hurt to get yourself some. Now . . .' He cocked his head. 'Do you want to get this mattress in here, or astound and amaze me by telling me what I had for lunch this afternoon?'

Her mouth opened as he walked out the door. Had he actually made a joke about it? People made fun of her, or rolled their eyes. Or backed cautiously away. Some came begging for her to solve all their problems and unhappiness. But no one, in her experience, made a casual joke.

She rolled the tension out of her shoulders, then walked outside to help him carry in the mattress.

They worked in silence now, her stewing, and his mind elsewhere. When the bed was in place, Cade polished off his tea, took the glass into the kitchen, then headed out.

'You should be able to handle it from here. I'm a bit behind schedule.'

Oh no you don't, she thought, and rushed after him. 'I appreciate the help. I really do.' Whether it was impulse or annoyance, she followed it and wrapped her fingers around his arm until he stopped and glanced down.

'Well then, you just think of me when you're sliding off to dreamland tonight.'

'I know it cost you some time. Oh, you said something about lunch?'

Baffled, he shook his head. 'Lunch?'

It was just enough. 'Yes, your lunch today. Half a ham sandwich with Swiss and brown mustard. You gave the other half to that skinny black dog who comes begging in the fields when he sees you.' She smiled now, stepped away. 'You ought to be ready for supper soon.'

He pondered a minute, then decided to go with instinct. 'Tory, why don't you come back here and tell me what I'm thinking now.'

She felt something like a laugh rumble in her chest. 'I believe I'll just let you keep that to yourself.'

She let the screen door slam behind her.

Chapter Seven

It was the flowers, Margaret always thought, that kept her sane. When she tended her flowers, they never talked back, never told her she didn't understand, never yanked up their roots and stalked away in a huff.

She could prune away the wild parts, those sudden growth sprigs that thought they could go their own way, until the plant was shaped as she intended for it to be shaped.

She'd have been much better off, she imagined, if she'd stayed a spinster and had raised peonies instead of children.

Children broke hearts just by being children.

But marriage had been expected of her. She had done, for as long as she could remember, what had been expected of her. Occasionally she did a little more, but rarely, very rarely did she do less.

And she had loved her husband, for surely that had been expected as well. Jasper Lavelle had been a handsome young man when he'd come courting her. Oh, and he'd had charm as well, the same slow, sly grin she sometimes saw cruise across the face of the son they'd made together.

He'd had a temper, but that had been exciting when she'd been young enough to find such things exciting. She recognized that same temper, the quick flash of it, in her daughter. The daughter who'd lived.

He'd been big and strong, a dramatic kind of man with a loud laugh and hard hands. Perhaps that was why she saw so much of him, and so little of herself, in the children who had been left to them.

It angered her, when she took stock, how vague and blurred her imprint was on the clay of those lives she'd helped create. She had opted, sensibly she was sure, to concentrate on leaving her mark on Beaux Reves instead. There her touch, her vision, ran deep as the roots of the old oaks that lined the drive.

And that, more than son or daughter, had become her pride.

If Hope had lived, it would have been different. She snipped off the faded head of a dianthus without sentiment or regret for the loss of the once fragrant bloom. If Hope had lived, she would have reflected, and realized, all the hopes and dreams a mother instilled in a daughter. She would have given a new luster to the polish of the Lavelle name.

Jasper would have stayed strong and stayed steady and never have disgraced himself with loose women and casual scandal. He would never have strayed from the path they had both started on and left his wife to rub the smudges from the name they shared.

But in the end, Jasper had been a storm, and when he hadn't been crashing, he'd been brewing. Life with him had been a series of events, she supposed. His last had been the poor taste to suffer a fatal heart attack in the bed of his mistress. The fact that the woman had had the sense and the dignity to step back while the incident was hushed up sat in Margaret's craw like a jagged bone.

Still, all said and done, it was so much easier to be his widow than it had been to be his wife.

She couldn't say why he was so much on her mind just now, on this blissfully cool morning when the dew lay wet kisses on her blossoms and the sky was the soft and gentle blue of spring.

He'd been a good husband. For the first stage of their marriage, he'd been a strong and solid provider, a man who'd made the decisions so she didn't have to mind the details. He'd been an attentive father, if perhaps a mite too indulgent.

The passion between them had quieted by the first anniversary of their wedding night. But passion was a difficult and distracting element in a life, such a demanding and unstable emotion. Not that she'd ever refused him, of course, never once since their wedding night had she turned from him in their bed.

Margaret was proud of that, proud she'd been a good and dutiful wife. Even when the idea of sex sickened her, hadn't she lain silent and allowed him his release?

She clipped off more deadheads with a sharp clack of blades, placed the faded flowers in her discard basket.

It was he who had turned away, he who had changed. Nothing had been the same in their marriage, in their lives, in their home since that terrible morning, that hot, sticky August morning when they'd found their Hope in the marsh.

Sweet, good-natured Hope, she thought, with a grief that had become both duller and more heavy through the years. Hope, her bright little angel, the only one of the children who'd come from her who had seemed truly connected. Truly hers.

There were times, after all these years there were still times she wondered if that loss had been a kind of punishment. The taking away of the child she'd loved most. But what crime, what sin had she committed that had merited that kind of punishment?

Indulgence perhaps. Indulging the little girl when it would have been wiser – it was so easy to be wise with distance – to have discouraged, even to have forbade her sweet, innocent Hope from associating with the Bodeen girl. That had been a mistake, but surely not a sin.

And if it had been a sin, it had been more Jasper's. He'd brushed away her concerns when she'd voiced them, even laughed at them. The Bodeen girl was harmless, that's what he'd said. Harmless.

Jasper had paid for that misconception, that mistake, that sin, the whole rest of his life. And still it wasn't enough. It would never be enough.

The Bodeen girl had killed Hope as surely as if she'd choked the life from her with her own small and dirty hands.

Now she was back. Back to Progress, back to the Marsh House, back to their lives. As if she had the right.

Margaret yanked out some bindweed, tossed it into her basket. Her grandmother had liked to say that weeds were just wildflowers that bloomed in the wrong place. But they weren't. They were invaders and needed to be pulled out, cut down, destroyed however it could be done.

Victoria Bodeen could not be allowed to set roots and bloom in Progress.

She looked so pretty, Cade mused. His mother, that admirable and unreachable woman. She dressed for gardening as she dressed for everything. With care, precision, and perfection.

She wore a wide-brimmed straw hat to shade her head, the

ribbon around it a soft blue to match the long cotton skirt and crisp blouse she protected with a dull gray gardening apron.

There were pearls at her ears, round moons of white as luminous as the gardenias she so treasured.

She'd let her hair go white as well, though she was only fifty-three. It was as if she wanted that symbol of age and dignity. Her skin was smooth. Worry never seemed to show on it. The contrast of that pretty, youthful face and the shock of white hair was striking.

She'd kept her figure. She sculpted it ruthlessly with diet and exercise. Unwanted pounds weren't tolerated any more than the stray weed in her gardens.

She'd been a widow eight years now, and had slid so slickly into that slot, it was hard to remember her being otherwise.

He knew she was displeased with him, but that was nothing new. Her displeasure was most usually expressed in the same way as her approval. With a few cool words.

He couldn't remember the last time she'd touched him with feeling, or with warmth. He couldn't remember if he had ever expected her to do so.

But she remained his mother, and he would do what he could to close the rift between them. He knew, too well, how a rift could widen into a gulf with silence.

A small yellow butterfly flitted around her head, and was ignored. She knew it was there, just as she knew he walked to her with long strides along the bricked path. But she acknowledged neither.

'It's a nice morning for being outside,' Cade began. 'Spring's been good to the flowers.'

'We could use some rain.'

'They're calling for some tonight, and none too soon. April's been drier than I like.' He crouched down, leaving an arm span between them. Nearby bees hummed madly in the hills of azaleas. 'Most of the first cultivating's done. I've got to go 'round and check on how the cattle's doing. We've got some bull calves ready to become steers. I've got some errands here and there. Is there anything I can pick up for you?'

'I could use some weed killer.' She lifted her head then. Her eyes were a paler, quieter blue than his own. But they were just as direct. 'Unless you have some moral objection to my using it in my gardens.'

'They're your gardens, Mama.'

'And your fields, as I have been reminded. You'll deal with them as you choose. Just as the properties are your properties. You'll rent them to whom you please.'

'That's right.' He could be as cool as she when he chose. 'And the income from those fields, and those properties, will keep Beaux Reves in the black, well into it. As long as it's in my hands.'

She pinched off a pansy with quick, ruthless fingers. 'Income is not the standard by which one lives one's life.'

'It sure as hell makes life easier.'

'There is no call to take that tone with me.'

'I beg your pardon. I thought there was.' He set his hands on his knees, waited for them to relax. 'I changed the way the farm's run, started changing it over five years back. And it works. Still you refuse to accept or acknowledge that I've made it work. There's nothing I can do about that. As for the properties, I do that my own way as well. Papa's way isn't mine.'

'Do you think he would have let that Bodeen girl set foot on what was ours?'

'I don't know.'

'Or care,' she said, and went back to her weeding.

'Maybe not.' He looked away. 'I can't live my life asking myself what he would've done or wanted or expected. But I do know Tory Bodeen isn't responsible for what happened eighteen years ago.'

'You're wrong.'

'Well, one of us is.' He got to his feet. 'Either way, she's here. Has a right to be here. There's nothing to be done about it.'

They would see, Margaret thought as her son left her alone. They would see what could be done about it.

His mood stayed raw throughout the day. No matter how many times he tried and failed to reach his mother, he felt the sting of that rejection as fresh as the first.

He'd stopped trying to explain and justify his changes to the farm. He still remembered the night he'd shown her charts and graphs and projections, still remembered how she'd stared at him, had stonily informed him before she'd walked away that Beaux Reves was something that couldn't be put on paper and analyzed.

It had hurt, more, he supposed, because she'd been right. It couldn't be put on paper. Neither could the land itself that he was so determined to protect, preserve, and pass on to the next generation of Lavelles.

His pride in it, his duty to it, were no less fierce than hers. But to Cade it was, had always been, a living thing that breathed and grew and changed with the seasons. And to her it was static, like a monument carefully tended. Or a grave.

He tolerated her lack of belief in him, just as he tolerated the amusement and the resentment of his neighbors. He'd dealt with countless sleepless nights during the first three years he'd been in charge of the farm. The fear and worry that he was wrong, that he would fail, that the legacy that had come into his hands would somehow slip through them in his eagerness, in the sheer stubbornness to do things his way.

But he hadn't been wrong, not about the farm. Yes, it cost more in time, effort, and money to grow cotton organically. But the land – oh, the land thrived. He could see it bursting in the summer, resting in the winter, and in spring thirsty for what he would put into it.

He refused to poison it, no matter how many told him that by that refusal he was dooming earth and crop. They'd called him wrongheaded, stubborn, foolish, and worse.

And the first year he'd met government standards for organic cotton, had harvested and sold his crop, he'd celebrated by getting quietly drunk, alone in the tower office that had been his father's.

He bought more cattle because he believed in diversification. He added on more horses because he loved them. And because both horses and cattle made manure.

He believed in the strength and value of green cotton. He studied, he experimented. He learned. He stood by his beliefs enough to hand-chop weeds when it was necessary, and to nurse his blisters without complaint. He watched the skies and the stock reports with equal devotion, and he plowed the profits back into the land just as he plowed the cotton after harvest.

Other areas of the operation were necessary, the leases and rentals and factories. He used them, worked them, juggled them. But they didn't own his heart.

The land did.

He couldn't explain it, and had never tried. But he loved Beaux

Reves the way some men love a woman. Completely, obsessively, jealously. Every year his blood thrilled when it gave birth for him.

Cool morning had become steamy afternoon by the time he finished the bulk of his chores and errands. He carried the list in his head, ticking them off systematically.

He stopped by the nursery two blocks off the town square to pick up his mother's weed killer. The flats of flowers distracted him. He selected a tray of pink rosebud impatient on impulse and carried them inside.

The Clampetts had run the nursery for ten years, starting it as a roadside operation to supplement their soybean farm. Over the decade, they'd done better with flowers than crop. The more successful the nursery, the bigger the burr that lodged in the craw of the Clampett men.

'Get another one of them for twenty percent off.' Billy Clampett puffed on a Camel, directly under the 'No Smoking' sign his mother had tacked to the wall.

'Charge me for two then. I'll pick the other up on the way out.' Cade set the flat on the counter. He'd gone to school with Billy, though they'd never really been friends. 'How's it going?'

'Slow but sure.' Billy squinted through smoke. His eyes were dark and discontented. He wore his hair in a vicious buzz cut that looked sharp as needles to the touch and was no particular color at all. He'd put on weight since high school, or more accurately, had lost the muscle that had made him a star tackle.

'You gonna plant those as another cover crop?'

'No.' Unwilling to get into a pissing match, Cade wandered over to study a selection of pots. He picked two in a verdigris shade, set them on the counter. 'I need some Roundup.'

Billy pinched off the cigarette, dropped the butt into the bottle he kept under the counter. He knew better than to leave evidence his ma would find and scald him over. 'Well now, didn't think you approved of such things. When'd you stop hugging trees?'

'And a bag of potting soil for the impatient,' Cade said easily.

'Might could get you some aldicarb, too; you in the market for insecticide?'

'No, thanks.'

'No, that's right.' Billy gave a wheezy laugh. 'You don't go for insecticides and pesticides and that nasty chemical fertilizer. Your crops, they're virgin pure. Got yourself wrote up in a magazine 'cause of it.'

'When did you start reading?' Cade said pleasantly. 'Or did you just look at the pictures?'

'Fancy magazines and speeches don't mean squat around here. Everybody knows you just sit back and take the benefits from the expense your neighbors put into their fields.'

'Is that so?'

'Yeah, that's so,' Billy lashed out. 'You've had a couple of good years. Just dumbass luck if you ask me.'

'I don't recall asking you, Billy. You want to ring me up here?'

'Sooner or later it's going to cave in on you. You're just inviting pest and disease.' It had been a long, boring day, and Cade Lavelle was one of Billy's favorite targets. The pussy never fought back. 'Your crops get infected, others will, too. Then there'll be hell to pay.'

'I'll keep that in mind.' Cade took some bills from his wallet, tossed them on the counter. 'I'll just carry this out to the truck while you ring it up.'

He kept a choke chain on his temper, much as he would a vicious dog. Unleashed, it was a cold and savage thing. Billy Clampett wasn't worth the time and the effort it would take to yank it back in line once it was loose.

That's what he told himself as he set the pots and the two flats in the truck.

When he came back, the Roundup and a twenty-pound bag of potting soil were on the counter.

'You got three dollars and six cents coming.' With deliberate slowness, Billy counted out the change. 'Saw that sister of yours a time or two 'round town. She sure looks good these days.' He raised his eyes, smiled. 'Real good.'

Cade shoved the change in his pocket, kept his fist in there, as it wanted to plant itself on that sneering mouth. 'How's your wife these days, Billy?'

'Darlene, she's just fine. Pregnant again, third time. I expect I planted another strong son in her. When I plow a field, or a woman, I do it right.' His eyes glinted as his smile spread. 'Just ask your sister.'

Cade's hand was out of his pocket and yanking Billy to his toes by the collar before either of them was prepared for it. 'Just one

89

thing,' Cade said softly. 'You want to remember who holds the deed on that house you're living in. You want to remember that, Billy. And you want to stay clear of my sister.'

'You wave your money around fast enough, but you haven't got the balls to try your fists like a man.'

'Stay clear of my sister,' Cade repeated, 'or you'll find out just what I've got the balls for.'

Cade released him, picked up the rest of his purchases, and strode out. He drove out of the lot, and to the first stop sign. There he simply sat, eyes closed, until the red wash of fury dulled.

He wasn't sure which was worse, all but coming to blows with Clampett while the two of them were surrounded by posies, or having the seed rooting in his mind that his sister had let scum like Clampett put his hands on her.

Shoving the truck into first, he turned and headed over to Market. He found a spot half a block from Tory's shop, just behind Dwight's truck. Doing his best to smother his temper, he hauled the pots out, carried them down to set them outside the door.

He could hear the high whine of a skill saw before he walked inside.

The base of the counters was in place, and the first line of shelves set. She'd gone with pine, and had them clear-varnished. A smart choice, Cade thought. Simple and clean, they'd show off her wares instead of distracting from them. The floor was covered with tarp and tools, and the air smelled of sawdust and sweat.

'Hey, Cade.' Dwight walked over, skirting tools.

Cade gave Dwight's blue and gold striped tie a tap. 'Now, aren't you pretty?'

'Had a meeting. Bunch of bankers.' As if just remembering it was over, Dwight reached up and loosened the knot in the tie. 'Just came by to check on the job before I go into the office.'

'You're making progress.'

'The client has definite ideas about what she wants and when she wants it.' Dwight rolled his eyes. 'We're here to accommodate, and let me tell you, she don't give you an inch of wiggle room. That skinny little girl grew up to be one hardheaded businesswoman.'

'Where is she?'

'In the back.' Dwight nodded toward the closed door. 'Stays out of the way, I'll give her that. Stays out once she *gets* her way is more like it.'

Cade took another moment to scan the work-in-progress. 'Her way looks good,' he decided.

'Gotta admit, it does. Listen, Cade . . .' Dwight shifted his feet. 'Lissy's got this friend.'

'No.'

'Well, Jesus, just hear me out.'

'I don't have to. She's got a friend, a single female friend who'd be just perfect for me. Why don't I give this single female friend a call, or come on by and have dinner with this single female friend and y'all at the house, or meet for drinks?'

'Well, why don't you? Lissy's going to be on my back until you do.'

'Your wife, your back, your problem. Tell Lissy you just found out I'm gay or something.'

'Oh yeah, that'll work.' The idea amused Dwight so much his laughter rolled up from the gut. 'That'll work just fine. Way things are, she'll just start lining up men for you.'

'God almighty.' It wasn't, Cade realized, out of the realm of possibility. 'Then tell her I'm having a blazing, backstreet affair with someone.'

'Who?'

'Pick somebody,' Cade said, waving it off, and heading for the back-room door. 'Just tell her no.' He knocked, then shoved inside without waiting for an answer.

Tory stood on a stepladder, replacing a fluorescent tube in the overhead light fixture.

'Here, let me do that.'

'I've got it. This is a tenant's obligation, not the landlord's.' It still grated, just a little, to realize he owned the building.

'I see they got the glass replaced on the front door.'

'Yes. Thank you.'

'Feels like they fixed the air-conditioning.'

'That's right.'

'If you need to be pissed off at me today, you're going to have to get in line. There's quite a wait.'

He turned away, hands in pockets. She'd gone for metal shelves in here, he noted. Gray, ugly, sturdy, and practical. They were already jammed with cardboard boxes, and the boxes meticulously labeled by stock number.

She'd bought a desk, again sturdy and practical. A computer and a phone were already on it as was a neatly stacked pile of paperwork.

In ten days, she'd organized considerably. Not once had she asked for, or accepted, his help. He wished it didn't irk him.

She was wearing black shorts, a gray T-shirt, and gray sneakers. He wished they didn't appeal to him.

He turned back as she came down the ladder, took hold of it to fold up just as she did. 'I'll put it away for you.'

'I can do it.'

He tugged, so did she. 'Goddamn it, Tory.'

The sudden hiss of temper, the dangerous flash in his eyes, had her stepping back, clasping her hands. He slapped the ladder together, shoved it into a small closet.

When he just stood there, his back to her, she felt a pang of guilt, and of sympathy. It was odd to realize she didn't feel fear or trepidation as she usually did around angry men. 'Sit down, Cade.'

'Why?'

'Because you look like you need to.' She walked over to where she'd hauled in a minifridge, found a bottle of Coke, twisted the top. 'Here, cool off.'

'Thanks.' He dropped down on the chair at her desk, took a long swig from the bottle.

'Bad day?'

'I've had a score of better ones.'

Saying nothing, she opened her purse and found the cloisonné pillbox where she kept aspirin. When she offered him two, he lifted his brows.

She felt heat rise fast and dark to her cheeks. 'I didn't . . . It just shows, that's all.'

'Appreciate it.' He popped the aspirin, sighed, rolled his shoulders. 'I don't suppose you'd be willing to make it some better by coming over here and sitting on my lap.'

'No, I wouldn't.'

'Had to ask. How about dinner and a movie? No, don't say no without even thinking about it,' he said before she could speak. 'Just dinner and a movie. Hell, a pizza, a burger, something friendly. I promise not to ask you to marry me.'

'That's a relief, but not much of an incentive.'

'Just think about it for five minutes.' He set the bottle on her desk, then rose. 'Come on outside. I got something for you.'

'I haven't finished in here.'

'Woman, do you have to argue about every damn thing? It wears me out.' To solve the problem, he took her hand, pulled her to the door and through.

She might have taken a stand, just on principle. But there were two carpenters in the shop, which meant two sets of eyes and ears. There would be less for them to talk about if she calmly stepped outside with Cade.

'I liked the look of these,' he began, gesturing toward the pots while he continued to pull her down the sidewalk to his truck. 'If you don't you can exchange them at Clampett's. Same goes for these, I suppose.'

He stopped, took one flat out of the truck bed. 'But I think they suit well enough.'

'Suit what?'

'You, your place. Consider them a kind of good luck gift, even though you have to pot them yourself.' He pushed the first flat into her hand, took out the second and the bag of soil.

She stood there, baffled and touched. She'd wanted flowers, she remembered, flowers in pots for the front of the shop. She'd thought of petunias, but these were prettier and every bit as friendly.

'This was kind of you. And thoughtful. Thank you.'

'Could you look at me?' He waited until she shifted her gaze, met his eyes. 'You're welcome. Where do you want them?'

'We'll just set them out front. I'll pot them.'

As they started up the sidewalk together, she gave him one sidelong glance. 'Oh hell. You could come by around six. I wouldn't mind the pizza. If we get through that all right, we can talk about the movie.'

'Fine.' He set the flowers and soil down in front of her display window. 'I'll be back.'

'Yes, I know,' she murmured when he strolled off.

Chapter Eight

Maybe people didn't actually die of boredom, Faith decided, but she didn't know how the hell they lived with it, either.

When she'd been a child and complained she had nothing to do, the words had fallen on unsympathetic adult ears, and chores had been assigned. She'd hated chores nearly as much as she'd hated boredom. But some lessons are hard-learned.

'There's nothing to do around here.' Faith lounged at the kitchen table, picking at a breakfast biscuit. It was after eleven, but she hadn't bothered to dress. She wore the silk robe she'd bought on a trip to Savannah in April.

She was already bored with that, too.

'Everything's the same around here, day after day, month after month. I swear, it's a wonder every blessed one of us doesn't run screaming into the night.'

'Got yourself a case of ennui, do you, Miss Faith?' Lilah's rough-as-sandstone voice cruised over the French pronunciation. She used it partly because her grandmother had been Creole, but mostly because it just tickled her.

'Nothing ever happens around here. Every morning's the same as the one before, and the whole day stretches out in a long thin line of more nothing.'

Lilah continued to scrub at the counter. The truth was, she'd had the kitchen tidied up for more than an hour, but she'd known Faith would wander in. She'd been lying in wait.

'I guess you're hankering for some activity.' She sent Faith a soft look out of guileless brown eyes. As guile was something Lilah had in spades, this look had taken some practice.

But she knew her target. She'd looked after Miss Faith since the day the girl had been born – born, Lilah recalled with some affection, wailing and waving bunched fists at the world. Lilah herself had been part of the Lavelle household since her own twentieth year, when she'd been hired on to help with the cleaning while Mrs. Lavelle had been carrying Mr. Cade.

Her hair had been black then, instead of the salt-and-pepper it was now. Her hips had been a mite more narrow, but she hadn't let herself go. She'd matured, she liked to think, into a fine figure of a woman.

Her skin was the color of the dark caramels she melted to coat apples every Halloween. She liked to set it off with a good strong red lipstick, and carried a tube in her apron pocket.

She'd never married. Not that she hadn't had the opportunity. Lilah Jackson had had plenty of beaux in her day. And since her day was far from over, she still enjoyed getting herself gussied up to go on the town with a good-looking man.

But marrying one? Well, that was a different kettle.

She preferred things just as they were, and that meant having a man come calling at the door and escorting her where she liked to go. If he expected to escort her again, he'd best remember to bring along a nice box of chocolates or some posies, and open doors for her like a gentleman.

Marry one, and you spent your life picking up after him, watching him fart and scratch and God knew what while you sweated to make the paycheck stretch to keep body and soul together and buy a few pretty things of your own.

No, this way she had a fine house – as tell the truth and shame the devil, Beaux Reves was as much hers as anyone's. She'd raised three babies, and grieved her heart sick over the lost one, and had, to her way of thinking, all the benefits of male companions without any of the problems.

She didn't mind a good snuggle now and again, either. If the good Lord hadn't meant for His children to snuggle, he wouldn't have put the need for it inside them.

Now, Miss Faith, she mused, was just packed full of needs and had yet to figure out how to meet them without causing herself grief. That meant the girl was equally full of problems. Most of her own making. Some chicks, Lilah knew, just took longer to find their way around the barnyard.

'Maybe you could take yourself a nice long drive,' Lilah suggested.

'To where?' Faith sipped her coffee without interest. 'Everything looks the same, any direction.'

Lilah took out her lipstick, touched it up in the chrome reflection of the toaster. 'I know what perks me up when I got the blues. A good spurt of shopping.'

'I suppose.' Faith sighed and toyed with the idea of driving down to Charleston. 'Nothing better to do.'

'That's fine, then. You go on shopping and brighten up your spirits. Here's the list.'

Faith blinked, then stared at the shopping list Lilah waved in front of her face. 'Groceries? I'm not going shopping for groceries.'

'You got nothing better to do, and said so yourself. You make sure those tomatoes are ripe, you hear? And you get the floor cleaner I got written down. The TV commercial made me laugh, and that's worth giving it a try.'

She turned back to the sink to rinse her dish rag and had to hold in a cackle at the way her girl's mouth was hanging open. 'Then you go on by the drugstore and get me some of my Oil of Olay, the kind in the jar, not the bottle. And the bath bubbles. The milk-and-honey ones. On the way back, you stop by the dry cleaners and pick up all the stuff I hauled down there last week, mostly yours anyway. God knows what you need with half a hundred silk blouses.'

Faith narrowed her eyes. 'Anything else?' she said sweetly.

'It's all written down there, plain as day. Give you something to do with your bored self for a couple hours. Now, go get some clothes on, it's going on noon. Sinful, just sinful to be lazing around in your robe half the damn day. Go on, get.'

Lilah made shooing motions, then snatched up Faith's plate and cup.

'I haven't finished my breakfast.'

'I didn't see you eating it. Picking and pouting's what you were doing. Now, out of my kitchen, and make yourself useful for a change.'

Lilah folded her arms, angled her head, and stared. She had a way of staring that could wither the bravest soul. Faith shoved back from the table, sniffed, and stalked out. 'I'll be back when I'm back,' she called out.

With a shake of her head and a chuckle, Lilah finished off

Faith's coffee herself. 'Some chicks, they just never learn who rules the roost.'

It had taken Wade three years and eighteen pups to convince Dottie Betrum to have her oversexed Lab-retriever mix spayed. The last litter of six were just weaned, and while their mama slept off the effects of the surgery, he gave each of the cheerfully barking puppies the necessary shots.

'I just can't look at the needles, Wade. Makes me light-headed.'

'You don't need to look, Mrs. Betrum. Why don't you go on out and wait? We'll be done here in just a few minutes.'

'Oh.' Her hands butterflied up to her cheeks, and her myopic eyes shone with distress behind the thick lenses of her glasses. 'I feel like I should stay. Doesn't seem right to just . . .' She trailed off when Wade slid the needle under fur.

'Maxine, take Mrs. Betrum on out to the waiting room.' He gave his assistant a quick wink. 'I can handle this.'

Handle it better, he thought, as Maxine helped the staggering woman out of the room, without sweet, little old ladies fainting on the floor.

'Here you go, little guy.' Wade rubbed the puppy's belly to soothe it and completed the inoculations. He weighed, scratched ears, checked for parasites, and filled out charts while yips and barks echoed off the walls.

Mrs. Betrum's Sadie slept peacefully in postop, old Mr. Klingle's cat, Silvester, hissed and squalled in his cage, and Speedy Petey, Progress Elementary's third-grade hamster mascot, raced on his wheel, proving he was recovered from a mild bladder infection.

It was, for Dr. Wade Mooney, his own little paradise.

He finished up the last pup while the siblings tumbled over each other, tugged at his shoelaces, or piddled on the floor. Mrs. Betrum had assured him she'd found good homes for five of the puppies already. He had, as always, gently declined her offer to take one for himself.

But he had an idea just where the last of the lot could make his home.

'Doc Wade?' Maxine peeked back in.

'All done here. Let's gather up the troops.'

'They're so cute.' Her dark eyes danced. 'I thought you were going to give in and take one of this batch.'

'Once you start, you'll never stop.' But his dimples deepened as a pup wormed and wiggled in his hands.

'Wish I could take one.' Maxine picked up a puppy, cuddling while it licked her face with desperate love and speed.

She adored animals, which is why the opportunity to work for Doc Wade had been heaven-sent. There were already two dogs at home, and she knew better than to think she could talk her parents into indulging her with another.

She'd been born in the holler, and her parents had worked their fingers raw lifting themselves, their daughter, and their two young sons out of it. Money was still tight, she reminded herself, as she cuddled and pined for the puppy.

And money would stay tight awhile longer, she thought with a sigh. She was the first of her family to get into college, and every penny had to be saved.

'They're so sweet, Doc Wade. But between work and school, I wouldn't have time to give it enough attention.' She set the pup down again. 'Besides the fact my daddy'd kill me.'

Wade only grinned. Maxine's father adored her. 'Classes going all right?'

She rolled her eyes. She was in her second year of college and time was as tight as money. If it hadn't been for Doc Wade giving her the most flexible of hours and letting her study when things were quiet, she'd never have made it this far.

He was her hero, and she'd once had a wonderfully painful crush on him. Now she only hoped to one day be as good and clever a veterinarian as he was.

'Finals coming up. I got so much in my head it feels like it's going to burst. I'll take these babies out, Doc Wade.' She hefted the basket full of puppies. 'What should I tell Miz Betrum about Sadie?'

'She can pick her up later this afternoon. Tell her around four. Oh, and ask her not to give that last pup away. I've got a line on someone.'

'Will do. Is it all right if I take lunch now? We're clear for an hour, and I thought I'd go study some in the park.'

'Go ahead.' He turned to the sink to scrub his hands. 'Take the full hour, Maxine. Let's see how much more you can fit in that brain of yours.'

'Thanks.'

He was going to be sorry to lose her. Which Wade imagined he would as soon as she had a degree hot in her hand. It wasn't going to be easy to find someone as competent, as willing, or as good with the animals, who could also type, deal with frantic pet owners, and answer the phone.

But life moved on.

He started toward the back to check on Sadie just as Faith came in the rear door.

'Dr. Mooney. Just who I was looking for.'

'I'm easy to find this time of day.'

'Well, me, I'm just passing through.'

He cocked an eyebrow. 'That's quite a dress for just passing through.'

'Oh.' She ran a finger down the soft cotton fabric of the thin-strapped, fully skirted number in bold poppy red. 'Like it? I'm in a red kind of mood.' She shook her hair back, sent out seductive clouds of scent. Stepping forward, she skimmed her hands up his chest, over his shoulders. 'Guess what I've got on under it?'

Every time, he thought, like a finger snap, just one look at her had him ready to beg. 'Why don't you give me a hint?'

'You're such a smart man. Got that college degree and those letters after your name.' She took his hand, and covered with hers, trailed it up her thigh. 'I bet you could find out right quick.'

'Jesus.' His blood took a violent panther's leap. 'You go walking around town with next to nothing on?'

'And you and me, we're the only ones who know.' She leaned forward, her eyes bright on his, and nipped his lower lip. 'Whatcha gonna do about it, Wade?'

'Come upstairs.'

'Too far.' With a throaty laugh, she nudged the door open behind him. 'I want you now. And I want you fast.'

The dog slept quietly, her breathing regular. The room smelled of canine and antiseptic. The old chair where he spent many hours watching over patients was pricked with hair shed from countless dogs and cats.

'I haven't locked up.'

'Let's live dangerously.' She flipped open the button of his jeans, dragged down the zipper. 'Why, look what I found.' She wrapped her hand around him, watched his melted chocolate eyes go blurry before he crushed his mouth on hers.

The sly excitement she'd felt when dressing, when driving into town knowing she'd go to him, seduce him, turned into something tangled and needy. Nearly painful.

'Take me someplace.' She arched back while his mouth fed on her throat. 'Take me someplace hot and dark and wild. I need to go. Hurry and take me there.'

The jagged edge of her desperation knifed through his blood, leaving him raw. There was nothing tame between them when they came together like this, nothing soft, nothing sweet. When she was panting his name and her hands were on him, he forgot he wanted the soft and sweet.

All he wanted was Faith.

He tossed up the red skirts, gripped her hips. She was hot and she was wet and seemed to clamp over him like a greedy jaw when he drove himself into her.

She wrapped one leg around his waist and moaned, long and deep. He filled the empty places. It didn't matter if it was only for the moment, if the emptiness came back. He filled them, and no one else ever had.

Harsh animal pants, the solid, rhythmic thud of body against body, bodies against wood, and the slick strong feel of him pounding into her. She let go, with a small, strangled cry in her throat as the orgasm sprang free. She always came fast and hard with Wade, such a surprise, such a lovely little shock to the system.

Then it would start again, slower, deeper, a long and gradual rip that opened something inside her to him.

And because it was him, she could cling, she could surrender to it. She could hold on and know he'd be there with her when she fell.

The phone was ringing. Or his ears were. Every breath he took was ripe with her. She moved with him, thrust for thrust, never stopping, never slowing. There were times when he could think about her sanely, and when he wondered why the two of them didn't just devour each other until nothing was left.

She was saying his name, over and over, punctuating the word with gasps and whimpers. And he saw, just before he emptied into her, her eyes close as if in prayer.

'God.' She shuddered once, let her head rest back against the door, kept her eyes shut. 'God. I feel wonderful. Like gold inside and out.' She opened her eyes, stretching lazily. 'How about you?'

He knew what she expected, so resisted burying his face in her hair, murmuring words she wouldn't believe. Words that hadn't mattered to her years before when he'd been foolish enough to say them. 'That was a lot more appetizing than the BLT I planned for lunch.'

It made her laugh and hook her arms around his neck in a manner that was as friendly as it was intimate. 'There are still some parts of me you didn't nibble on. So if—'

'Wade? Wade, honey, you upstairs?'

'Jesus.' The part of him that was still nestled cozily inside Faith shriveled. 'My mother.'

'Well, isn't this . . . interesting.'

Even as Faith snorted out a laugh, Wade was clamping his hand over her mouth. 'Hush. Christ Jesus, this is all I need.'

Eyes dancing, Faith muttered against his hand while her body shook with laughter.

'It's not funny.' He hissed it out, but had to struggle back a laugh of his own. He could hear his mother wandering around, cheerfully calling him in the same chirpy singsong she'd used to call him for supper when he'd been ten.

'Just be quiet,' he whispered to Faith. 'And stay here. Stay right in here and don't make a sound.'

He eased back slowly, eyes narrowed as Faith bit her lip and snickered.

'Wade, honey,' she said when he reached for the door, then she squeezed her own mouth shut with her fingers when he turned to snarl at her.

'Not a sound,' he repeated.

'Okay, but I just thought you might want to put that away.'

He glanced down, swore, and hurriedly stuffed himself back into his jeans and zipped. 'Mama?' He shot Faith one last warning look, then stepped outside, firmly closing the door behind him. 'I'm down here. I was just checking on a patient.'

He sprinted up the steps, grateful his mother had gone up to search him out.

'There you are, my baby. I was just going to leave you a little love note.'

Boots Mooney was a package of contradictions. She was a tall

101

woman, but everyone thought of her as little. She had a voice like a cartoon kitten and a will of iron. She'd been the Cotton Queen her senior year of high school and had gone on to reign as Miss Georgetown County.

Her looks, wholesome, rosy, and candy pretty, had served her well. She preserved them religiously, not out of vanity but out of a spirit of obligation. Her husband was an important man, and she would never allow him to be seen with less than he deserved.

Boots enjoyed pretty things. Including herself.

She threw her arms open for Wade, as if it had been two years rather than two days since she'd seen him. When he bent toward her, she kissed both his cheeks, then quickly drew back.

'Honey, you're flushed. Are you feverish?'

'No.' To his credit, he didn't wince when she laid the back of her hand on his brow. 'No, I'm fine. I was . . . in postop. It's a little warm in there.'

Distracting her was imperative, and he knew the surefire way. 'Look at you.' He took her hands, spread her arms and gave her a long, approving once-over. 'Don't you look pretty today.'

'Oh now.' She laughed, but pinked up with pleasure. 'I just had my hair done, is all. You should've seen me before Lori got done with me. I looked like a ragpicker.'

'Impossible.'

'You're just biased. I had a fistful of errands to do, and couldn't go home until I'd seen my baby.' She gave his cheek a pat, then immediately turned toward the kitchen. 'I bet you haven't had lunch. I'm just going to fix you something.'

'Mama, I have a patient. Miss Dottie's Sadie.'

'Oh dear, what's wrong with her? Why Dottie'd just be lost without that dog.'

'Nothing's wrong. She's just been fixed.'

'If nothing's wrong, what needed to be fixed?'

Wade dragged a hand through his hair while his mother poked in his refrigerator. 'Fixed so she'd stop having a litter of puppies every year.'

'Oh. Wade, you don't have enough food in this house to keep body and soul together. I'm just going to pick a few things up for you at the market.'

'Mama—'

'Don't Mama me. You don't eat right since you left home, and you can't tell me different. Wish you'd come home for supper more often. I'm going to bring you over a nice tuna casserole tomorrow. That's your favorite.'

He hated tuna casserole. Loathed it. But he'd never been able to convince her of it. 'I'd appreciate that.'

'Maybe I'll take one out to little Tory, too. I just stopped over to see her. She looks so grown-up.' Boots put three eggs on to boil. 'That shop of hers is coming along so fast. I don't know where that girl gets the energy. God knows her mother never had any I could see, and her daddy, well, it's best not to speak if you can't speak kind.'

Boots folded her lips and hunted up a jar of pickles. 'Always had a soft spot for that child, though for one reason or another I never could get close to her. Poor little lamb. I used to wish I could just gather her up and bring her on home with me.'

Love, Wade thought, made you helpless. Wherever, however it came. He walked over, wrapped his arms around Boots, and rested his cheek on her newly lacquered hair. 'I love you, Mama.'

'Why, honey, I love you, too. That's why I'm going to make you a nice egg salad here, so I don't have to stand around watching my only son starve to death. You're getting too thin.'

'I haven't lost an ounce.'

'Then you were too thin to start with.'

He had to laugh. 'Why don't you put another egg on, Mama, so there'll be enough for both of us. I'll just go down and see to Sadie, and I'll come back and we'll have lunch together.'

'That'd be nice. You take your time.'

She slid another egg into the water, and glanced over her shoulder as he went out.

Boots was well aware her son was a grown man, but he was still her baby. And a mother never stopped worrying about or looking out for her own.

Men, she thought with a sigh, were such delicate, such *oblivious* creatures. And women, well, certain women, could take advantage of that.

The doors of the old building weren't as thick as her son might believe. And a woman didn't reach the age of fifty-three without recognizing certain sounds for what they were. She had a pretty good idea just who'd been on the other side of that door with her boy. She'd reserve judgment on that matter, she told herself, as she sliced up pickles.

But she'd be watching Faith Lavelle like a hawk.

She was gone. Wade realized he should have figured she would be. She'd stuck a Post-it to the door, drawn a heart on it, and had pressed her lips to the center, leaving a sexy red kiss for him.

He peeled it off, and though he told himself he was an idiot, tucked it into a drawer for safekeeping. She'd come back when she was in the mood. And he'd let her. He'd let her until he came to despise himself, or if he was lucky, until his heart was whole and his again, and she was just an interesting diversion.

He stroked a hand over Sadie's head, then checked her vitals, her incision, and stitches. Because she was awake now, her deep brown eyes glassy and confused, he picked her up carefully. He'd take her upstairs with him, so she wouldn't be alone.

Chapter Nine

Sex made her thirsty. In a much happier frame of mind than she'd been in, Faith decided to wander up to Hanson's and buy herself a bottle of something cold and sweet to enjoy on the way to the market.

She glanced back at the vet's office, then up at Wade's apartment windows. Blew him a mental kiss. She thought she might just give him a call later and see how he felt about taking a drive that evening. Maybe they could head over to Georgetown and find some pretty spot near the water.

It was nice being with Wade, comfortable on one hand, exciting on the other. He was as dependable as sunrise, always there when she needed him.

Memories of a long-ago summer when he'd spoken so easily of love and marriage, of houses and children, tried to wind through her mind, through her heart. She cast them out and set her mind on the thrill of fast, secret sex instead.

That's what she wanted, and luckily, so did he. She'd oblige them both later. She'd borrow Cade's convertible, then they'd take that drive toward the coast. They'd park somewhere and neck like teenagers.

She'd parked her own car several storefronts up from Wade's office. No point in giving tongues an excuse to wag, though God knew they wagged anyway over everything and nothing. She was about to slide in when she spotted Tory walk out of her shop door, then just stand back on the sidewalk and stare.

There's an odd duck who never did grow out of her funny feathers, Faith thought, but curiosity had her crossing the street.

'This one of your trances?'

Tory jerked, then deliberately relaxed the shoulders that had tensed. 'I was just seeing how the window looks. The sign painter finished not long ago.'

'Hmm.' Faith planted a hand on her hip and took a long look herself. The black scrolled letters looked fresh and classy. 'Southern Comfort. Is that what you're selling?'

'Yes.' Because her pleasure in the moment had been dulled, Tory walked back to the door.

'You sure aren't very friendly to a potential customer.'

Tory glanced back, eyes mild. Faith looked gorgeous, she thought. Sharp, smug, and satisfied. And she wasn't in the mood for it. 'I'm not open yet.'

Annoyed, Faith grabbed the door before it could shut in her face, and squeezed inside. 'You don't look near ready to me,' she commented, scanning the nearly empty shelves.

'Closer than it looks. I have work to do, Faith.'

'Oh, don't mind me. You go on and do whatever.' Faith wagged a hand, and as much out of stubbornness as interest, began to wander.

The place was clean as a whistle, she had to admit. The glass sparkled on the displays Dwight's men had built, the wood was polished to a gleam. Even the storage boxes were neatly stacked, and a large plastic bag held the Styrofoam bits used for packing. There was a laptop computer and a clipboard on the counter.

'You got enough stuff to fill all this space?'

'I will have.' Resigned to the intrusion, Tory continued to unpack stock. If she knew Faith Lavelle, her companion would shortly be bored and wander out again. 'If you're interested, I plan to open next Saturday. Selected stock will be ten percent off, that day only.'

Faith shrugged a shoulder. 'I'm usually busy over the weekends.' She roamed by a waist-high counter with a glass top. Inside, on a drape of white satin, were examples of handcrafted jewelry – silver and beads and colored stones, artistically scattered, designed to catch the eye and the imagination.

Forgetting herself, she started to lift the top, found it locked, and swore under her breath. She shot a cautious look toward Tory, glad the other woman hadn't noticed.

'You got some pretty enough baubles here.' She wanted the silver dangle earrings with the little lapis balls, and wanted them

106

immediately. 'I didn't think you went in for baubles. Hardly ever wear any yourself.'

'I have three artists right now for baubles,' Tory added dryly. 'I particularly like the brooch in the center section. The wire's sterling, and the stones are garnet, citrine, and carnelian.'

'I see it. They're all scattered on the wire like stars, like one of those sparklers the kids light on the Fourth of July.'

'Yes, very like that.'

'It's nice enough, I suppose, but I'm not much for pins and brooches.' She bit her lip, but avarice won over pride. 'I like these earrings here.'

'Come back Saturday.'

'I might be busy.' And she wanted them now. 'Why don't you sell them to me, make yourself an early sale. That's what you're in business for, isn't it? To make sales.'

Tory set a pottery oil lamp on the shelf. She was careful to wipe the smile off her face before she turned. 'I'm not open for business yet, but . . .' She started toward the display. 'For old times' sake.'

'We never had any old times.'

'I suppose you're right.' She unhooked the keys that dangled from her belt loop. 'Which one caught your eye?'

'That one. Those.' She tapped the glass. 'The silver and lapis.'

'Yes, they're lovely. They suit you.' Tory took them off the satin, held them to the light before passing them to Faith. 'You can use one of the mirrors if you want to try them on. The artist lives outside of Charleston. She does beautiful work.'

As Faith walked to a trio of mirrors framed in bronze and copper, Tory slipped a long pendant out of the case. Why make one sale if you could make two? 'This is one of my favorite pieces of hers. It'd go well with those.'

Trying not to be overly interested, Faith glanced down. The pendant was a thick barrel of lapis clasped in silver hands. 'Unusual.' She switched her earrings for the new ones, then gave in and took the necklace. 'You won't see this walking back at you down the street.'

'No.' Tory allowed herself a smile. 'I plan to offer the unique.'

'I suppose I should have both. Haven't treated myself in ages. Seems like everything you see around Progress is the same as the other.'

Quietly, Tory closed the top of the display. 'Not anymore.'

Lips pursed, Faith swiveled the chain around to look at the tag. 'Some people will say you're outpricing yourself.' She skimmed her finger down the chain as she looked back at Tory. 'They'd be wrong. This is fair enough. Fact is, you could charge more if you were in Charleston.'

'But I'm not. I'll get your boxes.'

'Don't bother, I'll just wear them out.' She opened her purse, dropped her other earrings carelessly inside. 'You just cut the tags off for me, and ring it up.'

'Add it up,' Tory corrected. 'I don't have the cash register set up yet.'

'Whatever.' She slipped off the necklace, the tagged earring. 'I'll write you a check.' Faith lifted her eyebrows when Tory held out a hand. 'I can't write it until you give me the total.'

'No, give me your other earrings. That's no way to treat them. I'll give you a box.'

With a short laugh, Faith dug them out again. 'All right, little mother.'

Sex and shopping, Faith thought, as she wandered again. There couldn't be a better way to spend the day. And from the looks of things she could spend a lot of pleasant time in Tory's shop.

Who'd have thought little, spook-eyed Tory Bodeen would grow into such fine taste? And learn how to use it so cleverly.

It must've been a powerful lot of work to hunt up the right things, to find the people who made those things, to calculate what to charge for them, to design the space to display them.

Likely more to it than that, Faith mused. Bookkeeping and that kind of nasty thing.

She found herself impressed, and a little envious, by the idea of having the gumption and the skill to create a business from nothing.

Not that she'd want any part of such an undertaking, and all that responsibility, herself. A shop like this would tie you down tighter than a coil of hemp. But wasn't it nice the shop was so convenient to Wade? Maybe life in Progress was about to pick up for a while.

'You ought to tip this bowl up on a stand.' She stopped, tipped the big serving bowl herself. 'So people can see the inside design from across the room.'

Tory had intended to, once she'd unpacked her stands. Adding figures, she barely glanced up. 'Want a job? I've got your total here, tax included, but you should check my math.'

'You always got better grades there than I did.' She started over, and the shop door opened. Faith would have sworn she heard Tory groan.

Lissy's squeal was, in Tory's opinion, only one of her annoying habits. Among the others were her tendency to douse herself in a lily-of-the-valley scent that entered the room before she did, and remained in it long after she'd left.

As both the scent and the squeal entered her shop, Tory gritted her teeth in what she hoped would be mistaken for a smile.

'Oh, isn't this fun! I just got my hair done and was walking on down to the office when I saw y'all in here.'

As Lissy clapped her hands together and took a turn around, Tory shot Faith a single, deadly look. It was answered by a lightning grin of perfect understanding, and a coy flutter of lashes.

'I happened along just after Tory's sign was finished.'

'And it looks just fine, too. Everything's coming right along, isn't it?' With one hand on the weight of her belly, Lissy turned back to scan the shelves. 'It's all looking so pretty, Tory. Why, you must've worked like six mules to get so much done in so little time. And didn't my Dwight do a fine job.'

'Yes, I couldn't be happier with the work.'

'Course not. He's the best there is. Oh, isn't this dear!'

She snatched the oil lamp Tory had just placed on the shelf. 'I just love things that sit around the house. Dust catchers, Dwight calls them, but it's those touches that make a home, isn't it?'

Tory took a deep breath. Just one more of those annoying traits was Lissy's habit of turning every sentence into an exclamation. 'Yes, I think so. If dust doesn't have someplace to catch, it'll just fall on an empty table.'

'Why, that's so true!' Discreetly, Lissy turned the price tag over, then rounded her mouth into an O of surprise. 'My, it's dear, isn't it?'

'It's handcrafted and signed,' Tory began, but Faith rolled right over her.

'You get what you pay for, don't you, Lissy? And Dwight makes enough to indulge you, especially since you're about to pop with another baby. I swear if I ever carried a weight around for nine months, the man who planted it there would have to buy me the moon and the stars.'

Not entirely sure if she was being complimented or insulted, Lissy frowned. 'Dwight just spoils me rotten.'

' 'Course he does. I just bought me these earrings.' She gave the one still in her ear a spin with a fingertip. 'And a pendant, too. Tory's giving me a little jump on her Saturday opening.'

'Really?' Lissy's eyes went sharp and narrow.

As Faith knew, she wasn't one to tolerate anyone getting ahead of her. She clutched the lamp greedily to her breasts. 'Tory, you just have to let me have this now. My heart's just set on it. I don't know if I can get in here first thing on Saturday, and somebody else might snap it up. Be a doll, won't you, and let me buy it today?'

Tory circled Faith's total so that she could begin calculating. 'It'll have to be cash or check, Lissy. I'm not set up for credit cards today. But I'd be happy to set it aside for you if—'

'No, no, I can write you a check. Maybe, since I'm here and all, I could just poke about for a bit? It's just like playing store.'

'Yeah.' Tory took the lamp, set it on the counter.

It looked like she was open for business after all.

'Oh! Are these mirrors for sale?'

'Everything's for sale.' Tory got a small navy blue box from under the counter, placed Faith's earrings inside. 'I'm going to put the artist's card in with your old earrings.'

'Fine. You don't have to thank me,' she added under her breath.

'I'm debating whether you did it to be helpful or to irritate me,' Tory said equably. 'Or irritate her. But . . .' She noted down the price of the lamp. 'A sale's a sale, so I will thank you. You knew just which button to push.'

'On that one?' Faith glanced over to where Lissy was oohing and aahing and chattering. 'She's as simple as they come.'

'She buys one of those mirrors, and she can be my new best friend.'

'Well, I like that.' Enjoying herself more than she'd imagined, Faith pulled out her checkbook. 'I get shoved aside, and after I gave you your first sale, too.'

'I just have to have this mirror, Tory. The oval one with the lilies going up the side. I've just never seen anything like it. It'll look so sweet in my little sitting room.'

Tory's eyes met Faith's over the counter, gleamed. 'Sorry, she just outbought you.' To Lissy, she called out, 'I'll get the box out of the back room.'

'I appreciate that. I swear there's just so much to choose from already, and I guess you're not half set up. I was telling Dwight just the other night that I don't see where you find the time. Between moving into the house, setting things up here, handling deliveries, and spending evenings with Cade, you must've found yourself a twenty-six-hour day.'

'Cade?'

The name popped simultaneously from Tory's and Faith's lips.

'That man moved faster than I gave him credit for.' Lissy wandered back. 'I have to say, I never pictured the two of you together, as a couple. But you know what they say about still waters.'

'Yes. No.' Tory held up a hand. 'I don't know what you're talking about. Cade and I aren't together.'

'Oh, there's no need to be coy when it's just us girls. Dwight told me all about it, explained you'd probably want to keep it quiet awhile. I haven't told a soul, don't you worry.'

'There's nothing to tell. Absolutely nothing to tell. We just . . .' She saw two pair of eyes sharpen, and felt her tongue go thick. 'Nothing. Dwight's mistaken. I'll go get the box.'

'Don't know why she's so hell-bent to keep it secret,' Lissy commented, when Tory rushed into the storeroom. 'After all, it's not like either of them's married or anything. Of course,' she added with a smirk, 'I guess the idea she's rolling on the sheets with Cade after being back here less than a month doesn't go with that quiet, proper-lady attitude she's painting herself with.'

'Oh?' Cade's business was Cade's business, Faith told herself. But she'd be damned if she'd let this little cat claw at him. 'Don't quiet, proper ladies have sex?' With a viciously bright smile, she tapped a finger on Lissy's belly. 'I guess that bump you got there's from eating too much chocolate.'

'I'm a married woman.'

'You weren't when you and Dwight were bouncing around in the backseat of the secondhand Camaro his daddy bought him when he lettered in track.'

'Oh, for heaven's sake, Faith, you did plenty of bouncing of your own back then.'

'Exactly. That's why I'm damned careful where I aim my stone if I get an urge to throw one.' She signed her check with a flourish, then picked up the mate to her new earring.

'All I'm saying is that for somebody who's barely back in Progress and who's been doing God knows what all these years, she sure has latched on to a Lavelle mighty fast.'

'Nobody latches on to a Lavelle until we want them to.' But she was going to think about this. She was going to think about it good and hard.

Tory was tempted to close up as soon as she nudged her two unexpected customers out the door. But that would have thrown her off schedule, and given Lissy's foolish gossip too much importance.

She worked on her stock another three hours, systematically pricing, logging, and arranging. The manual labor and the tedium of paperwork kept her from brooding.

But the drive home gave her ample opportunity.

This was not the way she intended to establish herself in Progress again. She wasn't going to tolerate, not for one minute, being the focus of town gossip. The way to quash it, she told herself, was to ignore it, to rise above it.

And to keep her distance from Cade.

None of that would cause her any problem at all.

She was used to ignoring wagging tongues, and over matters a great deal more vital than some trumped-up romance. She certainly didn't have to spend any time with Cade Lavelle. She barely had, in any case. A couple of meals, a movie or two, maybe a drive. All harmless occupations where they'd just happened to go together.

From now on, she'd just go alone.

And that, she thought, was that.

It might have been, if she hadn't spotted his truck at the edge of a field.

She told herself to drive by. Really, there was no point in stopping, no reason to discuss it. It would be much more sensible to continue home and let the entire foolish matter die a natural death.

And she kept seeing the hungry, predatory gleam in Lissy's eyes.

She jerked the wheel, pulled to the side of the road where the grass was choppy and thick. She was just going to mention it, that was all. Just mention that Cade should shut the hell up and stop talking about her with his idiot buddies. This wasn't high school, damn it.

Piney Cobb took a long, contemplative drag from the last Marlboro in his pack. He'd watched the station wagon swerve to the shoulder, watched the woman – damn if it wasn't the little Bodeen girl, all grown up – start her march to the field, and he kept watching as she aimed her feet between the rows and kept on coming.

Beside him, Cade stood studying the day's work and the progress of the crop. Boy had funny ideas if you asked him, but those funny ideas were working. It was none of his never mind, anyway. He got paid all the same whether he sprayed hell out of the crop, or babied it with cow shit and ladybugs.

'Could use another good rain like we had the other night,' Cade mused.

'Could.' Piney scratched his grizzled chin, pursed his lips. 'What you got here's a good three inches higher than the traditional fields.'

'Organic cotton grows faster,' Cade said absently. 'Chemicals stunt growth.'

'Yeah, so you've said.' And so, despite Piney's doubts, it had been proven true. It made him think maybe, all in all, college educations weren't all bullshit.

Not that he'd say so right out loud. But it was something to mull on.

'Boss?' Piney took a last pull on his cigarette, then carefully tramped it out underfoot. 'You got female problems?'

Since his mind was full of work, it took Cade a minute. 'Excuse me?'

'See, myself, I've kept pretty clear of females, but I been around this world long enough to recognize a woman getting up a head of steam.'

He shifted his gaze, squinting against the sun, and nodded lazily to where Tory was plowing her way up the rows. 'There's one now. From the look of things, you're dead in her sights.'

'I got no problems.'

'I'd say you're wrong about that one,' Piney muttered, and eased a step back so as not to be hit with the fallout.

'Cade.'

It was a pleasure to see her, a simple, easy pleasure. 'Tory. This is a nice surprise.'

'Really? We'll see about that. I need to talk to you.'

'All right.'

'Alone.'

'I'll just mosey along.'

Tory sucked in her breath, remembered her manners. 'I beg your pardon, Mr. Cobb.'

'No need for that. Didn't think you'd remember me.'

She hadn't, or hadn't consciously. She'd said his name without thinking about it. Now, for a moment, her temper was coated with an old image of a scrawny, thin-chested man with wheat-colored hair who smelled most usually of liquor and snuck her little peppermint drops.

He was still scrawny, she noted, but age and drink had ravaged his face. It was red and worn and saggy, and the wheat-colored hair, if he still owned it, was thin enough to be covered completely by an old gray cap.

'I remember you used to give me candy, and you worked the field next to my father's.'

'Did.' His lips stretched out in a smile, revealing teeth as tilted and gapped as an old picket fence. 'Work for the college boy now. Pays better. I'll just be getting on. See you in the morning, boss man.'

He tipped his cap, then took a peppermint out of his pocket and handed it to Tory. 'As I recollect, you always favored these.'

'I still do. Thank you.'

'It pleased him that you remembered,' Cade said, as Piney walked across the field toward the road.

'My father used to shout at him about the evils of whiskey, then about once a month they'd get drunk together. Next day, Piney'd be out in the field, working as usual. And my father'd go back to shouting at him across the rows.'

She shook her head, turned to face Cade. 'I didn't stop for a trip down memory lane. Just what do you mean telling your friend Dwight that we're seeing each other?'

'I'm not sure—'

'We're *not* seeing each other.'

Cade arched a brow, slipped off his sunglasses, hooked them on

114

his shirt. 'Well now, Tory, yes, we are. I'm standing here seeing you right now.'

'You know very well what I mean. We're not dating.'

He didn't smile, but he wanted to. He settled for scratching his head instead, and looking bemused. 'Seems to me we're doing something pretty close to that. We've gone out, what, four times in the last ten days or so. To my thinking, when a man and a woman go out to dinner and such, it's a date.'

'Your thinking's wrong. We're not dating, so just get that straight.'

'Yes'm.'

'Don't grin at me.' A trio of crows cawed by, sleek and shiny. 'And even if you had that idea in your head, you had no business, no *right*, to tell Dwight we were involved. He went right off and told Lissy, and now she's got it in her pea-brained head we're having some sort of wild sexual affair. I do not want or intend for people around here to assume I'm your latest fling.'

'My latest?' He hooked his thumbs in his pockets, rocked back on the worn heels of his work boots. As far as entertainment went, he considered this the day's highlight. 'Just how many flings do you think I've had?'

'I have no interest.'

'You're the one who brought it up,' he pointed out, just for the pleasure of seeing her snarl.

'The point is you told Dwight we were involved.'

'No, I didn't. But I don't see . . .' It came back to him. 'Oh yeah. Hmm.'

'There!' With a kind of triumph, she jabbed a finger at him. 'You're a grown man, and should have gotten over the locker room talk.'

'It was a misunderstanding.' And a fascinating one, in his opinion. 'Lissy keeps trying to set me up. Can't appear to stand having a single man running loose. It's a pain in the ass. Last time it came up, I told Dwight to get her off my back, to tell her I was having a hot affair or something.'

'With me?' She wondered steam didn't stream from her ears. 'Why, of all the—'

'I didn't say you,' Cade broke in. 'I imagine Dwight just picked you out, as we were in your place at the time of the conversation. You want to jump somebody, jump him. But personally, I don't see what you're all het up about. We're both single, we're seeing each other – now, we are, Tory,' he added, before she could argue the point. 'And if Lissy wants to think things between us have progressed to what would be a natural stage, where's the harm?'

She wasn't sure she could speak. He was amused. She could see it in his eyes, hear it in his voice. 'You think this is funny?'

'Not so much funny as anecdotal,' he decided. 'Makes for an amusing little anecdote.'

'Anecdotal, my butt. Lissy'll have this spread all over the county, if she hasn't already.'

The crows came back, circling. 'Oh well, now, there's a tragedy. Maybe we should issue a press release denying all.'

She made a sound, something perilously close to a growl. When she whirled away, he took her arm, held her in place. 'Just simmer down, Victoria.'

'Don't you tell me to simmer down. I'm trying to establish a business, a home here, and I don't want to be the subject of back fence gossip.'

'Back fence gossip's the fuel that powers up small towns. You've lived in the city too long if you've forgotten that. And if people are talking, people are going to stroll into your shop to get a close-up look. Where's the harm in that?'

He made it sound gentle, reasonable. 'I don't like being gawked at. I've had enough of being gawked at.'

'You knew there'd be some of that before you came back here. And if people want to gawk a bit at the woman who's caught Cade Lavelle's eye, all they'll have to do is look at you to see why.'

'You're turning this around.' She wasn't entirely sure how, but she knew she wasn't on solid ground any longer. 'Faith was in the shop when Lissy made her announcement.' He did wince, which gave her some satisfaction. 'There, not so cheerful about it now, are you?'

'If Faith's going to poke at me about it, and she won't be able to resist, it's about time I got something out of it.' He tightened his grip on her arm, tossed his sunglasses on the ground beside them. Then brought her a step closer.

Alarm bells shrilled, and her hand slapped against his chest. 'What are you doing?'

'No need to jump out of your skin.' With his free hand he cupped the back of her neck. 'I'm just going to taste you.'

116

'Don't.' But his lips were already skimming over hers.

'Won't hurt. Promise.'

He kept his word. It didn't hurt. It soothed and aroused, it eased and it stirred up those needs she'd locked so carefully away. But it didn't hurt.

His mouth was soft, gentle, coaxing hers to taste. As he was. Warmth spread into her belly even as ropes of tension and awareness tangled together. And as that mix rose up toward her heart, he eased back.

'I had a feeling,' he murmured. His hand continued to rub and stroke the back of her neck. 'Had it the first time I saw you again.'

Her head was spinning. It wasn't a sensation she enjoyed. 'This is a mistake. I don't—' She stepped back in defense and felt something crunch under her heel.

'Damn, second pair this week.' Cade only shook his head over the broken sunglasses. 'Life's full of mistakes,' he went on, and kissed her again, lightly. 'This doesn't feel like one, but we're just going to have to see it through to find out.'

'Cade, I'm no good at this sort of thing.'

'Which sort? The kissing sort?'

'No.' Her own laugh came as a surprise. How could he make her laugh when she was terrified? 'The man-woman thing, the relationship thing.'

'Then you'll just have to practice.'

'I don't want to practice.' She could do nothing but sigh when he pressed his lips to her forehead. 'Cade, there's so much you don't know about me.'

'That goes both ways. So let's find out. It's a nice evening.' He slid his hand down to hers. 'Why don't we go for a drive?'

'This isn't dealing with the issue.'

'We can stop and get something to eat when the mood strikes.' He turned her, rather elegantly bent down to pick up his ruined glasses. He began to walk, with the young cotton between them. 'One step at a time, Tory,' he said quietly. 'I'm a patient man. You look around here, pay attention, you can see how patient. It took me three seasons to turn the farm around to where I wanted it. To what I believed in, and I did that against a couple of generations of tradition. There are people who still point and snicker, or grumble and curse. All because I didn't go the way most are comfortable

117

with, that most understand. And what people don't understand usually scares them.'

She looked at him, then away. The charmingly careless man who'd chuckled at her temper had a line of steel running through him. It wouldn't be wise, she mused, to forget it. 'I know that. I live with that.'

'So why don't we just consider ourselves two misfits, and see where that takes us?'

'I don't know what you're talking about. No Lavelle's a misfit in Progress.'

'You think that because I've yet to bore you senseless with the wonders of organic farming and the beauty of green cotton.' Casually, he lifted her hand, kissed the back of it. 'But I will, as I haven't had a new victim in months. Tell you what, you go on home. I need to clean up some. I'll come by and get you in about an hour.'

'I have things to do.'

'God knows there isn't a day goes by there aren't things to do.' He opened her car door. 'I'll be by in an hour,' he told her as she slid behind the wheel. 'And Tory? Just so there's no confusion. This is a date.'

He closed the door, then, tucking his hands in his pockets, strolled over to his truck.

Chapter Ten

'Oh, don't be mean, Cade. I'm just asking one little favor.' Faith stretched out across her brother's bed, her chin on her fists, and aimed her most winsome look.

She'd developed the habit of coming into his room for company after Hope had died and being alone was unbearable. Now she most often dropped in when she wanted something.

They both knew it, and he didn't seem to mind.

'You're wasting those eyes on me.' Stripped to the waist, his hair still damp from his shower, Cade pulled a fresh shirt from his closet. 'I'm using the car tonight.'

'You can use it anytime.' She tried a pout.

'That's right, I can. And I'm using it tonight.' He gave her the smug smile reserved for irritating siblings.

'I'm the one who did the marketing for the food you stuffed in your mouth.' She scrambled up to kneel on the bed. 'And went to the dry cleaners to pick up your stupid clothes, and all I'm asking is to borrow your damn car for one evening. But you're too selfish.'

He slipped on his shirt, began to button it, with that same satisfied smile on his face. 'And your point would be?'

'I *hate* you.' She yanked up a pillow, heaved it, and missed by a good foot and a half. She'd never had decent aim.

'I hope you wreck the goddamn car and end up trapped in a heap of twisting, burning metal.' The next pillow sailed over his head. He didn't even bother to duck. 'I hope glass gets in your eyes and you go blind, and if you do I'll laugh when you walk into walls.'

He turned away from her, a deliberate and calculated insult.

'Well then, I guess you won't want to borrow what's left of the car tomorrow night.'

'I want it now!'

'Faith, my treasure . . .' He tucked the shirt in, picked up his watch from the bureau. 'You want everything now.' Unable to resist, he picked up the keys, dangled them. 'But you can't have it.'

She screamed, a primal war cry, and launched herself off the bed. He could have sidestepped, but it was more entertaining to brace and catch her arms before she could use those pretty, lethal nails on his face.

Besides, if he'd nipped out of her way, she'd have plowed straight, blind with temper, into his dresser. 'You're going to hurt yourself,' he warned, dancing with her as he held her trembling arms high.

'No, I'm going to *kill* you. I'm going to rip your eyes right out of your head.'

'You've got a real obsession with me going blind tonight. You rip my eyes out, how can I see how pretty you are?'

'Let me go, you bastard. Fight like a man.'

'If I fought like a man. I'd just coldcock you and be done with it.' To infuriate her, he leaned down to give her a quick kiss. 'It'd take less energy.'

She slumped, eyes tearing up in defeat. 'Oh, just let go. I don't want your ugly old car anyway.'

'Those won't work, either. Tears come too easy to you.' But he kissed her cheek. 'You can have the car tomorrow, all day and half the night if you want.' He gave her arms an affectionate squeeze, started to step back.

And saw stars when she kicked his shin.

'Goddamn it. Jesus Christ.' He shoved her aside, tried to pace off the pain. 'You sneaky bitch.'

'Be glad I didn't go with my first instinct and use my knee. It was a near thing.' When he leaned over to rub at the sting, she made a leap for the keys still in his hand. She nearly had them, then he pivoted and her forward motion shot her past him and down onto the floor with a thud.

'Kincade! Faith Ellen!' The voice was a whip snapping on satin. Margaret stood in the doorway, body rigid, face pale. Instantly all movement stopped.

'Mama.' Cade cleared his throat.

'I could hear the shouting and the swearing all the way downstairs. As could Judge Purcell, whom I am entertaining this evening. As could Lilah, and the day maid, and the young man who's just come to take her home.'

She waited a full beat, for the weight of the impropriety to lie heavy on the shoulders of her children. 'Perhaps you feel this sort of behavior is acceptable, but I do not, and do not wish to have guests, servants, and strangers come to believe that I have raised two hyenas in this house.'

'I apologize.'

'Make him apologize to me,' Faith demanded, sulking as she rubbed her jarred elbow. 'He pushed me down.'

'I certainly did not. You tripped over your own feet.'

'He was being cruel and unreasonable.' She had one shot left, Faith calculated, and meant to take it. 'All I did was ask, and ask politely, to borrow his car for the evening, and he started calling me names and pushing me around.' She winced, gingerly touching her arm. 'I have bruises.'

'I suspect there was more than a little provocation, but there is no excuse for laying your hands on your sister.'

'No, ma'am.' Cade acknowledged this with a stiff nod, and the regret that a foolish interlude could be pressed into such cold, implacable lines. 'You're right on both counts. I apologize.'

'Very well.' Margaret shifted her gaze to Faith's. 'Cade's property is his to use or lend as he pleases. Now, let that be an end to it.'

'I just want to get out of this house for a few hours.' Temper spiked, spilling out of her mouth. 'He can use the truck just as easy as anything else. All he wants to do is drive someplace dark and quiet so he can grope Tory Bodeen.'

'That's pretty talk, Faith,' Cade murmured. 'Very attractive.'

'Well, it's true. Everyone in town knows the two of you are at each other.'

Margaret took two steps forward before her control snapped back. 'Are you – do you intend to see Victoria Bodeen tonight?'

'Yes.'

'Could you be unaware of my feelings about her?'

'No, Mama. I'm not unaware of them.'

'Obviously those feelings don't matter. The fact that she played

121

a part in your sister's death, the fact that she is a constant reminder of that loss, mean nothing to you.'

'I don't blame her for Hope's death. I'm sorry that you do, and sorrier that my friendship with her causes you any pain or distress.'

'Save your sorries,' Margaret said coldly. 'Sorry is nothing but an excuse for poor behavior. You may choose to bring that woman into your life, but you will keep her out of mine. Is that understood?'

'Yes, ma'am.' His voice iced in a direct reflection of hers. 'It's well understood.'

Without another word, she turned and walked away, her footsteps measured and slow.

Cade stared after her, wishing he hadn't seen that one quick flash of grief in her eyes. Wishing he didn't feel responsible for it. To cut at the guilt, he shot Faith one violent look.

'Very nice job, as always. Be sure to enjoy your evening.'

She squeezed her eyes shut as he strode out. There was a hole in her stomach, burned there by her own thoughtlessness. For a moment, she indulged herself, sat and rocked, then she leaped up, dashed toward the stairs. And heard the front door slam.

'I'm sorry,' she murmured, and sat on the landing. 'I didn't think. I didn't mean it. Don't hate me.' She dropped her head on her knees. 'I already hate myself.'

'I hope you'll pardon the behavior of my children, Gerald.' Margaret swept back into the main drawing room where her old friend waited.

There would have been no such outbursts in his house when his children lived under his roof. But then, he thought, his daughters had been raised to behave as ladies at all times.

Still, he offered Margaret a sympathetic and affectionate smile. 'No, Margaret, no need to apologize. Just high spirits.' He took the glass of sherry she'd set down before going upstairs and offered it back to her.

There was music playing on low. Bach. A favorite of both of them. He'd brought roses, as he always did, and Lilah had already put them into the Baccarat vase on the broad sweep of the piano.

The room, with its deep blue divans and old, polished wood, was perfect, peaceful, and precisely as Margaret demanded. The

122

piano was rarely played, but kept in tune just the same. It had been her wish that her daughters become accomplished on that instrument, but there she had been disappointed.

There were no family photos in this room. Every memento had been carefully selected for how it would fit into the scheme so that heirlooms blended seamlessly with her own acquisitions.

It was not a room where a man would prop his boots on a table, or a child would scatter toys on the rug.

'High spirits,' she repeated. 'It's kind of you to say so.' She paced over to the window, watched Cade's car roar down the drive. Dissatisfaction scratched her skin like wool. 'I'm afraid it's a great deal more, and less, than high spirits.'

'Our children grow up, Margaret.'

'Some of them do.'

He said nothing for a moment. He knew the subject of Hope was never an easy one for her. And as he preferred things easy, would let it drift by as if it had never been said.

He'd known her for thirty-five years, and had once, briefly, courted her himself. She had chosen Jasper Lavelle, who had been wealthier and with bluer blood. It hadn't put more than a hitch in Gerald's stride, or so he liked to think.

He'd had ambitions even then, as a young lawyer. He had married well himself, raised two children, and had comfortably widowed for five years.

Like his old friend, he preferred his widowed status to marriage. So much less demanding of time and energies.

He was a tall and strapping sixty with the dramatic features of enormous black eyebrows that winged up like ruffled feathers on his otherwise dignified, square face.

He had made the law, all the ins and slippery outs of it, his life, prospered and carved out a respected niche in the community.

He enjoyed Margaret's company, their discussions of art and literature, and was her usual escort at events and affairs. They had never exchanged more than a cool sociable kiss on the cheek.

For sex he enjoyed the favors of young prostitutes, who exchanged sexual fantasies for cash and remained nameless.

He was a staunch Republican, a devout Baptist. He considered his sexual adventures a kind of hobby. After all, he didn't golf.

'I don't know that I'm good company tonight, Gerald.'

He was also a creature of habit. It was their night for a quiet dinner at Beaux Reves, a dinner that would be followed by coffee and a pleasant thirty minutes in the gardens.

'I'm too old a friend for you to worry about that.'

'I suppose I could use a friend. I'm upset, Gerald. Victoria Bodeen. I had hoped I could resolve myself to her coming back to Progress. But now I've learned that Cade is seeing her, socially.'

'He's a grown man, Margaret.'

'He is my son.' She turned back then, her face hard as stone. 'I won't have it.'

He nearly sighed. 'It seems to me that if you press the matter with him, you'll make it, and her, too important.'

'I don't intend to press it with him.' No, she knew what needed to be done, and would see to it. 'He should have married your Deborah, Gerald.'

It was a mutual regret, mild on his part, and made him smile sadly. 'We might have had grandchildren together.'

'What a thought,' Margaret murmured, and decided she could use another sherry.

Tory was waiting for him to drive up. She had it all figured out. It always took a bit of time and distance for her to realize Cade had maneuvered her. He did so very smoothly, very quietly, and very skillfully. But it was still maneuvering.

She'd been in charge of her life for too long now to allow anyone a turn at the wheel.

He was a nice man, and she couldn't deny she enjoyed his company. She was proud of how calm and mature that sounded when she practiced it in front of her mirror. Just as she was pleased with the rest of the little speech she intended to make.

She was simply too involved with setting up her new business, establishing herself in town, reacquainting herself with the area, to put any time or effort into a relationship with him, or anyone else.

Naturally she was flattered he was interested in her, but it would be best all around if they simply stepped back now. She hoped they'd continue to be friends, but that was all they could be. Now or ever.

She scraped her teeth over her bottom lip. She could bring his taste back. She was good at bringing tastes back, even when she didn't want to be.

The hot, sweet flavor of the windfall peaches under the twisted

124

old tree by the river outside of town. Bees, drunk on the fermented juice, swarmed the fallen fruit and buzzed cozily.

She hadn't expected his taste to be as hot and sweet, or as potent.

She hadn't expected to be linked so perfectly with him for that moment, as if he were one of the missing pieces of the puzzle of her life.

That was romanticizing the casual, she reminded herself. It was foolish to pretend she hadn't imagined what it would be like to kiss him. She was human, after all.

She was normal.

But when she'd imagined it, everything had been rather mild and pleasant and simple. The reality of it hadn't really been a kiss at all, but more of a sample. And she supposed he'd done that on purpose, just to intrigue her.

Clever of him, she decided. He was a clever man. But it wasn't going to work.

She was ready for him now, and her mind was set. There was no temper or embarrassment to blur her senses. She'd walk outside when he pulled up. In that way she'd block him from coming inside and having any opportunity to confuse the issue again. She'd make her tidy speech, wish him well, then go back inside and close the door.

And stay where it was safe.

The plan put her at ease again, in control again. So when she heard him drive up, she gave a little sigh of relief. Everything was about to be put back in order again.

Then she stepped out, saw his face.

He sat in the pretty convertible, his streaked mass of hair already windblown, his hands resting on the wheel. He gave her an easy smile, but behind it she saw anger and frustration. Most of all she saw bitter unhappiness.

No maneuver he could have devised, no plan he could have calculated, could have hit her weakness more effectively.

'That's one of the things I like best about you, Tory. You're prompt.' He got out, started to round the hood to open the passenger door.

She didn't touch him. The connection tended to become too close with physical contact. 'Tell me what's wrong.'

'Wrong?' He glanced down, started to make light of it, then the

125

shield went up. He stepped back, went around to his own side as she climbed in. 'Do you just crack open a mind and take a peek at what's inside?'

Her head snapped back, as one would from a blow. Then she folded her hands in her lap. It was better this way. It would have happened eventually anyway, she reminded herself. Better to get it over with quick and early.

'No. That would be rude.'

He laughed, dropped back behind the wheel. 'Oh, I see. There's an etiquette to mind reading.'

'I don't read minds.' She gripped her fingers together – taut wires, white at the stress points. She let out a breath to relieve the pressure in her chest, and stared straight ahead. 'It's more a reading of feelings. I've learned to block it out, as it's not pleasant, whatever you might think, to have other people's emotions pounding at you. It's fairly easy to filter it, but now and again, if I'm not paying attention, something, particularly strong emotions, slide through. I apologize for intruding on your privacy.'

He said nothing for a moment, just sat with his head back and his eyes closed. 'No, I'm sorry. That was nasty. I'm feeling nasty, as you picked up on. I guess I needed to take a swipe at somebody, and you were elected.'

'I understand that it's uncomfortable to be with someone you can't trust. Someone you feel can and will take advantage of your own thoughts and feelings, use them to control you or hurt you or direct your life. That's one of the reasons I tried to explain to you why I'm not good at relationships, why I don't want to be involved in one. It's perfectly understandable to have questions and doubts, and for those questions and doubts to lead to resentment and distrust.'

She fell silent, used the silence to gear herself up for the rest.

'That,' Cade said mildly, 'is an amazing pile of bullshit. Mind if I ask whose words you just put in my mouth?'

'They were your own words.' She shifted, leaning on her own crutch of bitterness to face him. 'I am what I am and I can't change it. I know how to cope and how to get by. I don't want or expect anyone to stand with me. I don't need anyone to. I've learned to accept my life just the way it is, and I don't give a damn if you or anyone else doesn't.'

126

'You'd better watch out for gopher holes, Tory. That's a very high horse you're sitting on.' When she reached for the door handle, he just lifted an eyebrow. 'Coward.'

Her fingers tightened on it, then released. 'Bastard.'

'That's right, I was, for taking out a piss-poor mood on you. I was told tonight that sorries are just excuses for bad behavior, but I'm sorry anyway. You, however, are dumping opinions on me that I haven't expressed and don't have. I can't give them to you, as I haven't finished making them yet. When something's important, I like to take the time to study on it. You seem to be important.'

He leaned over. Instinctively she pressed back into the seat. 'You know, that's something that irritates me right down to the bone.' Calmly, he drew her seat belt over, hooked it. 'And it's a challenge at the same time. You see, I'm just bound and determined to keep touching you, to keep getting closer until you stop pulling back.'

He started the engine, tossed an arm over the seat, let his gaze rest on hers before he backed the car up the lane. 'You can chalk it up to pride and ego, if you like. I don't mind a bit.'

He swung onto the road, punched the gas. 'I've never hit a woman.' He said it conversationally, but she heard the viciously controlled anger beneath. 'I won't start with you. I'd like to have my hands on you. I damn well intend to have them on you eventually. But I won't hurt you.'

'I don't think every man uses his fists on women.' She looked out the window, gathering her composure the way she gathered bricks for her wall. 'I worked that, and several other issues, out in therapy.'

'Good.' He said it simply. 'Then I won't have to worry every move I make comes off as a threat to you. I don't mind making you nervous, but I do mind scaring you.'

'If I were afraid of you, I wouldn't be here.' The wind flowed over her face, through her hair. 'I'm not a pushover, Cade, or anyone's doormat. Not anymore.'

He waited a beat. 'If you were, I wouldn't want you here.'

She turned her head just a little, studied him with a sidelong glance. 'That was a very smart thing to say. Maybe the best thing that could be said. Even better, I believe you mean it.'

'I'm one of those peculiar creatures who tries to mean what they say.'

'I believe that, too.' She took a deep breath. 'I wasn't going to come tonight. I was going to walk out of the house, tell you I wasn't coming, explain how things were going to be. And here I am.'

'You felt sorry for me.' He shot her a glance. 'That was your first mistake.'

She gave a short laugh. 'I suppose. Where are we going?'

'No place special.'

'Good.' She settled back, surprised at how quickly, how easily she relaxed. 'That's a fine spot.'

He drove farther than he'd intended, choosing back roads at random, but always winding his way east. Toward the sea. The sun dipped lower behind them, shooting streaks of red across the sky that seemed to bleed down into the fields, pour through the stands of trees, drip into the snaking curve of the river.

He let her choose the music, and though Mozart blasted out rather than the rock he would have selected, it seemed to suit the oncoming twilight.

He found a little waterside restaurant, well south of the crowds that flocked to Myrtle Beach. It was warm enough to sit outside, at a little table where a squat white candle sputtered in a glass globe and the conversation around them was muted under the steady rise and slap of the surf.

On the beach children chased the bug-eyed sand crabs into their holes or threw bread crumbs into the air for the crying gulls. A group of young people thrashed in the surf and sent out the squeals and shouts that were caught between mating calls and childhood.

In a sky still deep blue with the last gasp of day, the first star winked to life and shone like a single diamond.

The tension and temper of the day melted out of her mind.

She didn't think she was hungry. Her appetite was never particularly keen. But she poked at her salad while he began to tell her of his work.

'When you feel your eyes begin to glaze over, just stop me.'

'I don't bore that easy. And I know something about organic cotton. The gift shop where I worked in Charleston sold organic cotton shirts. We got them from California. They were pricey, but sold well for us.'

'Give me the name of the shop. Lavelle Cotton started manufacturing organic last year. I can guarantee we'll beat the price from California. That's part of what I haven't been able to get across as well as I'd like. Growing organically, after you're established, competes head-on with chemical methods. And the product commands a premium in the marketplace.'

'Which equals more profit.'

'Exactly.' He buttered a roll, passed it to her. 'People listen to profit more than they listen to environmental concerns. I can talk about pesticide drift, the effect on wildlife and edge species—'

'Edge species?'

'Quail and other birds that nest in the grass along the fields. Hunters shoot the quail, eat the quail, and consume the pesticide. Then there's insecticide. Sure they kill off the pests, but they also kill off the good bugs, infect birds, reduce the food chain. A chick eats a dead or dying insect after spraying, then the chick's infected. It's a cycle you can't break until you try another method.'

Odd, she thought, to realize she'd carried her father's view of farming inside her, where nature was the enemy to be fought day after day, with the government running a close second.

'You love it. Farming.'

'Yes. Why wouldn't I?'

She shook her head. 'A great many people make a living doing things they don't enjoy and have no real talent for. I was supposed to go on and work at the tool and dye factory after high school. I took business courses in secret rather than argue about it. So I suppose I know what it's like to go against the grain to do what you want to do.'

'How did you know what you wanted to do?'

'I just wanted to be smart.' To escape, she thought, but steered the conversation back to him. 'The organic method's sensible, and certainly forward-thinking, but if you don't spray, you've got weeds and disease and pests. You've got a sick crop.'

'Cotton's been cultivated over four thousand years. What do you think people did up until sixty, seventy years ago, before we started using aldicarb and methyl parathion and trifluralin?'

It intrigued her, interested her; to see him getting worked up. To feel the passion for his work vibrating out of him. 'They had slaves. And after that, field hands they could work obscene hours for slave wages. That's just one of the reasons, in case you were wondering, why the South lost the War Between the States.'

'We can discuss history another time.' He leaned forward, needing to make his point. 'Organically grown cotton can and does use more hand labor, but it also makes use of natural resources. Animal manure, compost, instead of chemical fertilizers that can pollute groundwater. Cover crops to help control weeds and pests and add to revenue, and the basic soil conservation of rotation. Good bugs – ladybugs, mantis, and so on – to feed on the cotton pests instead of exposing farmworkers, neighbors, children to pesticide drift. We let the plants die naturally instead of using a defoliant.'

He sat back as their entrées were served, topped off the wine in their glasses, but he was on a roll. 'We keep up the process through the ginning. We clear the gin of residue from conventional cotton, that's federal regulation. So when it's sold, it's pure, free of chemicals. Not everyone thinks that such a big deal for a shirt or your jockey shorts, but cotton's seed as well as fiber. And cottonseed's in a whole lot of prepared food. How much pesticide do you figure you're taking in every time you eat a bag of potato chips.'

'I don't think I want to know.' But she remembered her father coming home, cursing the land. She remembered watching the crop dusters dropping their clouds, and how the filaments would linger and drift toward the house. The stench of it. And the burn in the air.

She remembered the stench of it. And the burn in the air.

'How did you get interested in the whole organic method?'

'First year of college. I started reading about it and, well, the fact is, there was this girl.'

'Ah.' Amused, Tory, cut into her trout. 'Now we see the picture form.'

'Her name was Lorilinda Dorset, from Mill Valley, California. My tongue fell onto my toes the first time I saw her. A long, lanky brunette in tight jeans.'

He gave a sigh at the memory, sweet with distance. 'And a card-carrying member of PETA, Greenpeace, the Nature Conservancy, and God knows what all. So of course, to impress her, I read up on animal rights and natural farming and whatnot. Gave up meat for two months.'

She lifted a brow at the steak on his plate. 'Must have been love.'

'For a few bright, shiny weeks it was. I let her drag me to a seminar on organic farming, and she let me get her out of those tight jeans.' His smile was slow and wicked. 'Of course, eventually, my desperate need for a hamburger outweighed my devotion and Lorilinda turned in disgust from the carnivore.'

'What else could she do?'

'Exactly. But I kept thinking about what I'd heard in that seminar, and what I read in those books, and it made more and more sense to me. I saw how it could be done, and why it should be. So when Beaux Reves came to me, I started the long and not entirely without conflict process.'

'Lorilinda would be proud.'

'No, she'll never forgive me for the cheeseburger. It was a serious breech of faith. For months afterward, I could barely choke one down over the guilt.'

'Men are bastards.'

'I know it.' He also knew that she might actually eat a full meal if he kept her mind engaged. 'But forgiving that genetic flaw, how would you feel about being Progress's exclusive outlet for Lavelle's Green Cotton products?'

'You want me to sell your shirts in my shop?' she asked, surprised.

'Not necessarily shirts, if that doesn't fit the ambiance. But linens? Tablecloths, napkins, that sort of thing.'

'Well.' Caught off-guard, she shifted gears to business. 'I'd want to see some samples, of course. But as the product would be produced here in the state, it should fit in with my stock. We'll need to discuss cost and supply and quality and style, of course. I'm keeping clear of assembly-line type products. I'm providing the unique, and celebrating South Carolina's impressive variety of artists and craftsmen.'

She paused to sip her wine and think. 'Organic cotton linens,' she murmured. 'From field to display to table, all within Georgetown County. That could be very appealing.'

'Good.' He lifted his glass, tapped hers. 'We'll find a way to make it work for both of us. To make it all work,' he added.

The evening was certainly ending on a much nicer note than it had begun. With a full moon riding overhead, and a lovely fog of wine in the brain. She hadn't meant to drink, she did so rarely, but it had been so pleasant to sit by the water and sip at wine.

So pleasant that she'd had two glasses instead of one, and was now comfortably sleepy. The car ran smooth and fast, and the wind that blew over her smelled of the approaching summer.

It made her think of honeysuckle and overblown roses, the smell of tar melting in the sun and the lazy hum of bees courting the magnolia blossoms in the marsh.

Wishing to God it'd get a little cooler now that the sun'd gone down. If a ride didn't come along soon she could hook her thumb around, she'd end up walking all the way to the goddamn beach. 'Course it was Marcie's fault, the bitch, ditching her so she could go off and make it with that asshole Tim. Well, she didn't give a flying fuck about Marcie, she'd hitch her way up to Myrtle Beach and have a fine time.

All she needed was a fricking ride. Come on, sweetheart, stop the car! There you go. Hot damn.

Tory reared up in the seat, eyes wide, sucking at air like a swimmer surfacing from a long, lung-bursting dive.

'She got in the car. She tossed her pack in the back and got in the car.'

'Tory?' Cade pulled to the side of the road, shifted to take her shoulders. 'It's all right. You just fell asleep for a minute.'

'No.' She shoved at him, sick and desperate, and yanked at her seat belt. There were hands squeezing her heart so it beat in hitchy strikes. 'No.' She wrenched open the door, leaped out, and began a stumbling run along the shoulder. 'She's hitchhiking, to the beach. He picked her up, back there, somewhere back there.'

'Wait. Hold on.' He caught up with her, had to drag her around. 'Honey, you're shaking.'

'He took her.' It was sliding into her head, images and shapes, sounds and scents. There was a burn in her throat, a smoker's rasp from pulling deep on one too many cigarettes. 'He took her, pulled off the road, pulled off and into the trees. And he hit her with something. She doesn't see what it is, she only feels the pain, and she's dazed. What's happening? What's the matter? She pushes at him, but he's dragging her out of the car.'

'Who?'

She shook her head, fighting to find herself in the confusion, in the pain. In the terror. 'That way. Just up that way.'

'All right.' Her eyes were huge, unfocused, and her skin had gone clammy under his hands. 'You want to walk up there a little ways?'

'I have to. Leave me alone.'

'No.' He wrapped an arm firmly around her. 'That I won't. We'll walk. I'm right here. You can feel me right here.'

'I don't want this. I don't want it.' But she began to walk. She opened herself, overriding her instinct for self-preservation. She didn't struggle when the images shifted, solidified.

The stars wheeled overhead, blindingly bright. Heat closed around her like a fist.

'She wanted to go to the beach. She couldn't get a ride. She was angry at her friend. Marcie. A friend named Marcie, they were supposed to drive together, spend the weekend. Now she's going to hitchhike because, by God, she's not going to let that stupid bitch ruin her trip. He comes along, and she's happy. She's tired and she's thirsty, and he says he's going all the way to Myrtle. It's less than an hour by car.'

She stopped, held up a hand. Her head lolled back, but her eyes stayed open. Wide open. 'He gives you a bottle. Jack Black. Blackjack. You take a drink, a long one. To kill your thirst and because it's so cool to be riding along and drinking whiskey.

'It must've been the bottle he hit you with. Must've been, because you passed it back to him, and were laughing, then something crashed into the side of your head. Christ! It hurts!'

She staggered, and her hand flew to her cheek. The taste of blood filled her mouth.

'No. Don't.' Cade pulled her against him, surprised she didn't slide out of his arms like smoke.

'I can't see. Can't. There's nothing in him. Just blank. Wait. Wait.' With her hands fisted, her breath in rags, she pushed. Sickness rolled in her stomach, but she slipped through, and saw.

'He took her in there.' She began to rock. 'I can't. I just can't.'

'You don't have to. It's all right now. Come on back to the car.'

'He took her in there.' Pity and grief overwhelmed everything else. 'He rapes her.' Now she closed her eyes, let it come, let it burn. 'You fight for a while. He's hurting you, and you're so scared, so you fight. He hits you again, twice, hard in the face. Oh it hurts, it hurts, it hurts. You don't want to be here. You want your mother. You just cry while he grunts and pants and finishes.

'You smell his sweat and his sex and your own blood, and you can't fight anymore.'

Tory lifted her hands, ran them over her own face. She needed to feel the lines of her own cheeks, nose, mouth. She needed to remember who she was.

'I can't see him. It's dark and he's just a thing. There's nothing from him for me to feel that seems real. She doesn't see him, either, not really. Not even when he uses his hands to strangle her. It doesn't take long because she's barely conscious anyway and hardly struggles. She hasn't been with him more than half an hour, and she's dead. Lying naked in the shadow of the trees. That's where he leaves her. He – he was whistling on his way back to the car.'

She stepped back from Cade then, in that deliberate way of hers. All he could see was her face, pale as the moon, with those eyes swirling smoke.

'She was only sixteen. A pretty girl with long blond hair and long legs. Her name was Alice, but she didn't like it, so everyone called her Ally.'

The strain and the sorrow swallowed her up.

Cade caught her, lifted her. She was limp as the dead. Shaken as much by her utter stillness as the story she'd told, he carried her away quickly. He thought, hoped, if he got her away from that spot, that place, she'd be better.

Even as he bent to lay her back in the car she stirred. When her eyes opened, they were dark and glazed:

'It's all right. You're all right. I'm going to get you home.'

'I just need a minute.' The queasiness came on, and the chill. But they would pass. The horror would take longer. 'I'm sorry.' She shrugged helplessly. 'I'm sorry.'

'For what?' He skirted the hood, got back behind the wheel. Then just sat. 'I don't know what to do for you. There ought to be something I could do. I'm going to get you home, then I'll come back and . . . I'll find her.'

Confused, Tory stared at him. 'She isn't there now. It happened a long time ago. Years ago.'

He started to speak, then stopped himself. Alice, she'd said. A young blond girl named Alice. It stirred his memory, and a kind of sickness in his gut. 'Does it always come on you like that? Out of nowhere?'

'Sometimes.'

'It hurts you.'

'No, it wears you out, makes you a little sick, but it doesn't hurt.'

'It hurts you,' he said again, and reached down to turn the key.

'Cade.' Tentatively she touched a hand to his. 'It was . . . I'm sorry to bring this back to you, but you have to know. It was like Hope. That's why it came so strong. It was like Hope.'

'I know it.'

'No, you don't understand. The man who killed that poor girl, left her there in the trees, it was the same man who killed Hope.'

Progress

Would you realize what Revolution is, call it Progress;
and would you realize what Progress is, call it
Tomorrow.

– Victor Hugo

Chapter Eleven

I didn't want to believe it. There were – are – dozens of rational, logical reasons why Tory is wrong. Small points and majors ones that make her claim about the teenager killed along the roadside impossible. The girl couldn't have been murdered by the same monster who killed my sister.

Little Hope with her flyaway hair and eyes full of fun and secrets.

I can list those reasons here in a straightforward manner, the way I couldn't seem to relate to Tory last night. I know I let her down. I know by the way she looked at me, by the way she slipped back behind that barricaded silence of hers. I know I hurt her by the way I turned aside her claim, the way I suggested, no, insisted, that she let it alone.

But what she told me, what she let me see through her eyes, the horror she relived right in front of me, and later spoke of with such quiet restraint, brought it all back. Brought me back to that long-ago summer when everything in the world changed.

Maybe it'll help more to write of Hope than of that doomed young girl I never knew.

As I sit here at my father's desk – for it will forever be my father's desk in everyone's mind, including my own – I can turn back the days and months and years until I'm twelve again, still innocent enough to be careless with people I love, still seeing my friends as superior in every way to family, still dreaming of the day when I'm old enough to drive, or to drink, or to do any of the magical things that belong to the coveted world of adulthood.

139

I'd done my chores that morning, as always. My father had been a stickler for responsibilities, and for hammering what was expected of me into my head. At least he was before we lost Hope. I'd gone out with him, midmorning, to look over the fields. I remember standing, looking over that ocean of cotton. My father stuck mostly with cotton, even when many of the neighboring farms turned heavily to soybeans or tomatoes or tobacco. Beaux Reves was cotton, and I was never to forget it.

I never did.

And that day it was so simple to see why, to stand and look out over that vast space, to see the magic of the bolls burst open by the straining lint. To watch the stalks bend with the weight − some of them carrying what must have been a hundred bolls, all cracked open like eggs. And that late in the year, with the fields so rich with it, the very air smelled of cotton. The hot smell of summer dying.

It was to be a good harvest that year. The cotton would spill into the fields, be picked and bagged and processed. Beaux Reves would go on, even with those who lived in it little more than ghosts.

I was set free shortly after noon. While my father expected me to work, to learn, to sweat, he also expected me to be a boy. He was a good man, a good father, and for the first twelve years of my life he was everything solid and warm and fine.

I missed him long before he died.

But when he cut me loose that day, I took my bike, the streamlined twelve-speed I'd been given for Christmas, and drove through the thick, hot wall of air all the way to Wade's. We had a tree house, back of Wade's yard, up in an old sycamore. Dwight and Wade were already there, drinking lemonade and reading comic books. It was too damn hot to do much else, even if we were twelve.

But Wade's mama never could leave us be. She was forever coming out and calling up asking didn't we want this or why didn't we come in and have a nice cold drink and a tuna fish sandwich. Miss Boots always did have a sweet heart, but she was a royal pain in our collective asses that summer. We were on the cusp of manhood, or so we considered ourselves, and it was more than mortifying to be offered tuna fish and Pepsi-Cola by a mother wearing a starched apron and an indulgent smile that turned us back into children again.

We escaped, headed down to the river for a swim. I believe, out of duty, we made rude, and to us, brilliantly clever insults regarding Dwight's plump white ass. He, in turn, retaliated by comparing our male parts to various unattractive vegetables. Naturally, such activities kept us all in hysterics for an hour.

It was very easy being twelve. We discussed important matters: Would the Rebel Alliance come back and defeat Darth Vader and the Evil Empire? Who was cooler – Superman or Batman? How would we con one of our parents into taking us to see the latest Friday the Thirteenth movie? We would never be able to face our schoolmates if we hadn't seen the insane Jason slaughter his annual quota of teenagers.

Such were the vital questions of our lives at the moment.

Sometime after four, I suppose it was, after we'd made ourselves half sick on wasp-stung peaches and underripe pears, Dwight had to get home. His aunt Charlotte was coming in from Lexington for a visit, and he was expected to be clean and on time for supper. Dwight's parents were strict, and it would not pay him to be late.

We knew he would be forced to wear pressed shorts and a bow tie for the evening, and with the generosity of friends, we waited until he was out of earshot to snicker about it.

Wade and I left soon after, parting ways on the road. He for town and me for Beaux Reves.

I passed Tory on the way. She didn't have a bike. She was walking home, toward me. I imagine she'd been up playing with Hope. Her feet were bare and dusty, and her shirt was too small. I didn't really notice any of that at the time, but I remember now just how she looked, that heavy brown hair pulled back from her face, those big gray eyes that stared right into mine as I zoomed by without a word. I could hardly have taken a moment to speak to a girl and maintain my manly dignity. But I recall glancing back, and seeing her walking away on strong legs tanned with summer.

The next time I saw her legs, there were fresh welts scoring them.

Hope was on the veranda when I got there, playing at jacks. I wonder if young girls still play at jacks. Hope was a terror at it, and could whoop anyone she persuaded to challenge her. She tried to get me to play, even promised to give me a handicap. Which, of course, insulted me beyond bearing. I think I told her jacks were for babies and I had more important things to do. Her laugh, and the sound of the ball bouncing, followed me inside.

I would give a year of my life to go back to that moment and sit on the veranda while she beat me at jacks.

The evening passed as others had. Lilah shooed me upstairs to bathe, saying I smelled of river skunk.

Mama was in the front parlor. I knew because the music she liked was playing. I didn't go in, as I knew from experience she didn't care much for smelly, sweaty boys in the front parlor.

It's funny, looking back I see how much we were, Wade, Dwight, and I, ruled by our mothers. Wade's with her fluttery hands and warm eyes, Dwight's with her bags of cookies and candy, and mine with her unbending notions of what was tolerable, and what was not.

I never realized that before, and don't suppose it matters at this point. It might have mattered then, if we'd understood it.

On this evening, what mattered was avoiding my mother's disapproval, so I headed straight up the stairs. Faith was in her room, putting some fancy dress on one of her pack of Barbie dolls. I know because I took the time and trouble to stop at her door and sneer.

I had a shower, as I had, shortly before, decided baths were for girls and old wrinkled men. I'm sure I put my dirty clothes in the hamper, as Lilah would have twisted the lobe of my ear if I'd done otherwise. I put on clean clothes, combed my hair, likely took a few moments to flex my biceps and study the results in the mirror. Then I went downstairs.

We had chicken for supper. Roast chicken with mashed potatoes and gravy, and the peas that were fresh from the garden. Faith didn't care for peas and refused to eat hers, which might have been tolerated, but she made an issue of it, as Faith often did, and ended up sassing Mama and being sent from the table in disgrace.

I believe Chauncy, Papa's faithful old hound who died the next winter, got what was left on her plate.

After supper, I poked around outside, devising a way I would talk Papa into letting me build a fort. Thus far my efforts in this area had been a dismal failure, but I thought if I could locate the right spot, one that would conceal the proposed structure so that it wouldn't be the eyesore Papa imagined, I would succeed.

It was during this reconnoiter that I found Hope's bike where she'd hidden it behind the camellias.

I never thought of tattling. It just wasn't the way we worked as siblings, unless temper or self-interest outweighed loyalty. It didn't even concern me, though I imagined she planned to sneak out and meet Tory somewhere that night as they were thick as thieves all that summer. I knew she'd done so before, and didn't blame her. Mama was much more strict on her daughters than she was on her son. So I said nothing about the bike and set my mind on the fort.

One word from me, and her plans would have been shattered. She'd have shot me one of her hot, angry looks under her lashes, and likely have refused to speak to me for a day, two if she could hold out.

And she'd have been alive.

Instead, I went back into the house around dusk and planted myself in front of the TV as was my right on a long summer night. Being twelve, I had a powerful appetite and eventually wandered out to hunt up some appropriate snack. I ate potato chips and watched Hill Street Blues *and wondered what it was like to be a policeman.*

By the time I went to bed, with a full stomach and tired eyes, my sister was already dead.

He'd thought he could write more, but he couldn't manage it. He'd intended to write down what he knew about his sister's murder, and the murder of a young girl named Alice, but his thoughts had veered away from the facts and the logic and had left him steeped in memories and grief.

He hadn't realized how completely she would come alive for him if he wrote of her. How the pictures of that night, and the horrible images of the next morning, would run through his mind like a film.

Was that, he wondered, how it was for Tory? Like a movie playing in the mind that would not be stopped?

No, it was more. Did she know that when she'd been caught in that vision the night before she'd spoken *to* the girl rather than about her? Perhaps the girl Alice had spoken through her.

What kind of strength did it take to face that, to survive it and build a life?

He picked up what he'd written, started to lock it in a drawer of the old desk. Instead he folded the pages, sealed them in an envelope.

He would need to see Tory again. Need to speak with her again. He'd been right on that first day when he'd told her the ghost of his sister stood right there between them.

There would be no going forward or back until they'd each come to terms with what they'd lost.

He heard the old grandfather clock call the hour with its hollow, echoing bongs. Two lonely beats. He would be up again in four hours, dressing in the pale light, eating the breakfast Lilah would insist on fixing, then driving from field to field, eyeing the crops with all the faith and fatalism every farmer was born with, checking for pests, studying the sky.

Despite, or perhaps because of, all the science he studied and implemented, Cade's Beaux Reves was more plantation than the farm of his father. He hired more laborers, stuck with more hand-work than the generation before him. He put more effort, and more of the profits, into the ginning and the compression and storage and processing than his father, and his grandfather, had been willing to do. It made Beaux Reves a self-contained ante-bellum plantation, and at the same time, a kind of busy, diversified factory.

And still, with his charts and his science and his careful business plans, he would stand and study the sky and hope nature cooperated.

In the end, he thought, as he picked up the envelope, it all came down to fate.

He switched off the desk lamp and used the moonlight spilling through the windows to guide him down the curving stairs and out of the tower office. He'd need those four hours' sleep, he told himself, as after the morning work he had afternoon meetings at the plant. He reminded himself to pick up some samples for Tory, and work up a proposal.

If he could pull all that together, he could go see her the next night. As he stepped into his room, he weighed the envelope in his hand, then switched on the light and tucked the envelope into the briefcase that sat beside his field boots.

He was unbuttoning his shirt when the faint breeze and the drift of smoke it carried had him glancing toward his terrace doors. He stepped over, noted they were open a chink, and through the glass saw the red glow of a burning cigarette.

'I wondered if you'd ever come down.' Faith turned. She was wearing the robe she favored these days, and spreading her arms on the stone, struck a kind of pose.

'Why don't you smoke out your own window?'

'I don't have this fine terrace, like the master of the house.' That had been another bone of contention. And though he agreed that she'd have made more of the master suite than he, it hadn't been worth fighting their mother over her insistence he take it after his father's death.

She lifted the cigarette, drew slowly. 'You're still mad at me. I don't blame you. That was a lousy thing to do. I just don't think when my temper's up.'

'If that's an apology, fine. Now, go on and let me go to bed.'

'I'm sleeping with Wade.'

'Jesus.' Cade pressed his fingers to his eyes and wondered why they didn't just bore through his brain. 'You figure that's something I need to know?'

'I found out one of your secrets, so I'm telling you one of mine. We'll be even.'

'I'll make a note to take an ad on it out in the paper. Wade.' He dropped down into the iron chair on the terrace, slumped. 'Goddamn it.'

'Oh, don't be that way. We're getting along just fine.'

'Until you chew him up and spit him out.'

'I don't plan to.' Then she gave a short, humorless laugh. 'I never plan to, it just happens.' She sent the butt of the cigarette sailing over the rail, never thinking that her mother would find it

145

and be annoyed. 'He makes me feel good. Why does something have to be wrong with that?'

'It doesn't. It's your business.'

'The way you and Tory is yours.' She stepped over, crouched down so their eyes were level. 'I am sorry, Cade. It was mean and spiteful of me to say what I did, and I wish I could take it back.'

'You always do.'

'No, I might say I do, but half the time I don't mean it. This time I do.' Since there was more fatigue than anger in his eyes, she reached up to dance her fingers in his hair. She'd always envied the weight and the curl of his hair.

'But you don't pay any attention to Mama. She's got no business telling you what to do. Even if she's probably right.'

He caught a drift of his mother's jasmine, the night bloomer. 'She's not right.'

'Well, I'm the last one to give advice on romantic entanglements—'

'Exactly.'

She arched a brow. 'Ouch. That was a quick little stab. But, as I was going to say before I started bleeding, this family is screwed up enough on its own without adding a strange element like Tory Bodeen to the mix.'

'She's a part of what happened that night.'

'Oh Lord, Cade, we were screwed up long before Hope died.'

He looked so frustrated at that statement, and so tired, she nearly backed off, made some joke out of the whole thing. But she'd been doing a lot of thinking since Tory had come back to town. It was time to say it.

'You think about it.' Anger with him, and more than a little self-loathing, made her voice sharp as honed tacks. 'We were made the minute we were born, all three of us. And Mama and Papa before us. You think their marriage was some sort of love match? You might like to look at the pretty side of things, but you know better than that.'

'They had a good marriage, Faith, until—'

'A good marriage?' With a sound of disgust, she pushed to her feet, dragged her cigarettes from her robe pocket. 'What the hell does that mean? A good marriage? That they were suited for each other, that it was smart and convenient for the heir of the country's biggest and richest plantation to marry the well-to-do debutante?

146

Fine, it was a good marriage. Maybe they even had feelings for each other, for a while anyway. They did their duty,' she said bitterly, and snapped on her lighter. 'They made us.'

'They did their best,' Cade said wearily. 'You never wanted to see that.'

'Maybe their best was never good enough, not for me. And I don't see why it was for you. What choice did they ever give you, Cade? All your life you were expected and groomed to be the master of Beaux Reves. What if you'd wanted to be a plumber, for God's sake.'

'That always was my secret life's ambition. I often fix a leaky faucet just to give myself a thrill.'

She laughed, and the roughest edge of her anger smoothed. 'You know very well what I mean. You might have wanted to be an engineer or a writer or a doctor, or something, but you weren't given the chance to choose. You were the oldest son, the only son, and your path was set.'

'You're right. And I don't know what might have happened if I'd wanted to be any of those things. But the point is, Faith, I didn't.'

'Well, how could you, growing up and hearing "When Cade runs Beaux Reves," and "When Cade's in charge"? You never got to be anything else, never got to say "I'm going to play guitar in a rock-and-roll band."'

This time he laughed and she sighed and leaned back against the rail. It reminded her why she so often came to his room, so often sought out his company. With Cade she could say what she needed to. He'd let her. He'd listen.

'Don't you see, Cade, they made us what we are, and maybe you got what you wanted in the end. I'm glad you did, and I mean that.'

'I know you do.'

'That still doesn't make it right. You were expected to be smart, to know things, to figure things. And while you were off learning your life's work, I was here being told to behave, to speak softly, not to run in the house.'

'You can take comfort that you rarely listened.'

'I might've,' she murmured. 'I might've if I hadn't already figured out that this house was a training ground for a good wife, a good marriage, just like Mama'd made before me. No one ever asked me if I wanted something more, something else, and when I questioned I was shushed. "Let your father worry about that, or your brother. Practice your piano, Faith. Read a good book so that you can discuss it intelligently. But not too intelligently. Wouldn't want some man to think you might be smarter than he is. When you marry, it'll be your job to make a pleasant home."'

She stared at the tip of her cigarette. 'A pleasant home. That was to be the sum total of my ambitions, according to the rules of the Lavelles. So, of course, being me, I was bound and determined to do just the opposite. I wasn't going to discover myself some dried-up repressed woman at thirty, no indeed. I made sure that wouldn't happen to me. Ran off with the first slick-talking, wild-eyed boy who asked me, one who was everything I wasn't supposed to want. Married and divorced before I was twenty.'

'That showed them, didn't it?' Cade murmured.

'Yes, it did. As did my next foray into marriage and divorce. Marriage was all I'd been trained for, after all. Not Mama's kind of marriage. I twisted that around and strangled myself doing it. Now here I am, twenty-six years old and two strikes against me. And no place to go but here.'

'Here you are,' Cade commented. 'Twenty-six years old, beautiful, smart, and experienced enough to know better than to repeat your mistakes. You never asked for any part in the farm, or the plant. If you want to learn, if you want work—'

The look she sent him stopped the words. It was so quietly indulgent. 'You really are too good for the rest of us. Christ knows how you manage it. It's too late for that, Cade. I'm a product of my upbringing and my own rebellion against it. I'm lazy and I like it. One of these days I'll find me a rich and doddering old man and charm him into marrying me. I'll take good care of him, of course, and spend his money like water. I might even be faithful, too. I was with the others, for all the good it did me. Then, with luck and time, I'll be a rich widow, and that, I think, will suit me best.'

The way it suits Mama, she thought bitterly. Bitterly.

'You're more than you think you are, Faith. A hell of a lot more.'

'No, honey, it's likely I'm a great deal less. Maybe it would've all turned out different, just a few shades different, anyway, if Hope had lived. You see, she never even had the chance to live.'

'That's no one's fault but the bastard who killed her.'

'You think not?' Faith said quietly. 'I wonder, would she have gone out that night, gone off to have her adventure with Tory, if she hadn't felt as closed-in here as I did? Would she have climbed out that window if she'd known that she'd be free to do as she pleased, with whom she pleased, the next morning? I knew her, better than anyone else in this house. That's the way of twins. She'd have made something of herself, Cade, because she'd have quietly chipped away at the bars. But she never got the chance. And when she died, the illusion of balance in this house went with her. They loved her best, you know.'

Faith pressed her lips together, heaved the cigarette over the rail. 'Better than you or me. I can't count the times afterward, one of them would look at me, me who shared her face, and I'd see in their eyes what they were thinking. Why hadn't it been me out there in the swamp instead of Hope.'

'Don't.' He got to his feet. 'That's not true. No one ever thought that.'

'I did. And it's what I felt from them. And I was a constant reminder that she'd died. I was not to be forgiven for that.'

'No.' He touched her face, saw the woman, and the child who'd been. 'That she'd lived.'

'But I couldn't be her, Cade.' The tears that sheened her eyes shone in the dim light, made them, he thought, so brutally alive. 'She was something they shared the way they couldn't share anything or anyone else. But they couldn't share the loss of her.'

'No, they couldn't.'

'So Papa built his shrine to her, and found his solace in the bed of another woman. And Mama got colder and harder. You and me, we just went the way we'd already been directed. So here we are in the middle of the night, with no one to call our own. And we still have nobody who loves us best.'

It hurt to hear it, and know it was true. 'We don't have to stay that way.'

'Cade, we *are* that way.' She leaned against him, rested her head when his arms came around her. 'Neither one of us has ever loved anyone, not enough to put that balance back. Maybe we loved Hope enough, maybe even back then we knew she was the one who held it all steady.'

'We can't change what happened, any of it. Only what we do about it now.'

'That's it, isn't it? I just don't want to do anything, about anything. I hate Tory Bodeen for coming back here, for making me remember Hope, miss her, grieve for her again.'

'She's not to blame, Faith.'

'Maybe not.' She closed her eyes. 'But I've got to blame someone.'

Chapter Twelve

The matter had to be dealt with, and as quickly and efficiently as possible. Money, Margaret knew, spoke to a certain class of people. It bought their silence, their loyalty, and what passed for their honor.

She dressed carefully for the meeting, but then she always dressed carefully. She wore a crisp suit in dignified navy, and her grandmother's single-strand pearls at her throat. She'd sat, as she did every morning, at her vanity, not so much disguising the signs of age, as she considered age an advantage, but using them to show her character and her station.

Character and station were both sword and shield.

She left the house at precisely eight-fifty, telling Lilah that she had an early appointment and would then be attending a luncheon in Charleston. She could be expected back at three-thirty.

She would, of course, be on time.

Margaret calculated the business she had to attend to before making the drive south would take no more than thirty minutes, but she had allowed forty-five, which would still give her time to tend to her short list of errands before the lunch.

She could have hired a driver, even kept one on staff. She could have assigned the errands to a servant. These were indulgences, and therefore weaknesses she would not permit.

The mistress of Beaux Reves was required, in her opinion, to be visible in town, to patronize certain shops and maintain the proper relationship with the right merchants and civil servants.

This civic responsibility was never to be shrugged aside for convenience.

Margaret did more than write generous checks to her selected charities. She held positions on committees. The local art council and the historical society might have been personal interests, but that bent did not negate the time, energy, and funds she funneled into them.

In more than thirty-two years as mistress of Beaux Reves, she had never once failed in her duties. She did not intend to fail today.

She didn't wince when she drove past the stand of moss-draped trees that cloaked the entrance to the swamp, nor did she slow down or speed up. She didn't notice that the planks on the little bridge had been replaced, and the sumac hacked down.

She drove steadily past the site of her daughter's death. If there was a pang, it would not have shown on her face.

It had not shown the day that child had been buried, even when her own heart lay ripped open and bleeding out.

Her face remained set and composed as she turned in to the narrow lane that led to the Marsh House. She parked behind Tory's station wagon, retrieved her purse. She didn't take one last look at herself in the rearview mirror. That would have been vain, and it would have been weak.

She stepped out of the car, closed the door, locked it.

She hadn't been to the Marsh House in sixteen years. She knew there had been work done on it, work Cade had arranged and paid for over her silent disapproval. As far as she was concerned, fresh paint and flowering bushes didn't change what it was.

A shanty. A slum. Better bulldozed into the ground than lived in. There had been a time, in the swarm of her grief, when she'd wanted to burn it, to set fire to the swamp, to see it all scorched to hell.

But that, of course, was foolish. And she was not a foolish woman.

It was Lavelle property, and despite everything, must be maintained and passed on to the next generation.

She climbed the steps, ignoring the charm of the long clay troth full of spilling flowers and vines, and knocked briskly on the wooden frame of the screen door.

Inside, Tory paused in the act of reaching for a cup. She was running behind, and didn't much give a damn. Tired to the bone, she'd slept late, had yet to dress. She was trying to gear herself up for a lecture on responsibility, to scold herself for self-indulgence.

She hoped the coffee would help snap her system to life so she could work up the enthusiasm it would take to go into the shop and finish preparing for her opening.

The interruption wasn't just unwelcome, it was almost intolerable. There was no one she wanted to see, no words she wanted to exchange. She wanted, more than anything, to go back to bed and fight her way into the dreamless sleep that had eluded her through the night.

But she answered the knock because to ignore it would have been weak. That, at least, Margaret would have understood.

Faced with Hope's mother, Tory felt immediately guilty, frazzled, and embarrassed. 'Mrs. Lavelle.'

'Victoria.' Margaret skimmed her ice-edged gaze up from Tory's bare feet, over the rumpled robe, to the top of her tousled hair. This sloth, she told herself with cold satisfaction, was no more or less than what she'd expected from a Bodeen. 'I beg your pardon. I assumed you would be up by nine, and preparing for the day.'

'Yes. Yes, I should be.' Miserably self-conscious, Tory tugged at the belt of her robe. 'I was . . . I'm afraid I overslept.'

'I need a few moments of your time. If I might come in.'

'Yes. Of course.' With all her carefully learned layers of composure shredded, Tory fumbled with the screen door. 'I'm sorry, the house isn't much more presentable than I am.'

She'd found a chair she'd liked, a big, overstuffed wingback in soft, faded blue. That and the little pie-crust table she planned to refinish eventually were the sum total of her living room furniture.

There was no rug, no curtains, no lamp. Neither was there dirt or dust, but Tory stepped back feeling as though she were inviting a queen into a hovel.

Her voice echoed uncomfortably in the near-empty room as Margaret stood taking a silent and damning assessment.

'I've been concentrating on setting up my shop and haven't . . .' Tory caught herself clutching her hands together, deliberately unlaced her fingers. Damn it, she wasn't eight years old any longer, a child to be mortified and awed by the regal disapproval of a friend's mother.

'I've just made coffee,' she said, rigidly polite. 'Would you like some?'

'Is there a seat?'

'Yes. It seems I live primarily in the kitchen and the bedroom, and will until I have my business up and running smoothly.' Babbling, Tory told herself, as she led the way. Stop babbling. You've nothing to apologize for.

Everything to apologize for.

'Please, sit down.'

At least she'd bought a good solid kitchen table and chairs, she thought. And the kitchen was clean, nearly cheerful with the little herbs she'd potted on the windowsill and the darkly glazed bowl from her own stock on the table.

It helped to pour the coffee, to set the sugar bowl out, but when she opened the refrigerator, fresh mortification reared up and bit pink into her cheeks.

'I'm afraid I don't have any cream. Or milk.'

'This will do.' Margaret nudged her cup aside a bare inch. A subtle and deliberate slap. 'If you would sit down, please?' Margaret let the silence hang a moment. She knew the value of silences, and of timing.

When Tory was seated, Margaret folded her hands on the edge of the table, and with her eyes mild and level, began.

'It has come to my attention that you have become involved with my son.' Another beat of silence while she watched surprise flicker over Tory's face. 'Small-town gossip is as unattractive as it is unavoidable.'

'Mrs. Lavelle—'

'Please.' Margaret cut her off with the lift of one finger. 'You've been away for a number of years. Though you do have family connections in Progress, you are, virtually, a newcomer. A stranger. Virtually,' Margaret repeated. 'But not entirely. For whatever reason, you've decided to return, to establish a business here.'

'Are you here to ask me my reasons, Mrs. Lavelle?'

'They hold no interest for me. I will be frank and tell you I did not approve of my son renting you space for your business, or renting you this house. However, Cade is the head of the family, and as such, business decisions are his alone. When those decisions, and their results, affect our family position, it becomes a different matter.'

The longer Margaret spoke in that soft, implacable tone, the easier it was for Tory to settle. Her stomach continued to jump, but when she spoke her voice was equally soft, and equally implacable. 'And how, Mrs. Lavelle, do my business and my choice of residence affect your family position?'

'That alone would have been difficult enough to tolerate. The circumstances are inconvenient, as I'm sure you're aware. But this personal element is not in any way acceptable.'

'So while you will tolerate, for now, my business association with your family, you're asking me not to see Cade in a personal manner? Is that correct?'

'Yes.' Who was this cool-eyed woman who remained so still, so composed? Margaret wondered. Where was the spindly child who'd slunk away or stared out from shadows?

'That is problematic, seeing as he's the landlord of both my home and business and seems to take those responsibilities seriously.'

'I'm prepared to compensate you for the time and effort it takes to relocate. Perhaps back to Charleston, or to Florence, where you again have family.'

'Compensate me? I see.' With deadly calm, Tory picked up her coffee. 'Would it be crass for me to ask just what form of compensation you had in mind?' She smiled a little, and saw Margaret's jaw tighten like a bow pulled. 'After all, I'm a businesswoman.'

'The entire matter is crass, and deplorable to me. I see no choice but to sink to your level in order to preserve my family and its reputation.' She opened the purse on her lap. 'I'm willing to write you a check for fifty thousand dollars upon your agreement to sever ties with Cade, and with Progress. I will give you half that amount today, and the rest will be sent to you upon your relocation. I will give you two weeks to remove yourself.'

Tory said nothing. She also knew the weapon of silence.

'That amount,' Margaret continued with her voice sharpening, 'will allow you to live quite comfortably during your transition.'

'Oh, undoubtedly.' Tory sipped her coffee again, then set the cup neatly back in its saucer. 'I do have a question. I wonder, Mrs. Lavelle, what makes you think that I would be, in any way, receptive to the insult of a bribe?'

'Don't pretend a sensibility you don't possess. I know you,' Margaret said, leaning forward. 'I know where and who you come from. You may think you can hide behind a quiet manner, behind the mask of some borrowed respectability. But I *know* you.'

'You think you do. But I can promise you I'm not feeling quiet or respectable right at this moment.'

It was Margaret's composure that unraveled, that had to be gathered back, tightly rewound like a ball of yarn. 'Your parents were trash and let you run wild as a cat, sidling down the road to push yourself on my child. Luring her away from her family, and finally to her death. You cost me one child, and you won't cost me another. You'll take my money, Victoria. Just as your father did.'

She was shaken now, down to the heart, but she held on. 'What do you mean, as my father did?'

'It only took five thousand for them. Five thousand for them to take you out of my sight. My husband wouldn't turn them out, though I begged him to do so.'

Her lips trembled open, then firmed. It had been the first and last time she had begged him for anything. Had begged anyone for anything. 'Finally, it was up to me to see to it. Just as it is now. You'll go, you'll take the life you should have lost that night instead of her and live it somewhere else. And you'll stay away from my son.'

'You paid him to leave. Five thousand,' Tory mused. 'That would've been a lot of money for us. I wonder why we never saw it. I wonder what he did with it. Well, it doesn't matter. I'm sorry to disappoint you, Mrs. Lavelle, but I'm not my father. Nothing he ever did to me could make me like him, and your money won't change that. I'm staying, because I need to stay. It'd be easier not to. You won't understand that, but it'd be easier. As for Cade . . .'

She remembered how distant he'd been, how removed after her episode the night before. 'There's not as much between us as you seem to think. He's been kind to me, that's all, because he is a kind man. I don't intend to repay that kindness by breaking a friendship, or by telling him of this conversation.'

'If you go against my wishes in this, I'll ruin you. You'll lose everything, as you did before. When you killed that child in New York.'

Tory went white, and for the first time, her hands shook. 'I didn't kill Jonah Mansfield.' She gulped in air, let it out in a broken sigh. 'I just didn't save him.'

Here was the chink. Margaret dug her fingers into it. 'The family held you responsible, and the police. And the press. A second child dead because of you. If you stay here, there will be talk about that. Talk about the part you played. Ugly talk.'

How foolish, Tory thought, to have believed no one would connect her with the woman she'd been in New York. With the life she'd built and destroyed there.

Nothing could be done to change it. Nothing could be done but face it. 'Mrs. Lavelle, I've lived with ugly talk all my life. But I've learned I don't have to tolerate it in my own home.' Tory got to her feet. 'You'll have to leave now.'

'I will not make this offer again.'

'No, I don't suppose you will. I'll see you out.'

Tight-lipped, Margaret rose, picked up her bag. 'I know the way.'

Tory waited until the length of the living room separated them. 'Mrs. Lavelle,' she said quietly, 'Cade is so much more than you believe him to be. So was Hope.'

Rigid with pain, and with fury, Margaret gripped the doorknob. 'You would dare speak to me of my children?'

'Yes,' Tory murmured as the door snapped shut and left her alone in the house. 'I would.'

She locked the door. The click was like a symbol. Nothing she didn't allow in would get in. And nothing, she told herself, that was already inside would hurt her now. She walked to the bathroom and stripped, couldn't get her nightclothes off fast enough. She ran the shower hot, almost too hot to bear, and stepped into the vicious heat and steam.

There, she let herself weep. Not an indulgence, she told herself. But because, as the water beat on her skin to make her feel clean again, the tears washed away the scum of bitterness inside her.

Memories of another dead child, and her helplessness.

She cried until she was empty, and the water ran cool. Then she turned her face up to the chilling spray and let it soothe.

When she was dry, she used the towel to wipe the steam from the mirror. Without compassion, without excuses, she studied her face. Fear, denial, evasion. They were all there, she admitted. Had been there. She'd come back, then she'd buried herself. Hidden herself in work and routine and details.

Not once had she opened herself to Hope. Not once had she gone beyond the trees and visited the place they'd made there. Not once had she gone to the grave of her only real friend.

157

Not once had she faced the true reason she was here.

Was that any different from running away? she wondered. Was it any different from taking the money that had been offered and running anywhere that wasn't here?

Coward. Cade had called her a coward. And he had been right.

She put on her robe again, and went back into the kitchen to look up the number, dialed, waited.

'Good morning. Biddle, Lawrence, and Wheeler.'

'Victoria Bodeen calling. Is Ms. Lawrence available?'

'One moment please, Ms. Bodeen.'

It took no more than that for Abigail to come on the line. 'Tory, how nice to hear from you. How are you? Are you settling in?'

'Yes, thanks. I'll be opening the store on Saturday.'

'So soon? You must've been working night and day. Well, I'm just going to have to take a trip up your way sometime soon.'

'I hope you do. Abigail, I have a favor to ask.'

'Name it. I owe you a big one for my mama's ring.'

'What? Oh. I'd forgotten.'

'I doubt I'd have come across it for years, if then. Hardly ever use those old files. What can I do for you, Tory?'

'I . . . I'm hoping you might have some contact with the police. Someone who could get you information on an old case. I don't – I think you'll understand that I don't want to contact the police myself.'

'I know some people. I'll do what I can.'

'It was a sexual homicide.' Unconsciously, Tory began to press and rub her right temple. 'A young girl. Sixteen. Her name was Alice. The last name—' She pressed harder. 'I'm not completely sure. Lowell or Powell, I think. She was hitchhiking on, ah, 513, heading east on her way to Myrtle Beach. She was taken off the road, into the trees, raped and strangled. Manual strangulation.'

She let out a huge breath, relieved the pressure in her chest.

'I haven't heard anything about this on the news.'

'No, it's not recent. I don't know exactly when, not exactly. I'm sorry. Ten years ago, maybe less, maybe more. In the summer. Sometime in the summer. It was very hot. Even at night it was very hot. I'm not giving you very much.'

'No, that's quite a bit. Let me see what I can find out.'

'Thank you. Thanks so much. I'll be home for only a little while longer. I'll give you the number here, and at the store. Anything you can tell me, anything at all, would help.'

She kept herself busy, and had nearly five uninterrupted hours and still Abigail didn't call back.

People stopped by the window off and on during the day and admired the display she'd created out of old crate boxes, homespun cloth, and cannily selected samples of pottery, handblown glass, and iron work. She filled her shelves and cabinets, hung wind chimes and watercolors.

She arranged point-of-purchase items on the checkout counter, then changed her mind and chose different ones. Willing the phone to ring, she organized boxes and shopping bags.

When someone rapped on the door, she was almost relieved. Until she saw Faith on the other side of the glass. Couldn't the Lavelles leave her be for one damn day?

'I need a gift,' Faith said, the minute Tory wrenched open the door, and would have pushed past if Tory hadn't shifted and blocked.

'I'm not open.'

'Oh hell, you weren't open yesterday, either, were you? I only need one thing, and ten minutes. I forgot my aunt Rosie's birthday, and she just called to say she's coming to visit. I can't hurt her feelings now, can I?' Faith tried a pleading smile. 'She's half crazy anyway, and this might push her over the edge.'

'Buy her something on Saturday.'

'But she's going to be here tomorrow. And if she likes her present, she'll come on down on Saturday herself. Aunt Rosie's loaded. I'll buy something very expensive.'

'See that you do.' Grudgingly, Tory gave way.

'All right, help me out here.' Faith swirled in, spun around. 'What does she like?'

'Oh, she likes everything. I could make her a paper hat and she'd be pleased as punch. Lord, you've got a lot more in here than I imagined.' Faith reached up, sent a metal wind chime whirling and tinkling. 'Nothing practical. I mean I don't want to get her a set of salad bowls or that kind of thing.'

'I have some nice trinket boxes.'

'Trinkets? That's Aunt Rosie's middle name.'

'Then she should have the big one.' In the interest of getting it over and done, Tory walked over and chose a large beveled glass box. The panels were mullioned in diamond shapes and hand-painted with tiny violets and pink roses.

'Does it play music or anything?'

'No, it doesn't.'

'Just as well. She'd have it going all day and half the night and drive us all mad. She'll probably fill it with old buttons or rusted screws, but she'll love it.'

Faith flipped over the tag, whistled. 'Well, I see I'm keeping my word.'

'The panels are hand-cut and painted. There are no two alike.' Satisfied, Tory carried it to the counter. 'I'll box it for you, and throw in the gift tag and ribbon.'

'Very generous.' Faith took out her checkbook. 'Seems to me you're ready for business. Why wait till Saturday?'

'There are a few stray details yet. And Saturday's the day after tomorrow.'

'Time does fly.' She glanced at the amount Tory had totaled and dashed off the check while the present was boxed.

'Pick out a gift tag from the display there, and write what you want. I'll loop it on the cord.'

'Hmm.' Faith chose one with a little rose in the center, scrawled off a birthday greeting and added *xxx*'s and *ooo*'s after her name. 'Perfect. I'll be top of her list for months now.'

She watched Tory secure the box with shiny white ribbon, slide on the card, then twist and loop the business into an elegant bow.

'I hope she enjoys it.' She passed the box over just as the phone rang. 'If you'll excuse me.'

'Sure.' Something in Tory's eyes had Faith stalling. 'Just let me enter that figure in my checkbook. I'm always forgetting.' The phone rang a second time. 'You just go ahead and get that. I'll toddle on out in just a second.'

Trapped, Tory picked up the phone. 'Good afternoon, Southern Comfort.'

'Tory. I'm sorry it took me so long to get back to you.'

'No, that's all right. I appreciate it. Were you able to get the information?'

'Yes, I think I have what you're looking for.'

'Would you hold on a moment? I'll get the door for you, Faith.'

With a little shrug, Faith picked up the box. But as she walked out she wondered who was on the phone, and why the call had made Tory's quick and clever hands tremble.

'I'm sorry, I had someone in the shop.'

'Not a problem. The victim's name was Alice Barbara Powell, white female. Sixteen. Her body wasn't discovered until five days after the murder. She wasn't reported missing for three days, as her parents thought she was at the beach with friends. The remains . . . well, Tory, the animals had been at her by then. I'm told it wasn't pretty.'

'Did they catch him?' She already knew the answer, but she had to hear it.

'No. The case is still open, but inactive. It's been ten years.'

'What was the date? The exact date of the murder.'

'I have that here. Just a minute. It was August twenty-third, 1990.'

'God.' A chill ran through her, into heart and bone.

'Tory? What is it? What can I do?'

'I can't explain, not right now. I have to ask you, Abigail, if you can use your contact again. If there's a way you can find out if there's any like crime, in the six years before, and the ten years after. If you can find out if there were any other victims of that kind of murder on that date. Or right near that date in August.'

'All right, Tory, I'll ask. But when I find out, one way or the other, I'm going to need you to tell me why.'

'I need the answer first. I'm sorry, Abigail, I need the answer. I have to go. I'm sorry.'

She hung up quickly, then simply sat down on the floor.

On August 23, 1990, Hope had been dead exactly eight years. She would have been sixteen years old that summer.

Chapter Thirteen

The living brought flowers for the dead, elegant lilies or simple daisies. But flowers died quickly when laid on the earth. Tory had never understood the symbolism of leaving what would fade and wither on the grave of a loved one.

She supposed they brought comfort to those left behind.

She brought no flowers to Hope. Instead she brought one of the few keepsakes she'd allowed herself. Inside the small globe a winged horse flew, and when it was shaken, silver stars sparkled.

It had been a gift, the last birthday gift from a lost friend.

She carried it across the long, sloping field where generations of Lavelles, generations of the people of Progress, were laid to rest. There were markers, simple as a brick of stone, elaborate as the rearing horse and rider cast in bronze.

Hope had called the horseman Uncle Clyde, and indeed he was the likeness of one of her ancestors, a cavalry officer who'd died in the War of Northern Aggression.

Once, Hope had dared her to climb up behind Uncle Clyde and ride his great steed. Tory remembered hitching herself up, sliding over the sun-baked metal that reddened her skin, and wondering if God would strike her dead with a handy bolt of lightning for blasphemy.

He hadn't, and for a moment, clinging to the cast bronze, the world spread out in greens and browns beneath her, the sun beating on her head like a dull hammer, she'd felt invincible. The towers of Beaux Reves had seemed closer, approachable. She'd shouted down to Hope that she and the horse would fly to them, land on the top turret.

She'd nearly broken her neck on the way down, and had been

lucky to land on her butt instead of her head. But the bruised tail-bone had been nothing compared to that moment so high on the rearing horse.

For her next birthday, her eighth, Hope had given her the globe. It was the only thing Tory had kept from that year of her life.

Now, as they had then, live oaks and fragrant magnolia guarded the stones and bones, and offered shade in dapples of light and shadows. They also provided a screen between that testament to mortality and the regal house that had outlasted its many owners and occupants.

It was a pleasant enough walk from the cemetery to the family home. She and Hope had walked it countless times, in blistering summer, in rainy winter. Hope had liked to look at the names carved in the stone, to say them out loud for luck, she'd said.

Now Tory walked to the grave, and the marble angel that serenaded it with a harp. And said the name out loud.

'Hope Angelica Lavelle. Hello, Hope.'

She knelt on the soft grass, sat back on her heels. The breeze was soft and warm, and carried the sweet perfume of the pink baby rose bushes that flanked the angel. 'I'm sorry I didn't come before. I kept putting it off, but I've thought of you so often over the years. I've never had another friend like you, someone I could tell everything to. I was so lucky to have you.'

As she closed her eyes, opened herself to the memories, someone watched from the shelter of trees. Someone with fists clenched to white bone. Someone who knew what it was to crave the unspeakable. To live, year after year, with the desire for it hidden in a heart that thundered now with both that craving, and with the knowledge it could feed.

Sixteen years, and she'd come back. He'd waited, and he'd watched, always knowing there was a chance some day she could circle around, despite everything, and come back here where it had all begun.

What a pretty picture they'd made. Hope and Tory, Tory and Hope. The dark and the bright, the pampered and the damaged. Nothing he'd done before, nothing he'd done after that night in August, had brought him the same thrill. He'd tried to recapture it; when the pressure built so high and hot inside him, he'd reconstruct that night and its sheer, speechless glory.

Nothing had matched it.

Now it was Tory who was a threat. He could deal with her, quickly, easily. But then he would lose this fresh excitement of living on the edge. Maybe, maybe this was just what he'd been waiting for, all this time. For her to come back, for him to have her in place again.

He would have to wait until August, if he could. A hot night in August when everything would be as it had been eighteen years before.

He could have dealt with her any time over the years. Finished her. But he was a man who believed in symbols, in grand pictures. It had to be here. Where it began, he thought, and watching her, imagining her, stroked himself to climax, as he had other times when in secret he'd watched Tory. Hope and Tory. Tory and Hope.

Where it all began, he thought again. Where it would end.

A shudder ran through her, a chilly finger from nape to the base of her spine. Even as Tory glanced uneasily over her shoulder, she dismissed it as a product of the atmosphere and her own thoughts.

After all, she was trespassing here, an intruder among the dead and beloved. The light was going, fat gray clouds rolling in from the east to smother the sun. There would be a farmer's rain that night.

She wouldn't linger much longer.

'I'm so sorry I didn't come that night. I should have, even after the beating. He'd never have considered that I would defy him and leave the house. No one would have checked on me. I could never explain to you back then what it was like when he took his belt to me. The way every lash stripped away my courage, stripped away my self, until there was nothing left but fear and humiliation. If I'd found the courage and gone out the window that night, I might have saved us both. I'll never know.'

Birds were singing, trills and chorus. It was a bright, insistent sound that should have been out of place, and was instead perfect. Birds, the hum of bees going lazy in the roses, and the strong, living scent of the roses themselves.

Overhead the sky was brooding, turgid with the storm clouds pushed by the wind that stayed high, too high to cool the air where she knelt.

When she breathed it was like breathing in water. It felt like drowning.

She lifted the globe again, and sent the silver stars shimmering.

'But I'm back. For whatever it's worth, I'm back. And I'll do whatever I can to make it up. I never told you what you meant to me, how just by being my friend you opened up something inside me, and how when I lost you, I let it close again. For too long. I'm going to try to unlock it, to be what I was when you were here.'

She glanced back again toward the screen of trees and the towers of Beaux Reves that rose behind them. Could they see her from there, in the stone tower? Was someone standing, closed behind the glass and watching?

It felt that way, as if eyes and mind and heart shut behind glass watched. Waited.

Let them watch, she thought. Let them wait. She looked back at the angel, looked down at the stone. 'They never found him. The man who did this to you. If I can, I will.'

She turned the globe, then lay it under the angel so the horse could fly and the stars sparkle. And leaving it there, she walked away.

The rain was coming down strong and cool when Cade swung away from town and took the road toward home. It was a good rain, a soaker that wouldn't pound the young crops. If his luck was in, the rain would last most of the night, and leave the fields wet and satisfied.

He wanted to get samples of the soil from several of his fields and compare the success of his various cover crops. He'd put in fava beans the year before, as they added the nitrogen his cotton was so greedy for.

He'd test it the next day, after the rain, then compare and study the last four years of charts. The fava bean crop had done reasonably well, but it hadn't produced a solid profit. If he was going to try them again, he had to be able to justify it.

To himself, Cade thought. No one else paid attention to his charts. Even Piney, who could usually be depended on to at least pretend an interest, had glazed over when presented with the graphics.

Didn't matter, Cade decided. No one had to understand them but himself.

And if he was honest, he'd admit that he wasn't all that interested in them at the moment, either. He was using them to keep his mind off Tory, and what had happened the night before.

So it was best to deal with her, with all of it. To clear the decks before he went home and washed off the day's work.

Cade's brows drew together as the red Mustang convertible he'd been following took the turn into Tory's lane. He swung in behind it, and those brows arched up as J.R. climbed out.

'Well, what do you think?' Grinning ear to ear, J.R. patted the bright fender as Cade walked over.

'Yours?'

'Just picked her up this morning. Boots says I'm going through a midlife crisis. Woman watches too many talk shows, if you ask me. I say if it feels good and you can afford it, what's wrong with that?'

'She's a beauty, all right.' With the rain streaming down, both men walked to the hood so J.R. could pop it. They stood, hands on hips, admiring the engine.

'Loaded, too.' Cade nodded in admiration. 'What'll she do?'

'Between you, me, and the gatepost, I had her up to ninety-five and she stays smooth as glass. Handles the curves like a champ, too. I went on over to Broderick's yesterday. Time to trade in my sedan. Planned to get another one, then I saw this baby on the lot.' J.R. grinned and ran his fingers over his thick silver mustache. 'Love at first sight.'

'Four-speed?' Cade strolled around to peer into the cockpit.

'Bet your ass. Four on the floor. Haven't had me one of them since, hell, since I was younger than you. Didn't know until I popped the clutch how much I've missed it. Hated having to put the top up when the rain started.'

'You pop the clutch and drive around at ninety, you're going to be stacking up tickets like cordwood.'

'It'll be worth it.' J.R. gave the car another affectionate pat, then glanced toward the house. 'You stopping by to see Tory?'

'Thought I might.'

'Good. I got some news to give her she might not take well. Just as soon she have a friend around when I do.'

'What's wrong, what's happened?'

'It's nothing dire, Cade, but it'll trouble her. Let's just get it said all at once.' He stepped up on the porch, knocked. 'Feels

166

funny knocking on family's door, but I got into the habit with my sister. She wasn't one for leaving the door open for company. There's my girl!' He said it heartily when Tory opened the door.

'Uncle Jimmy. Cade.' Though her stomach did a quick pitch and jolt at seeing both of them on her porch, she stepped back. 'Come in out of the wet.'

'Ran into Cade here, seeing as both of us had in mind to stop by. I was just showing off my new car.'

Obligingly, Tory looked out. 'That's quite a . . .' She started to say toy, and realized that was likely to hurt his feelings. 'A machine.'

'Purrs like a big old cat. I'll take you for a spin first fine day.'

'I'd like that.' But just now she had two big wet men in her living room, one chair, and a nagging headache. 'Why don't y'all come out to the kitchen. There's a place to sit, and I just made some hot tea to chase the damp away.'

'Sounds good, but I don't want to track through the house.'

'Don't worry about it.' She led the way, hoping the aspirin she'd taken would kick in without the ten-minute nap she'd planned to go with it. The house smelled of the rain, of the ripe, wet scent of the marsh. Any other time, she would have enjoyed it, but now it made her feel closed in.

'I've got some cookies. They're store-bought, but better than I could make.'

'Don't you go to any trouble now, honey. I've got to get back home here directly.' But since she was already putting cookies on a plate, he reached for one. 'Boots won't buy sweets these days. She's on a diet, and that means I am, too.'

'Aunt Boots looks wonderful.' Tory got out cups. 'So do you.'

'Now, that's what I tell her, but she fusses over the scale every blessed morning. You'd think gaining a pound here and there was the end of the world. Till she's satisfied, I'll be on rabbit food.' He took another cookie. 'Surprised my nose doesn't start to twitch.'

He waited while she poured the tea, sat. 'Heard your store's coming right along. Haven't had a minute to get down and see for myself.'

'I hope you'll make it in on Saturday.'

'Wouldn't miss that on a bet.' He sipped his tea, shifted in his chair, sighed. 'Tory, I hate coming over here with something that might upset you, but seems to me you ought to know what's what.'

'It'll be easier if you tell me straight out.'

'I'm not sure I can, exactly. I had a call from your mother just a bit ago. Just as Boots and I were finishing up our supper. She's in a state, or I guess you know she wouldn't have called me. We don't telephone regular.'

'Is she ill?'

'No, not as what you'd call sick.' He blew out a breath. 'It has to do with your father. Seems like he got in some trouble a little while back. Damn it.' J.R. pushed his cup around its saucer, then raised his eyes to Tory's. 'Appears he assaulted a woman.'

In her mind, Tory heard the snake-slither of the thick leather belt. The three harsh snaps. Her fingers jerked once, then settled steady. 'Assaulted?'

'Your mother said it was all a mistake, and I had to pry what I got out of her with both hands. What she told me is some woman claimed your father, ah, roughed her up. Tried to, ah . . . molest her.'

'He tried to rape a woman?'

Miserable, J.R. shifted in his chair again. 'Well, Sari, she wasn't real clear on the details. But whatever happened, it got Han arrested. He's been drinking again. Sarabeth didn't want to tell me that part, but I pushed it out of her. He got probation, contingent on his going to alcohol rehab and such. I don't figure he took it well, but he didn't have much choice.'

He picked up the tea to wet his dry throat. 'Then a couple weeks ago, he lit out.'

'Lit out?'

'Hasn't been home. Sarabeth said she hadn't seen him in more'n two weeks now, and he's violated his probation. When they pick him up, he'll . . . they'll put him in jail.'

'Yes, I suppose.' She'd always been surprised, in a mild, distant way, that he'd never found himself on the wrong side of iron bars before.

God provided, she thought.

'Sarabeth, she's frantic.' Without thinking, J.R. dunked his cookie in his tea, a habit his wife despaired over. 'She's running low on money and she's worrying herself sick. I'm going to drive up and see her tomorrow, see if I can get a clearer picture of things.'

'You think I should come with you.'

'Now, honey, that's up to you. No reason I can't handle this on my own.'

'And no reason you should. I'll go with you.'

'If that's what you want, I'd be pleased to have the company. I thought to leave bright and early. You be ready 'round seven?'

'Yes, of course.'

'Good. That's good. Fine.' Awkward now, he got to his feet. 'We'll get this all straightened out, you'll see. I'll come 'round and get you in the morning. No, you just sit still and drink your tea.' He patted her head before she could rise. 'I'll let myself out.'

'He's embarrassed,' Tory murmured, as she heard the front door open. 'For himself, for me, for my mother. He told me while you were here because he'd have heard the gossip Lissy Frazier's passing around and thought I'd be better with you than alone.'

Cade kept his eyes on her face. She hadn't shown any reaction. He marveled at her control even while it frustrated him. 'Is he right?'

'I don't know. I'm more used to being alone. Are you wondering why I'm not particularly concerned about my father, or my mother?'

'No. I'm wondering what happened between you so that you're not particularly concerned. Or why you're determined not to be or show that you're upset by what J.R. just told you.'

'What's the point in being upset? What's done's already been done. My mother chooses to believe my father didn't do what he was arrested for doing. But of course he did. If he'd been drinking he wouldn't have been as careful to keep the violence inside his own doors.'

'Did he abuse your mother?'

A corner of Tory's mouth twitched into a parody of a smile. 'Not while I was around. He didn't need to.'

Cade nodded. He'd known. A part of him had known since the morning she'd come to his door to tell them all about Hope. 'Because you were the easier target.'

'He hasn't been able to aim at me for quite some time. I've made sure of that.'

'Why are you blaming yourself?'

'I'm not.' Because his eyes were steady, she closed hers. 'Habit. I know he used her for his punching bag after I was gone.

169

I never tried to do anything to change that. Not that either of them would have let me, but I never tried. I've only seen him twice since I was eighteen. Once, when I was living in New York, when I was happy, I had this notion that we could mend the things that were broken, or at least some of them. They were living in a trailer then, near the Georgia border. They moved around a lot after we left Progress.'

She sat like that, with her eyes closed, in the quiet, while the rain pattered on the roof. 'Daddy couldn't keep a job for long. Someone was always in for him, so he said. Or there was a better job another place. I lost track of how many other places there were – different schools, different rooms, different faces. I never made any real friends, so it didn't matter so much. I was just biding time until I could get away. Save up money on the sly and wait until the law said I could leave home. If I'd left before, he'd've made me come back, and he'd've made me pay.'

'Couldn't you have gone for help? Your grandmother.'

'He'd have hurt her.' Tory opened her eyes, looked straight into Cade's. 'He was afraid of her, the same as he was afraid of me, and he'd have done something to her. And my mother would've sided with him. She always did. That's why I didn't go to her when I left. If he'd found out, that wouldn't have set right with him. I can't explain it to you, I could never explain it to anyone, the way a fear can live inside you. The way it dictates how you think and how you act, what you say, what you don't dare say.'

'You just did.'

She opened her mouth, then closed it again before something leaped out she hadn't thought through. 'Do you want more tea?'

'Sit. I'll get it.' He rose before she could, and put the kettle back on to boil. 'Tell me. Tell me the rest.'

'I didn't tell them I was leaving home, though I'd planned every step of what I would do, where I would go. I packed and ran off in the middle of the night, walked into town, to the bus station, and bought a ticket to New York City. When the sun came up I was miles away, and I never intended to come back again. But . . .'

She lifted her laced fingers, then closed them again, like a prayer. 'I went to see them that time,' she said carefully. 'I'd just turned twenty. Been gone two years. I had a job, working at a store downtown. A store with lovely things. I made a good salary, and I had my own place. It wasn't much bigger than a closet, but it was mine. I had my vacation coming and I took the bus all the way to the Georgia border to see them, well, maybe part of it was to show them that I'd made something of myself. Two years I'd been away, and inside of two minutes, it was like I'd never left.'

He nodded. He'd gone away to college, become a man, he supposed, during those four years. And when he'd come back the rhythm was the same.

But for him it had been the right rhythm, one keenly missed.

'Nothing I did,' she went on, 'had done, could do, was right. Look how I'd tarted myself up. He knew the kind of life I was living up north. He figured I'd just come home because I was pregnant from one of the men I'd let get at me. I was still a virgin, but to him, I was a whore. I'd gotten some spine in those two years, just enough steel that I stood up to him. The first time in my life I dared to stand up to him. It took the rest of my vacation week for the bruises on my face to heal enough that I could cover them with makeup and go back to work.'

'Christ, Tory.'

'He only hit me once. But God, he had big hands. Big, hard hands, and they bunched so easily into fists.' Absently, she lifted her hand to her face, traced the slightly crooked line of her nose. 'Knocked me right off my feet and into the counter of that grubby little kitchen. I didn't realize my nose was broken. The pain was so familiar, you see.'

Under the table Cade's own hands curled into fists that felt useless and late.

'When he came at me again, I grabbed the knife out of the sink. A big, black-handled kitchen knife. I didn't even think about it,' she said in that calm, thoughtful voice. 'It was just in my hand. He must've seen in my face that I'd have used it. That I'd have loved to use it. He stormed out of the trailer, with my mother running after him, begging him not to go. He flung her off like a gnat, right into the dirt, and still she called after him. God, she crawled after him on her goddamn hands and knees. I'll never forget that. Never.'

Cade walked back to the stove, to the spitting kettle, to give her time to settle. In silence, he measured tea, poured the hot water. He sat again, and waited.

'You have a gift for listening.'

'Finish it out. Get rid of it.'

'All right.' Calm now, Tory opened her eyes. If there had been pity in his, the words might not have come. But what she saw was patience.

'I felt sorry for her. I was disgusted with her. And I hated her. In that moment, I think I hated her more than him. I put down the knife and picked up my bag. I hadn't even unpacked, hadn't been there an hour. When I walked out, she was still sitting in the dirt and crying. But she looked at me, so much anger in her eyes. 'Why'd you have to go and make him mad? You always caused nothing but trouble.' She sat in the dirt, with her lip bleeding, either from where he hit her or from biting it when she fell. I just kept walking, never said a word to her. I haven't spoken to her since. My own mother, and I haven't had a word with her since I was twenty.'

'It's not your fault.'

'No, it's not my fault. I've had years of therapy so I can say that with assurance. It was none of it my fault. But I was still the cause. He, I think, he fed on punishing me, for being born. For being born the way I was. Up till the time I showed that I was different, he left me pretty much alone. I was my mother's problem, and he rarely took time for more than an absent swat. After that, I don't think a week ever went by without him abusing me.

'Not sexually,' she said when she saw Cade's face. 'He never laid hands on me that way. He wanted to. God, he wanted to, and that frightened him more, so he beat me more. And got twisted pleasure from it. Sex and violence are wrapped up tight inside him. Whatever they said he did to that woman, he did. Not rape, at least not that could be proved, or they'd never have given him probation so easily. But rape's only one way a man can hurt and humiliate a woman.'

'I know it.' He got up to fetch the pot and pour her tea. 'You said you'd seen them twice.'

'Not them, him. Three years ago he came to Charleston. He came to my house. He followed me home from work. He'd found out where I worked, and he followed me home. He caught me as I was walking from the car. I was scared to death. Didn't have much of that steel I'd forged in New York left in me. He said my mother was sick and they needed money. I didn't believe him. He'd been drinking. I could smell it on him.'

She could smell it now, if she let herself. The stale, hot stench like a bad taste in the air. She lifted her cup, breathed in the steam instead. 'He had his hand around my arm. I could see what he wanted to do. To twist my arm, to snap the bone, and he was aroused by the images in his own head. I wrote him a check for five hundred dollars, wrote it on the spot. I didn't let him into the house. I would not let him into my home. I told him if he hurt me, or tried to get in the house, that if he came to where I worked, any of those things, I'd stop payment on the check and there'd never be any more money. But if he took it and left, and he never came back, I'd send a hundred dollars every month.'

She let out a short laugh. 'He was so surprised at the idea, he let me go. He'd always liked money. Just the having of it. He liked to lecture about rich men and eyes of needles, but he liked having money. I got into the house and locked the door. All that night I sat up with the phone and the fireplace poker in my lap. But he didn't try to get in. Not then, not ever. A hundred dollars a month bought me a kind of peace of mind. Not a bad price for it.'

She drank now, a long drink of tea that was too hot and too strong, and nonetheless bolstered her. Unable to sit, she rose to stare out at the steady rain. 'So, there you have it. Just some of the ugly secrets of the Bodeen family.'

'The Lavelles have some ugly secrets of their own.' He got up to walk to her, ran his hand down the length of the tidy braid that hung down her back. 'You still had your steel, Tory. You had what you needed. He couldn't break it. He couldn't even bend it.'

He brushed his lips on the top of her head, pleased when she didn't step aside as she usually did. 'Have you eaten?'

'What?'

'Probably not. Sit down. I'll scramble some eggs.'

'What are you talking about?'

'I'm hungry, and if you're not, you should be. We'll have some eggs.'

She turned, jerked once when he slid his arms around her. Tears swam into her eyes, quick and stinging, to be blinked ruthlessly away. 'Cade, this can't go anywhere. You and me.'

'Tory.' He cupped the back of her neck until her head settled on his shoulder. 'It's already gone somewhere. Why don't we stay there awhile, see how we like it.'

It felt so good, so steady to be held this way, this easy and familiar way. 'I don't have any eggs.' She drew back, met his eyes. 'I'll make soup.'

Sometimes food was only a prop. She was using it now, Cade thought. Maybe they both were as she stirred canned soup on the stove and he put together the makings for grilled cheese sandwiches. A nice, homey meal for a rainy evening. The kind a couple might share with light conversation, and for the hell of it, a good bottle of wine.

He could have used an evening like that, he thought. Instead here he was slathering butter on bread the way Lilah had taught him and trying to figure out the way through Tory's thin and prickly shield.

'You could do better than soup and a sandwich down at Beaux Reves.'

'I could.' He set the skillet on the stove and stood beside her. Close, but not close enough to touch. 'But I like the company here.'

'Then something's wrong with you.'

She said it so dryly, it took him a minute. With a laugh he laid the two sandwiches on the heated skillet. 'You're likely right about that. After all, I'm a hell of a catch, you know. Healthy, not overly hard on the eyes, got me a big house, good land, and money enough to keep the wolf from the door. And in addition to that, and my subtle charm, I make a terrific cheese sandwich.'

'All that being the case, why hasn't some smart woman snatched you up?'

'Thousands have tried.'

'Slippery, are you?'

'Agile.' He flipped the sandwiches. 'I like to think of it as agile. I was engaged once.'

'Were you?' She said it casually as she reached for bowls, but her focus had sharpened.

'Um-hmm.' He knew human nature well enough to be certain leaving it at that would swell her curiosity until she either burst or surrendered.

She held until they'd set plates and bowls on the table, sat. 'You think you're clever, don't you?'

'Darling, a man in my position has to be. Cozy in here with the rain and all, isn't it?'

'All right, damn it. What happened?'

'About what?' The way her eyes narrowed delighted him. 'Oh, about Deborah? The woman I was on the point of vowing to love, honor, and cherish until death and so on? Judge Purcell's daughter. You might remember the judge, except I don't think he was a judge yet when you left.'

'No, I don't remember him. I doubt the Bodeens moved in his social sphere.'

'In any case, he has a lovely daughter and she loved me for a while, then decided she didn't want to be a farmer's wife after all. At least not one who actually worked at it.'

'I'm sorry.'

'It wasn't a tragedy. I didn't love her. Liked her considerably,' Cade mused as he sampled the soup. 'She was lovely to look at, interesting to talk to, and . . . we'll say we were compatible in certain vital areas. But one. We just didn't want the same thing. We discovered that, much to our mutual embarrassment, a few months after we were engaged. We broke things off amicably enough, which goes to show there was considerable relief on both sides, and she went off to live in London for a few months.'

'How could you—' She broke off, filled her mouth with sandwich.

'Go on. You can ask.'

'I just wondered how you could ask someone to marry you that you could let go again without a qualm.'

He considered it, kicking back to chew the sandwich as if he were also chewing his thoughts. 'I suppose there were some minor qualms. But the fact is, in hindsight, I was twenty-five, and there was a bit of family pressure. My mother and the judge are good friends, and he was a friend of my father's as well. Time to settle down and make myself an heir or two, was the idea.'

'That's awfully cold-blooded.'

'Not entirely. I was attracted to her, we knew a lot of the same people. Her daddy was mine's lawyer for years. It was easy to slide into an arrangement, one that pleased both our families. Then as time got closer, I for one began to feel like you do when your tie's just a mite too tight. So you can't quite get a good gulp of air. So I asked myself, what would my life be like without her? And what would it be like with her, in five years.'

He took another bite of his sandwich, shrugged. 'Turned out I

175

liked the answer to the first part a whole lot better than I did the second. And as luck would have it, so did she. The only ones who were truly upset were our families.' He paused, watching her eat. 'And we just can't live our lives around what our parents want or don't want for us, can we, Tory?'

'No. But we do live our lives carrying around the weight of it anyway. Mine could never accept me for who and what I was. For a long time I tried to be someone and something else.' She lifted her gaze. 'I can't.'

'I like who you are.'

'Last night you had trouble with it.'

'Some,' he admitted. 'You worried me. You were frantic,' he added, laying a hand over hers before she could pull away. 'Then fragile. Made me feel clumsy. I didn't know what to do, and I'm used to knowing.'

'You didn't believe me.'

'I don't doubt what you saw, or felt. But I have to think part of it could be mixed up with coming here, with remembering what happened to Hope.'

She thought about the call from Abigail, about the dates of both murders. But she held back. She'd trusted before, shared before. And had lost everything.

'It is all mixed up with me coming here. And with Hope. If it wasn't for Hope, you wouldn't be sitting here now.'

On more even ground again, he sat back, continued to eat. 'If I'd seen you for the first time four, five weeks ago, if we'd never met before and there'd been nothing between us till then, I'd damn well have figured out how to get myself sitting here now. Fact is, if we'd started weeks ago instead of years, I do believe I'd already have you in that very interesting bed.'

He smiled, slow and easy, when she set the spoon back down in her soup with a little plop. 'I figure it's time we got that out in the open, so you can think about it.'

Chapter Fourteen

The drive was pleasant enough and reminded her of all she'd missed by not staying close to J.R. There was such a hugeness to him, in his voice, his laugh, his gestures. Twice she'd had to dodge his arm as he'd thrown it toward her to point out something along the highway.

He seemed to swallow you up with his simple joy of being.

He sat in the little car, his knees all but up to his chin, his big, wide hand clutching the gearshift the way she'd seen some young boys clutch a joystick during a video game.

For the fun and competition.

The way he dived into the day they might have been racing to some mad picnic rather than a painful family duty.

Living in the now, she thought, that was his gift, and a skill she'd struggled to master all her life.

He got such a kick out of his new car, zipping and roaring up the interstate with his CDs of Clint Black and Garth Brooks blasting, and a natty glen plaid cap snugged down on his lamb's wool mat of gingercolored hair.

He lost the cap just past the exit for Sumter when a frisky tail of wind caught it and flipped it toward the ramp and under the wheels of a Dodge minivan. J.R. never slowed down, and laughed like a lunatic.

With the top down and the music up, conversation was exchanged in shouts, but J.R. still managed to hold one, with his topics of interest bouncing like a big rubber ball from Tory's store, politics, fat-free ice cream, and the stock market.

As they approached the exit to Florence, he allowed as he hoped they'd have just a bit of time to slip by and visit his mother.

It was the first time since he'd picked her up that he mentioned family.

Tory shouted out that she'd love to stop and see her grandmother. Then she thought of Cecil and wondered if J.R. knew about the new arrangements. Thinking about that kept her mind occupied and entertained until they bypassed Florence and headed northeast.

She'd never been to her parent's place outside of Hartsville. She had no idea what either of them did now for a living, or how they spent their time together or apart.

She'd never asked her grandmother, and Iris never brought it up.

'Nearly there.' J.R. shifted in his seat. Tory felt his mood shift as well. 'Last I heard, Han, he was doing some factory work. They, ah, leased a patch of land and were raising chickens.'

'I see.'

J.R. cleared his throat as if about to speak again, then fell silent until he turned off the main road onto a shoulderless twist of pitted asphalt. 'I haven't been up to see their place. Ah, Sarabeth gave me the directions when I said I'd come to see what was what.'

'It's all right, Uncle Jimmy, don't fret about me. We both know what to expect.'

The scatter of houses that could be seen were small and skeletal, yellowed bones stuck on overgrown yards or dust bowl lots. A rusted pickup with its windshield cracked like an eggshell tilted on cinder blocks. An ugly black dog leaped on its chain and barked viciously while less than a foot away a child wearing nothing but grayed cotton underwear and a tangle of dark hair sat on an old dented washing machine abandoned in a scrub-grass yard. She sucked her thumb and stared vacantly as the spiffy convertible drove by.

Yes, Tory thought. They knew what to expect.

The road turned, climbed a little, then veered off in a fork. J.R. switched off the music and slowed to a crawl to navigate the dirt and gravel path.

'Your county taxes at work,' he said, with an attempt at a joke, then only sighed and eased his car into the hardpack driveway that butted up to the house.

No, not a house, Tory corrected. A shack. You couldn't call such a thing a house, and never a home. The roof sagged, and like

178

an old man's smile, showed gaps where shingles had blown away or fallen off. The ancient speckled gray siding was torn and ragged. One of the windows was plugged with cardboard. The yard, such as it was, was choked with weeds. Dandelion and thistle grew in nasty abundance. An old cast-iron sink lay on its side and showed a black fist-sized hole in the bowl.

Beside and back from the house was a metal building gray with grime and spotted with blood-colored rust. A wire fence spit out from its side and in this enclosure a dozen or so scrawny chickens pecked at the dirt and complained.

The stench of them stung the air.

'Jesus. Jesus Christ,' J.R. muttered. 'Didn't think it would be this bad. You never think it'll be this bad. No call for this. No call for it to come to this.'

'She knows we're here,' Tory said dully, and pushed the car door open. 'She's been waiting.'

J.R. slammed his own door, then as they walked toward the house lay his hand on Tory's shoulder.

She wondered if he was giving her support, or asking for it.

The woman who appeared had gray hair. Stone gray that was scraped back pitilessly from a thin face. The skin seemed to be scraped back as well, so that the bones jutted out like knobs. The lines that bracketed her mouth might have been carved with a knife, and the deep gouge of them pulled the lips down into misery.

She wore a wrinkled cotton dress, too big for her, and a small silver cross between her lifeless breasts.

Her eyes, rimmed red as fire, glanced at Tory, then away, fast, as if a look could burn.

'You didn't say you were bringing her.'

'Hello, Mama.'

'You didn't say you were bringing her,' Sarabeth said again, then pushed open the screen. 'Haven't I got worries enough?'

J.R. gave Tory's shoulder a squeeze. 'We're here to do what we can to help, Sari.' With his hand still on Tory's shoulder, J.R. stepped inside.

The air stank of garbage gone over, of stale sweat. Of hopelessness.

'I don't know what you can do, 'less you can get that woman, that lying slut, down to Hartsville to tell the truth.' She pulled a

179

tattered tissue out of her dress pocket and blew her nose. 'I'm at my wit's end, J.R. I think something awful's happened to my Han. He's never stayed away so long as this.'

'Why don't we sit down?' He transferred his hand from Tory to his sister, then scanned the room.

His stomach clenched.

There was a sagging sofa draped in a dingy yellow slipcover, and a vile green recliner patched with duct tape. The tables were littered with paper plates, plastic cups, and what he supposed was the remains of last night's dinner. A woodstove, streaked with soot, stood in the corner, hobbled on three legs with a block of wood for the fourth.

There was a picture of a mournful Jesus, exposing his Sacred Heart, inside a cheap wire frame.

As his sister's face was still buried in her tissue, J.R. led her to the sofa and sent a pleading look at Tory.

'Why don't I make some coffee?'

'Got some instant left.' Sarabeth lowered the tissue and stared at the wall rather than look at her daughter. 'I haven't felt much like going to the store, didn't want to go far from home in case Han . . .'

Saying nothing, Tory turned away. The house was shotgun style, so she walked straight back into the kitchen. Dishes were piled in the sink, and the splatters on the stove were old and crusted. Her shoes stuck to the torn linoleum floor.

During Tory's childhood, Sarabeth had cleaned like a tornado, chasing dust and grime, whirling through them as though they were sins against the soul. As Tory filled the kettle she wondered when her mother had given up this nervous habit, when poverty and disinterest had out-weighed the illusion that she was making a home, or that God would come into it as long as the floor was swept.

Then she stopped wondering, stopped thinking, blocked everything out but the mechanical chore of heating water and hacking a spoon at coffee grains gone to brown concrete in a little glass jar.

The milk was sour, and there was no sugar to be found. She carried two mugs of dismal-looking liquid back to the living room. Her stomach would have rejected even the appearance of drinking.

'That woman,' Sarabeth was saying. 'She tried to lure my Han.

She played on his weaknesses, tempted him. But he resisted. He told me all about it. I don't know where she got herself beat up, probably some pervert she sold herself to, but she said it was Han to pay him back for refusing her. That's what happened.'

'All right, Sari.' J.R. sat on the sofa beside her, patted her hand. 'We won't worry about that part of it right now, okay? Do you have any notion, any notion at all where Han might go?'

'No!' She shouted it, jerking away from him and nearly upending the coffee Tory put on the table. 'You think I wouldn't go to him if I knew? A woman cleaves to her husband. I told the cops the same thing. Told them just what I'm telling you. I don't expect a bunch of corrupt, godforsaken cops to take my word, but I'd think my own flesh and blood would believe me.'

'I do. 'Course I do.' He picked up a mug of coffee and gently pushed it into her hands. 'I just thought maybe something occurred to you, that maybe you remembered a couple of places that he went when he went off before.'

'It's not like he went off.' Sarabeth's lips trembled as she sipped. 'He just needs to get away and think sometimes is all. Men got a lot of pressure, providing. And sometimes, Han, he just needs to be off by himself, to think things through, to pray on them. But he's been gone too long now. I'm thinking maybe he's hurt.'

Tears spurted into her eyes again. 'That woman lying about him, getting him in all that trouble, it was weighing heavy on his mind. Now the police are talking like he's a fugitive. They just don't understand.'

'Was he going to the alcohol rehab program?'

'I guess he was.' She sniffed. 'Han didn't need no program. He wasn't a drunk. Just now and then he took a bit to relax. Jesus drank wine, didn't he?'

Jesus, Tory thought, hadn't made a habit of downing the best part of a bottle of Wild Turkey and stomping hell out of the womenfolk. But her mother wouldn't see the difference.

'They're always on his back at work, you know, pushing at him 'cause they know he's smarter than they are. And the chickens cost more to keep than we figured. That bastard down at the feed and grain raised his prices so he can keep his on-the-side chickie in perfume. Han told me how it was.'

'Honey, you have to face the fact that by leaving this way, Han broke his probation. He broke the law.'

'Well, the law's *wrong*. What am I going to do, J.R.? I'm just frantic over it. And everybody's wanting money, and there's nothing coming in except what I get for eggs. I've been to the bank, but those thieving, sneaking liars took what we got in there and said how Han withdrew the funds. Withdrew the funds, they said, with their prissy lying-mouths.'

'I'll take care of the bills.' He had done so before. 'You don't worry about that. Here's what I think we should do. I think you should get some things together and come on home with me. You can stay with me and Boots until everything's straightened out.'

'I can't leave. Han could come back any minute.'

'You can leave him a note.'

'That'd just make him mad.' Her eyes began to dart around, wary birds looking for a safe place to light, away from her husband's righteous fury. 'A man's got a right to expect his wife to be home when he gets there. For her to be waiting under the roof he puts over her head.'

'Your roof has holes in it, Mama,' Tory said quietly, and earned a searing whip of a stare.

'Nothing was ever good enough for you, was it? No matter how hard your daddy worked and I sweated, it was never fine enough. Always wanting more.'

'I never asked for more.'

'You were smart enough not to say it out loud. But I saw it, saw it in your eyes. Sneaky's what you were, sneaky and sly,' Sarabeth said, with a violent twist of her mouth. 'And didn't you run off first chance you got, never looked back, either, never honored your father and mother. You were obliged to pay back what we sacrificed for you, but you were too selfish. We had a decent life in Progress, still would if you hadn't ruined it.'

'Sarabeth.' Helplessly, J.R. gave her hand quick, light pats. 'That's not fair and that's not true.'

'She brought shame on us. Brought it the minute she was born. We were happy before she came along.' She began to cry again, harsh, racking sobs that shook her shoulders.

At a loss, J.R. put an arm around her and made shushing noises.

With her face and mind blank, Tory bent down and began to clear the litter from the table.

Sarabeth was up like a thunderbolt. 'What do you think you're doing?'

182

'Since you're determined to stay, I thought I'd clean this up for you.'

'I don't need you criticizing me.' She slapped the plates to the floor. 'I don't need you coming here with your hoity-toity ways and your fancy clothes trying to make me look bad. You turned your back on me years ago, and as far as I'm concerned, you can keep on walking.'

'You turned yours on me the first time you sat quiet while he beat me bloody.'

'God made man master of his own house. You never got licked you didn't deserve it.'

Licked, Tory thought. Such a friendly word for horror. 'Is that how you sleep at night?'

'Don't you sass me. Don't you disrespect your daddy. You tell me where he is, damn you. You know, you can see. You tell me where he is so I can go take care of him.'

'I won't look for him. If I stumbled over him bleeding in a ditch, I'd leave him there.' Her head snapped back when Sarabeth slapped her, and the raw red print stained her cheek. But she barely flinched.

'Sarabeth! God Almighty, Sari.' J.R. grabbed her, pinned her arms while she struggled and sobbed and screamed.

'I was going to say I hope he's dead.' Tory spoke quietly. 'But I don't. I hope he comes back to you, Mama. I dearly hope he comes back and gives you the life you seem to want.'

She opened her purse, took out the hundred-dollar bill she'd put in it that morning. 'If and when he does, you tell him this is the last payment he'll ever get from me. You tell him I'm living back in Progress, that I'm making a life there for myself. If he wants to come and raise his hand to me again, then he better make it last, he better beat me dead this time. Because if he doesn't finish me, I will him.'

She closed her purse. 'I'll be in the car,' she said to J.R., and walked out.

Her legs didn't start to shake until she sat down and pulled the door closed. Then the trembling started at her knees and worked up so that she crossed her arms over her torso, pressed hard and with her eyes closed, waited for it to pass.

She could hear the weeping, rolling like lava out of the house, and the monotonous cluck and squawk of the chickens hunting for

183

food. From somewhere close by was the deep-throated, angry bark of a dog.

And still, she thought, over it all the birds sang, in determinedly cheerful notes.

She concentrated on that sound, and willed her mind away. Oddly, unexpectedly, she found herself standing in her kitchen, her head on Cade's shoulder, his lips brushing her hair.

Resting there, she didn't hear her uncle until he settled in the seat beside her and closed his door.

He said nothing as he pulled away from the house, nothing when he stopped a half mile away and just sat, his hands resting on the wheel and his eyes staring away at empty space.

'I shouldn't have let you come,' he said at last. 'I thought – I don't know what I was thinking, but I guess I had some idea that she'd want to see you, that the two of you might be able to make some of it up with Han gone off this way.'

'I'm not part of her life except to blame for things. He is her life. That's the way she wants it.'

'Why? For God's sake, Tory, why would she want to live like this, live with a man who's never given her any joy?'

'She loves him.'

'That's not love.' He spat the words out, along with anger and disgust. 'That's a sickness. You heard the way she made excuses for him, how she put it off on everybody but him. The woman he attacked, the police, even the goddamn bank.'

'She wants to believe it. She needs to.' Seeing he was more upset than she'd realized, Tory laid a hand on his arm. 'You did all you could.'

'All I could. Gave her money and left her there, in that hovel. And I'll tell you the truth, Tory, I'm thanking God right now she didn't want to come home with me, that I don't have to bring that sickness into my house. I'm ashamed of it.' His voice broke, and he dropped his forehead to the wheel.

Because he needed it, Tory unsnapped her seat belt and leaned into him, her head on his arm, her hand rubbing circles on his wide back. 'There's no shame in that, Uncle Jimmy, no shame in wanting to protect your home and Aunt Boots, to keep all of this away. I could've done what she asked me to do. I could have given her that. But I didn't, and I won't. I'm not going to be ashamed of it.'

He nodded, and struggling for composure sat back again. 'Hell of a family, aren't we, baby?' Gently, very gently, he touched his fingertips to the raw spot on her cheek. Then he shifted back into first, eased on the gas. 'Tory, if it's all the same to you, I don't have the heart to go by and see your gran just now.'

'Neither do I. Let's just go home.'

When her uncle dropped her off, Tory didn't go into her house, but transferred to her own car and drove directly to her shop. She had hours to make up for and was grateful the work and rush would keep her mind off how she'd spent her morning.

Her first call was to the florist, clearing them to deliver the ficus and the flower arrangement she'd ordered the week before. Her next was to the bakery to confirm the cookies and petits fours she'd selected would be ready for her to pick up first thing in the morning.

It was late into the day before she'd satisfied herself that all the arrangements were in the most attractive spots. For a celebrational touch, she began to string fairy lights through the graceful branches of the ficus.

The little bell on her door rang, reminding her she'd forgotten to lock it after the last delivery.

'Saw you as I was passing by.' Dwight stepped in, scanned the shop, then gave a low whistle. 'I was going to see if everything worked out for you, and if you needed any last-minute help. But seems like you've got it under control.'

'I think so.' She straightened, standing with the end of the string of lights still in her hand. 'Your crew did a wonderful job, Dwight. I couldn't be happier with the work.'

'Just make sure you mention Frazier's if anyone compliments your carpentry.'

'You can count on it.'

'Oh now, this is nice work.' He walked over to a cutting board fashioned of narrow strips of various tones of wood, and sanded smooth as glass. 'Beautiful work. I do some woodworking in my hobby room, but nothing as nice as this. Almost too pretty to use.'

'Form and function. That's the key here.'

'Lissy's happy with that candle thing she bought in here, and shows off the mirror every chance she gets. Said it wouldn't hurt her feelings if I took a look at the jewelry and found her something to brighten her mood.'

'Isn't she feeling well?'

'Oh, she's fine.' Dwight waved at the question as he wandered the shop. 'Gets the baby blues now and then, that's all.' He tucked his thumbs in his front pockets and gave her a sheepish grin. 'While I'm here I guess I ought to apologize.'

'Oh.' Since he appeared to be staying awhile longer, Tory continued to thread the lights through the branches. 'For?'

'For letting Lissy think you and Cade were enjoying each other's company.'

'I don't mind Cade's company.'

'Now, I don't know whether you're letting me off the hook or stringing me like you are those little lights. The thing is, well, Lissy just gets the bit between her teeth on some things. She keeps trying to match Cade up with someone, and if it's not him, it's Wade. She's got some wild hair about getting my friends married off. Cade just wanted to wiggle out of her last matchmaking attempt and told me to tell her he was . . .'

He flushed now as Tory simply studied him silently.

'That he was what you could say involved with someone. I told her how it was you, figuring since you'd pretty much just gotten back to town she'd believe it, and let things alone for a while.'

'Uh-huh.' Finished, Tory plugged the lights in, then stepped back to gauge the results.

'I should've known better,' Dwight went on, frantically digging the hole deeper. 'God knows I'm not deaf and know Lissy tends to talk. By the time Cade got back to me to ring a peel over my head, I'd already heard from six different people the two of you were half near engaged and planning a nursery.'

'It might've been simpler just to tell her the truth, that Cade wasn't interested in being fixed up.'

'Now, I wouldn't say simpler.' His handsome white teeth flashed again, quick, charming, and male. 'I tell her that, she wants to know why. I say something like some men aren't looking for marriage. She comes back and says it's good enough for you, isn't it? Or are you wishing you were footloose and fancy-free like your two best pals? I say, no, honeybunch, but by then I've got one foot in the doghouse.'

Trying to look pitiful, he scratched his head. 'I tell you, Tory, marriage is a walk on a greased-up tightrope, and any man who tells you he wouldn't sacrifice a friend to keep from slipping off's

186

a damn liar. Besides, the way I hear it, you and Cade've been seen around together a few times.'

'Are you making a statement or asking a question?'

He shook his head. 'I should've said dealing with a woman's like a walk on that tightrope. Better quit while I can still make it to safe ground.'

'Good idea.'

'Well, Lissy's having herself a hen party, a woman's get-together,' he corrected quickly, seeing Tory's brows shoot up. 'I'm going to wander over to Wade's, see if he wants to grab some supper and keep me company till it's safe to go home. I'll stop by tomorrow. Maybe you can help me pick out some earrings or something.'

'I'll be happy to.'

He walked to the door, paused. 'It looks nice in here, Tory. Classy. This place is going to be good for the town.'

She hoped so, she thought, as she went behind him to lock up. But more, she hoped the town was going to be good for her.

Dwight walked down to cross at the light. As mayor it was important to set a good example. He'd given up jaywalking, and drinking more than two beers a night in a bar, and driving over the posted limit. Small sacrifices, he thought, but every now and again he had the urge to shake off the restraints.

Came from being a late bloomer, he supposed, and gave a quick salute toward the beep of a horn as Betsy Gluck drove by. He hadn't started to hit his stride until his middle teens, then he'd been so dazzled that girls actually wanted to talk to him, he'd stumbled straight into the backseat of his first car with Lissy – well, a few others, then Lissy – found himself going steady with the prettiest and most popular girl in school. Before he knew it he was renting a tux for his wedding.

Not that he regretted it. Not for a minute. Lissy was just what he wanted. She was still as pretty as she'd been in high school. Maybe she fussed and pouted some, but name him a woman who didn't.

They had a fine house, a beautiful son, and another baby on the way. A damn good life, and he was mayor of the town in which he'd once been a joke.

A man had to appreciate the irony of that.

If now and again he got an itch, it was natural enough. But the fact was he didn't want to be married to anyone but his Lissy, didn't want to live anywhere but Progress, and wanted his life to keep right on going just as it was.

He opened the door to Wade's waiting room in time to be all but bowled over by a frantic sheepdog bent on escape.

'Sorry! Oh, Mongo.' The blonde struggling to hold the leash was both pretty and unfamiliar. She sent Dwight an apologetic look out of soft green eyes, even while her Kewpie-doll lips turned up in a quick smile. 'He just got his shots and he's feeling betrayed.'

'Can't say I blame him.' Since doing otherwise would compromise his manhood, Dwight risked his fingers and patted the dog through the mop of gray and white hair. 'Don't recall seeing you or Mongo around town before.'

'We've only been here a few weeks. I moved down from Dillon. I teach English at the high school – well, I'll be teaching summer classes, then I'll start full-time in the fall. Mongo, sit!' With a toss of her hair, she offered a hand. 'Sherry Bellows, and you can blame me for the dog hair covering your jeans.'

'Dwight Frazier, nice to meet you. I'm the town mayor, so I'm the one you come to if you've got any complaints.'

'Oh, everything's been just fine. But I'll keep that in mind.' She turned her head back toward the examining room. 'Everyone's been very friendly and helpful. I'd better get Mongo in the car before he breaks the leash and you have to give me a citation.'

'Need a hand?'

'No, I've got him.' She laughed as she and the dog lunged out the door. 'Barely. Nice to have met you, Mayor Frazier. Bye, Max!'

'Likewise,' he murmured, then rolled his eyes toward Maxine at reception. 'Didn't have English teachers like that when I was in Progress High. Might've taken me a few more years to graduate.'

'You men.' Maxine chuckled as she took her handbag out of the bottom drawer. 'So predictable. Mongo was our last patient, Mayor. Doc Wade's washing up in the back. You mind telling him I'm running off to make my evening lecture?'

'Go right on. Have a nice night, now.'

He wandered back to find Wade straightening the drug cabinet. 'Got any good stuff?'

'Got me some steroids that'll put hair on your chest. You never did grow any.'

' 'Cause you used it all on your ass,' Dwight said easily. 'So how about that blonde?'

'Hmm?'

'Jesus, Wade, you been hitting that cabinet for doggie downers? The blonde with the big dog who just left. English teacher.'

'Oh, Mongo.'

'Well, I see it's too late.' Dwight shook his head, boosted himself up to sit on the padded table. 'When you start missing pretty blondes who fill out their skinny jeans the way that one did, and remember a big, sloppy dog, you're too far gone even for Lissy to fix up.'

'I'm not going on another blind date. And I noticed the blonde.'

'I'd say she noticed you, too. You hit on her?'

'Jesus, Dwight, she's a patient.'

'The dog's the patient. You're missing a golden opportunity here, son.'

'Get your mind off my sex life.'

'You don't have one.' Dwight leaned back on his elbows, grinned. 'Now, if I was single and only half ugly like you, I'd have talked the blonde onto this table, instead of her big, hairy dog.'

'Maybe I did.'

'In your dreams.'

'Ah, but they're my dreams, aren't they? Why aren't you home washing your hands for supper like a good boy?'

'Lissy's got a bunch of women coming over to look at Tupperware or something. I'm steering clear.'

'It's makeup.' Wade closed the cabinet door. 'My mother's going.'

'Whatever the hell. Christ knows the woman doesn't need any more face paint or plastic bowls, but she gets bored to death when she's this pregnant. So how about we have a beer and something to eat? Like the old days.'

'I've got some things to do around here.' Faith could come by, he thought.

'Come on, Wade. A couple hours.'

He started to refuse again. What the hell was wrong with him, locking himself in his apartment, waiting for Faith to call? It was as bad as a teenage girl mooning after the football star. Worse.

'You're buying.'

'Shit.' Cheered, Dwight pushed off the table. 'Let's give Cade a call, get him to meet us. Then we'll make him pay for it.'

'That's a plan.'

Chapter Fifteen

She hadn't expected to be nervous. She was prepared, she'd checked and rechecked every detail down to the color and weight of the cord used to secure her boxes. She had experience and knew every piece of her merchandise almost as well as the craftsmen who created it.

She had gone through every step and stage of the creation of her shop with a calm and often cool eye, and a steady hand. There were no mistakes, no gaps, no flaws.

The shop itself looked perfect, warm and welcoming and bright. She herself looked casually professional and efficient. She should, as she'd spent the hour between three and four that morning agonizing over her choice of outfit before settling on the navy slacks and white linen shirt.

Now she worried it was too much like a uniform. Now she worried about everything.

Less than an hour before opening and all the nerves and doubts and fears she'd managed to ignore for months tumbled down on her like broken bricks.

She sat in her storeroom at her desk with her head between her knees.

The sick giddiness insulted her, shamed her. Even as she went limp with dizziness she berated herself. She was stronger than this. She had to be. She couldn't come so far, work so hard, then collapse inches from the goal.

They would come. She wasn't worried about drawing in people. They would come and they would gawk, and shoot her the quick, curious glances she was already used to seeing aimed at her around town.

The Bodeen girl. You remember her. Spooky little thing.

She couldn't let it matter. But oh, it mattered. She'd been insane to come back here where everyone knew her, where no secret was ever truly kept. Why hadn't she stayed in Charleston where it was safe, where her life had been quiet and her privacy complete?

Sitting there, skin clammy, stomach rolling, she wished desperately for her pretty, familiar house, her tidy garden, the routine of her demanding but impersonal job in someone else's shop. Sitting there, she wished for the anonymity she'd cloaked herself in for four steady years.

She should never have come back. She should never have risked herself, her savings, her peace of mind. What had she been thinking?

Of Hope, she admitted, and slowly raised her head. She'd been thinking of Hope.

Foolish, reckless, she thought. Hope was dead and gone and there was nothing she could do to change it. Now everything she'd worked for was on the line. And to preserve it, she would have to face the stares and the whispers.

When she heard the knock on the shop door her first instinct was to crawl under the desk, curl up, and slap her hands over her ears. The fact that she nearly did, could actually see herself huddled there, pushed her to her feet.

She had thirty minutes until opening, thirty precious minutes to pull herself together. Whoever was out there would just have to go away.

She straightened her shoulders, ran a hand over her hair to smooth it, then started out to tell the early arrival to come back at ten.

She saw her grandmother's face on the other side of the glass and sprinted to the door. 'Oh, Gran. Oh.' She flung her arms around Iris and clung like a woman dangling off a cliff clings to a rock. 'I'm so glad to see you. I didn't think you were coming. I'm so glad you're here.'

'Not come? For your grand opening? Why, I couldn't wait to get here.' Gently she nudged Tory into the shop. 'I drove Cecil crazy badgering him to push a little more speed out of his truck. That's Cecil behind the corn plant, and Boots behind the mountain of him.'

Tory sniffled, then managed a laugh when Cecil poked his head around the long, bladelike leaves. 'It's wonderful, and so are you. All of you. Let's put it . . .' She turned around, calculating space and impact. 'Right over there, at the end of the display along the wall. It's just what I needed.'

'Doesn't look to me like you needed a thing,' Iris commented. 'Tory, this place looks spiffy as a June bride. All these lovely things.' She hooked her arm around Tory's shoulder, studying the shop as Cecil grunted the ornamental tree into place. 'You always had an eye.'

'I just can't wait to buy something.' Boots, polished as a new penny in her yellow sundress, clapped her hands like a girl. 'I want to be your very first sale today, and I warned J.R. I was going to have his credit card smoking before I was done.'

'I've got a fire extinguisher.' Tory laughed and turned to hug her.

'And lots of breakables.' Mindful of them, Cecil put his hands safely in his pockets. 'Makes me feel clumsy.'

'You break it, you bought it,' Iris said with a wink. 'All right, honey-pot, what can we do?'

'Just be here.' Tory let out a long breath. 'There's nothing left, really. I'm as ready as I'm going to be.'

'Nervous?'

'Terrified. I just need to put out the tea and cookies, keep my hands busy for the next little while. Then—' She turned as the door jangled.

'Delivery for you, Miz Bodeen.' The young boy from the florist carried a glossy white box.

'Thank you.'

'My ma's coming over later today. Said she wanted to see how her arrangements look, but I expect she wants to see what you got.'

'I'll look forward to seeing her.'

'Sure got a lot of stuff.' He craned his neck to look around while Tory took a dollar out of the cash drawer. 'I expect people'll be coming in soon. Everybody's talking about it.'

'I hope so.'

He stuffed the bill Tory handed him into his pocket. 'Thanks. See ya later.'

Tory set the box on the counter and took off the lid. It was full of gerber daisies in bright, cheerful colors and fat, sassy sunflowers.

'Aren't they pretty!' Iris leaned over her shoulder for a better look. 'And just exactly right. Roses wouldn't go with your pottery and wood. Somebody knew enough to send you nice, friendly flowers.'

'Yes.' She'd already opened the card. 'Somebody always seems to know the right thing.'

'Oooh, aren't they sweet, aren't they pretty.' Boots fluttered her hands over the flowers. 'Tory honey, you'll drive me crazy if you don't tell me who sent them.'

Boots snatched the card Tory offered. ' "Good luck on your first day. Cade." Awww.'

Head cocked, Iris pursed her lips. 'Would that be Kincade Lavelle?'

'Yes. Yes, it would.'

'Hmmm.'

'Don't *hmmm*. He's just being thoughtful.'

'Man sends a woman flowers, the right flowers, he's got a woman on his mind. Right, Cecil?'

'Seems to me. Thoughtful's a plant. Flowers are romance.'

'Now there. See why I love this man?' Iris tugged on his shirt to bring him down for a kiss, and made Boots beam.

'Daisies and sunflowers are friendly,' Tory corrected, but she had to struggle not to sigh over them.

'Flowers are flowers,' Boots said firmly. 'A man sends them, means he's thinking about a woman.' And she dearly loved the notion of Cade Lavelle thinking about her niece. 'Now, you go on and fuss with them, and I'll put your cookies out. Nothing I love more'n getting ready for a party.'

'Would you mind? I've got one of the raku pots in the store-room. It's perfect for these, and they'll add a nice splash to the counter.'

'Go on, then.' Iris waved her away. 'You just point us in the direction things need to be done. We'll get this show on the road.'

The first customers walked in at ten-fifteen, headed by Lissy. Tory decided to take back every unkind thought she'd ever had about the former prom queen as Lissy proceeded to escort her friends around the shop and coo over merchandise.

By eleven, she had fifteen customers browsing and debating and had already rung up four sales.

By lunchtime, she was too busy to be nervous. There were stares, and there were whispers. Her eye or ear caught more than one, but she coated steel over the prickles of discomfort and boxed up the choices of the curious.

'You used to be friends with the little Lavelle girl, didn't you?'

Tory continued to wrap the iron candlesticks in brown paper. 'Yes.'

'Terrible shame what happened to her.' The woman, with her sharp eagle eyes fixed on Tory's face, leaned closer. 'Hardly more than a baby. Was you who found her, wasn't it?'

'Her father found her. Would you like a box or a bag for these?'

'A box. They're for my sister's girl. Getting married next month. Seems you went to school with her. Kelly Anne Frisk.'

'I don't remember many of the people I went to school with.' Tory lied with a pleasant smile as she boxed the purchase. 'It was so long ago. Would you like this gift-wrapped?'

'I'll do that, honey-pot. You've got other customers.' Iris stepped in. 'So, Kelly Anne's getting married. I believe I remember her quite well. That'd be Marsha's oldest girl, wouldn't it? My, where do the years go?'

'Kelly Anne had nightmares for a month after the Lavelle girl.' The woman said it with a quiet satisfaction that rang in Tory's ears as she walked away.

Tory was tempted to slip into the back, just to breathe until her heart stopped pounding. Instead she turned to a tall brunette who was debating over the selections of serving bowls. 'Can I help you with anything?'

'It's hard to make up your mind with so many nice choices. JoBeth Hardy – Kelly Anne's aunt there? She's a very disagreeable woman. And you can hardly say anything to that. You always were a careful, composed creature. You won't remember me.'

The brunette held out a hand.

'No, I'm sorry.'

'Well, I was considerably younger then, and you weren't in my class. I taught, still teach, second grade at Progress Elementary. Marietta Singleton.'

'Oh, Miss Singleton. I do remember. I'm sorry. It's nice to see you again.'

'I've been looking forward to your opening. I've wondered about you off and on over the years. You might not have known I

194

was friendly with your mother once. Years before you were born, of course. It's a small old world.'

'Yes, it is.'

'Sometimes a little too close for comfort.' She glanced toward the door as Faith walked in. The two of them locked eyes, and that contact sparked before Marietta turned back to study the bowls again. 'But it's all we have to live with. I think I'll take this one here, the blue on white's very charming. Why don't you put it behind the counter for me while I wander around a little more?'

'I'd be happy to. I'll get you one out of the stockroom.'

'Victoria.' Marietta lowered her voice, brushed her hand over the back of Tory's. 'You were very brave to come back here. You always were very brave.'

She moved away while Tory stood, puzzled and surprised by the wave of grief that had flowed off the woman and into the air.

She stepped into the stockroom to clear her mind and fetch the bowl, and was annoyed when Faith marched in behind her.

'What did that woman want?'

'I beg your pardon? This is employees only.'

'What did she want? Marietta.'

Coolly, Tory reached on the shelf for the bowl. 'This. A number of people who come here want merchandise. That's why I call it a store.'

'What did she say to you?'

'And why would that be your business?'

Faith hissed between her teeth and dug a pack of cigarettes out of her purse.

'No smoking.'

'Damn it.' She shoved them back in and began to pace. 'That woman has no business flouncing around town.'

'That woman seemed perfectly nice to me. And I don't have time for your snits or your gossip.' Though she couldn't deny her curiosity was peaked. 'Now, unless you'd like to help me replace stock, or refill the iced tea pitcher, I'll need you to step back out.'

'You wouldn't think she was so nice if she'd been fucking your daddy.' With that one snarling outburst, Faith whirled for the door. Tory remembered Faith's temper very well and, anticipating her mood, Tory shifted the bowl and slapped a hand on the door before Faith could wrench it open.

'Don't you make a scene. Don't you dare bring your family

troubles into my place. You want to have a catfight, then you just go somewhere else.'

'I won't make a scene.' But she was vibrating. 'I have no intention of giving the people around here anything to snicker about. And you just forget what I said. I shouldn't have said it. We've gone to considerable trouble to keep my father's association with that woman quiet. So if I hear any talk, I'll know you started it.'

'Don't threaten me. The day you could push me around is long past, so you just pull in your claws around here because nowadays I fight back.'

She would have left it at that, was angry enough to, but Faith's lip trembled. One small quiver of emotion and Tory saw Hope. 'Why don't you stay in here a minute? Go on, sit down until you're calm again. You walk out looking like that and you won't have to make a scene to set people talking. Besides, right now they're having a fine time talking about me.'

She opened the door, glanced over. 'No smoking,' she repeated, and closed the door behind her.

Faith dropped into a chair and, glaring at the door, pulled her cigarettes out again. She stuffed them guiltily back into her purse when the door swung back open.

But instead of Tory, it was Boots who slipped into the room. Just because she was having a high time flitting around the store didn't mean she was blind to subtleties. She'd seen the hot rage on Faith's face, just as she saw the embarrassed misery on it now.

'We sure are hopping out there.' She spoke cheerfully and waved a hand in front of her face. 'I needed me a minute out of the crowd.' And thought it the perfect opportunity to corner the woman who had Wade wrapped in knots.

'Why don't you sit down, Miss Boots?' Faith got quickly to her feet. 'I was just going back out.'

'Oh, keep me company a minute, won't you, honey? Don't you look pretty today, then you always do.'

'Thanks. I can say the same for you.' Now that she was standing, Faith wished she had something to do with her hands. 'Ah, you must be very proud of Tory today.'

'I've always been proud of her. And how's your mama doing?'

'She's well.'

'Never known her to be otherwise for long. You be sure to give her my best now, won't you?' Smiling easily, Boots wandered over to the bakery box, selected a cookie. 'Haven't seen Wade today, have you? I expect he'll be over.'

'No, I haven't seen him today.' Yet.

'Boy works so hard.' She sighed, nibbled on the little frosted cookie. 'I wish he'd settle down, find a woman who'd help make a home with him.'

'Ah. Hmmm.'

'Oh, now no point in being flustered, sweetie.' Boots kept nibbling, and her eyes were sharp enough to pin even a clever butterfly like Faith. 'He's a grown man, and you're a beautiful woman. Why shouldn't you be attracted to each other? I know my boy has sex.'

Well, Faith thought, there you have it. 'But you'd prefer he didn't have it with me.'

'Now, I don't believe I said any such thing.' She selected another cookie, held it out to Faith. 'We're private here, Faith, and both of us women. That means we know just how to draw a man into doing what we want him to, at least most of the time. You got a wild streak. I don't mind that. Could be I'd pictured some other kind of woman for my Wade, but he pictures you. I love him, so I want for him what he wants for himself. That appears to be you.'

'It's not like that between us, Mrs. Mooney.'

The formal title amused Boots. If she wasn't mistaken, the use of it meant Faith was intimidated. 'Isn't it? You keep coming back to him, don't you? Ever ask yourself why? No,' she said, lifting a finger tipped with pearly pink polish. 'Maybe you should just think about that. I want you to know I've got an affection for you, always have. That surprises you?'

Stupefied her. 'Yes. I suppose.'

'It shouldn't. You're a smart and clever young woman, and haven't had it as easy as some like to think. I like you fine, Faith. But if you hurt my Wade this time around, why, I'll just have to snap that lovely neck of yours like a twig, that's all.'

'Well.' Faith bit into the cookie, narrowed her eyes. 'That clears everything up.'

Suddenly Boots's face was soft again and her eyes mild and dreamy as always. She let out a light, trilling laugh, and to Faith's confusion wrapped her in a hug, kissed her cheek.

'I do like you.' With her thumb, she wiped the imprint of her lipstick from Faith's cheek. 'Now, you sit down and eat your cookie till you feel a little better. Since I'm feeling just fine, I believe I'll go out and buy something else. There's nothing like shopping, is there?' she added as she pranced out the door.

'Jesus.' Speechless, Faith sat down. And ate her cookie.

Tory kept busy, but saw Faith go out ten minutes later. Just as she saw Cade come in, his aunt Rosie in tow, during the first lull of the afternoon.

It was impossible not to recognize Rosie Sikes LaRue Decater Smith. At sixty-four, the woman made just as much of a statement as she had at her debutante ball, when she'd shocked society by doing an exuberant barefoot jitterbug on the tennis court of the country club. She'd married Henry LaRue, of the Savannah LaRues, when she'd been seventeen, and lost him to Korea before their first anniversary.

She'd grieved for six months, then had opted to play the merry widow, flaunted a hot-blooded affair with a struggling artist, and suspected Communist, whom she'd married for the hell of it at twenty. She and the artist both espoused free love and held what many considered orgies at their estate on Jekyll Island.

She buried husband number two there after nineteen tumultuous years, when he tumbled from a third-story window after spending the evening with a bottle of Napoleon brandy and a twenty-three-year-old model.

Some said foul play was involved, but nothing had been proved.

At the ripe age of fifty-eight, she married a longtime admirer, more out of pity than love. He died two years later, on their second anniversary, after being gored and partially devoured by a rogue lion during their second honeymoon trip to Africa.

Burying three husbands, and an untold number of lovers, hadn't dimmed Rosie's style. She wore a wig, at least Tory assumed it was a wig, of platinum blond, a flowing floor-length dress striped like a red-and-white awning, and enough jewelry to topple a lesser woman.

Tory spotted the gleam of diamonds among the plastic beads.

'Toys!' she said in her rusty squeak of a voice and rubbed her hands together. 'Stand back, boy. I'm in a shopping mood.'

She made a beeline for the display of blown-glass paperweights and began tucking them into the crook of her arm.

Torn between amusement and alarm, Tory hurried over. 'May I help you with those, Miss Rosie?'

'Need six of them. The prettiest six.'

'Yes, of course. Ah, for gifts?'

'Gifts, hell. For me.' She clanked glass carelessly together and made Tory's heart stop.

'Why don't I put these up on the counter for you?'

'Good, they're heavy.' Rosie's eyes, weighed down by false eyelashes that disconcertingly resembled spiders, finally fixed on Tory's face. 'You're the girl who used to play with little Hope.'

'Yes, ma'am.'

'Got a way about you. I recollect. I had my palm read once by a gypsy in Transylvania. Said how I'd have myself four husbands, but damned if I want another.' Rosie stuck out a hand crowded with rings and bracelets. 'What do you say?'

'I'm sorry.' Instead of feeling awkward, Tory was marvelously entertained. 'I don't read palms.'

'Tea leaves then, or some such. One of my lovers, young fellow from Boston, claimed he was Lord Byron in another life. Don't expect to hear that kind of thing from a Yankee, do you? Cade, get on over here and hold on to these glass things. What's the point in having a man around if you can't use him as a pack mule,' she said to Tory with a wink.

'I have no idea. Would you like some iced tea, Miss Rosie? Some cookies.'

'I'll just work up an appetite first. Now, what the blue hell is this thing?' She picked up a polished wooden stand with a hole in it.

'It's a wine rest.'

'Don't that beat all? Why anybody's want to give a decent bottle of wine time to rest is beyond me. Wrap me up two of those. Lucy Talbott!' She shouted across the room to another customer. 'What're you buying there?' And was off like a rocket, red and white stripes flapping.

'We just can't break Aunt Rosie out of her shell,' Cade said with a smile. 'And how's your day going?'

'Very well. Thank you for the flowers. They're lovely.'

'I'm glad you liked them. I'm hoping you'll let me take you out to dinner tonight, to celebrate your first day.'

'I—' She already begged off the evening at her uncle's,

switching that to a Sunday family dinner the following day. She was going to be tired, and wired, she reminded herself. Not fit company. 'I'd like that.'

'I'll come by your place around seven-thirty. That work for you?'

'Yes, that'll be perfect. Cade, does your aunt really want all these things? I don't know what anyone could want with six glass paperweights.'

'She'll enjoy them, then she'll forget where she bought them and make up some story about how she found them in a dusty little shop in Beirut. Or claim she stole them from her lover the Breton count when she left him. Then she'll give them away to the paperboy or the next Jehovah's Witness who comes to her door.'

'Oh. Well.'

'You'll want to keep an eye on her. She tends to slip things in her pockets. Absentmindedly,' he continued, when Tory's eyes went wide. 'You just keep track of what goes in, and add it to her bill at the end.'

'But—' Even as she glanced over, she saw Rosie slide a spoon rest into the wide slit pocket of her dress. 'Oh, for heaven's sakes!' Tory rushed over, leaving Cade chuckling.

'Rosie hasn't changed any,' Iris commented.

'No, ma'am, not a whit. Bless her for it. How are you, Miz Mooney?'

'Fiddle fit. You're looking fit yourself. Grew into your feet well enough. How's your family?'

'They're well, thank you.'

'I was sorry to hear about your daddy. He was a good man, and an interesting one. You don't always get both in one.'

'I suppose you don't. He always spoke highly of you.'

'He gave me a chance to earn a decent living after I lost my husband, to put food on my table for my children. I don't forget that. You got something of him around your eyes. Are you a fair man like he was, now that you're full-grown, Kincade?'

'I try to be.' As Rosie let out a cackle and batted at the wind chimes to send them singing, Cade glanced over, met Tory's exasperated eyes. 'Tory's got her hands full.'

'She can deal with it. She's good at dealing with things. Sometimes, maybe, a little too good.'

'She gets her back up when you want to help.'

'She can,' Iris agreed. 'From where I'm standing, I don't think the only thing you want to do about Tory is help her. I'd say there's something more basic on your mind along with that, and as I hope I'm correct in that assumption, I'd like to give you something everyone needs from time to time and no one likes to take.'

He adjusted the balance of the paperweights he still carried. 'And that would be advice?'

She beamed at him. 'You're a smart boy. Always thought so. Advice it is. Just one little bit of it. Don't drag your feet. If there's one thing every woman deserves at least once in her life, it's to be swept off hers. Now, give me some of those things before they get banged together and cracked.'

'She's not sure of me yet.' Cade transferred two of the paperweights and carried the other four to the counter. 'She needs some time.'

'She tell you that?'

'More or less.'

Iris just rolled her eyes. 'Men. Don't you know a woman who says that's either one of three things. She's not really interested, she's being coy, or she's been hurt before. Tory'd tell you straight out if she wasn't interested, there isn't a coy bone in her body, so that leaves number three. You see that man over there?'

Baffled, Cade glanced over to where Cecil was arranging fresh cookies on a plate with hands the size of whole smoked hams. 'Yes, ma'am.'

'You hurt my baby, and I'll send that big old bear after you with a pipe wrench. But since I don't think you're going to do that, I'd suggest you show her that there are some men worth trusting.'

'I'm working on that.'

'Since my girl is trying to convince herself that the two of you are no more than friendly acquaintances, I'd say work faster.'

Chew on that, Iris mused, then moved off to try to prod another customer into a sale.

'She put five napkin rings into her pocket.' At six-ten, with the door locked and Cecil nodding off in the stockroom, Tory plopped on her counter stool and threw up her hands. 'Five. Now, I could see, in a twisted way, taking four or six. But what kind of person takes five napkin rings?'

'Don't imagine she was thinking of them as a set.'

'Add two spoon rests, three wine toppers, and a pair of salad tongs. She put those in her pocket while I was standing right there talking to her. Put them in her pocket, smiled, then took off her pink plastic beads and gave them to me.'

Still bemused, Tory fingered the beads around her neck.

'She likes you. Rosie's always giving things to people she takes a shine to.'

'I don't feel right charging her for all those things. She might not even have wanted them. Lord, Gran, she spent over a thousand dollars. A thousand,' she repeated, and pressed a hand to her stomach. 'I think I might be sick after all.'

'No, you won't. You'll be happy soon as you let yourself be. Now, I'm going to go give Cecil a shake and move him along so you have a chance to catch your breath. You come on by J.R's around one tomorrow. It's too long since we had the family together.'

'I'll be there. Gran, I don't know how to thank you for staying all day. You must be tired.'

'My feet are smarting some, and I'm ready to put them up and let Boots give me a glass of wine.' She leaned over to kiss Tory's cheek. 'You celebrate, you hear?'

Celebrate, Tory thought, after she'd made her notes, tidied, and locked up. She could barely think, much less celebrate. She'd gotten through the day. More than gotten through it, she told herself on the dazed drive home. She'd proven that she was back, to stay, back to make a mark.

Not just survival this time, but success. Some might look at her and see the small, hollow-eyed girl in hand-me-downs. But it wasn't going to matter. More would look and see just what she'd made herself. What she wanted to be.

She would make that matter.

She wasn't going to fail, and she wasn't going to run. This time, finally, she was going to win.

The wonder of that began to set in as she turned into her lane, as she saw the house as it had been, and as it was. Herself as she had been. As she was.

Unable to fight them back any longer, she laid her head on the steering wheel and let the tears come.

She was sitting on the ground, trying not to cry. Only babies cried. And she was *not* a crybaby. But the tears leaked out despite her.

She'd skinned her knees and her elbow and the heel of her hand when she'd fallen off the bike. The scraped skin burned and seeped blood. She wanted to go to Lilah and be hugged and petted and soothed. Lilah would give her a cookie and make it all better.

She didn't care about learning how to ride a stupid bike anyway. She hated the stupid bike.

It lay beside her, a downed soldier with one wheel still spinning in a mocking whirl as she lay her head on her folded arms and sniffled.

She was just six.

'Hope! What the heck are you doing?' Cade rushed down the lane, his Nikes bulleting on the gravel. His father had dropped him off at the entrance to Beaux Reves, giving him his freedom for the rest of the Saturday morning. His whole world had been wrapped around how quickly he could get his bike and ride to the swamp to meet up with Wade and Dwight.

And here was his old and beloved three-speed, crashed, with his baby sister sprawled beside it.

He wasn't sure which he wanted to do more, yell at her or croon to his wounded bike.

'Oh man, look at this! You ruined the paint. Damn it.' He hissed the last. He was just beginning to try out swear words in secret. 'You got no business taking my bike. You got your own.'

'It's a baby bike.' She lifted her face and tears streaked through the fine layer of dirt on her cheeks. 'Mama won't let Daddy take off the training wheels.'

'Well, jeez, guess why.' Disgusted he righted his bike and sent her a superior look. 'Go on inside and get Lilah to wash you up. And keep your sticky fingers off my stuff.'

'I just want to learn.' She swiped a hand under her nose and through the tears shone a light of defiance. 'I could ride as good as you if somebody'd teach me.'

'Yeah, right.' He snorted, swung a leg over the bar. 'You're just a little girl.'

She sprang to her feet then, thin chest heaving with insult. 'I'll get bigger,' she said between her teeth. 'I'll get bigger and I'll ride faster than you or anybody. Then you'll be sorry.'

'Oh, now I'm shaking.' The amusement was coming back, sliding into his deep blue eyes, crinkling them at the corners. If a guy was going to be saddled with a couple of little sisters, the least he could do was tease them. 'I'll always be bigger, I'll always be older, I'll always be faster.'

Her bottom lip trembled, a sure sign more tears wanted to come. He sneered at her, shrugged, and began to pedal up the lane, popping a quick wheelie just to prove his superior talents.

When he glanced back, grin wide, to make sure she'd witnessed his prowess, he saw her head was bent, her tangled hair hanging forward in a curtain. A thin trickle of blood slid down her shin.

He stopped, rolled his eyes, shook his head. His friends were waiting. There were a zillion things to do. Half of Saturday was already *gone*. He didn't have time to waste on girls. Especially sisters.

But he heaved a weighty sigh and rode the bike back. As annoyed with himself as with her now, he hopped off.

'Get on. Damn it.'

She sniffled again, knuckled her eyes, and peered at him. 'Really?'

'Yeah, yeah, come on. I haven't got all day.'

Joy sprang into her, rushing her heartbeat as she climbed onto the seat. As her hands clutched the rubber tips of the handlebars, she giggled.

'Pay attention. This is serious business.' He glanced back, toward the house, and hoped to God his mother didn't chance to look out. She'd have them both skinned for supper.

'No, you gotta, like, center your body.' It embarrassed him to say *body*, though he couldn't say why. 'And keep looking forward.'

She looked up at him, all trust, her smile bright as the sunlight that streamed through the new spring leaves. 'Okay.'

He remembered the way his father had taught him to ride and kept his hand on the back of the seat, jogging lightly as she began to pedal.

The bike wobbled comically. They made it three yards before she went down.

She didn't cry, didn't hesitate to get back on. He had to give her points for it. They pedaled and jogged together, up the lane and down again, past the big oaks, the sunny-faced daffodils, the young tulips while late morning waned away to afternoon.

Her skin was slicked with sweat now, and her heart kept bumping, bumping, bumping. More than once she bit her bottom

204

lip hard to hold back a squeal as the bike tipped. She heard his breath near her ear, felt his hand reach to steady her. And was filled with love for him.

More than for herself now, it was for him she was determined to succeed.

'I can do it. I can do it,' she whispered to herself, as the bike tipped and was righted. Her eyes narrowed in the fierce concentration of a child with only one goal, one world, one path. Her legs trembled, and the muscles in her arms were tight as drums.

The bike wobbled under her, but didn't fall. And suddenly Cade was jogging along beside her, a grin splitting his face.

'You're doing it! Keep going, you're doing it.'

'I'm riding!' Under her the bike became a majestic steed. With her face lifted, she rode like the wind.

Tory woke on the ground beside her car, her muscles trembling, her pulse pounding, with an ache of joy and joys lost in her heart.

Chapter Sixteen

She'd forgotten about dinner until minutes before Cade knocked. There'd barely been time to wash her face and repair the damage from the crying jag and what had followed it, and no time at all to think of an acceptable excuse to send him away.

She couldn't get her mind around it. The bout with tears had left her hollow, head and body. The swing back into Hope's past brought both uneasiness and sorrow.

And a thrill. That was the oddest part of it, she admitted. This lingering thrill of that first solo ride, the sheer delight of wobbling down that lovely, shade-dappled lane with Cade running beside her.

The way his eyes, so blue, so bright, laughed into hers.

The love she'd felt for him, the innocent love of a sister, still shimmered through her and mixed, dangerously, she knew, with her own emotions that were very adult and had nothing to do with kinship.

The combination made her vulnerable, to herself and to him. Better, wiser, to be alone until it passed.

She'd tell him she was exhausted, too tired to eat. That, at least, would be the truth.

He was a reasonable man. Almost too reasonable, she told herself. He'd understand and let her be.

When she opened the door he was standing there, holding a casserole dish. Neighbors, she thought, brought food for death. Well, she was dead on her feet so it seemed appropriate enough.

'Lilah sent this.' He stepped in, handed it over. 'She said anyone who worked as hard as you shouldn't have to cook on top of it. You're instructed to put this in the freezer and pull it out the

206

next time you come home and just need to sit and put your feet up. Which,' he added, as he continued to study her face, 'looks like tonight.'

Yes, she thought, almost too reasonable. 'I hadn't realized how geared up I was about today. Now that it's over, I'm limp.'

'You've been crying.'

'Delayed reaction. Relief.' She carried the dish into the kitchen to put it away, then wondered what to do next. 'I'm sorry about tonight. It was a nice idea, going out to celebrate. Maybe in a couple of days, we could—' She turned, all but bumped into him, then backed hard against the counter.

There was a rough-and-ready jolt of lust. From her, from him, she couldn't be sure.

'You had a lot to deal with today.' He didn't give her room. He figured he'd already given her plenty. He simply laid his palms on the counter on either side of her. Caged her in. He saw her awareness of the move in her eyes. The wariness. 'A lot of people, and the memories they bring along with them.'

'Yes.' She started to shift, realized there wasn't anywhere to go. It was her blood that was hot, she thought with some embarrassment. Running hot, fast, and greedy. 'It seemed like memories were shooting out like pebbles from a slingshot.'

And had ultimately taken her down.

'All of them painful.'

'No.' Oh God, don't touch me. But even as she thought it his hands were on her shoulders, running down her arms. Everything inside her body began to pulse. 'It was wonderful to see Lilah . . . and Will Hanson. He looks just like his father now. When I was a girl, Mr. Hanson – old Mr. Hanson used to give me Grape Nehi on credit if I was a few pennies short. I often was. Cade . . .'

His name was almost a plea. She couldn't have said for what.

She was trembling. The little jumps under his palms were wonderfully arousing. 'I liked the way you looked today. All tidy and crisp. All calm and cool on the outside. Always makes me wonder what's going on under the surface.'

'I was nervous.'

'It didn't show. Not the way it's showing now. Defenses down, Tory. I want them down. I'm going to take advantage of it.'

'Cade, I've got nothing in me.'

'Then why are you trembling?' He tugged the band from her

hair, heard the quick catch in her breathing. His eyes stayed on hers, watching the irises darken as he combed his spread fingers through her hair and unwound the neat braid. 'Why aren't you stopping me?'

'I . . .' Was that her knees going weak? She'd forgotten that could be such a lovely sensation. Surrender wasn't always weakness. 'I'm thinking about it.'

He smiled then, a lazy slide of amusement with power at the edges. 'You just keep right on thinking. I'll keep right on taking advantage.' He undid the first button of her shirt, then the second.

He'd taught Hope to ride a bike, she thought. He'd only been ten years old, and already man enough to care.

He'd sent flowers today. The right flowers, because he'd known they'd please her.

Now he was touching her, as she hadn't been touched in so long.

'I'm out of practice.'

He flipped the third button open. 'Thinking?'

'No.' Her breath came out on a shaky laugh. 'I'm very good at thinking most of the time.'

'Then think about this.' He gave her shirt a little tug to pull it from the waistband of her slacks. 'I want to touch you. I want to feel your skin under my hands. Like this.' He skimmed them up her sides, down. Her stomach quivered when he unhooked her slacks. 'No, keep your eyes open.'

He leaned forward, caught her chin in his teeth. A brief nip that shot an ache down the center of her body. 'Since you're out of practice, I'll just guide you through. And I want you looking at me when I touch you.'

Look straight ahead, he'd told Hope. And had steadied her.

'I want to look at you,' she told him.

He lowered the zipper, slowly, knuckles grazing against her. Her own low moan echoed like thunder in her ears.

It had been so long since a man had wanted her. Since a man had made her want. She wanted to tense, go rigid at the thought of the invasion, of privacy, of self. But her body was already yearning.

'Step out,' he murmured when her slacks pooled at her feet. As she blinked, opened her mouth to speak, he simply covered it with his. Gentle and warm, somehow reassuring even as the edge of something reckless shimmered at the edges.

Then his arms were around her, sliding and skimming over her back as he circled her, a kind of seductive waltz toward the doorway.

Nerves chased after the heat that rose to her skin. 'Cade.'

'I want to take you in the light.' She was already his. No barrier of doubt would stop him. 'So I can see you when you're under me. When I'm inside you.'

At the door of the bedroom he lifted her. 'There are all manner of things I've imagined doing to you in this bed. Let me.'

The sun streamed, rich and gold with the spring evening. It washed over the bed, over her face as he laid her down. The mattress gave under his weight, and he linked his fingers with hers. Restraint and unity. And watching her, always watching her, he took her mouth.

Slowly at first, and sweetly until her hands relaxed under his, until her lips softened, parted, invited. He felt her heartbeat begin to slow, begin to thicken. And as she opened for him, he changed the texture and set to ravage.

The sudden demand stabbed into her, shocking the senses, scraping the nerves. She arched as heat balled in her belly, and the groan strangled in her throat. He aroused her to shudders with his mouth.

He didn't want her to anticipate. Wanted all her senses stunned and her mind empty of all but pleasure. She would think of him, only of him. He would see to it. When she was steeped in him, finally, he would have her.

Her body was slender, the muscles surprisingly firm, almost tough, with delicate skin a delightful contrast. He indulged himself in the taste of it, while part of him calculated how to exploit those nerves and destroy every barrier.

He dragged her up, hands rough, grip near to bruising, ripping another gasp from her as her head fell back, her hair tumbled. Then he used his fingertip to nudge the straps of her bra over each shoulder. He danced his fingers lightly over the swell, with his thumb circled her nipples through the cotton.

'Is it coming back to you yet?'

Her head was so heavy, her skin so hot. 'What?'

'Good.'

He unhooked her bra, drew it aside. But when she reached for him, he pressed her hands flat on the bed, sliding them back until her elbows locked. 'I want you to take this time. Take until you can't take anymore. Then you'll let go, and you'll give. Everything.' His mouth all but savaged hers, ripping down to her gut with one jagged and panicked thrill.

She wanted to resist, to push him back before he dragged her over a line she'd sworn never to cross again. But then his mouth was on hers again, the scrape of teeth, the flick of tongue whipping hot points of pleasure into her. Her back arched, willful invitation, and her hips began to rock.

Little cries and whimpers, she couldn't bite them back. Her arms trembled from the strain even as her body gloried in it. Something frantic was clawing inside her, fighting to break free.

A hard, fast orgasm shocked her eyes wide, left her stunned and embarrassed. Then he was pulling her against him, wrapping her close.

'Let go.'

He rolled her back on the bed, tugging off his shirt. Her eyes were blurred now, her breath as ragged as his. This time when she reached for him, he slid into her arms.

His mouth was urgent, his hands impatient as they molded and pressed and stroked. She dragged at his trousers, desperate now that nerves had been swallowed by needs. He stripped them aside, then sent her flying when he yanked up her hips and used his mouth on her.

Her hands locked around the rungs of the bed, as he'd once imagined. Her head whipped to the side as sensations, dark delights, swamped her. His taste, his scent flooded her senses, swelled them until there was nothing else. Her breath sobbed out an instant before her long, mindless cry of release.

Even as her hands went limp, he locked his around them. His heart was pounding, a rage of blood. The last lights of day, and the dying breeze of evening brushed over her face. Her hair was a wild mass over the pillows, her cheeks flushed.

He would remember this, always. And so, he promised himself, would she.

'Open your eyes. Tory, look at me.' When her lids fluttered up, he clung to the last link of control, bent his head, kissed her, long, deep. 'Say my name.'

The pressure had built again, the terrible, glorious heat of it. 'Cade.'

'Say it again.'

Her fingers flexed under his. She wanted to weep. Or scream. 'Cade.'

'Again.' And plunged into her.

Her mind went brilliant. She moved with him, matching each slow, smooth stroke. Absorbing him, feeding on each individual sensation until they became one glorious feast.

Cade, hot and hard inside her, the weight of him solid, strong. The spread soft and smooth on her back, the iron slick against her hands. And the last rays of light, going gray with dusk.

When the rhythm quickened, she was ready, she was eager, and enraptured by the way his eyes, the stunning blue of them, remained fixed on hers.

'Stay with me.' He was lost in her now. Drowning in her now. His heart beat brutally against hers as he buried his face in her hair.

With their hands still gripped, they let go.

She'd never been taken over so completely. Not by anyone. Not even the man she'd loved. Tory imagined she should be worried about it, but at the moment she couldn't work up the energy for concerns and calculations.

She lay under him while the air in the room softened in the twilight. For the first time in much, much too long to remember, she felt completely relaxed, body and mind.

She had a hand tangled in his hair. It seemed all right to leave it there.

When he turned his head, and his lips brushed the side of her breast, she smiled at the lazy pleasure of it.

'I guess we celebrated after all,' she murmured, and wondered if it would be terribly rude to slide into sleep, just like this.

'We'll be sure to find a lot more to celebrate from now on. I've been wanting to get you here since I helped you cart this bed in.'

'I know.' Her eyes were nearly closed, but she felt him move his head again, felt him look at her. 'You weren't all that subtle about it.'

'A lot more subtle than I wanted to be.' He thought of how he'd imagined gilding their first time with music, and candlelight.

'We did fine without them,' she said sleepily.

'Without what?'

'Without the music and . . .' Her eyes flew open, filled with horror, and met his considering ones. 'I'm sorry. I'm sorry.' She tried to push up, push away, but the weight of him held her in place.

'What are you sorry for?'

'I didn't mean to.' She pressed her hands into the bed, gripped the spread, and was already beginning to shake. 'It won't happen again. I'm so sorry. I didn't mean to.'

'Read my mind?' He shifted so that he could brace on his elbows and frame her face in his hands. 'Stop it.'

'I will. I'm terribly sorry.'

'No, damn it, Tory. Stop pulling in. Stop anticipating my reactions. And goddamn it, stop wondering if and when I'm going to take a crack at you.'

He shifted to sit up, then lifted her to face him. Her cheeks had lost that rosy, contented glow and were pale, her eyes looked strained, near to terrified. He hated it. 'Did it ever occur to you that there might be times a man wouldn't mind having a woman read his mind?'

'It's an inexcusable breach of privacy.'

'Yeah, yeah.' To her shock, he rolled over and pulled her with him so she was sprawled over his chest. 'Seems to me a few minutes back the two of us breached each other's privacy pretty damn effectively. You want to snatch a stray thought out of my head, I'll let you know if it pisses me off.'

'I don't understand you.'

'You ought to have a pretty good clue since I'm lying here naked in your bed.' He kept his voice deliberately careless. 'If that doesn't do it, take another look inside, see what you find.'

She didn't know whether to be insulted or horrified. 'It's not like that.'

'No? Tell me what it's like then.' When she shook her head, he cupped the back of her neck and began to rub. 'Tell me what it's like.'

'I don't read minds. It doesn't happen by accident, or hardly ever. It's just that we were very closely connected physically.'

'I can't argue with that.'

'And I was nearly asleep. Sometimes it can sneak up on you when you're drifting like that. You had an image in your head. It was a very clear, distinct thought, and it just came through.

212

Candlelight, music playing, the two of us standing by the bed. I saw it in mine.'

'So . . . what were you wearing?' When her head snapped up, he shrugged. 'Never mind. I can think that one through for myself. You get images, pictures of thoughts.'

'Sometimes.' He looked so relaxed, so at ease. Where was his anger? 'God, you confuse me.'

'Good, it'll keep you on your toes. Is that the way it always works?'

'No. No. Because if you have any decency, you don't go poking into someone else's private thoughts. I block them out. It's simple enough, as they only come through with effort anyway, or if there's a great deal of emotion on either side. Or if I'm very tired.'

'All right, then I'd say the next time we make love and you're drifting off to sleep, I'd better keep any fantasies about Meg Ryan out of my head.'

'Meg . . .' Baffled, Tory sat up again, automatically crossing an arm over her breasts. 'Meg Ryan.'

'Wholesome, sexy, smart.' Cade opened his eyes. 'Seems to be my type.' He cocked his head, studied her. 'Just trying to picture you as a blonde. It could work.'

'I'm not going to be a party to some prurient fantasy you've cooked up about a Hollywood actress.' Miffed, she started to climb off the bed, and found herself flat on her back again, and under him.

'Oh, come on, darling, just this once.'

'No.'

'God, you giggled. Meg, she's got this sexy little giggle.' He nipped Tory's shoulder. 'Now I'm excited.'

'Get off me, you idiot.'

'I can't.' He rushed wild kisses over her face, foolish and sweet as a puppy. 'I'm a victim of my own helpless fantasies. Giggle again. I'm begging you.'

'No!' But she did. 'Don't! Don't you even think about – Jesus.' Her laughing struggles stopped as he slid silkily inside her. Her hips arched up, and her hands gripped his hips. 'Don't you dare call me Meg.'

He lowered his head, chuckling as he took her.

They ate Lilah's casserole and washed it down with wine. And tumbled back into bed with the eagerness and energy that fuels

213

new lovers. They made love at moonrise, with the light shining silver over their joined bodies. Then slept with the windows open to a fitful breeze and the ripe green scents of the marsh.

'He's coming back.'

Hope sat cross-legged on the porch of the Marsh House. The porch that hadn't been there when she'd been alive. She tossed her handful of silver jacks, then began bouncing the little red ball while her hand darted, deft and quick, plucking the star-shaped metal.

'He's watching.'

'Who? Who is he watching?' Tory was eight again, her thin face wary, her legs bruised.

'He likes to hurt girls.' She scooped up the last jack, tossed them again. 'It makes him feel big, important. Twosies.' In that same steady rhythm she began snatching up pairs.

'He hurt other girls, too. Not just you.'

'Not just me,' Hope agreed. 'You already know. Threesies.' Jacks clattered, the ball thumped methodically on wood. A light breeze danced by, twined up with the scent of rambling roses and honeysuckle. 'You already know, like when you saw the little boy's picture that time. You knew.'

'I can't do that anymore.' Inside the child's chest, Tory's heart began to swell and bump. 'I don't want to do that anymore.'

'You came,' Hope said simply, and moved onto foursies. 'You have to be careful not to go too fast, not to go too slow,' she continued, as she swiped a set of four and nipped the ball on the bounce. 'Or you lose your turn.'

'Tell me who he is, Hope. Tell me where to find him.'

'I can't.' She swept for another set and knocked a finger against another jack, sent it spinning. 'Oops.' She looked over at Tory with clear eyes. 'It's your turn now. Be careful.'

Tory's eyes shot open. Her heart was knocking against her ribs and her hand was curled into a tight fist. So tight she was nearly surprised that a little red ball didn't roll out when she spread her aching fingers.

It was full dark now. The moon had set and left the world black and thick. The little breeze had gone with it so the air was still. Hushed.

She heard an owl, and the shrill bell sound of peepers. She heard Cade's steady breathing in the dark beside her, and realized she'd moved to the edge of the bed, as far from him as was possible.

No contact in sleep, she thought. The mind was too vulnerable then to permit the luxury of casual snuggling.

She slipped out of bed and tiptoed into the kitchen. At the sink she ran water until it chilled, then filled a tumbler.

The dream had given her a desperate thirst, and had reminded her why she had no business sleeping with Kincade Lavelle.

His sister was dead, and if she wasn't responsible, she was obligated. She'd felt obligated before, and had followed through. The path she'd taken had brought her great joy and shattering grief. She'd slept with another man then, given herself out of careless and innocent love.

When she'd lost him, lost everything, she'd promised herself she'd never make those choices, those mistakes again.

Yet here she was, opening herself to all that pain a second time.

Cade was the kind of man women fell in love with. The kind she could fall in love with. Once that step was taken, it colored everything you thought, everything you did and felt. In the bold hues of joy. In the drowning grays of despair.

So the step couldn't be taken. Not again.

She would have to be sensible enough to accept the physical attraction, enjoy the results of it, and keep her emotions separate and controlled. What else had she done, nearly all of her life?

Love was a reckless, dangerous thing. There was always something lurking in the shadows, greedy and spiteful, just waiting to snatch it away.

She lifted the glass to her lips, and saw. Beyond the window, beyond the dark. In the shadows, she thought dully. Waiting. And the glass slipped from her fingers to shatter in the sink.

'Tory?' Cade shot out of sleep, out of bed, and stumbled in the dark. Cursing, he rushed toward the kitchen.

She stood under the harsh light, both hands at her throat, staring, staring at the window. 'Someone's in the dark.'

'Tory.' He saw the sparkle of broken glass that had jumped from the sink to the floor. He grabbed her hands. 'Are you cut?'

'Someone's in the dark,' she said again, in a voice much like a child. 'Watching. From the dark. He's been here before. And he'll come back again.' Her eyes stared into Cade's, through them, and all she saw were shadows, silhouettes. What she felt was cold. So much cold.

'He'll have to kill me. I'm not the one, but he'll have to because I'm here. It's my fault, really. Anybody could see that. If I'd come with her that night, he'd have just watched. Like he'd done before. He'd have just watched and imagined doing it. Just imagined until he got hard and used his hand so he could feel like a man.'

Her knees went out from under her, but she protested as Cade swept her up. 'I'm all right. I just need to sit down.'

'Lie down,' he corrected. When he put her back on the bed, he hunted up his trousers. 'You stay in here.'

'Where are you going?' The sudden terror of being left alone brought strength back to her knees. She leaped up.

'You said someone was outside. I'm going to go look.'

'No.' Now the fear was all for him. 'It's not your turn.'

'What?'

She held up both hands and sank down onto the mattress. 'I'm sorry. My mind's confused. He's gone, Cade. He's not out there now. He was watching, earlier, I think earlier. When we were . . .' It made her queasy. 'When we were making love, he watched.'

Grimly, Cade nodded. 'I'll look anyway.'

'You won't find him,' she murmured, as Cade strode out.

But he wanted to. He wanted to find someone, and use his fists, use his fury. He switched on the outside lights, scanned the area washed in pale yellow. He walked to his truck, got a flashlight out of his toolbox, and the knife he kept there.

Armed, he circled the house, sweeping the light over the ground, into the shadows. Near the bedroom window, where the grass needed trimming, he crouched beside a flattened area where a man might have stood.

'Son of a bitch.' He hissed it between his teeth, and his hand tightened on the hilt of the knife. He straightened, spun around to stalk into the marsh.

He stood on the verge and strained against impotence. He could go in, thrash around, work off some of his anger. And by doing so leave Tory alone.

Instead he went back inside, left the knife and flashlight on the kitchen table.

She still sat there, her fists bunched on her knees. She lifted her head when he came in but said nothing. She didn't have to.

216

'What we did together in here was ours,' Cade said. 'He doesn't change that.' He sat beside her, took her hand. 'He can't, if we don't let him.'

'He made it dirty.'

'For him, not for us. Not for us, Tory,' he murmured, and turned her face to his.

She sighed once, touched the back of his hand with her fingers. 'You're so angry. How do you tie it up that way?'

'I kicked my truck a couple of times.' He pressed his lips to her hair. 'Will you tell me what you saw?'

'His anger. Blacker than yours ever could be, but not . . . I don't know how to explain, not substantial, not real. And a kind of pride. I don't know. Maybe it's more a satisfaction. I can't see it — see him. I'm not the one he wants, but he can't let me stay, he can't trust me this close to Hope.

'I don't know if those are my thoughts or his.' She squeezed her eyes shut, shook her head. 'I can't get him clear. It's as if something's missing. In him or in me, I don't know. But I can't see him.'

'It wasn't a drifter who killed her. The way we thought all these years.'

'No.' She opened her eyes again, turned away from her own grief and toward his. 'It was someone who knew her, who watched her. Us. I think I knew that even back then, but I was so afraid I closed it up. If I'd gone back the morning after, if I'd had the courage to go in with you and your father instead of telling you where she was, I might have seen. I can't be sure, but I might've. Then it would've been over.'

'We don't know that. But we can start to end it now. We'll call the police.'

'Cade, the police . . .' Her throat wanted to close. 'It's very rare that even the most forward-thinking, open-minded cop listens to someone like me. I don't expect to find that particular breed here in Progress.'

'Chief Russ might take some convincing, but he'll listen to you.' Cade would make sure of it. 'Why don't you get dressed.'

'You're going to call him now? At four in the morning.'

'Yeah.' Cade picked up the bedside phone. 'That's what he gets paid for.'

217

Chapter Seventeen

Police chief Carl D. Russ wasn't a big man. He'd reached the height of five-feet-six-and-a-quarter when he was sixteen, and had stayed plugged there.

He wasn't a handsome man. His face was wide and pitted with his ears stuck on either side like oversized cup handles. His hair was as grizzled as a used-up scouring pad.

He had a scrawny build and topped the scale at one thirty. Fully dressed and soaking wet.

His ancestors had been slaves, field-workers. Later they'd been share-croppers eking out stingy livings on another man's land.

His mother had wanted more for him, and had pushed, prodded, harangued, and browbeat until, mostly out of self-defense, he aimed for more.

Carl D.'s mother enjoyed the fact that her boy was police chief nearly as much as he did.

He wasn't a brilliant man. Information cruised into his brain, meandering about, taking winding paths and detours until it settled down into complete thoughts. He tended to be plodding.

He also tended to be thorough.

But above all, Carl D. was affable.

He didn't bitch and moan about being awakened at four in the morning. He'd simply gotten up and dressed in the dark so as not to disturb his wife. He'd left her a note on the kitchen board, and had tucked her latest honey-do list in his pocket on the way out.

What he thought about Kincade Lavelle being at Victoria Bodeen's house at four in the morning, he kept to himself.

Cade met him at the door. 'Thanks for coming, Chief.'

'Oh well, that's all right.' Carl D. chewed contentedly on the stick of Big Red gum he was never without since his wife had nagged him into quitting smoking. 'Had yourself a prowler, did you?'

'We had something. Let's take a look around the side, see what you think.'

'How's your family doing?'

'They're fine, thanks.'

'Heard your aunt Rosie was down for a visit. You be sure to give her my best, now.'

'I'll do that.' Cade shone his flashlight on the grass under the bedroom window, waited while Carl D. did the same, and pondered.

'Well, could be y'all had somebody standing there playing Peeping Tom. Might've been an animal.' He scanned with his light, chewed contemplatively.

'It's a quiet spot, off the road a ways. Don't see that anybody'd have good cause to be wandering 'round out here. Guess they could come across from the road, or out through the swamp. You get any kind of a look?'

'No, I didn't see anything. Tory did.'

'Guess I'll talk to her first, then do some poking around. Anybody was out here's hightailed it by now.'

He got creakily to his feet and swept his light over the darker shadows where the live oaks and tupelos closed in the swamp. 'Yeah, this here's a quiet spot, all right. Couldn't pay me to live out this-a-way. Bet you hear frogs and owls and such all blessed night long.'

'You get used to them,' Cade said, as they walked around to the back door. 'You don't really hear them.'

'I guess that's the way. You get so's you don't hear the usual sounds anymore. And something that's not usual gives you a kind of jolt. Would you say that?'

'I suppose I would. And no, I didn't hear anything.'

'Me, I'm what you call a light sleeper. Least little thing pops my eyes open. Now, Ida-Mae, she won't stir if a bomb goes off.' He stepped into the kitchen, blinked at the bright lights, then politely removed his cap. 'Morning, Miz Bodeen.'

'Chief Russ. I'm sorry for the trouble.'

'Don't you worry about that. Would that be coffee I smell?'

'Yes, I just made it. Let me pour you a cup.'

'Sure would appreciate that. Heard you had a nice turnout at your store today. My wife sure enjoyed herself. Got one of those wind chimes. Fussed about it the minute I got in the door. Nothing would do but I hang it up right off the bat. Makes a pretty sound.'

'Yes, they do. What would you like in your coffee?'

'Oh, a half a pound of sugar's all.' He winked at her. 'You don't mind, we'll sit down here and you can tell me about this prowler of yours.'

Tory shot Cade a look before she set out the coffee and sat. 'Someone was at the window, the bedroom window, while Cade and I were . . .'

Carl D. took out his notepad and one of the three chewed-up pencils in his pocket. 'I know this is a mite awkward for you, Miz Bodeen. You try to relax now. Did you get a look at the person at the window?'

'No. No, not really. I woke up, and came into the kitchen for a drink of water. While I was standing at the sink I . . . He was watching the house. Watching me, us. He doesn't want me here. He's stirred up that I came back.'

'Who?'

'The same man who killed Hope Lavelle.'

Carl D. set his pencil down, and tucking his gum in the pocket of his cheek, picked up his coffee to sip. 'How do you know that, Miz Bodeen?'

Oh, his tone was mild, she thought, but his eyes were the cool, flat eyes of a cop. She knew cops' eyes, intimately. 'The same way I knew where to find Hope the morning after she was killed. You were there.' She knew her voice was belligerent, her posture defensive. She couldn't help it. 'You weren't chief then.'

'No, I've only been chief for going on six years. Chief Tate, he retired, moved on down to Naples, Florida. Got himself a motorboat. Does a lot of fishing. Chief Tate, he always was one for fishing.'

Russ paused. 'I was a deputy the summer little Hope Lavelle was murdered. Terrible thing. Worst thing ever happened around these parts. Chief Tate, he figured it was a drifter did what was done to that little girl. Never found any evidence to the contrary.'

'You never found anything,' Tory corrected. 'Whoever killed her knew her. Just like he knows me and you and Cade. He knows Progress. He knows the swamp. Tonight he came up to the window of my house.'

'But you didn't see him?'

'Not in the way you mean.'

Carl D. sat back, pursed his lips. Considered. 'My wife's granny on her ma's side holds whole conversations with dead relatives. Now, I'm not saying that's the true case or that it's not, as I'm not the one having those chats. But in my job, Miz Bodeen, it comes around to facts.'

'The fact is I knew what had happened to Hope and where she could be found. The man who killed her knows that. Chief Tate didn't believe me. He decided I'd been out there with her, then had run off when I got scared. Left her there. Or that I found her after she was dead, and just went home and hid until morning.'

There was kindness in Carl D.'s eyes. He'd raised two girls of his own. 'You were hardly more than a baby yourself.'

'I'm grown up now, and I'm telling you the man who killed Hope was out there tonight. He's killed others, at least one other. A young girl he picked up hitchhiking on the way to Myrtle Beach. He's already targeted someone else. Not me. I'm not the one he wants.'

'You can tell me all this, but you can't tell me who he is.'

'No, I can't. I can tell you what he is. A sociopath who feels he has the right to do what he does. Because he needs it. Needs the excitement and the power of it. A misogynist who believes women are here to be used by men. A serial killer who has no intention of stopping or being stopped. He's had a run of eighteen years,' she said quietly. 'Why should he stop?'

'I didn't handle that very well.'

Cade closed the back door, sat back down at the table. He and Carl D. had walked the property, scouted the edges of the swamp. They'd found nothing, no fresh footprints, no handy torn swatch of material on a tree branch.

'You told him what you know.'

'He doesn't believe me.'

'Whether he does or not, he'll do his job.'

'Like they did their job eighteen years ago.'

He said nothing for a moment. The reminder of that morning was always a quick, sharp jab to the gut. 'Who are you blaming, Tory? The cops or yourself?'

'Both. No one believed me, and I couldn't explain myself. I was

221

afraid to. I knew I'd be punished, and the more I said, the worse the punishment. In the end, I did what I could to save myself.'

'Didn't we all?' He pushed away from the table, went to the stove to pour coffee he didn't want. 'I knew she was out of the house that night. Knew she planned to sneak out. I didn't say anything, not then, not the next day, not ever, about seeing her bike hidden. That night I considered it the code. You don't tattle unless you're going to get something out of it. So what if she wanted to ride off for a couple of hours?'

He turned back to see Tory watching him. 'The next day, when we found her, I didn't say anything. That was self-preservation. They'd blame me, as much as I blamed myself. After a while, there just didn't seem to be a point. We were all missing a piece, and could never get it back. But I can go back to that night, replay it in my head. Only this time I tell my father how Hope's stashed her bike, and he locks it up and gives her one hell of a talking-to. The next morning she wakes up safe in her bed.'

'I'm sorry.'

'Oh, Tory. So am I. I've been sorry for eighteen years. And over that time I've watched the sister I have left do whatever she could to ruin her life. I saw my father pull away from all of us as if being with us hurt more than he could stand. And my mother coat herself with layer on layer of bitterness and propriety. All because I was more interested in my own affairs than seeing to it Hope stayed in bed where she belonged.'

'Cade. There would have been another night.'

'There wouldn't have been that one. I can't fix it, Tory, and neither can you.'

'I can find him. Sooner or later, I will find him.' Or he'll find me, she thought. He's already found me.

'I have no intention of standing by this time while someone else I care about takes foolish risks.' He set the coffee aside. 'You need to pack some things, go stay with your aunt and uncle.'

'I can't do that. I have to stay here. I can't explain it to you except to say I have to stay here. If I'm wrong, there is no risk. If I'm right, it won't matter where I am.'

He wouldn't waste time arguing. He'd simply find a way to arrange it as he thought best.

'Then I'll pack a few things of my own.'

'Excuse me?'

'I'm going to be spending a lot of time here. It'll be more convenient to have what I need close at hand. Don't look so surprised. One night in bed doesn't make us lovers. But that,' he said, pulling her to her feet, 'is what we're going to be.'

'You're taking a lot for granted, Cade.'

'I don't think so.' He caught her face in his hands, kissed her, sliding her closer until her lips softened, warmed, beneath his. 'I don't think I'm taking a thing for granted. Most particularly you. Let's just say you get your feelings about things, Tory. Things you know without being able to explain them. So do I. I've had one of those feelings about you, and I'm going to stick close until I can explain it.'

'Attraction and sex aren't such a puzzle, Cade.'

'They are when you haven't found and fit in all the connecting pieces. You let me in, Tory. You won't get me out again half as easy.'

'It's a clever trick. How you manage to be annoying and comforting at the same time.' She drew away. 'And I'm not sure I let you in at all. You just pretty much go where you please.'

True enough, and he wouldn't bother to deny it. 'Going to try to kick me out?'

'It doesn't look like it.'

'Good, that saves us an argument. Well, since we're up and dressed, why don't we do some business?'

'Business?'

'I've got those samples out in the truck. I'll bring them in, and we can negotiate.'

Tory glanced at the clock. It was still shy of seven. 'Why not? This time you make the coffee.'

Faith waited until half past ten, when she was certain both her mother and Lilah had left for church. Her mother had long since given up expecting Faith to attend Sunday services, but Lilah was bullheaded about God and often considered herself His drill sergeant, whipping the troops out of bed and into church with threats of eternal damnation.

Whenever she was home, Faith was careful to hide and hide well on Sunday mornings. She made up for it by occasionally putting on a demure dress and presenting herself in the kitchen so Lilah could shuffle her off toward redemption.

223

But this particular Sunday she wasn't in the mood to be obliging, or to sit on a hard pew and listen to a sermon. She wanted to sulk over a breakfast bowl of chocolate ice cream, and remind herself what bastards men were.

When she thought of all the trouble she'd gone through for Wade Mooney, she could just spit. Hadn't she slathered herself all over with perfumed cream, slithered into the sexiest lingerie money could buy – and would have been perfectly willing for him to rip those bits of satin and lace right off her body, too. She'd dug out four-inch heels and had strapped herself in an excuse for a little black dress that shouted 'I want to sin.'

She'd raided the wine cellar for two bottles that cost more than a college education, and when Cade found out, he was going to skin her for it.

And when she'd arrived at Wade's primed, polished, and perfumed, he hadn't had the decency to be home.

Bastard.

Worse, she'd waited for him. She'd tidied up his bedroom like a little hausfrau, had lighted candles, put on music. Then had damn near nodded off during the vigil.

She'd waited another hour, till almost one in the morning, primed for a different purpose. Oh, how she'd wanted him to walk in the door so she could have kicked his inconsiderate ass all the way back down the steps.

It was his fault that she'd gotten half drunk on the wine, and certainly his that due to the alcohol content in her blood she'd misjudged the turn through the gates and had scraped the side of her car.

So it was absolutely his fault that she was sitting there on a Sunday morning, miserably hung over and stuffing ice cream in her face.

She never wanted to see him again.

In fact, she thought she would just give up men altogether. They weren't worth the time and trouble they drained out of a woman. She'd just cut them out of her life, and find other areas of interest.

Cade walked in the door as Faith was digging her spoon back into the half-gallon carton, and since he knew what mood dictated that particular behaviour, tried to slip right out again.

But he wasn't quite quick enough.

'Oh, sit down. I'm not going to bite you.' She lighted a cigarette, then proceeded to smoke with one hand and eat with the other. 'Everybody's gone off to church to save their immortal souls. Aunt Rosie went with Lilah, I think. She likes to go to Lilah's church more than she does Mama's. I caught a glimpse of them as they were leaving. Aunt Rosie had a hat on big as a turkey platter and lime-green tennis shoes, so she couldn't be going with Mama.'

'Sorry I missed it.' He got a spoon, sat, and scooped out some ice cream. 'So, what's wrong?'

'Why should anything be wrong? I'm just as content as a goose with a nest of golden eggs.' She blew out smoke, narrowed her eyes against it, and took a good look at him.

His hair was a little damp so the gilt edges of it stood out. That meant a recent shower, since Cade never bothered to do more than rub a towel over his hair to dry it off after one.

His eyes, blue as her own, were lazily content, his lips quirked in a half-assed smile.

She knew just what sort of activity put that look on a man's face.

'You haven't changed clothes since yesterday. Haven't been home, have you? Well, well, well. I guess somebody got lucky last night.'

Cade licked his spoon, studied her in turn. 'And I guess somebody didn't. I'm not going to sit here and discuss my sex life over your breakfast ice cream.'

'You and Tory Bodeen. Isn't that just perfect?'

'I like it.' Cade scraped out another spoonful. 'Don't get in the way of this, Faith.'

'Why should I? What do I care? Just don't know what you see in her is all. She's pretty enough, but she's got a coolness around her. Sooner or later, she'll freeze you out. She's not made the way the rest of us are.'

'You'd find out differently if you took time to get to know her. She could use a friend, Faith.'

'Well, don't look at me. I make a lousy friend. You can ask anyone. And I don't even much like her. You want to bang her a few times, that's your business. Hey!' She looked up, full of surprised insult, when he grabbed her wrist, thumped their joined hands to the table.

'It's not like that.' His voice had gone soft as silk, and there was the warning gleam of temper in his eyes. 'Sex isn't a casual pastime to everyone.'

'You're hurting me.'

'No, you're hurting yourself.' He let her go, then rose to toss his spoon in the sink.

Thoughtfully, Faith rubbed her wrist. 'What I'm doing is making damn sure I'm not hurt. You want to lay your heart out so somebody can stomp on it, that's fine for you. But I'll tell you one thing I know for sure. You don't want to be falling in love with Tory. That's something that's never going to work.'

'I don't know whether I want to or not. I don't know whether it'll work or not.' He turned back. 'What you don't seem to know, Faith, is how much you're like her. The two of you, barricaded against your own feelings in case, just on the off chance, that something might sting. She does it by closing in, and you do it by acting out. But it's the same damn thing.'

'I'm nothing like her!' She shouted it at him as he walked from the room. 'I'm nothing like anybody but myself.'

Furious, she heaved her spoon across the room, and leaving the ice cream melting on the table, stormed upstairs to dress.

She had to take it out on somebody, and since, through the maze of her thinking it all stemmed back to Wade, he was elected. She dressed for this bout, too. She had her pride, and wanted to look stunning when she skewered him straight through the heart, ripped him into little pieces, then dumped him and danced away singing a happy tune.

She wore silk, tailored and trim in a deep blue to bring out her eyes and make him remember them. She started to shove open the door to his apartment, stopped herself, and knocked formally.

She heard yips and whines on the other side and rolled her eyes. He'd brought one of his sick mutts upstairs. How had she ever let herself get to this stage with a man who thought more of a stray dog than he did of a woman willing to jump his bones?

Thank God she'd come to her senses.

Then he opened the door, rumpled, sleepy-eyed, wearing only jeans he hadn't bothered to button. And she remembered how she'd gotten to this stage with this particular man.

Her juices wanted to rise and churn, but she ignored them and, grabbing his hand, slapped the key into it.

'What?'

'That's for starters. I have a few things to say to you, then I'll take my leave.' She shoved him aside and strode in. She'd worn heels that showed off her legs in the short dress. Just to torment him.

'What time is it?'

She gritted her teeth. He was simply destroying her timing. 'It's nearly noon.'

'Oh Christ, it can't be. I have to be at my mother's in an hour.' He sank into a chair, buried his head in his hands. 'I'll probably be dead in an hour.'

'You will if I have anything to do with it.' She leaned down, sniffed, reared back. 'You smell like the inside of a cheap bottle of bourbon.'

'It was an expensive bottle of bourbon, and I'm not inside it. It's inside me.' His stomach rolled uneasily. 'For the moment.'

'So.' She slapped her hands on her hips. 'You were out getting drunk and tomcatting around half the night. I hope you enjoyed yourself.'

'I'm not entirely sure. I think I started out that way.'

'Because,' she continued, furious at the interruption, 'that's how you can spend every Saturday night from now on as far as I'm concerned.' Jealousy veered in and cut pride off at the pass. 'Who the hell was she?'

'Who?' He took a chance and let go of his head. He was vaguely disappointed when it didn't roll off his shoulders. 'Who was who?'

'The little slut you think you can two-time me with and live.' She picked up the closest thing at hand – a small lamp – yanked the cord free, and heaved it. The resulting crash had howls coming from the bedroom and brought Wade unsteadily to his feet. 'You son of a bitch. Is she still here?'

'Who? What the hell's wrong with you? You broke my lamp.'

'I'll break your neck before I'm done.' She whirled, raced into the bedroom intending to rake the eyes out of the woman who'd usurped her place.

On the bed stood a small black puppy, barking wildly and cowering against the pillows.

'Where is she?'

'Who?' Wade threw up his hands. His hair was standing on end and there was a kickboxer working out behind each of his eyes. 'Where is who? What the hell are you talking about, Faith?'

'The bitch you're sleeping with.'

'The only bitch I've slept with recently, besides you, is that one.' He gestured toward the bed. 'And she's only been here a couple of hours. Really, she means nothing to me.'

'You think you can joke about this? Just where were you last night?'

'I was out. Goddamn it.' He stalked to the bathroom, shoving bottles and tubes aside as he searched for aspirin in the medicine chest.

'You were out, all right. I came by at nine, and stayed till nearly one—' Damn it, she hadn't meant to tell him she'd waited so long. 'You never showed up.'

Ready to whimper, he shook out four pills, swallowed them with tepid tap water. 'I don't recall us having plans for last night. You don't like to make plans. Ties you down, takes the excitement out of things.' He leaned back on the sink, stared at her balefully. 'Well, this is exciting.'

'It was Saturday night. You had to know I'd come by.'

'No, Faith, I don't have to know anything. You don't want me to know anything.'

She tossed her head. They were getting off the subject. 'I want to know where you were and who you were with.'

'That's a lot of demands from someone who doesn't want any strings.' His eyes might have throbbed like drums, but they could still go hard. 'Straight sex, fun and games. Aren't those the ground rules?'

'I don't cheat,' she said with some dignity. 'When I'm with a man, I don't go off with another. I expect the same consideration.'

'I wasn't with another woman. I was with Dwight.'

'Oh, that's just a bullshit lie. Dwight Frazier's a married man and he wasn't out half the night drinking and carousing with you.'

'I don't know where he was after about ten. Home tucked in with Lissy, I expect. They went to the movies, and I tagged along.' His voice had gone flat, his eyes cold and dull. 'They went home. I bought a bottle, I went for a drive. I got drunk, I came home. If

228

I'd done anything else, with anyone else, I'd have been free to do so. Same as you are. That's the way you wanted it.'

'I never said that.'

'You never said different.'

'I'm saying different now.'

'You can't have it all your way, Faith. You want to change things, you want it to be you and me, then we start adding some of my rules.'

'I didn't say anything about rules.' He was twisting things. Just like a man. 'I'm speaking of common courtesy.'

'And that means I sit around here and wait until you're in the mood for my company? I don't think so. We both come and go as we please, unless we're pleased to be together. Or, we make this a relationship. No more sneaking in here or off to some motel. No more pretending we're not involved. We're either a couple or we're not.'

'You're making ultimatums?' Her voice snapped at the end, a whiplash of shock. 'You're making them to me after you kept me waiting here half the night?'

'Frustrating, isn't it? The waiting. Pisses you off.' He pushed away from the sink and walked toward her. 'Makes you feel used and sorry and hurt. I know.'

Stymied, she pushed a hand through her hair. 'You never said anything about that.'

'You'd have taken off like a shot. That's your style, Faith. Sometime last night while I was sitting down at the river with a bottle for company, it occurred to me that I didn't like that about you, and I didn't like it about myself that I let you be that way with me. So I'm telling you now. We try to make this work like people who give two damns about each other, or we walk away.'

'You know I care about you, Wade. What do you take me for?'

It was more, he thought, what she took herself for. 'There was a time I'd have taken you no matter what. That time's over. I want more now, Faith. If you can't give it to me, or won't, I'll live with it. But I'm not settling for crumbs anymore.'

'I don't understand this.' Shaken, she sat on the edge of the bed. The puppy crawled toward her on her belly, sniffing. 'I don't see how you can turn this around on me.'

'Not on you. On us. I want there to be an us, Faith. I'm in love with you.'

'What? Are you crazy?' She leaped up again, panic in every pore. 'Don't say that.'

'I've said it before, but you never listened. It didn't matter enough. This time it'll have to matter or I won't say it again. I'm in love with you.' He caught her shoulders. 'That's the way it is, whatever you do about it.'

'What am I supposed to do about it?' There was a loose and fluttery sensation in her stomach she recognized as pure panic. 'Oh, this is just a mess.'

'Your usual response to me telling you I love you is to run off and marry somebody else.' He lifted his brow as her mouth fell open.

'That's not – I don't—' Oh God, he was right. She did.

'We could try something new this time out. We could try dealing with this like normal people, and see where it goes. We could spend time with each other, do more together than jump into bed. There's more between us than sex.'

She sniffled. 'How do you know?'

He laughed a little, brushed at her hair. 'All right, let's say I want to find out if there's more between us than sex.'

'What if there isn't?'

'What if there is?'

'What if there isn't?'

He sighed. 'Then I guess we'll end up spending a lot of time in bed. If there's anything left of it,' he added, and stepped over to tug away the pillow the puppy was trying to chew to bits.

He was so solid, so smart and kind and handsome. And he loved her. But no one ever loved her for long. Lighten it up, Faith ordered herself, at least until her heart stopped jumping. 'I don't know about a relationship with a man who sleeps with little mongrel dogs.'

'Miss Dottie dropped her off this morning on her way to church. I was too hung over to do anything but plop us both in bed.'

'What's wrong with her?'

'Who? Oh, the puppy. Nothing.' He leaned over, ruffled fur, scratched ears. 'Bright-eyed and healthy. Had all her shots, and took them like a champ.'

'Then what are you doing with her?'

'Keeping her for you.'

'For me?' Faith took a full step back. 'I don't want a dog.'

'Sure you do.' He plucked the puppy from the bed, then pushed her into Faith's arms. 'Look, she likes you.'

'Puppies like everybody,' Faith protested, as she twisted her head to try to avoid the pup's cheerful tongue.

'Exactly.' With the dimples flickering in his cheeks, Wade slipped his arms around Faith's waist, sandwiching the puppy between them.

'And everybody likes puppies. She'll depend on you, entertain you, keep you company, and love you no matter what.'

'She'll pee on the rug. She'll chew my shoes.'

'Some. She'll need discipline and training and patience. She'll need you.'

They'd known each other most of their lives. Just because they'd spent most of their time together between the sheets didn't mean she didn't have clues as to how his mind worked.

'Is this a dog or a life lesson you're giving me?'

'Both.' He leaned over to kiss Faith's cheek. 'Give it a try. If it doesn't work out, I'll take her back.'

The puppy was warm and trying desperately to snuggle in the curve of Faith's neck and shoulder. What was going on? It seemed everyone was hammering at her all at once. First Boots, then Cade, and now Wade.

'You've got my head spinning. I can't keep up with you today, and that's the only reason I'm agreeing to this.'

'To us, or to the puppy?'

'A little bit of both.'

'That's a good enough start for me. There's puppy food in the kitchen. Why don't you go feed her while I get a shower? I'm going to be late for dinner at my folks'. Why don't you come with me?'

'Thanks, but I'm not ready for family dinners quite yet.' She remembered, all too well, the cool, clear gleam in his mother's eyes. 'Go on and shower. You stink worse than a litter of puppies.' She frowned as she carried the puppy into the kitchen. She wasn't sure if she was ready for any of this. Any of it at all.

Chapter Eighteen

Tory had barely unlocked the door on Monday morning when it chimed open.

'Morning. I'm Sherry Bellows. I tied my dog to your bench outside. Hope that's all right.'

Tory glanced out, saw a hairy mountain sitting docilely on the sidewalk. 'It's fine. He's big, isn't he? And beautiful.'

'He's a doll baby. We just got back from a morning run in the park, and I thought I'd stop in. I was here Saturday for a little while. You had quite a crowd.'

'Yes, it kept me busy. Is there something I can show you, or would you just like to browse?'

'Actually, I wondered if you were thinking of taking on any help.' Sherry flipped back her ponytail, lifted her arms. 'I'm not exactly dressed for job hunting,' she said with a smile, and tugged the damp T-shirt down over her running shorts. 'But I just followed impulse. I teach at the high school. Will teach. Summer classes starting middle of June, then full-time in the fall.'

'It doesn't sound like you need a job.'

'I've got the next couple of weeks, then Saturdays and half days through September. I'd enjoy working in a place like yours and the extra money a part-time job would bring in. I put myself through college working retail, so I know the ropes. I can give you references, and I don't have a problem working for minimum wage.'

'To tell you the truth, Sherry, I haven't really thought about hiring, at least not until I see how the business goes for the first few weeks.'

'It can't be easy to run the place solo.' If there was one thing

232

Sherry had learned while pursuing her teaching degree, it was persistence. 'No breaks, no time to do paperwork or check inventory or make your orders. Since you're open six days a week, that doesn't give you much opportunity to run errands. Do your banking, your shopping. I imagine you ship, don't you?'

'Well, yes—'

'You'd have to close the shop every time you needed to scoot down to the post office, or wait to ship orders until the next morning before you opened. That adds extra hours to your day. Anybody who can put together a business like this, on her own, knows her time is worth money.'

Tory took another good look. Sherry was young, pretty, damp from jogging. And very direct. And she had a point. Tory had been in the shop since eight, boxing orders for shipping, doing paperwork, rushing to the bank and the post office.

Not that she didn't enjoy it. It gave her a lovely flush of satisfaction. But it would become more and more demanding as time went on.

At the same time she wasn't sure she wanted to share her shop with anyone, even part-time. There was a deep pleasure in having it all to herself. And that, she admitted, was indulgent and impractical.

'You've caught me off guard. Why don't you write down your address and phone number, and those references.' Tory walked behind the counter for her clipboard. 'Give me some time to think about it.'

'Terrific.' Sherry took the pen Tory offered, tapped it on the clipboard. 'And I come with a partner, a two-for-one deal.' She nodded toward the window where two women had stopped to admire Mongo. 'He's so precious people can't help but want to give him a good pet. Since they're standing there, they'll just have to look at your display. I bet they come in.'

'Clever.' Tory lifted a brow. 'Maybe I should just buy a dog.'

Sherry laughed and began to write. 'Oh, you'd never find another like my Mongo. And as good as he is, he can't ring up sales.'

'Good point. And good call,' she added quietly, when the two women stepped into the shop.

'Is that your dog?'

'He's mine.' Sherry turned, beaming. 'I hope he didn't bother you.'

233

'Why, he's the sweetest thing. Just a great big ball of fur.'

'Gentle as a lamb,' Sherry assured them. 'We just had to stop in and see all the pretty things in here. Isn't this a wonderful place?'

'Very nice. I don't recall seeing it before.'

'We just opened Saturday,' Tory told her.

'I haven't been down this part of town for quite a while.' The woman glanced around. Her friend was already wandering. 'I do like those candle stands in the window. We've just moved into a new house and I'm doing some redecorating.'

'I'll get them out for you.' Tory glanced at Sherry. 'Excuse me.'

'Oh you go right on, take your time.'

Sherry watched as Tory assisted the customers. Low-key, she noted. Well, she could do low-key, let the merchandise sell itself. But she didn't think it would hurt if she chatted. It was so hard for her not to, and she thought it might be a nice balance against Tory's quiet class.

She'd get the job, Sherry determined, as she continued to write and keep one eye on the procedure. She was good at talking people into things, and she really could use the extra money.

To gild the lily a bit, she enthused over the customers' choices, drew them into friendly conversation while Tory boxed and wrapped. They left happy, and well loaded down.

'That was nice. But I think you could have talked Sally into those garden plaques.'

'If she wants them, she'll be back.' Amused, Tory filed the credit card receipts. 'And I'm banking on her friend talking her into it over lunch. You're good with people. Do you know anything about crafts?'

'I'm a very fast learner. And since I admire your taste in merchandise, it'll be an easy lesson. I can start right away.'

Tory was on the point of agreeing. Something about Sherry hit all the right notes. Then the door opened, and her mind emptied of everything but terrorized shock.

'Hello there, Tory.' Hannibal spread his lips in a wide, wide smile. 'Been a while.' He shifted his eyes, spread that bright look over Sherry. 'That your dog out there, missy?'

'Yes, that's Mongo. I hope you didn't mind him.'

'Oh no, indeed. Looks to be as friendly as a Sunday social. Mighty big dog for a little thing like you. Saw you running with

234

him in the park a while ago. Couldn't tell who was leading who.'

Sherry felt a quick ripple of unease, but managed a laugh. 'Oh, he lets me think I'm in charge.'

'A good dog's a faithful friend. More faithful than people, mostly. Tory, aren't you going to introduce me to your friend here? Hannibal Bodeen,' he said, before Tory could speak, and held out the big hand he'd so often used to silence her. 'I'm Victoria's daddy.'

'It's nice to meet you.' Relaxed again, Sherry gave his hand a warm shake. 'You must be so proud of your daughter, and what she's done here.'

'Hardly a day goes by I don't think of it.' His eyes pinned Tory again. 'And her.'

Tory shoved at the edges of shock. If he was here she had to deal with him. And deal with him alone. 'Sherry, I appreciate your coming in. I'll look this over, and call you soon.'

'I appreciate that. I'm trying to talk your daughter into hiring me. Maybe you could put in a good word. Nice to have met you, Mr. Bodeen. I'll wait to hear from you, Tory.'

She walked out, crouched by the dog. Tory could hear her delighted laughter and the dog's welcoming bark through the closed door.

'Well now.' He put his hands on his hips and turned to study the shop. 'This is quite a place you've got here. Looks like you're doing pretty well for yourself.'

He hadn't changed. Why hadn't he changed? Did he look older? He didn't seem to. He hadn't lost his girth or his hair or that dark gleam in his eyes. Time didn't seem to touch him. And when he turned back, she felt herself shrinking, she felt the years, and all the effort she'd put into remaking herself, slipping away.

'What do you want?'

'Real well for yourself.' He stepped up to the counter, closing the distance. And she saw she'd been wrong, at least partially wrong. There was some age on his face, carved into deep lines around his mouth, sagging in his jowls, scored across his brow like whiplashes. 'You come back here to flaunt that in your old hometown. Pride goeth before a fall, Victoria.'

'How did you know I was here? Did Mama tell you?'

'A father's a father all of his life. I've kept my eye on you. Did you come back here to boast, and to shame me?'

235

'I came back here for myself. It has nothing to do with you.' Lies, lies, lies.

'It was here you set the town talking, had them pointing fingers. It was here you defied me and the Lord for the first time. The shame of what you did and what you were drove me from here.'

'Margaret Lavelle's money in your pocket drove you from here.'

A muscle jumped in his cheek. A warning. 'So, people are talking already. I don't care for that. "A liar giveth ear to a naughty tongue." '

'They'll talk more if you spend any time around here. And those who are looking for you are bound to find you. I've been to see Mama. She's worried about you.'

'Got no cause to. I'm head of my own house. A man comes and goes as he sees fit.'

'Runs. You ran after you were caught and arrested and charged for assaulting that woman. You lit out and left Mama alone. And when they catch you this time, there won't be probation. They'll put you behind bars.'

'You mind your mouth.' His hand shot out. She was prepared for a blow, was braced for it, but he grabbed her shirtfront and hauled her half over the counter. 'You show me respect. You owe me your life. It was my seed started you into this world.'

'To my everlasting regret.' She thought of the scissors under the counter. Imagined them in her hand as he dragged her over another inch. And wondered, as she looked into the terrible and familiar rage in his face, if she was capable of using them. 'If you lay a hand on me, I swear I'll go straight to the police. You hit me, and I'll tell them, and I'll tell them of all the times you left me bruised and battered. When I'm done—'

She gasped, fought not to cry out when he yanked her hair back with his free hand and the rough edge of his fingers scraped like a burn over the side of her throat. Tears of pain leaked out of her eyes and made her voice rasp. 'When I'm done, they'll put more bars around you. I swear it. Now, you let me go, and you walk out of here. I'll forget I ever saw you.'

'You would dare to threaten me?'

'It's not a threat. It's a fact.' The fury and hate rolling out of him almost smothered her. She could feel her throat closing against it, her chest clogging. She wouldn't be able to hold out

236

much longer. 'Let me go.' She kept her eyes on his as she slid her hand under the counter, feeling for the scissors. 'Let me go before someone comes through and sees you.'

Emotions lit over his face. Fear added to the mix of violence pumping from him. Her fingers brushed the cool metal handles, and he jerked her to the side, all but rammed her into the cash register.

'I need money. You give me what you've got in there. You owe me for every breath you've ever taken.'

'There isn't much. It won't take you far.' She opened the cash drawer, pulled out money with both hands. Anything to get him out, anything to get him away.

'That lying whore back in Hartsville will burn in hell.' He kept his hand on her hair as he stuffed the money in his pocket. 'And so will you.'

'You'll already be there.' She didn't know why she did it. She couldn't foresee future events, she couldn't predict. That was one small blessing. But she focused her eyes on his and spoke as if ripe with visions. 'You won't live the year out, and you'll die in pain and fear and fire. You'll die screaming for mercy. The mercy you never gave me.'

He went white and shoved her away from him so that her back hit the wall and supplies tumbled. He lifted an arm, pointing. ' "Thou shalt not suffer a witch to live." You remember that. You tell anyone you saw me here today, I'll come back for you and do what should have been done the minute you were born. Born with a cowl over your face. Devil's mark. You're already damned.'

He shoved out the door, ducked his head, and hurried away. Tory simply slid down to the floor. Already damned? She stared blankly at the scissors, teetering on the edge of the under counter. She'd nearly had them in her hand, very nearly . . .

One of them would have been in hell if she'd firmed her grip on them. She wasn't sure she would have cared which one of them. At least it would've been over.

She brought her knees up, pressed her face into them, and curled into a ball as she'd done so often as a child.

That's how Faith found her when she came in with a wriggling puppy under her arm.

'Jesus, Tory!' With one glance she took in the open and empty register, the scatter of supplies, and the woman trembling on the floor. 'God, are you hurt?'

She set the puppy down, and as it scampered joyfully away, rushed behind the counter. 'Let's have a look, let me have a look at you.'

'I'm all right. It's nothing.'

'Getting robbed in broad daylight in this town is something. You're shaking all over. Did they have a gun, a knife?'

'No. No. It's okay.'

'I don't see any blood. Well, ouch, you're a little raw back here on the neck. I'll call the police. You want a doctor?'

'No! No police, no doctor.'

'No police? I just saw some big brute of a man skulking out of here, walk in, and see your cash register open, empty, and you sprawled behind the counter, and you don't want the police? What do they do in the big city when they get robbed, make cupcakes?'

'I wasn't robbed.' Exhausted, she let her head fall back and rest against the wall. 'I gave him the money. Under a hundred dollars. The money doesn't matter.'

'Then you want to give me some while you're at it, 'cause if that's how you plan to run your business, you won't be here very long.'

'I'm going to be here. I'm going to stay here. Nothing's going to make me run away again. Nothing. No one. Not ever again.'

Faith didn't have much experience with hysteria, unless it was her own, but she thought she recognized it in the rise of Tory's voice, the sudden wildness in her eyes.

'That's the spirit. Why don't we just get up off the floor here, go on in the back a minute.'

'I said I'm all right.'

'Then you're stupid or a liar. Either way, let's go.'

Tory tried to push her away, tried to stand on her own, but her legs wouldn't manage it. They buckled as Faith pulled her up and left her no choice but to lean.

'We'll just go on back. I'm going to leave the puppy out here.'

'The what?'

'Don't you worry about him. He's about half housebroken. You got anything back here to drink that's got a bite to it?'

'No.'

'That figures. Tidy Tory wouldn't have herself a bottle of Jim

Beam in the drawer. Now, sit down, catch your breath, then tell me why I'm not calling the police.'

'It would just make it worse.'

'Because?'

'Because it was my father you saw leaving the store. I gave the money to him so he'd go away.'

'He put that mark on you.' When Tory simply stared, Faith drew a deep breath in and out. 'Guess it's not the first time. Oh, Hope didn't tell me. I imagine you swore her to secrecy, but I had eyes. I saw you with bruises and welts plenty of times. Always had a story about falling down or running into something, but the funny thing was, I never noticed you being clumsy. As I recall, you had a number of those welts and bruises the morning you came to tell us about Hope.'

Faith walked over to the minifridge, found a bottle of water, opened it. 'Is that why you didn't meet her that night? Because he'd walloped you?' She held out the water, gauging Tory's silence. 'I guess I've been focusing my blame on what happened back then on the wrong person.'

Tory took the water, soothed her throat. 'The person to blame is the one who killed her.'

'We don't know who that is. It's more of a comfort to put blame on a face and a name. You can pick up that phone, call the police, and bring charges. Chief Russ'll go after him.'

'I just want him gone. I don't expect you to understand.'

'People never do. But surprise.' Considering Tory, Faith eased a hip onto the desk. 'My papa rarely raised a hand to me. I think I got a swat on the butt from time to time, and shame the devil, less often than I deserved it. But he sure knew how to shout, and how to strike terror in a young girl's heart.'

Oh God, she missed him. It catapulted into her. The longing for her father.

'Not because I thought he'd take a strap to me,' she said quietly now. 'But because he let me know every time I let him down. I was afraid to let him down. That's not the same thing as this, I know it. But I'm asking myself, if he'd been a different kind of father, a different kind of man, and I spent my life being afraid, what would I do?'

'You'd call the police and have him thrown in jail.'

'Damn right. But that doesn't mean I don't understand why you aren't. When Papa was cheating with that woman, I never told my mother. For a while I actually believed she didn't know, but I didn't tell her. I thought maybe it would all go away. I was wrong, but thinking it gave me some peace of mind.'

Steadier, Tory set the bottle of water on the desk. 'Why are you being nice to me?'

'I have no idea. Never did like you much, but that was mostly because Hope did and I was contrary. Right now you're sleeping with my brother, and it occurs to me that he means more to me than I realized. It makes sense to get to know you so I can see how I feel about all that.'

'So you're being nice to me because I'm having sex with Cade.'

The dry way it was phrased tickled Faith's humor. 'In a round-about way. And I'll tell you this because it'll piss you off. I feel sorry for you.'

'You're right.' Tory got to her feet, grateful the trembling had stopped. 'It pisses me off.'

'Figured. You don't like sympathy. But the fact is, no one should be afraid of her own father. And no man has the right, blood kin or not, to leave bruises and scars on a child. Now, I'd better go see what kind of trouble that puppy's gotten herself into out there.'

'Puppy?' Tory's eyes went wide. 'What puppy?'

'My puppy. Haven't named her yet.' Faith strolled out, and let out a hoot of laughter. 'Isn't that the cutest thing? She's just a little darling.'

The little darling had found the tissue paper and was currently waging a war on it. Casualties were many and scattered like snow over the floor. She'd managed to find a roll of ribbon as well, and most of that was wound around her chubby torso.

'Oh, for God's sake.'

'Don't take on so. Can't be more than five dollars' worth of supplies. I'll pay for them. There's my baby.'

The pup barked joyfully, tripped over a tail of ribbon, and sprawled adoringly at Faith's feet. 'I swear, I never thought a little bit of a thing like this could make me laugh so much. Look at you, Mama's baby doll, all wrapped up like Christmas.'

She lifted the puppy high and made cooing noises.

'You're acting like an idiot.'

'I know. But isn't she sweet? She just loves me to death, too.

240

Mama's got to clean up this mess now before the mean lady scolds my baby.'

Already on her hands and knees, Tory looked up. 'You set that shop wrecker down in here again, I'll bite your ankle.'

'I've been teaching her to sit. She's smart as a new hat. Just watch.' Despite the threat, Faith set the pup down, kept one hand on its rump. 'Sit. Be a good girl now. Sit for Mama.'

The puppy leaped forward, slapped its tongue against Tory's face, then chased its own tail.

'Some new hat.'

'Isn't she precious?'

'Downright adorable. But she doesn't belong in here.' Gathering up the bulk of the ruined supplies, Tory rose. 'Go take her for a walk or whatever.'

'We were going to buy a nice pretty set of bowls for her food and water.'

'Not my bowls. You are not buying handcrafted pottery bowls designed by artisans for puppy chow.'

'What do you care what I use it for as long as I pay the price?' Only more determined, Faith marched over, scooped up the pup, and picked out two matching bowls of royal blue with bold emerald swirls. 'We like these. Don't we, darling? Don't we, sweet-ums?'

'That's the most ridiculous thing I've ever heard.'

'A sale's a sale, isn't it?' Faith crossed to the counter, set the bowls down. 'Ring me up, and don't forget to add the cost of the supplies.'

'Forget the supplies.' Behind the counter, Tory dumped the tissue in the wastebasket, then dealt with the transaction. 'That's fifty-three dollars and twenty-six cents. For puppy bowls.'

'Fine. I'll pay cash. Here, hold her a minute.'

Faith pushed the pup at Tory so she could dig into her purse.

Charmed despite herself, Tory gave the puppy a nuzzle. 'You're going to be eating like a queen, aren't you? A regular queen bee.'

'Queen Bee. Why, that's just perfect.' Faith laid the money on the counter and snatched the puppy back. 'That's who you are, Queen Bee. I'm going to get you a fancy collar that sparkles.'

Tory shook her head as she made change. 'I'm seeing a whole new side of you, Faith.'

'So am I. I kinda like it. Come on, Bee, we've got places to go and people to see.' She gathered up the shopping bag. 'I don't think I can get the door.'

'I'll get it.' Tory opened it, and after a minute's hesitation, touched Faith's arm. 'Faith. Thank you.'

'You're welcome. Your makeup could use a little freshening,' she added, and left.

She didn't intend to get involved. The way Faith looked at it, other people's personal lives were fascinating to speculate about, to gossip about, but all from a safe and smug distance.

But she kept seeing the way Tory had looked curled up behind the counter, with ribbon and tape and silver cords scattered around her.

She kept seeing that ugly red mark on Tory's neck.

There'd been marks on Hope. She hadn't seen them, no one had let her see them. But she'd known.

She didn't hold with a man pushing a woman around, that's all there was to it. When it was kin, you didn't run to the police. But there were other ways to make things right.

She bent to kiss Bee's head, then walked straight to the bank to tell J.R. what had happened to his niece.

He didn't waste time. J.R. canceled his next appointment, told his assistant manager he had to leave on personal business, and set out for Tory's shop at such a brisk pace his shirt was damp with sweat by the time he got there.

She had customers, a young couple who were debating over a blue-and-white serving platter. Tory was giving them room, staying on the other side of the shop replacing the candle stands she'd sold that morning.

'Uncle Jimmy. Is it heating up out there? You're flushed. Can I get you something cold?'

'No — yes,' he decided. It would give him time to compose himself. 'Whatever you've got handy, honey.'

'I'll just be a minute.' She went into the back, then leaned on the door and cursed. She'd seen it in his eyes. Faith must've made a beeline to the bank. So much for trust, Tory thought, wrenching open the refrigerator. So much for understanding.

Then drawing a cleansing breath, she carried the can of ginger ale out to her uncle.

'Thanks, honey.' He took a good long swig. 'Ah, why don't I buy you lunch?'

'It's not even noon, and I brought something from home. I don't want to close the shop in the middle of the day. But thanks. Gran and Cecil get off all right this morning?'

'First thing. Boots tried to talk them into staying a few days, but you know your gran. She likes to be in her own. Always itchy when she's away from home.'

The young couple started out, with the woman glancing back wistfully. 'We'll come back.'

'I hope you do. Enjoy your day.'

'All right, now let me see.' The door had hardly closed when J.R. set down the ginger ale and took Tory's shoulders. He studied the raw skin on the side of her neck. 'Oh, sweetie. That bastard. Why didn't you call me?'

'Because there was nothing you could do. Because it was over. And because there wasn't a point in worrying you, which is all Faith's done by running down and telling you.'

'Now, you stop that. She did exactly what was right, and I'm beholden to her for it. You didn't want to call the police, and maybe, well, maybe it's easier on your mother if we don't. But I'm family.'

'I know.' She let him draw her into a hug. 'He's gone now. All he wanted was money. He's scared, running scared. They'll catch him before long. I just want it to be away from here. Away from me. I can't help it.'

'Of course you can't. I want a promise from you.' Gently, J.R. held her out at arm's length. 'If you see him around again, even if he doesn't try to get near you, I want you to promise you'll tell me right off.'

'All right. But don't worry. He got what he came for. He's miles away by now.'

She needed to believe it.

Chapter Nineteen

She believed it for the rest of the day. She covered herself with the thin, battle-scarred armor of that belief through the long afternoon. And though she knew it was foolish, she opened one of the candles wrapped and ribboned on display and set it on the counter.

She hoped the light and scent of it would help dispel some of the ugly film her father's visit had smeared on the air.

At six, she locked up, then caught herself scanning the street as she had done for weeks when she'd escaped to New York. It angered her that he could put that cautious anxiety back in her step, that jolt back in her heart.

Had she really stood in the ruin of her mother's house and claimed she could and would face down her father and all that fear if he dared slither into her life again?

Where was her courage now?

All she could do was promise herself she would find it again.

But she locked the car doors the minute she was inside, and her pulse jittered as she constantly shifted her glance from the road ahead to the rearview mirror on the drive home.

She passed cars, even stirred herself to wave at Piney as his pickup rumbled by with a quick toot of the horn. Fieldwork would be done for the day, she thought. Hands would be heading home. And so would the boss.

So it was with an irritating bump of disappointment that she turned into her lane and found it empty. She hadn't realized she'd been expecting Cade to be there, anticipating it. True, she hadn't greeted his statement that he was basically moving in with any real enthusiasm. But the more she thought of it, the easier it had been to accept. And once accepted, enjoyed.

It had been a very long time since she'd wanted companionship. Someone to share the day with, to talk over inconsequential things with, to find little things to laugh over, complain about.

To have someone there when the night seemed too full of sound, and movement, and memories.

And what was she giving back? Resistance, arguments, irritable and unstated agreement.

'Just general bitchiness,' she murmured, as she climbed out of the car. That, at least, she could stop. She could do what women traditionally did to make up for petty crimes. She could fix him a nice dinner, and seduce him.

The idea lifted her mood. Wouldn't he be surprised when she made the moves for a change? She hoped she remembered how, because it was about time she took back a little control. By doing so she'd take some of the responsibility for whatever was going on between them off his shoulders.

She'd tried to please Jack that way, and then . . .

No. She pushed that train of thought firmly away as she unlocked her front door. Cade wasn't Jack, and she wasn't the same woman she'd been in New York. Past and present didn't have to connect.

When she entered she knew that was just one more delusion. She knew he'd been there, inside what she'd tried to make her own home. Her father.

There'd been little for him to destroy, and she didn't think he'd put much effort into it. He hadn't come in to break her few pieces of furniture, or punch holes in the walls. Though he had done some of both.

Her chair was overturned, and he'd taken something sharp to the underside. The lamp she bought only days before was shattered, the table she'd hoped to refinish tossed into the corner with one of its legs snapped like a twig.

She recognized the size and shape of the dents in the wallboard. It was his signature mark, left when for whatever reason he chose to use fists on inanimate objects instead of his daughter.

She left the door open, an escape route in case her instincts were off and he was still in the house.

But the bedroom was empty. He'd yanked off the bedclothes, ripped at the mattress. She supposed the iron bed frame had been more trouble to him than it was worth, as he'd left it be.

The drawers of her dressers were pulled out, her clothes heaped in piles. No, he hadn't really wanted to destroy her things, she mused, or he'd have taken that sharp tool to her clothing as well. He'd done that before, to teach her a lesson about dressing appropriately.

He'd been looking for more money, or for things he could easily sell for cash. If he'd been drinking, it would have been worse. If he'd been drinking, he'd have waited for her. As it was . . . She bent down to pick up a rumpled blouse, then let out a cry of despair when she saw the small carved wooden box she used to hold her jewelry.

She pounced on it, sinking down when she found it empty. Most of what she'd owned had been trinkets, really. Good trinkets, carefully selected, but easily replaced.

But among them had been the garnet and gold earrings her grandmother had given her when she'd turned twenty-one. Earrings that had been her own great-grandmother's. Her only heirloom. Priceless. Irreplaceable. Lost.

'Tory!'

The alarm in Cade's voice, the rush of footsteps, brought her quickly to her feet. 'I'm all right. I'm here.'

He burst into the room, had her pinned against him before she could say another word. Tangled waves of fear and release pumped from him, over and into her.

'I'm all right,' she repeated. 'I just got here. Minutes ago. He was already gone.'

'I saw your car, the living room. I thought—' He tightened his grip, pressed his face into her hair. 'Just hold on a second.'

He knew what it was to have terror dig slick claws into his throat. He'd never thought he'd feel it again.

'Thank God you're all right. I meant to be here before you, but I got hung up. We'll call the police, then you're coming to Beaux Reves. I should have taken you there this morning.'

'Cade, there's no point in all that. It was my father.' She drew away, set the box down on the dresser. 'He came to the shop this morning. We had words. This is just his way of letting me know he can still punish me.'

'Did he hurt you?'

'No.' The denial was quick and automatic, but his gaze had already landed on the side of her neck.

246

He said nothing. He didn't have to. His eyes went dark, narrowed into slits, as violence – she knew how to recognize violence – swam into them. Then he turned away and found the phone.

'Cade, wait. Please. I don't want to call the police.'

His head snapped up, and that same narrowed rage snapped out at her. 'You don't always get what you want.'

Sherry Bellows celebrated her potential job by opening a bottle of wine, turning up her Sheryl Crow CD as loud as her neighbors would tolerate, and dancing around her apartment.

Everything was working out perfectly.

She loved Progress. It was exactly the sort of small, close-knit town she wanted to be a part of. The stars, she thought, had been well aligned when she'd followed instinct and applied for the position at Progress High.

She liked the other teachers. Though Sherry didn't know all her associates very well as yet, that would all change in the fall when she started full-time.

She was going to be a wonderful teacher, someone her students could come to with their problems and their questions. Her classes were going to be fun, and she'd inspire her students to read, to enjoy, to seek out books for pleasure, planting the seeds for a life-long love affair with literature.

Oh, she'd make them work, and work hard, but she had so many ideas, so many fresh and wonderful notions on how to make the work interesting, even entertaining.

Years from now, when her students looked back, they'd remember her fondly. Miss Bellows, they'd say. She made a difference in my life.

It was all she'd ever wanted.

Wanted it enough, she thought now, to study like a demon, to work long and hard to subsidize her scholarship. It had been worth every penny.

She had the bills to prove it.

But that was only money, and she'd found a way to deal with that.

Working at Southern Comfort was going to be a delight. It would help ease the burden of those student loans, give her a little financial breathing room. But more, it would provide her with one more access to the community. She'd meet people, make friends, and before long she'd be a familiar face in Progress.

She was already widening her circle. Her neighbors in the building, Maxine at the vet's. And she planned to cement that connection by giving a party, a kind of potluck get-together sometime in June. A summer kickoff, she mused, that wouldn't conflict with anyone's plans.

She'd invite Tory, too, of course. And Dr. Hunk, the dreamily dimpled vet. She'd definitely like to get to know him better, she decided, as she poured a second glass of wine.

She'd ask the Mooneys. Mr. Mooney at the bank had been so helpful when she'd set up her new accounts. Then there was Lissy at the realtors. A tongue wagger, Sherry admitted, but it was always good to have the town gossip in your camp. You found out such interesting things. And she was married to the mayor.

Another looker, Sherry remembered, with a great smile and a superior butt. A bit of a flirt, too. It was a good thing she'd found out he was married.

She wondered if it would be presumptuous to invite the Lavelles. They were, after all, the VIPs of Progress. Still, Kincade Lavelle had been very nice, very friendly whenever they'd bumped into each other around town.

And talk about gorgeous.

She could make the invitation very casual. It couldn't do any harm. She wanted lots and lots of people. She'd keep the patio doors open as she always did, let guests spill outside.

She loved her pretty little garden apartment, and she could buy another lounge chair to sit outside. The one she had looked lonely out there, and she didn't intend to be lonely.

One day she'd meet the right man, and they'd fall in love over warm nights, and marry in the spring. Start a life together.

She just wasn't meant to stay single. She wanted a family. Not that she'd give up teaching, of course. A teacher was what she was, but there was no reason she couldn't be a wife and mother, too.

She wanted it all, and the sooner the better.

Humming to the music, she stepped out onto the patio, where Mongo was dozing. He stirred enough to thump his tail, and rolled over in case she wanted to scratch his belly.

Obliging, she crouched down, giving him a good rub as she

sipped and glanced idly around. Her patio opened up to a nice grassy area that was bordered by the trees of the park on one side and a quiet residential avenue on the other.

She'd chosen the apartment first because they allowed pets, and where she went, Mongo went. As a bonus it was convenient for their morning runs in the park.

The apartment was small, but she didn't need much room as long as Mongo had a place to exercise. And in a town like Progress, housing didn't cost an arm and two legs as it did in Charleston or Columbia.

'This is the right place for us, Mongo. This is home for us.'

Straightening, she wandered back inside, into the small galley kitchen, as she sang along with Sheryl about her favorite mistake. She'd continue her celebration by fixing herself a huge salad for dinner.

Life, she thought, as she chopped and diced, was good.

Twilight was edging closer by the time she finished. Made too much again, she thought. That was one of the problems with living alone. Still, Mongo liked his carrots and celery, too, so she'd add them to his evening meal. They'd have it on the patio, and she'd treat herself to one more glass of wine, get a little tipsy. Then they'd take a nice long walk, she decided, as she squatted down to scoop Mongo's kibble out of the plastic bin. Maybe get some ice cream.

She lifted the bowl. A movement at the corner of her eye had her heart wheeling into her throat. The bowl flew out of her hands, and she managed one short scream.

Then a hand clamped over her mouth. The knife she'd used to make her dinner pricked at her throat.

'Be quiet. Be very, very quiet, and I won't cut you. Understand?'

Her eyes were already circling wildly. Wings of fear beat in her belly, had her skin going hot and damp. But confusion rode over it. She couldn't see his face, but thought she recognized the voice. It made no sense. No sense at all.

His hand slid slowly away from her mouth to grip her chin. 'Don't hurt me. Please don't hurt me.'

'Now, why would I do that?' Her hair smelled sweet. A whore's blond hair. 'Let's go in the bedroom where we can be comfortable.'

'Don't.' She gasped as the edge of the knife teased along her throat, tipped up her chin. The scream was inside her, desperate to burst out, but the knife turned it into silent tears as he pushed her out of the kitchen.

Her patio doors were closed now, the blinds shut. 'Mongo. What did you do with Mongo?'

'You don't think I'd hurt a nice, friendly dog like that, do you?' The power of the moment cruised through him, spread, made him hard and hot and invincible. 'He's just taking a quiet nap. Don't you worry about your dog, honey. Don't you worry about a thing. This is going to be good. This is going to be just what you want.'

He shoved her belly down on the bed, put his knee in the small of her back and added weight. He'd brought precautions. A man had to be prepared, even for a whore. Especially for a whore.

After a while, they screamed no matter what. And he didn't want to use the knife. Not when he was so good with his hands. He took the bandanna from his pocket, gagged her.

When she began to stir, when she began to struggle, he was in heaven.

She wasn't weak. She kept the body she liked to flaunt and tease men with in good shape. It only excited him to have her struggle. The first time he hit her, the thrill of it slammed into him like sex. He hit her again so they both understood who was in charge.

He tied her hands behind her back. He couldn't afford those nails with their sluttish pink polish scraping any of his skin.

Quietly, he walked over to shut the curtain and close them into the dark.

She was moaning against the gag, dazed from the blows. The sound of it made him tremble so that he nicked her skin a little as he used the knife to cut her clothes away. She tried to roll, tried to buck, but when he put the point of the blade just under her eye, pressed, she went very still.

'This is what you want.' He unzipped, then flipped her onto her back and straddled her. 'It's what you asked for. What you all ask for.'

When it was done, he wept. Tears of self-pity ran down his face. She wasn't the one, but what else could he do? She'd put herself in his path, she'd given him no choice.

It wasn't perfect! He'd done everything he'd wanted and still it wasn't perfect.

Her eyes were glazed and empty as he took off the gag, kissed her cheeks. He cut the cord from her wrists, stuffed it back in his pockets.

He turned her music off, and left the way he'd come in.

'I can't come to Beaux Reves.'

Tory sat on the front porch in the soft night air. She couldn't face going back inside quite yet, wasn't yet prepared to deal with the mess left by her father and compounded by the police.

Cade contemplated the cigar he'd lighted to ease his own nerves, wished fleetingly he had a whiskey to go with it. 'You're going to have to tell me why. Staying here the way things are doesn't make any sense, and you're a sensible woman.'

'Most of the time,' she agreed. 'Being sensible cuts down on complications and saves energy. You were right about calling the police, I realize that now. I wasn't being sensible. It was pure raw emotion. He frightens me, and embarrasses me. By trying to keep it contained, as always, I thought I'd limit the fear and humiliation. It's hateful to be a victim, Cade. Makes you feel exposed and angry and somehow guilty at the same time.'

'I won't argue with that, even though you're smart enough to know that guilt has no part in what you should be feeling.'

'Smart enough to know it, but not clever enough to figure out how not to feel it. It'll be easier once I put the house back to rights and get rid of what he left behind in it. But I'll still remember the way Chief Russ sat writing in his little book and watching my face, how my father intimidated me today, how he's done so all my life.'

'There's no cause for your pride to be wounded over this, Tory.'

' "Pride goeth before a fall." My father reminded me of that this morning. He does love to use the Bible to hammer his point home.'

'They'll find him. There are police in two counties looking for him now.'

'The world's a lot bigger than two counties. Hell, South Carolina's a lot bigger than two counties. Swamps and mountains and glades. Lots and lots of places to hide.' She rocked restlessly, needing movement. 'If he finds a way to contact my mother, she'll help him. Out of love and out of duty.'

'That being the case, it just makes my point about you coming with me to Beaux Reves.'

'I can't do that.'

'Why?'

'A number of reasons. First, your mother would object.'

'My mother has nothing to say about it.'

'Oh, don't say that, Cade.' She pushed out of her chair, walked to the end of the porch. Was he out there? she wondered. Watching? Waiting? 'You don't mean it, or you shouldn't. That's her home, and she has a right in saying who comes into it.'

'Why should she object? Especially after I explain it to her.'

'Explain what?' She turned back. 'That you're installing your lover in her house, because your lover's daddy is a crazy man?'

He drew on his cigar, took his time about it. 'I wouldn't choose those particular words, but more or less.'

'And I'm sure she'll greet me with fresh flowers and a box of fine chocolates. Oh, don't be such a man about this,' she said with a wave of her hand before he could speak. 'Whatever it says on the damn deed, Cade, the house belongs to the woman in it, and I will not intrude on your mother's home.'

'She's a difficult woman at times ... most of the time,' he admitted. 'But she isn't heartless.'

'No, and her heart will not accept the woman she holds responsible for a beloved daughter's death. Don't argue with me about that.' Tory's voice shook, nearly broke. 'It hurts me.'

'All right.' He tossed the cigar aside with one violent gesture, but his hands were gentle enough as he laid them on Tory's shoulders. 'If you won't or can't come with me, then I'll take you to your uncle's.'

'And there we come to the second part of the problem.' She lifted her hands to his. 'Irrational, bullheaded, illogical. I'll admit all that now, so you don't have to feel obliged to point it out to me. I have to make a stand here, Cade.'

'This isn't a strategic hill on a battlefield.'

'For me, it's very much like that. I never thought about it quite that way,' she said with a quiet laugh. 'But yes, this is very much my hill on my own personal battlefield. I've retreated so often. You once called me a coward to get my dander up, but the fact is, I've been one most of my life. I've had small spurts of courage,

252

and that makes it only worse when I see myself fall back yet again. I can't do it this time.'

'How does staying here make you brave instead of stupid?'

'Not brave, and yes, maybe stupid. But whole. I want so much to be whole again. I think I'd risk anything not to have this empty place in me. I can't let him run me out.'

She gazed toward the marsh that grew thicker, deeper, greener with encroaching summer. Mosquitoes whined in there, breeding in the dark water. Alligators slid through it, silent death. It was a place where snakes could slither and bogs could suck the shoe right off your foot.

And it was a place, she thought, that went bright and beautiful with the twinkling of fireflies, where wildflowers thrived in the shade and the stingy light. Where an eagle could soar like a king.

There was no beauty without risk. No life without it.

'When I was a child I lived scared in this house. It was a way of life,' she said, 'and you got used to it the way you get used to certain smells, I suppose. When I came back, I made it mine, shaking out all those bad memories like dust from a rug. Airing out that smell, Cade. Now he's tried to bring the fear back. I can't let him. I won't let him,' she added, shifting until her eyes met his again.

'That's what I did this morning. Don't tell anyone, keep it quiet. One more dirty little secret. If you hadn't pushed me, that's what I'd have done here, too.

'I'm staying. I'm cleaning him out of this place and staying. I hope he knows it.'

'I wish I didn't admire you for it.' He ran a hand down the sleek tail of her hair. 'Make it easier to bully you into doing things my way.'

'You don't have much bully in you.' Maybe it was relief, maybe it was something else that made her stroke her hand over his cheek. 'You maneuver, you don't push.'

'Well, it speaks well for the future of our relationship that you've figured that out and can live with it.' He drew her in, laid his lips on the top of her head. 'You matter to me. No, don't go stiff on me. I'll just have to maneuver you. You matter, Tory, more than I'd planned for you to matter.'

When she remained silent, he let frustration lead. Sometimes it was the most honest way. 'Give me something back. Damn it.'

He jerked her back, then up, crushing his mouth to hers.

She tasted the demand, the heat, the little licks of rage he'd concealed so well. And it was that shot of pure, unfiltered emotion from him that turned another bolt inside her.

God, she didn't want to be loved or needed, didn't want to have those same feelings stirred to life again inside her. But he was here, and just by being made her feel again.

'I've already given you more than I thought I had. I don't know how much more there is.' She held on to him, burrowed into him. 'There's so much happening inside me, I can't keep up with it. It all circles back to you. Isn't that enough?'

'Yeah.' He eased her back to kiss her again, softly this time. 'Yeah, that's enough for now. As long as you make room for more.' He skimmed his thumbs over her cheeks. 'Had a hell of a day, haven't you?'

'I can't say it's been one of my best so far.'

'Let's finish it right, then. We'll get started.'

'On what?'

He opened the screen door. 'You wanted to clean him out. Let's do it.'

They worked together for two hours. He turned on music. She wouldn't have thought of it, would have stayed focused on the details, kept her mind channeled down those strict lines. But the music drifted through the house, into her head, just distracting enough to keep her from brooding.

She wanted to burn the clothes he'd touched, could visualize carrying them outside, heaping them up, striking a match. But she couldn't afford the indulgence. Instead, she washed, folded, put away.

They turned the damaged mattress over. It would have to be replaced, but it would do for now. And with fresh linens, you hardly noticed.

He talked about his work, in a way that had his voice drifting pleasantly through her mind like the music. They dealt with the wreckage of the kitchen, ate sandwiches, and she told him that she was considering hiring on help.

'It's a good idea.' He helped himself to a beer, quietly pleased that she'd stocked some for him. 'You'll enjoy your business more if it doesn't strangle all your time. Sherry Bellows, that's the new high school teacher, isn't it? I met her and her dog a few weeks ago out at the minimart. Seems like a bundle of energy.'

'That was my impression.'

'In a very attractive package.' He grinned and sipped his beer when Tory merely lifted her brows. 'Just thinking of you, darling. An attractive clerk is a business asset. You think she'll wear those little shorts?'

'No,' Tory said firmly. 'I don't.'

'Bound to draw a lot of male customers if you let that be her uniform. That's a girl with very nice pins.'

'Pins. Hmmm. Well, she and her pins depend on how her references check out. But I imagine they will.' Tory swept up the last of the debris, dumped it in the trash. 'That seems to be the best that can be done.'

'Feel better?'

'Yes.' She crossed the room to put away the broom and dustpan. 'Considerably. And I'm very grateful for the help.'

'I'm always open to gratitude.'

She took the pitcher from the refrigerator, poured herself a glass of iced tea. 'The bedroom closet's not very big, but I made some room. And there's an empty drawer in the dresser.'

He said nothing, only drank his beer. Waited.

'You wanted to be able to have some of your things here, didn't you?'

'That's right.'

'So.'

'So?'

'We're not living together.' She set down her glass. 'I've never lived with anyone, and that's not what this is.'

'All right.'

'But if you're going to be spending so much time here, you might as well have a place for some of your things.'

'Very practical.'

'Oh, go to hell.' But there wasn't any heat in the response.

'You're not supposed to smile when you say that.' He set his beer aside, then slid his arms around her.

'What do you think you're doing?'

'Dancing. I never took you dancing. It's something people who aren't really living together ought to do now and then.'

255

It was an old, shuffling number with a boy asking a girl to stand by him when the land was dark.

'Are you trying to be charming?'

'I don't have to try. It's just part of my makeup.' He dipped her, made her laugh.

'Very smooth.'

'All those miserable hours of cotillion had to pay off.'

'Poor little rich boy.' She rested her head on his shoulder and let herself enjoy the dance, the feel of him against her, the scent of him. 'Thanks.'

'You're welcome.'

'When I was driving home tonight, I was thinking of you.'

'I like the sound of that.'

'And I was thinking, so far he's made all the moves. I let him because I wasn't sure if I really wanted to make any of my own, or counter any of his. It was sort of easy to be . . .'

'Maneuvered?'

'I suppose. And I was thinking, I just wonder how Kincade Lavelle would react if I got home and I fixed us a nice supper.'

'He'd have appreciated that.'

'Yes, well, some other time. That part of the thought process didn't pan out. But there was this second part.'

'Which was?'

She lifted her head from his shoulder, met his eyes. 'How would Kincade Lavelle react if after that, once we were all relaxed and quiet, just what would he do if I set out to seduce him?'

'Well . . .' was all he could manage as she pressed closer, ran her hands intimately down his hips. The stirring in his blood was a not-so-quiet delight. 'I think the least I can do, as a gentleman, is let you find out.'

This time it was she who unfastened buttons, his shirt, then her own. She laid her lips over his heart, on the warm skin and vibrant beat.

'I've had your taste with me since the first time you kissed me.' While her lips played over him, she eased the shirt away. 'I can bring tastes back, and I've done that with yours so many times already.'

She trailed her hands over his chest; his belly – a quiver – up to his shoulders. Such broad, tough shoulders. 'I like the feel of you. Long, hard muscles. It excites me. And your hands, roughened from work, riding over me.' She peeled her shirt open, and let it fall to the floor to join his. Watching him, she unhooked her bra, let it slide away.

'Touch me now.'

He cupped her breasts in his hands, the warm, soft weight of them, skimmed the nipples with the edges of his thumbs.

'Yes, like that.' Her head fell back as heat balled in her belly. 'Exactly like that. My insides go liquid when you touch me. Can you see it?' Her eyes, long and dark, met his. 'I want . . .'

'Tell me.'

She moistened her lips, reached for the button of his jeans. His hands flexed on her, one hard caress. 'I want to feel what you feel. I want what's inside you inside me. I've never tried that with anyone else. Never wanted to. Will you let me?'

He bent his head, rubbed his lips over hers. 'Take what you want.'

It was a risk. She would be open, gaping, so much more defenseless than he. But she wanted it, all of it, and that exquisite bond of trust.

Once more she lay her lips on him, and opened mind, heart, body.

It was a bolt, a lightning strike, the power of those coupled needs, images. His desire, layered and tangled inside her with her own. It slashed through her, dark, bright, swollen with energy. Her head snapped back from the punch of it, and she came in one long erotic gush.

'God. God. Wait.'

'No.' He'd never experienced anything like it. The twisted bonds of unity only knotted tighter in a bold and beautiful mass of arousal. 'More.' He set his teeth on her shoulder, craving flesh. 'Again. Now.'

She couldn't stop it, it lashed through her like a storm full of fury and brilliance. It was she who dragged him to the floor, she who panted out pleas, demands, threats as they tore at clothes.

She clawed at him, nipped as they rolled over the floor. His pulse was inside her, a savage beat that crashed against her own. The taste of him, the taste of herself, brewed together to saturate her.

When he plunged into her she felt the urgent pumping of his blood, the desperate maze of his thoughts. Lost. She cried out, once, twice. They were both lost.

She heard her name, his voice calling it inside her mind seconds before it burst from his lips. When he came inside her, dragged her with him, the glory of it made her weep.

Chapter Twenty

Wade had his hands full – what was left of them after the ornery tabby badly misnamed Fluffy mangled them during her shots. Maxine was deep into finals, and he'd given her the day off, which meant he had only two hands to pit against four claws and a number of very sharp teeth.

He'd concluded, an hour before, that he'd made a mistake of horrendous proportions by springing Maxine. He'd started the day with an emergency that required a house call and put him solidly behind. Add the minor war in the waiting area set off by a personality clash between a setter and a bichon, the Olsons' baby goat who'd managed to eat the best part of Malibu Barbie until her arm became lodged in his throat, and Fluffy's vile temper, and he'd had a pisser of a morning.

He was cursing, sweating, bleeding, when Faith rushed in through the back. 'Wade, honey, can you take a look at Bee for me? I think she's feeling poorly.'

'Take a number.'

'It'll only take a minute.'

'I haven't got a minute.'

'Oh now . . . goodness, what happened to your hands?' Faith watched as Wade narrowly avoided another swipe and tucked the cat firmly under his arm. 'Did that mean old pussycat scratch you, darling?'

'Kiss my ass,' was his best response.

'Did she get you there, too?' Faith called out as he marched into the waiting area. 'It's all right, baby.' She nuzzled the puppy. 'Daddy's going to take good care of you in just a minute.'

He came back in to scrub up and dug out antiseptic.

258

'She's been whimpering and sort of moaning all morning. And her nose is a little warm. She doesn't want to play. Just lies there. See?'

Faith set Bee down, and the pup squatted by Wade's feet, looked up at him pitifully, then proceeded to throw up on his shoes.

'Oh! Oh! For goodness sake. Must've been something she ate. Lilah said I shouldn't give her all those cookies.' Faith bit her lip but couldn't quite hold in the giggle. Wade simply stood staring at her, antiseptic in one hand, a thin trickle of blood on the other, and puppy vomit on his shoes.

'We're awfully sorry. Bee, don't you eat that. That's just nasty.' She scooped up the puppy. 'I bet you feel so much better now, don't you, sweetheart? There, see that, Wade? She's wagging her tail again. I just knew if I brought her in to you, everything would be fine.'

'Is that how it looks to you? Like everything's fine?'

'Well, Bee's sicked up what was worrying her, and I don't imagine it's the first time you've had a little doggie puke on you.'

'I've got a waiting room full of patients, my hands are scratched to shit, and now my shoes are going to stink for the rest of the day.'

'Well, go on up and change them then.' She stepped back when he made one of his hands into a claw. She loved the light that came into his eyes when his dander was up. 'Now, Wade.'

He bunched the claw into a fist, then punched it lightly between his own eyes. 'I'm going to go ditch these shoes, and when I come back, I want you to have cleaned this up.'

'Clean it up? Myself?'

'That's right. Put your dog back in surgery, get a mop and bucket, and deal with it. I don't have time for this.' He reached down, pulled off the ruined shoes at the heels. 'And make it fast. I'm behind schedule.'

'Daddy's a little cross this morning,' she murmured to Bee, as Wade strode out to the garbage. She looked at the floor, grimaced. 'Well, at least you got the best part of it on his shoes. It's not so bad.'

When he came back she was dutifully if inexpertly mopping. There were suds gliding across the linoleum on little waves of water. It almost seemed to him they had a current. But he didn't have the heart to complain.

'Almost done here. Bee's in the back playing with her squeaky bone. She's bright-eyed and frisky again.' Faith dumped the mop in the bucket, sloshed more water. 'I guess this needs to dry off some.'

As an alternative to screaming, he rubbed his hands over his face and laughed. 'Faith, you are unique.'

'Of course I am.'

She stepped back as he picked up the bucket, emptied it, rinsed off the mop, then began to slop up suds and water.

'Oh. Well, I suppose that works, too.'

'Do me a favor. Go on out there and tell Mrs. Jenkins to bring Mitch on back. That's the beagle who's been howling the last half hour. And if you can find a way to maintain some sort of order out there for the next twenty minutes, I'll buy you a fancy dinner at your choice of restaurants.'

'Champagne?'

'A magnum.'

'Let's just see what I can do.'

He got his twenty minutes, barely, when he heard the urgent cry.

'Wade! Wade, come quick!'

He bolted out, saw Piney Cobb staggering under the weight of Mongo.

'Ran out into the road, right in front of me. God almighty. He's bleeding pretty bad.'

'Bring him in the back.'

He moved fast. The dog's breathing was labored, his pupils fixed and dilated. His thick fur was matted with blood; and more was dripping on the floor.

'Here, on the table.'

'I hit the brakes,' Piney muttered and stood back. 'Swerved, but I clipped him anyway. I was heading into the hardware for some parts, and he come barreling out of the park right into the street.'

'Do you know if you ran over him?'

'Don't think I did.' With trembling hands he pulled out a faded red bandanna and wiped his sweaty face. 'Knocked him's what I think, but it happened fast.'

'Okay.' Wade grabbed toweling, and since Faith was standing beside him, he simply took her hands, pushed them onto the cloth.

260

'Press down, hard. I want that bleeding under control. He's in shock.'

He yanked open the drug cabinet, grabbed a bottle to prepare a hypo. 'You just hang in there, boy. Just hang on,' he murmured, as the dog began to stir and whimper. 'Keep the pressure firm,' he ordered Faith. 'I'm giving him a sedative. I need to check for internal injuries.'

Her hands had shaken when he'd pressed them to the wound. She thought she'd seen straight down to the bone in the gash gaping down the dog's back leg. And her stomach had flipped over.

She wanted to snatch her hands away from all that blood, to rush out of the room. Why couldn't Piney do it? Why couldn't someone else be here? She started to say so, the words jumping into her throat. She could smell the blood, the antiseptic, and the sour stench of Piney's panic sweat.

But her gaze landed on Wade's face.

Cool, composed, strong. His eyes were flat with concentration, his mouth firmed into one determined line. She stared at him, breathing through her teeth. Watching him work, the quick efficiency of it, the focus, calmed her even as the dog went still again beneath her hands.

'No broken ribs. I don't think the wheel went over him. Might have a bruised kidney. We'll deal with that later. Head wound's pretty superficial. No blood in the ears. The leg's the worst of it.'

And that, he thought, was bad enough. Saving it, and the dog, was going to be tricky.

'I need to move him into surgery.' He glanced back, saw that Piney had dropped into the chair and had his head on his knees. 'I need your hands, Faith. I'm going to lift and carry him, you have to stay with me. Keep the pressure firm. He's lost too much blood. Ready?'

'Oh but, Wade, I—'

'Let's go.'

She did what she was told because he left her no choice. She jogged beside him, fumbling for the door with her free hand. Bee sent up a joyful bark and ran between her feet.

'Sit!' Wade said so sharply, Bee's butt plopped obediently to the floor. The minute he'd laid the sedated dog down he grabbed a thick apron, tossed it to Faith. 'Put that on. I've got to get pictures.'

'Pictures.'

'X rays. Go to his head. Hold him steady as you can.'

The apron weighed like lead, but she dragged it on, did what she was told. Mongo's eyes were slitted, but it seemed to her he was watching her, pleading with her to help.

'It's going to be all right, baby. Wade's going to make everything all right. You'll see.'

The sound of her voice had Bee whining and scooting over to huddle by her feet.

'Get rid of the apron now.' While he waited for the film to develop, Wade shot out orders. 'Come back here and apply pressure again. Keep talking to him. Just let him hear your voice.'

'Okay, all right. Um.' Swallowing what tasted like bile, she pressed the thick padding over the gash. 'Wade's going to fix you up just fine again. You . . . you have to look both ways before you cross the street. You remember that next time. Oh Wade, is he going to die?'

'Not if I can help it.' He slapped the X rays onto a lighted panel, nodded grimly. 'Not if I can help it,' he said again, and started gathering instruments.

Sharp silver tools glinted in the hard overhead light. Her head seemed to circle in time with her stomach. 'You're going to operate? Now? Just like that?'

'I have to try to save the leg.'

'Save it? You mean—'

'Just do what I say, and don't think.'

When he peeled back the compress, her stomach gave a nasty lurch, but he didn't give her time to be sick.

'You hold this, press this button here when I tell you I need suction. You can do that one-handed. When I need an instrument, I'll describe it. Give it to me handle first. I'm going to knock him out now.'

He lowered the light, cleaned the field. All Faith could hear now was the slurping noises of her hose when he demanded suction, the click and clatter of tools. She averted her eyes, wanted to keep them that way, but he kept snapping out orders that required her to look.

Before long, it was like a movie.

Wade's head was bent, his eyes cool and calm, though she saw beads of sweat pearling on his forehead. It seemed to her his hands were like magic, moving so delicately through blood, flesh, and bone.

She didn't even blink when he slid the protruding bone back into place. None of it was real.

She watched him suture impossibly tiny stitches inside the gash. The raw yellow of the sterile wash he'd used stained his hands, mixed with the blood until it was all the color of an aging bruise.

'I need you to check his heart rate manually. Just use your hand, gauge his heartbeat for me.'

'It's kind of slow,' she said when she pressed down. 'But it seems steady. Like, bump, bump, bump.'

'Good, take a look at his eyes.'

'Pupils are awfully big.'

'Any blood in the whites?'

'No, I don't think so.'

'Okay, he needs some pins in this leg. Bone shattered more than broke. Once that's done I'll close it. Then we'll set the leg.'

'Is he going to be all right?'

'He's healthy.' Wade used his forearm to wipe his brow. 'And he's young. He's got a good chance to keep the leg.'

He worried about the bone chips. Had he gotten them all? There'd been muscle damage, some badly ripped tendons, but he felt confident he'd repaired the worst of it.

All this ran through one part of his mind while the rest was focused on securing bone with steel.

'I'll know better in a day or two. I need gauze and tape. That cabinet there.'

Once he'd closed the wound, Wade bandaged and set the leg, then checked the dog's vitals himself. He treated the raw scrape on the muzzle, behind the left ear. 'He held up,' Wade murmured, then for the first time in over an hour, looked directly at Faith. 'So did you.'

'Yeah, well, I was a little queasy at first, then . . .' She lifted her hands, started to gesture. They were streaked with blood, as was her blouse. 'Oh. Oh my,' was all she managed before her eyes rolled back.

He caught her, barely, then stretched her out on the floor. She was already coming around when he lifted her head and brought a paper cup of water to her lips.

'What happened?'

'You fainted, gracefully and at a convenient moment.' He brushed his lips over her cheek. 'I'll take you upstairs. You can clean up and lie down for a bit.'

'I'm all right.' But when he helped her stand, her legs wobbled. 'Okay, maybe not. I might be better off flat out for a while longer.'

She dropped her head on his shoulder, half floating as he carried her up. 'I don't think I'm cut out to be a nurse.'

'You did great.'

'No, you did. I never thought, never understood why you do what you do. Always figured it as giving out shots and cleaning up dog poop.'

'There's a lot of that.'

He carried her into the bathroom where he could brace her on the sink and run warm water in the bowl. 'Just put your hands in here. You'll feel better when they're clean.'

'There's a lot more, Wade, to what you do. And to you.' Her eyes met his in the mirror. 'I haven't been paying attention, haven't bothered to look close enough. You saved a life today. You're a hero.'

'I did what I was trained to do.'

'I know what I saw, and what I saw was heroic.' She turned, kissed him. 'Now, if you don't mind, I'm going to strip to the skin and get in the shower.'

'You steady enough?'

'Yeah, I'm fine. You go check on your patient.'

'I love you, Faith.'

'I think you do,' she said quietly. 'And it's nicer than I expected. Go on now, my head's still light enough for me to say something I'll regret later.'

'I'll be back up when I can.'

He checked on Mongo first, then cleaned up before stepping out into the examining room. Piney was still in the chair, and now Bee was curled sleeping in his lap.

Wade had forgotten about both of them.

'That dog gonna make it?'

'It looks good.'

'Oh Jesus, Wade. I'm just sick about it. I've been going over it in my head, and if I'd been paying more attention. I was just driving along and my mind was wandering, and next thing I knew that dog jumped right out in the road. Could've been a kid.'

'It wasn't your fault.'

'Hit me a deer a time or two. Don't know why it didn't bother me like this. Mostly I'd just get pissed off. Deer can do a hell of a number on a truck. Some kid's gonna come home from school looking for that dog.'

'I know the owner. I'll give her a call. You getting him here fast made a big difference. That's what you ought to remember.'

'Yeah, well.' He sighed hugely. 'This little gal's right cute,' he said, stroking Bee's head. 'She came out here looking for trouble, chewed on my bootlaces for a bit, then she conked right out.'

'I appreciate your looking out for her.' Wade reached down and picked her up. Bee yawned hugely, then licked at the cat scratches on his hand. 'Are you going to be all right?'

'Yeah. Tell the God's truth, I'm going to go get me a drink. Cade's probably sent out the marines for me by now, but that's just gonna have to wait.' He got to his feet. 'You let me know how that dog goes on, now, will you?'

'Sure.' He slapped Piney's shoulder as they walked out.

The waiting room was clear. Wade imagined most of his patients got tired of the delay and left. He could only be grateful for the quiet.

He set Bee down with one of the dog treats Maxine kept in her desk drawer, then looked up Sherry Bellow's number in his files.

The answering machine picked up, so he left a message. She'd be out looking for her dog, he supposed. More than likely she'd run into someone who'd seen the accident.

He left it at that and went back in to Mongo.

Minutes after Wade talked to Sherry's machine, Tory listened to the same cheery voice announcing she wasn't able to come to the phone. 'Sherry, this is Tory Bodeen at Southern Comfort. I'd like you to call or come by when you get a chance. If you're still interested, you've got a job.'

The decision felt good, Tory thought, as she replaced the receiver. Not only had Sherry's references been glowing, but it might even be fun to have a bright face and willing hands around the shop for a few hours a week.

Business was slow today, but she wasn't discouraged. It took time to establish yourself, to become part of people's routines. And she'd had a handful of browsers that morning.

She used the downtime to work out an affordable schedule for her new employee. She got out the forms she'd need to fill out for tax records and added the list of store policies she'd typed.

She toyed with the wording for an ad in the Sunday paper that would include the linens she'd decided to carry. When her bells chimed, she looked up quickly, with the same bump in the heart she'd experienced at the sound all day.

But the sight of Abigail Lawrence made her set down her pen and smile. 'What a nice surprise.'

'Told you I'd find my way here. Tory, this is just lovely. You have beautiful things.'

'We have some very talented artists.'

'And you know just how to display their work.' Abigail held out a hand as Tory came around the counter. 'I'm going to have a wonderful time spending money here.'

'Don't let me stop you. Can I get you anything? A cold drink, a cup of tea?'

'No, not a thing. Oh, is that batik?'

Abigail crossed over to admire a framed portrait of a young woman standing on a garden path.

'She does wonderful work. I have a few of her scarves in stock as well.'

'I'll have to take a look. I want to see everything. But I can tell you I want this batik. It's perfect for my husband to give me for our anniversary.'

Amused, Tory turned to lift it from the wall. 'And does he want it gift wrapped?'

'Naturally.'

'How long have you been married?'

Abigail cocked her head as Tory carried the batik to the counter. In all the time she'd been Tory's lawyer, she never remembered her asking a personal question. 'Twenty-six years.'

'So you were married at ten?'

Abigail beamed, examined a box of polished burl wood. 'Shopkeeping agrees with you.' She carried the box to the counter herself. 'I think this town does, too. You're at home here.'

'Yes. This is home. Abigail, did you really come up from Charleston to shop?'

'That, and to see you. And to talk to you.'

Tory nodded. 'If you found out more about the girl who was murdered, you don't have to ease me into it.'

'I didn't learn any more about her. But I did ask my friend to do that check on like crimes, crimes that had taken place during the last two weeks of August.'

'There are others.'

'You already knew.'

'No, felt. Feared. How many more?'

'Three that fit the profile and time frame. A twelve-year-old girl who went missing during a family trip to Hilton Head in August 1975. A nineteen-year-old coed taking summer classes at the university in Charleston in August 1982, and a twenty-six-year-old woman who'd been camping with friends in Sumter National Forest. August 1989.'

'So many,' Tory whispered.

'All were sexual homicides. Raped and strangled. There was no semen. There was some physical violence, particularly in the facial area. That escalates with each victim.'

'Because their faces aren't right. Their faces aren't hers. Hope's.'

'I don't understand.'

Tory wished she didn't. Wished the sickness of it wasn't so horribly clear. 'They were all blondes, weren't they? Pretty, slim builds?'

'Yes.'

'He keeps killing her. Once wasn't enough.'

Abigail shook her head, a little concerned at the way Tory's eyes went vague and dark. 'It's possible they were killed by the same man, but—'

'They were killed by the same man.'

'The length of time between the murders deviates from the typical serial-killer profile. So many years between. Now, I'm not a criminal lawyer, and I'm not a psychologist, but I have done some studying up on this subject in the last week or two. The ages of the victims don't fit the standard profile.'

'This isn't standard, Abigail.' Tory opened the burl box, closed it again. 'It isn't typical.'

'There has to be a basis. Your friend and the twelve-year-old indicate a pedophile. It appears to me a man who chooses children as victims doesn't switch to young women.'

'But he's not switching anything. Their ages have everything to do with it. Every one was the age Hope would have been if she'd lived. That's the pattern.'

'Yes, I agree with you, though neither of us is experts in this area. I suppose I felt obligated to point out the flaws.'

'There may be more.'

'That's being investigated as well, though at this point, my contact assures me, none has been found. The FBI is looking into it.' Abigail's pretty mouth firmed. 'Tory, my contact wanted to know why I was interested, how I'd learned of the hitchhiker. I didn't tell him.'

'Thank you.'

'You could help.'

'I don't know that I can. Even if they'd let me, I don't know if I'm capable. It freezes me up inside. It was never easy. Always wrenching. And now, I don't want to face that again, to put myself through that again. I can't help them. This is for the police.'

'If that's really how you feel, then why did you ask me to find out?'

'I had to know.'

'Tory—'

'Please don't. Please. I don't want to go back there again. I'm not sure I'd come out whole again this time.' To keep her hands busy, she began shifting items on a shelf. 'The police, the FBI, they're the experts here. This is their job, not mine. I don't want the faces of all those people in my head, what happened to them, inside my head. I already have Hope.'

Coward. The voice whispered the taunt in her ear throughout the rest of the day. She didn't ignore it, she accepted it. And she was going to learn how to live with it.

She knew what she needed to know. Whoever had killed Hope was still killing, selectively. Efficiently. And it was the job of the police, or the FBI, or some special task force to hunt him down and stop him.

It was not up to her.

And if her deepest and most personal fears were realized and that killer had her father's face, could she live with that?

They would find Hannibal Bodeen soon. Then she would decide.

When she locked up for the day, she thought it might do her good to walk around town, through the park. She could drop by Sherry's and speak with her instead of her answering machine. Take care of business, Tory reminded herself. Take care of yourself.

Traffic was light. Most would already be home from work, sitting down to supper. Children had already been called in to wash up, and the evening, long and bright, would stretch out with television and porch sitting, homework and dirty dishes.

Normal. Everyday. Precious for its simple monotony. And she wanted it for herself with a quiet desperation.

She cut through the park. Roses were blooming and pools of wax begonias spread in crimson and white. Trees cast long shadows and welcome shade, and a few people sat or stretched under them. Young people, Tory noted, not yet stone-set in the tradition of five-thirty supper. They'd go out for pizza later, or a burger, then flock somewhere with others like them to listen to music or their own voices.

She'd done the same once, briefly. But it seemed like decades ago. It seemed like another woman entirely who had elbowed her way into a crowded club, to dance, to laugh. To be young.

She'd already lost all that once. She would not lose the new life she'd just begun.

Deep in thought, she came out of the line of trees and started across the green slope that led to the apartment building.

Bee shot across the lawn like a bullet, yapping insanely.

'You sure get around, don't you?' Charmed, Tory crouched and let herself be attacked.

'She's been inside most of the day.' Faith strolled up, pleased when her pup deserted Tory to leap on her. 'She's got a lot of energy.'

'So I see.' Tory glanced up, pursed her lips as she straightened. 'That's not your usual look,' she commented, studying the over-large T-shirt over Faith's linen slacks.

'Still works for me, doesn't it? I spilled something on my blouse earlier. Borrowed this from Wade.'

'I see.'

'Yes, I suppose you do. You have a problem with that?'

'Why should I? Wade's a big boy.'

'I could say something crude about that, but I'll let it pass.' Faith skimmed her sleek hair behind her ear, smiled broadly. 'Tired of the solitude of the marsh? Going apartment hunting?'

'No, I like my house. I'm just dropping by to see a potential employee. Sherry Bellows.'

'Well, that's a coincidence. I'm here to see her myself. Wade's still tied up at his office, and he hasn't been able to reach her all day. Her dog was hit by a car late this morning.'

'Oh no.' Instantly the reserve fled. 'She'll be heartbroken.'

'He's doing all right. Wade went right to work on him. Saved his life.' It was said with such pride, Tory could only stare. 'He's not sure how well the dog's leg will heal, but I'm betting it'll be right as rain.'

'I'm glad to hear it. He's a beautiful dog, and she seems to love him so much. I can't believe she'd go off for the day and leave him running loose.'

'You just never know about people. Her apartment's there.' Faith pointed. 'I was around front, but she didn't answer the knock, so I thought I'd poke back here. Her neighbor said she uses this door more than the front.'

'Blinds are closed.'

'Maybe the door's open. We can slip in and leave her a note, anyway. Wade really wants to get ahold of her.' She crossed the patio, reached for the handle of the sliding glass door.

'Don't!' Tory gripped her shoulder, jerked her back.

'What in the hell's wrong with you? It's not breaking and entering, for Christ's sake. I'm just going to poke my head in.'

'Don't go in there. Don't go in.' Tory's fingers dug into Faith's shoulder.

She'd already seen. It had slapped in front of her face, jumped there almost gleefully, and the copper penny taste of blood and fear pooled in her mouth.

'It's too late. He's been here.'

'What are you talking about?' Faith gave her arm an impatient jerk. 'Would you please let go?'

'She's dead,' Tory said flatly. 'We have to call the police.'

Hope

'Hope' is the thing with feathers –
That perches in the soul –
And sings the tune without the words –
And never stops – at all –
                          – Emily Dickinson

Chapter Twenty-One

She couldn't go in. She couldn't make herself leave.

The deputy who'd answered the call had been both skeptical and annoyed, but he hadn't been able to hold out against what he considered two overreacting females.

He'd hitched at his belt, tugged on his cap, then had knocked loudly on the glass panel of the door. Tory could have told him Sherry was incapable of answering, but he wouldn't have listened or understood.

But two minutes after he'd stepped inside, he was back out again. And the irritated smirk was no longer on his face.

It didn't take long to get the wheels rolling. When Chief Russ arrived the scene was closed off with yellow police tape and those who moved in and out carried the tools of their trade and their badges.

Tory sat on the ground and waited.

'I called Wade.' Since there was nothing else to do, Faith sat down beside her. 'He has to wait until Maxine comes to look after Mongo, but he's coming.'

'There's nothing for him to do.'

'There's nothing for any of us to do.' Faith stared at the tape, the door, the shadows of men moving around behind the blinds. 'How did you know she was dead?'

'Sherry? Or Hope?'

Faith clutched the puppy to her breast, rubbed her cheek against warm fur for comfort. 'I've never seen anything like this. They wouldn't let me near where Hope was. I was too young. You saw it.'

'Yes.'

273

'You saw it all.'

'Not quite all.' She pressed her palms together, squeezed her hands between her knees as if they were very cold. 'I knew when we got to the door. There's darkness about death. Violent death especially. And he left something of himself behind. Maybe just the madness of it. It's the same as before. He's the same.' She closed her eyes. 'I thought he would come for me – I never considered . . . I never imagined this.'

And that was the guilt she would live with now.

'You're saying whoever did this to Sherry killed Hope? After all these years?'

Tory started to speak, then shook her head. 'I can't be sure. I haven't been sure of anything in a long time.' She glanced over as she heard Faith's name called. Wade ran across the grass toward them.

It surprised her when Faith leaped up. It was rare to see Faith bother to move quickly. Then she watched them take each other. One long, hard embrace.

He loves her, Tory realized. She's the center of things for him. How odd.

'You're all right?' He put his hands on Faith's face, cupped it there.

'I don't know what I am.' She had been all right. Everything had seemed to hold at a distance, far enough away not to touch her. Now her hands wanted to shake and her stomach jump. The same way she'd reacted after the surgery when there had been blood on her hands. 'I think I need to sit down again.'

'Here.' When she lowered to the grass, he knelt, his hand still clutching Faith's while he studied Tory's face. Too calm, he decided. Too controlled. It only meant when she broke, she'd shatter. 'Why don't y'all come back with me. You need to get away from here.'

'I can't, but you should take Faith.'

'So you can see it through and I can't? I don't think so,' Faith said.

'It's not a competition.'

'Between you and me? It's always been. There's Dwight.'

People had started to gather in small pockets of murmurs and curiosity. Word traveled lightning fast in Progress, Tory thought dully. She watched Dwight move through the gatherings and head straight for Sherry's door.

274

'Maybe you can talk to him, Wade.' Faith gestured in Dwight's direction. 'Maybe he'll be able to tell us something.'

'I'll see.' He touched Tory's knee before he rose. 'Cade's on his way.'

'Why?'

'Because I called him. Just wait here.'

'There was no need for that,' Tory said, frowning at Wade's back as he slipped through the crowd of onlookers.

'Oh, shut up.' Annoyed, Faith dug in her purse for a chewy bone to keep Bee occupied. 'You're no more iron woman than I am. It doesn't make us less to lean on a man.'

'I don't intend to lean on Cade.'

'For Christ's sake, if he's good enough to sleep with, he's good enough to hold on to at a time like this. I swear, you just hunt up things to be bitchy about.'

'Why don't we all go out on a double date later? We can go dancing.'

Faith's smile was scalpel sharp. 'You're a real pain in the ass, Tory. I'm starting to like that about you. Well shit, there's Billy Clampett, and he's spotted me. That just makes it perfect. I was nearly pissed off enough, and drunk enough, one night a thousand years ago to have sex with him. Fortunately I came to my senses in time, but he's never stopped trying to finish things off.'

Tory watched Billy stroll toward them, thumbs tucked in his front pockets, fingers beating out a tune on either side of his zipper. 'There couldn't be enough liquor in the country for that.'

'Finally, a point of agreement. Billy.'

'Ladies.' He crouched down. 'Heard there was some excitement 'round here. Some girl went and got herself killed.'

'Careless of her.' Faith didn't shift away, wouldn't give him the satisfaction, though she could smell his evening beer on his breath.

'Heard it was Sherry Bellows. She's the one who runs around town with that big shaggy dog. Wears little shorts and low-cut tops. Sort of advertising the wares.'

He took a cigarette out of the pack he had rolled in the sleeve of his T-shirt. He thought the effect made him look like James Dean. 'Sold her some annuals a couple weeks back. She was mighty friendly, if you catch my meaning.'

'Tell me, Billy, do you practice being disgusting or is it just a gift?'

It took him a minute, but his smile went sour as old milk as he struck a match and puffed the cigarette to life. 'Aren't you Miss High and Mighty all of a sudden.'

'Nothing sudden about it. I've always been high and mighty. Isn't that right, Tory?'

'I've never known you to be otherwise. It's a bit like a birth-mark.'

'Exactly.' Delighted, Faith slapped a hand on Tory's thigh. She took out a cigarette of her own. 'We Lavelles,' she began, lighting it and blowing smoke, coolly, into Billy's face, 'are destined to be superior. It's just stamped on our DNA.'

'You weren't so superior that night behind Grogan's when I had your tits in my hands.'

'Oh.' Faith smiled, blew more smoke. 'Was that you?'

'Ever since you grew tits you've been a slut. You better watch yourself.' He glanced deliberately at Sherry's door. 'Sluts end up getting just what they ask for.'

'I remember you now,' Tory said quietly. 'You used to tie fire-crackers to cats' tails and light them, and then you'd go home and masturbate. Is that still how you spend your leisure time?'

He jerked back. There was no smile on his face now, and fear had replaced the sneer in his eyes. 'We don't need you around here. We don't need your kind.'

He might have left it at that, he was frightened enough to, but Bee decided his pant leg was more interesting than her bone. Billy sent her flying with the back of his hand.

With a cry of outrage, Faith scrambled to her feet to scoop up the whining dog. 'You yellow-bellied, beer-soaked, half-peckered asshole. No wonder your wife's shopping for a new man. You can't get it up with your own fist.'

He started to lunge at Faith. Tory didn't know how it happened, and it seemed to be happening to someone else. But her fist popped out of her lap and connected with his eyes. The force and shock of the blow knocked him on his ass. Dimly she heard shouts and squeals and running feet, but as Billy leaped up so did she.

All of her rage rolled into one hot ball inside her. She could already taste the blood.

'Fucking bitch.'

When he charged she planted her feet. She wanted violence. Welcomed it. Even as he swung back, he went sprawling.

'Try me,' Cade suggested, and hauled him to his feet. 'Stay out of it,' he snapped, as people rushed up to interfere. 'Come on, Billy. Let's see how you handle me instead of a woman half your size.'

'You've had this coming for years.' The sneer was back. He crouched, burning with the need to restore himself in front of the town, desperate to pound his bunched fists into the haughty face of one of the Lavelles. 'When I'm done with you, I'm going to have some fun with your whore sister and your cunt.'

He came in hard. Cade simply sidestepped. It only took two blows, an uppercut that snapped Billy's head back and a fast, vicious jab to the gut.

Cade bent down and, pressing his thumb on Billy's windpipe, whispered in his ear, 'If you ever touch my sister or my woman, if you ever speak to them, ever look at them, I'll wrap your balls around your throat and choke you with them.'

He dropped Billy's head back to the ground and walked toward Tory without a backward glance. 'This isn't the place for you now.'

She couldn't find her voice. She'd never seen fury burst, then retreat so easily. Almost elegantly, she thought. He'd battered a man to the ground without breaking a sweat and now he was speaking to her gently. And his eyes were cold as winter.

'Come on away with me now.'

'I have to stay.'

'No, you don't.'

'Sorry to say, she does.' Carl D. walked up, turned his gaze down at Billy, rubbed his chin in a thoughtful manner. 'Have some trouble out here?'

'Billy Clampett made insulting remarks.' Instantly soft tears swam into Faith's eyes and turned them the color of dew-drenched bluebells. 'He was – well, I can't even begin, but he was very offensive to me and to Tory, then he . . .' She sniffled delicately. 'Then he struck my poor little Bee here, and when Tory tried to stop him, he . . . If it hadn't been for Cade, I don't know what might have happened.'

She turned to Tory, sobbing quietly. 'You could've taken him,' she murmured. 'Fat, puss-faced asshole.'

Carl D. tucked his tongue in his cheek. After what he'd seen inside, this little comedy was an entertaining relief. 'That about how it was?' he asked Cade.

'More or less.'

'I'll have him taken in so's he cools off some.' He glanced around, making eye contact with faces in the crowd as he gently chewed his gum. 'Don't think anybody wants to press charges here.'

'No, we'll let it lay.'

'Good enough. I'm gonna need to talk to Tory here, and Faith, too. We can be a little more private down at the station.'

'Chief.' Wade joined them, stepping so casually over the half-conscious Billy, Faith had to disguise a snort of laughter with a wet sniffle. 'My place is closer. I think it'd be more comfortable for the ladies.'

'We might could do that, for a start; anyway. I'm going to have one of my deputies take you on over. I'll be along directly.'

'I'll take them,' Wade said.

'You and Cade know most of these people. I'd appreciate if you'd give me a hand getting them to go on home. One of my men'll see to the ladies here. I need to get their statements,' he said, before Cade could object. 'That's police business.'

'We can get there by ourselves.'

'Well now, Miss Faith, I'll just send one of my men along with you. It's procedure.' He signaled, and set the wheels in motion.

'Jesus, how does something like this happen in the middle of town?' Dwight rubbed at the tension in the back of his neck.

They'd managed to nudge most of the curious away from the building. Now it was darkness that gathered as he stood with his two oldest friends on the quiet lawn outside the apartment where death wore the symbol of yellow police tape.

'How much do you know?' Wade asked him.

'No more than anyone else, I expect. Carl D. didn't let me past the edges, and I only got that far because I'm mayor. It looks like somebody broke into her place sometime yesterday. Maybe it was a robbery.' He pinched the bridge of his nose, shook his head. 'Doesn't seem like it. Didn't look to me like she had a lot.'

'How'd they get by the dog?' Wade wondered.

'Dog?' Dwight looked blank a moment, then nodded. 'Oh yeah. I don't know. Maybe it was someone she knew. That makes more sense, doesn't it? Maybe it was someone she knew, and they had an argument that got out of hand. She was in the bedroom,' he added on a sigh. 'That much I know. The – well, the bits and pieces I heard said she was raped.'

'How was she killed?' Cade asked him.

'I don't know. Carl D. was keeping a tight lid on most of it. Jesus, Wade, we were just talking about her the other night, remember. I ran into her coming out of your place.'

'Yeah, I remember.' He got a picture of her, bubbling over, flirting, while he examined Mongo.

'There were some murmurs in there.' Dwight jerked his head toward the sealed door. 'About Tory Bodeen. Edgy talk,' he added. 'I figure you'd want to know.' He sighed again. 'This shouldn't happen in the middle of damn town. People ought to be safe in their own houses. This is going to worry Lissy sick.'

'There'll be a run on the hardware store and gun shop tomorrow,' Cade predicted. 'Locks and ammo.'

'Oh Christ. I'd best call a town meeting, see if I can calm people down. I hope to God Carl D. has something on this by tomorrow. I've got to get back to Lissy. She'll be in a state by now.' He shot one last look at the door. 'This shouldn't have happened here,' he repeated, and walked away.

'I only met her once. Just yesterday.'

Tory sat on Wade's sofa with her hands neatly folded in her lap. She knew it was important to be calm and clear when talking to the police. They picked at emotion, used weaknesses as levers to pry out more than you wanted to say.

Then they made you ridiculous.

Then they betrayed you.

'You only met her the once.' Carl D. nodded, made his notes. He'd asked Faith to wait downstairs. He wanted his interviews, and the facts he gleaned from them, on separate pages. 'Why'd you happen to go by her place today?'

'She applied for a job at my store.'

'That so?' He cocked a brow. 'I thought she had herself a job. Teaching at the high school.'

'Yes, so she told me.' Answer the questions exactly, she reminded herself. Don't add, don't elaborate. 'Not full-time until fall, though, and she wanted something part-time to supplement her income. And to keep her busy, I think. She seemed to have a lot of energy.'

'Uh-huh. So you went on and hired her.'

'No, not immediately. She gave me references.' Wrote them

279

down, she remembered, along with her address, on the clipboard. The clipboard that she'd left on the counter when her father had come in. Oh God. Oh God.

'Well, that's a sensible thing. Didn't know you were hiring at your place.'

'I hadn't really thought about it, until she came in. She was persuasive. I took some time to go over my budget and decided I could afford light part-time help. I checked her references this morning, then I called her. I got her machine and left a message.'

'Um-hmm.' He'd already heard her message, and the ones from Wade's office. The one from her upstairs neighbor, the one from Lissy Frazier. Sherry Bellows had been a popular lady. 'Then you decided to go on over in person.'

'After I closed for the day, I wanted a walk. I decided I'd take one through the park and drop by her apartment. That way, if she was in, I could discuss the job with her.'

'You went over there with Faith Lavelle?'

'No. I went over alone. I ran into Faith outside the building, the back of the building. She said Sherry's dog had been injured earlier in the day. He'd been hit by a car and Wade had treated him. She'd come over as a favor to Wade, as they'd been unable to reach her.'

'So you got there at the same time.'

'Yes, more or less. That would have been around six-thirty, as I closed up and left the shop about six-ten or six-fifteen.'

'And when Miss Bellows didn't answer, you went on in looking for her.'

'No. Neither of us went inside.'

'But you saw something that worried you.' He looked up from his pad. She sat perfectly still, kept her eyes on his, and said nothing. 'You were worried enough to call the police.'

'She didn't return my call, though she appeared to be very eager for the job. She didn't return Wade's, though it was obvious to me from our one and only meeting that she adored her dog. Her blinds were shut, the door was closed. I called the police. Neither Faith nor I went inside. Neither of us saw anything. So I can't tell you anything.'

He sat back, gnawed on his pencil. 'Did you try the door?'

'No.'

'It wasn't locked.' He let the silence hang, filled the time by getting out his pack of gum, offering it to Tory. When she shook her head he took out a stick, unwrapped it, carefully folded the wrapper.

Tory's heart began to dance in her chest.

'So . . .' Carl D. folded the gum as carefully as he had its wrapper, slipped it into his mouth. 'You two had gone over. Now, knowing Faith Lavelle, I'd say she'd have poked her head in — curiosity if nothing else. What's this new teacher got in her place, that kind of thing.'

'She didn't.'

'You knocked? Called out?'

'No, we—' She broke off, fell silent.

'You just stopped there at the door and decided to call the police.' He let out a sigh. 'You're going to make me pull some teeth here. Now, I'm a simple man, got simple ways. And I've been a cop more'n twenty years. Cop's got instincts, gets hunches in the gut. Can't always explain them. They just are. Could be you got like a hunch today outside the door of Sherry Bellows's apartment.'

'It's possible.'

'Some people tend toward hunches. You might say you had one eighteen years ago when you led us to Hope Lavelle. You had more of them up in New York. A lot of people were glad you did.'

His voice was kind, a soft roll of words, but his eyes, she noted, were watchful. 'What happened in New York has nothing to do with this.'

'It has to do with you. Six kids got back home because you had hunches.'

'And one didn't.'

'Six did,' Carl D. repeated.

'I can't tell you any more than I've told you.'

'Maybe you can't. Strikes me as more that you won't. I was there eighteen years ago when you led us to that little girl. I'm a simple man with simple ways, but I was there. And I was there today, looking down at that young woman and what had been done to her. It took me back. I was at both those places, saw both those things. And so did you.'

'I didn't go in.'

'But you saw.'

'No!' She surged to her feet. 'I didn't. I felt. I didn't see, and I didn't look. There was nothing I could do. She was dead, and

281

there was nothing I could do for her. Or for Hope. Or any of them. I don't want that inside me again. I've told you everything I know, exactly as it happened. Why isn't that enough?'

'All right. Now, all right, Miss Tory. Why don't you sit down there, try to relax, while I go down and talk to Faith.'

'I'd like to go home now.'

'You just sit down and catch your breath a little. We'll see you get home soon enough.'

He chewed over his thoughts on her and her reaction to his questions as he walked downstairs. The girl, he decided, was a basket of troubles. He could be sorry for it. But that wouldn't stop him from using her if it suited his purposes. He had a murder in his town. It wasn't the first, but it was damn near the ugliest in a good many years.

And he was a man who had hunches. His gut told him Tory Bodeen was the key.

He found Cade pacing at the bottom of the stairs. 'You can go on up to her. I expect she could use a shoulder. Your sister around?'

'She's in the back, with Wade. He's checking on the dog.'

'Too bad that dog can't talk. Was Piney clipped him, wasn't it?'

'So I'm told.'

'Yeah, too bad that dog can't talk.' He patted his notebook pocket and wandered into the back.

Cade found Tory still sitting on the sofa.

'I should have just walked away. Or better, smarter, I should have let Faith go in the way she wanted to. Faith would have found her, we'd have called the police, and there'd have been no questions.'

He moved over to sit beside her. 'Why didn't you?'

'I didn't want her to see what was in there. I didn't want to see it, either. And now Chief Russ expects me to go into a trance and give him the name of the killer. It was Professor Plum in the conservatory with the candlestick. I'm not a goddamn board game.'

He took her hand. 'You've every right to be angry. With him, with the situation. Why are you angry with yourself?'

'I'm not. Why would I be?' She looked down at their joined hands. 'You bruised your knuckles.'

'Hurts like a son of a bitch.'

'Really? It didn't seem like it when you hit him. It didn't seem like you felt anything but mild annoyance. I really must swat this pesky fly, then get back to my book.'

He grinned at that, brought her hand to his lips. 'As a Lavelle, one must maintain one's dignity.'

'Bull. I said that's what it seemed like, but that wasn't the reality of it. Rage and disgust were the reality, and you enjoyed flattening him. I know,' she said with a sigh. 'Because that's what I was feeling. He's an ugly man, and he'll try to find another way to hurt you now. But he'll come at your back, because he's afraid of you. And no, that's just good sense and a reasonable understanding of human nature, not my fabulous psychic powers.'

'Clampett doesn't worry me.' He rubbed his bruised knuckles over her cheek. 'Don't let him worry you.'

'I wish I could.' She got to her feet. 'I wish I could worry about him so it would occupy my mind. Why should I feel guilty?'

'I don't know, Tory. Why should you?'

'I barely knew Sherry Bellows. I spent less than an hour with her, no more than a brush on my life. I'm sorry for what happened to her, but does that mean I have to get involved?'

'No.'

'It won't change what happened to her. Nothing I do will change what happened. So what's the point? Even if Chief Russ pretends he's open to whatever I could do, in the end he'll be just like the others. Why should I put myself in the middle of it only to be laughed at and dismissed?'

She rounded on him. 'Don't you have anything to say?'

'I'm waiting for you to come around to it.'

'You think you're smart, don't you? You think you know me so well. You don't know me at all. I didn't come back here to right wrongs or avenge a dead friend. I came back here to live my life and run my business.'

'All right.'

'Don't say all right to me in that patient tone, when your eyes are telling me I'm a liar.'

Because her breath was starting to hitch, he rose and went to her. 'I'll go with you.'

She stared at him another moment, then just went into his arms. 'God. Oh God.'

'We'll go on down and tell the chief. I'll stay with you.'

She nodded, held on another minute. And she accepted that after she was done in Sherry's apartment, he might never want to hold her again.

Chapter Twenty-Two

'You need anything before we go in?'

Tory was still fighting to calm her nerves, but met Carl D.'s gaze levelly. 'What, like a crystal ball? A pack of tarot cards?'

He'd gone in the front as she'd requested, and unlocked the patio door from the inside, cut the seal, and stepped out where she waited with Cade.

There was less chance of being seen going in through the rear. The killer had known that, too.

Now Carl D. pushed back his hat to scratch his wide brow. 'Guess you're a mite put-out with me.'

'You pushed where I don't like to be pushed. This isn't going to be pleasant for me, and could very well be useless to you.'

'Miss Tory, I got a young woman about your age lying on a table down at the funeral parlor. County ME's got his job to do on her. Her family's coming down tomorrow morning. Wouldn't call any of that pleasant for anybody.'

He'd wanted her to have that picture in her head. Tory acknowledged it with a nod. 'You're a harder man than I remember.'

'You're a harder woman. I guess we both got reason.'

'Don't talk to me.' She opened the door herself, stepped inside.

She'd braced herself, and concentrated on the light first. The light in the room as he'd flicked the switch. The light Sherry had permeated through the air.

It was a long time before she spoke. A long time, while what was left in the room slid inside her.

'She liked music. She liked noise. Being alone just wasn't natural to her. She liked to have people over. Voices, movement. They're all so fascinating to her. She loved to talk.'

There was fingerprint dust on the phone. She didn't notice that it smeared her own fingers as she trailed them over it.

Who was Sherry Bellows? That had to come first.

'Conversations were like food to her. She'd have starved to death without them. She liked to find out about people, to listen to them talk about themselves. She was very happy here.'

She paused, letting her fingers brush over picture frames, the arm of a chair.

'Most people don't really want to hear what people say, but she did. Her questions weren't a ploy to wheedle an opening to talk about herself. She had such plans. Teaching was an adventure to her. All those minds to feed.'

She walked past Cade and Carl D. Though she was aware of them, they were becoming less important to her, their presence less real.

'She loved to read.' Tory spoke quietly as she wandered toward a cheap, brass-plated shelf filled with books.

Images floated through her mind of a pretty young woman tucking books on the shelf, taking them out, curled up with them on the chair on the patio with a big, shaggy dog snoring at her feet.

It was easy to blend into those images, to open to them, become part of them. She tasted salt – potato chips – on her tongue, and felt a lovely wave of contentment.

'But that's just another way to be with people. You slide into the book. You become a character, your favorite character. You experience.

'The dog gets up on the sofa with you, or in the bed. He leaves hair everywhere. You swear you could make a coat out of the hair he sheds, but he's such a sweetheart. So you run the vacuum most every day. Turn the music up so you can hear it over the motor.'

Music pulsed inside her head. Loud, cheerfully loud. Her foot tapped to it.

'Mr. Rice next door, he complained about that. But you bake him some cookies and bring him around. Everyone's so nice in this town. It's just where you wanted to be.'

She turned from the bookshelf. Her eyes were blurry, blank, but she was smiling.

Cade's heart skipped a beat as her smoky gaze passed over him. Passed through him.

'Jerry, the little boy from upstairs, he's just crazy about Mongo.

Jerry's just as cute as a bug and twice as pesky. One day you want a little boy just like him, all eyes and grins and sticky fingers.'

She turned in a circle, her lips curved, her eyes blind.

'Sometimes in the afternoon after school they'll go out and run around together, or he'll throw Mongo tennis balls. Fuzzy yellow balls that get all wet and messy. It's fun to sit on the patio and watch them. Jerry has to go in, his mother called him in to do his chores before supper. Mongo's just plain worn out, so he'll sleep out on the patio. You want the music on, loud as you can without bothering Mr. Rice, because you're feeling so happy. So hopeful. A glass of wine. White wine. Not really good wine, but you can't afford better. Still it's nice enough and you can sip and listen to the music and plan.'

She walked to the patio doors, looked out. Instead of dark she saw early twilight. The big dog spread out on the concrete like a shaggy welcome mat and snoring lightly.

'Lots to think about, so many plans. So much to do. You feel so good about things and just can't wait to get started. You want to have a party, have the rooms crowded with people, and flirt with that gorgeous vet, and that slick-looking Cade Lavelle. My, my, they sure grow them handsome in Progress. But now you should make a meal. You have to feed the dog. Maybe another glass of wine while you're putting it together.'

She strolled into the kitchen, humming the tune she heard in her head. Sheryl Crow. 'A salad. A nice big salad, with extra carrots because Mongo likes them. You'll mix them in with his kibble.' She reached down, brushed her fingers over the handle of the cupboard, then let out a gasp, stumbled back.

Instinctively Cade moved toward her, but Carl D. gripped his arm. 'Don't.' He spoke in a whisper, as though in church. 'Let her be.'

'He was there. Just there.' Tory's breathing came in quick, short bursts now. She had both hands fisted at her throat. 'You didn't hear him. You can't see him. There's a knife. He has a knife. Oh God, oh God, oh God. His hand's over your mouth, squeezing. The knife's at your throat. You're so scared. So scared. You won't scream. You won't. You'll do anything if he doesn't hurt you.

'His voice is at your ear, soft, quiet. What did he do with Mongo? Did he hurt him? It's all tumbling in your head. It's not real. It can't be real. But the knife's so sharp. He pushes you and you're afraid you'll stumble and the knife . . .'

She shuffled out of the kitchen, braced a hand on the wall when she swayed. 'The blinds are drawn. No one can see. No one can help. He wants you in the bedroom, and you know what he's going to do. If you could only get away, away from the knife.'

Tory froze at the door to the bedroom. Nausea rolled into her in short, choppy waves. 'I can't. I can't.' She turned her face to the wall, struggling to find herself through all the fear and violence. 'I don't want to see this. He killed her here, why do I have to see it?'

'That's enough.' Cade shoved away Carl D.'s restraining hand. 'Goddamn it, that's enough.'

But when he reached for Tory, she stumbled away. 'It's in my head. I'll never get it out of my head. Don't talk to me. Don't touch me.'

She pressed her hands to her face, trapping her own breath, and let it claw back inside her.

'Oh. Oh. He pushes you on the bed, facedown. And he's on top of you. He's already hard, and feeling him, feeling him pressing against you, you struggle. The fear's wild inside you. Huge, choking. There's a heat to it. Fear burns.'

She moaned, went down to her knees beside the bed. 'He hits you. Hard. The back of the neck. The pain's so sharp, it rushes through you, stuns you. He hits you again, the side of your face explodes with it. You taste blood. Your own blood. Blood tastes the same as terror. The same. He yanks your arms behind your back, and the pain of that's just another layer.'

Tentacles of that pain slithered and groped inside her, tangled with a horror so huge it seemed the mass of it all would burst out of her brain. She pressed her face to the side of the mattress, dug her fingers into it.

'It's dark. The room's dark, and the music's playing and you can't think over the pain. You're crying. You try to plead with him, but he's tied a cloth over your mouth. He hits you again and you start sliding away somewhere. Half conscious, you hardly feel it when he cuts your clothes away. The knife nicks you, but it's worse, so much worse when he uses his hands on you.'

Tory doubled over, wrapped her arms around her belly, and began to rock. 'It hurts. It hurts. You can't even cry when he's raping you. Just let it be over, but he keeps beating himself into

287

you and you have to go away. You have to be somewhere else. You have to go away.'

Exhausted, Tory laid her head on the side of the bed, closed her eyes. It was like being smothered, she thought dimly. Like being buried alive, so the blood rings in your ears like a thousand bells and the sweat that coats your body is cold. So viciously cold.

She had to fight her way back into the air.

Back into self.

'When he was finished with her, he strangled her with his hands. She couldn't fight anymore. She cried, or he did. I can't tell. But he cut the rope from around her wrists. He took it with him. He didn't want to leave any of himself behind, but he did. Like an ice rime on glass. I can't stay here. Please get me out of here. Please get me away from here.'

'It's all right.' Cade bent down to gather her into his arms. Her skin was cold, slicked with sweat. 'It's all right, baby.'

'I'm sick. I can't breathe in here.' She lay her head on his shoulder and let herself drop away.

He drove her home. She didn't speak, didn't move throughout the drive. She sat like a ghost, pale and silent, while the wind through the open windows of the truck blew over her face and hair.

There was an anger in him that had lashed out at Carl D. when the chief said he would follow them back. But she'd said to let him come. That was the last thing she'd said. So his anger had no target or release and built steadily inside him. His silence was like a bruise, gathering dark and full of violence.

He pulled up to the Marsh House, and she was out of the truck before he could come around to help her. 'You don't have to talk to him.' His voice was clipped, his eyes brutally cold.

'Yes, I do. You can't see what I see, then not do whatever you can.' She shifted her exhausted eyes toward the police cruiser. 'He knew that, and used it. There's no need for you to stay.'

'Don't be stupid,' he snapped, and turned to wait for Carl D. as she walked to the door.

'You watch your step.' Cade faced the chief the minute he was out of his cruiser. 'You be very, very careful with her, or I'll use whatever comes to hand to make you pay for it.'

'I expect you're upset.'

'Upset?' Cade took a fistful of Carl D.'s shirt. He felt he could

288

break the man in half. One quick snap. 'You put her through that. And so did I,' he said, dropping his hand in disgust. 'And for what?'

'I don't know, not yet. Fact is, I'm a bit shaken by this. But I gotta use whatever comes to hand, too. And right now, that's Tory. I'm feeling my way here, Cade.'

There was regret in his voice, in his eyes, a veneer over duty. 'I don't want to hurt that girl. If it makes you feel any better, I'm going to be careful. As careful as I know how. And I'm going to remember, probably the rest of my life, the way she looked back there.'

'So will I,' Cade said, and turned away.

She was making tea, an herbal blend she hoped would soothe her stomach and stop her hands from trembling. She said nothing when the two men walked in, but got out a bottle of bourbon, set it on the counter, then sat.

'I could use a shot of that. Ain't supposed to on duty, but we got extenuating circumstances.'

Cade got out two glasses, poured doubles.

'He came in through the back,' Tory began. 'You know that. You'll already know a great deal that I can tell you.'

'I appreciate it.' Carl D. scraped back a chair. 'You just tell me, how it feels best to you, and take your time.'

'She was alone in the apartment. She had a couple of glasses of wine. She felt good, excited, hopeful. She had music playing. She was in the kitchen when he came in. Fixing a salad for dinner, getting ready to feed the dog. He took her from behind, used the knife she'd set aside when she pulled out the dog food.'

Tory's voice was flat, dull, her face expressionless. She lifted her tea, sipped, set it down. 'She didn't see him. He kept behind her, kept the knife to her throat. He'd closed the blinds to the patio. I think he locked the door, but it doesn't matter. She didn't try to run, she was too afraid of the knife.'

Absently, she lifted her hand to her throat, skimmed her fingers along her windpipe as if nursing a sting. 'I don't know what he said to her. Everything she felt was so much stronger than what he felt. He didn't particularly want her. What was left of him there was rage and confusion and a kind of horrible pride. She was a substitute, a handy outlet for a . . . a need he doesn't even understand. He took her into the bedroom, kept her facedown on the

289

bed. He struck her several times, the back of the neck, the face. He tied her hands behind her back, good strong rope. He closed the curtains, so that they could be private, so that it would be dark. He didn't want her to see his face, but more, I think more, he didn't want to see hers. He sees another face when he rapes her. He uses the knife to cut off her clothes, he's very careful, but he still nicks her, on the back, and up by her shoulder.'

Carl D. nodded, took a long drink. 'That's right. She had two shallow cuts, and there were ligature marks on her wrists, but we didn't find any rope.'

'He took it with him. He's never done this inside before. It's always been out-of-doors, and there's something exciting about doing these things to her in bed. When he hits her, it gives him pleasure. He likes to hurt women. But more than pleasure it provides him with a kind of relief for this pent-up hunger in him. This need to prove himself a man. He's a man when he makes a woman bend to his will. While he rapes her he's happier, someone stronger inside himself, than he is any other time. He celebrates his manhood this way, in a way he can't in any other.'

Trying to see him, to crawl inside him, hurt her head. She rubbed at her temple, pushed harder. 'It is sexual for him, and he believes she was meant to be taken, to be dominated. He's convinced himself of that, and still he's careful. He uses a condom. How does he know who she's fucked? She's a whore, like all the others. A man has to look out for himself.'

'You said he didn't want to leave any of himself behind.'

'Yes, he won't leave his seed inside her. She doesn't deserve it. I – this isn't what I feel from him, I feel almost nothing from him.' Her fingers drilled at her throbbing temple. 'There are blanks and dead ends. Turns in him. I don't know how to tell you.'

'That's fine,' Carl D. told her. 'Go ahead.'

'This isn't an act of procreation, but of punishment for her, and ego for him. During the process, she ceases to exist for him. She's nothing, so it's easy to kill her. When it's over, he's proud, but he's angry, too. It's never exactly what he hoped it would be, it never completely purges him. Her fault, of course. The next time will be better. He cuts the rope, he turns off her music, and he leaves her in the dark.'

'Who is he?'

'I don't see his face. I can see some of his thoughts, some of the more desperate of his emotions, but I don't see him.'

'He knew her.'

'He'd seen her, I think he's spoken to her. He knew enough to know about the dog.' Tory closed her eyes a moment, tried to focus. 'He drugged the dog. I think he drugged the dog. Burger laced with something. Risky. This was all very risky and that added to the excitement. Someone might have seen him. All the other times there was no one to see.'

'What other times?'

'The first was Hope.' Her voice broke. She lifted her tea again, calmed herself. 'There were four others that I know of. I had a friend look into it. She found out there've been five over the last eighteen years. All of them killed in late August, all of them young blondes. Each one was the age Hope would have been if she'd lived. I think Sherry was younger, but she wasn't the one he wanted.'

'A serial killer? Over eighteen years.'

'You can verify it with the FBI.' She looked at Cade then, for the first time since they'd sat down. 'He's still killing Hope. I'm sorry. I'm so sorry.'

She rose, and her cup clattered in the saucer as she carried it to the counter. 'I'm afraid it could be my father.'

'Why?' Cade kept his eyes on her face. 'Why would you believe that?'

'He has — when he hurt me, it aroused him.' The shame of it sliced through her, shards of glass jagged and edged with bitter heat. 'He never touched me sexually, but it aroused him to hurt me. I think, looking back, I can't be sure he didn't know of my plans to meet Hope that night. When he came in for supper he was in a good mood, a rare one. It was as if he was waiting for me to make a mistake, to open the door so that he could pounce. When I did, when I told my mother she could find the canning wax up in the top of the cupboard — such a stupid mistake — he had me. He didn't always beat me that bad, but that night . . . When he was finished he could be sure I wasn't going anywhere.'

She came back to the table. 'Sherry was in the store when he came in yesterday. He asked her about her dog, and she'd just filled out an application for a job. I had the paper on the counter. Her name, her address, her phone number. He would have been certain of me, certain I'd be too afraid to tell anyone I'd seen him. He wouldn't have expected me to go to the police. But he couldn't have been sure of her.'

'You believe Hannibal Bodeen killed Sherry Bellows because she'd seen him?'

'It would have been his excuse, his justification for what he wanted to do. I only know he's capable of it. I can't tell you any more. I'm sorry. I'm not feeling well.'

She walked away from the table and closed herself in the bathroom.

She couldn't fight off the sickness anymore and let it come. Let it empty her out. Afterward she lay on the floor, on the cool tiles, and waited for the weakness to abate. The quiet seemed to echo in her ears along with her own heartbeat.

When she could she got to her feet, and turned the shower to blistering hot. She was chilled to the bone. It seemed nothing could warm her, but the water helped her imagine all the ugliness, the smear of it being washed off her skin if not out of her mind.

Steadier, she wrapped herself in a towel, dosed herself with three aspirin, and stepped out, prepared to curl into bed and lose herself in sleep.

Cade was standing by the window, looking out over the moon-washed dark. He'd left the lights off so that silvered glow silhouetted him there. She could hear the flutter of night beyond the screen, the wings and whines that were the music of the marsh.

Her heart ached for everything she couldn't stop herself from loving.

'I thought you'd gone.' She walked to the closet for her robe.

He didn't turn. 'Are you feeling any better?'

'Yes, I'm fine.'

'Hardly that. I just want to know if you're any better.'

'Yes.' Decisively, she belted the robe. 'I'm better. Thank you. You're under no obligation here, Cade. I know what to do for myself.'

'Good.' He turned, but his face remained in shadows. She couldn't read it, refused to try to see anything else. 'Tell me what to do for you.'

'Nothing. I'm grateful you went with me, and that you brought me home. It's more than you had to do, more than can be expected of anyone.'

'Now back off? Or is that just what you expect? For me to go, to leave you alone, to take myself off to a nice comfortable distance. Comfortable for whom? You or me?'

'Both, I imagine.'

'You don't think any more of me than that? Any more of us?'

'I'm awfully tired.' Her voice wavered, shaming her. 'I'm sure you are, too. It couldn't have been pleasant for you.'

He stepped toward her then and she saw what she'd known she would see. Anger, black waves of it. So she shut her eyes.

'For God's sake, Tory.' His hand brushed over her cheek, back into the wet tangle of her hair. 'Has everyone always let you down?'

She didn't speak, couldn't. A tear slid down her cheek and lay glistening on his thumb. She went, biddable as a child, as he led her to the bed, lifted her onto his lap.

'Just rest,' he murmured. 'I'm not going anywhere.'

She pressed her face into his shoulder. Here was comfort, and strength, and above all the solidity no one had ever offered her. He asked no questions, so neither would she. Instead she curled into him, lifted her mouth to his.

'Touch me. Please. I need to feel.'

Gently, so gently, he ran his hands over her. He could give her the comfort of his body, take his own in hers. Trembling she reached for him, her lips parting under his and going warm.

Slowly, so slowly, he loosened the tie of the robe, slipped it from her. Laid his hand on her heart. It beat frantically, and her breathing still caught on sobs she fought back.

'Think of me,' he murmured, and lay her on the bed. 'Look at me.'

He touched his lips to her throat, her shoulders, skimming his hands through her hair when she reached up to unbutton his shirt.

'I need to feel,' she repeated. 'I need to feel you.' She put her palms against his chest. 'You're warm. You're real. Make me real, Cade.'

She sank into him when his mouth came back to hers, sank deep into the tenderness of it, the kindness that erased the horror she'd seen. The calm came first, the understanding that this brush and slide of flesh, this meeting of bodies, had nothing to do with pain or fear.

His mouth on her breast, feeding, arousing, sped the beat of her

293

blood. His hands, strong, patient, washed her mind clear of everything but the need to join.

She sighed out his name as he danced over the first peak.

She was fluid, and open, rising toward him, sliding against him. When she rolled, he found her mouth again, then let her set the pace. She rose over him, her hair like wet ropes gleaming over her shoulders. Her face was flushed with life, damp with tears.

She took him into her, bowing back, her breath catching, releasing, her fingers locking with his as she began to move.

There was nothing in his world now but her, the heat of her surrounding him, the steady rise and fall of her hips as she rode him. The dark smoke of her eyes stayed wide and fixed on his even as her breath began to tear.

He saw her come, watched the force of it ripple through her.

'God.' She brought their joined hands to her breasts. 'More. Again. Touch me, touch me, touch me.'

He took her breasts in his hands, reared up, and took them into his mouth so that she arched back. When she gripped his hair, he drove deeper. Filling her, taking her. Taking himself.

They stayed wrapped around each other. Even when he shifted to lie with her, they remained tangled and close. She breathed him in.

'You should sleep now,' he murmured.

'I'm afraid to sleep.'

'I'll be right here.'

'I thought you would go.'

'I know.'

'You were so angry. I thought . . .' No, she needed another minute. Courage didn't come without effort. 'Would you get me some water?'

'All right.' He shifted, and rising, pulled on his jeans before he went out into the kitchen.

She heard him open a cupboard for a glass, close it again. And when he came back she was sitting on the side of the bed in her robe. 'Thank you.'

'Tory, are you always sick afterward?'

'No.' Her hand tightened on the glass. 'I've never done anything like . . . I can't talk about that yet. But I need to talk. I need to tell you about something else. About when I was in New York.'

'I know what happened. It wasn't your fault.'

'You only know parts and pieces. What you heard in the news. I need to explain.'

Because she'd tightened up again, he combed his fingers through her hair. 'You wore your hair differently there. You'd lightened it, cut it shorter.'

She managed a laugh. 'My attempt at a new me.'

'I like it better this way.'

'I changed a lot more than my hair when I went there. Escaped there. I was only eighteen. Terrified but exhilarated. They couldn't make me go back, and even if he came after me, he couldn't make me go back. I was free. I'd saved some money. I've always been good at saving money, and Gran gave me two thousand dollars. I suppose it saved my life. I was able to afford a little apartment. Well, a room. It was on the West Side, this cramped little space. I loved it. It was all mine.'

She could remember, could bring back inside her, the sheer joy of standing in that empty box of a room, of hugging herself as she stared out the window at the dour brick face of the next building. She could hear the riot of noise from the street below as New York shoved its way toward the business of the day.

She could remember the absolute bliss of being free.

'I got a job at a souvenir shop, sold a lot of Empire State Building paperweights and T-shirts. After a couple of months, I found a better job, at a classy gift shop. It was a longer commute, but the pay was a little better and it was so nice to be around all those lovely things. I was good at it.'

'I don't doubt it.'

'The first year, I was so happy. I was promoted to assistant manager, and I made some friends. Dated. It was so blessedly normal. I'd forget for long periods that I hadn't always lived there, then someone would comment on my accent and it would bring me back here. But that was all right. I'd gotten away. I was exactly where I wanted to be, who I wanted to be.'

She looked at him then. 'I didn't think of Hope. I didn't let myself think of her.'

'You had a right to your own life, Tory.'

'That's what I told myself. God knows that's what I wanted more than anything else in the world. My own. I'd gone back to see my parents during that period, partly out of obligation. Partly,

295

too, because things never seem as bad as they were when you're away from them. I suppose I thought that since I felt so . . . normal, that I could have a normal relationship with them.'

She paused, shut her eyes. 'But mostly I went back because I wanted to show them what I'd made of myself despite them. Look at me: I have nice clothes, a good job, a happy life. So there.' She gave a weak laugh. 'I failed on all three levels.'

'No, they did.'

'Doesn't matter. I guess I was a little off balance because of the visit even after I got back to New York. Then one day after work, not long after that, I went by the market. Picked up a few things. I don't even remember exactly. But I took my bag home and started to put everything away.'

She looked down at her water, clear water in a clear glass. 'Then I was standing there in that tiny kitchen, with the refrigerator open and a carton of milk in my hand. A carton of milk,' she repeated, her voice hardly a whisper. 'With a picture of a little girl on the side. Karen Anne Wilcox, age four. Missing. But I wasn't seeing the picture, I was seeing her. Little Karen, only she didn't have blond hair like in the picture. It was brown and cut nearly short as a boy's. She was sitting in a room by herself playing with dolls. It was February, but I could see the sky out her window. Pretty blue sky, and I could hear the water. The sea. Why, Karen Anne's in Florida, I thought. She's at the beach. And when I came back to myself, the milk carton was on the floor with the milk spilling out of it.'

She drank again, then set the glass aside. 'I was so angry. What business of it was mine? I didn't know this girl, or her parents. I didn't *want* to know them. How dare they interfere with my life that way? Why should I have to be involved? Then I thought of Hope.'

She rose, walked to the window. 'I couldn't stop thinking about her, about the little girl. I went to the police. They thought I was just one more lunatic, passed me off, rolled their eyes while they spoke very slowly, as if I were stupid as well as crazy. I was embarrassed and angry, but I couldn't get the child out of my head. While two of the detectives were interviewing me, I lost my temper. I said something to one of them about how if he weren't so damned closed-minded he'd listen instead of worrying how much the mechanic was going to hose him for over the transmission job.

'That got their attention. Turned out the older one, Detective Michaels, had his car in the shop. They still didn't believe me, but now I worried them. The interview turned into more of a grilling. They kept pushing and pushing, and my nerves were fraying. The younger one, I guess he was playing good cop, he went out and got me a Coke. He brought back this plastic bag. Evidence bag. Inside were mittens. Bright red mittens. They'd found them on the floor of Macy's, where she'd been snatched while her mother was shopping. At Christmas. She'd been missing since December. He tossed them on the table, like a dare.'

She remembered his eyes. Jack's eyes. The hardness in the beautiful green brilliance of Jack's eyes.

'I wasn't going to pick them up. I was so angry and ashamed. But I couldn't help it. I picked up the bag, and I saw her so clear, in her little red coat. All the people crowded in, trying to buy presents. The noise. Her mama was right there at the counter, working on picking out a sweater. But she wasn't paying attention, and the little girl wandered off. Just a few feet. Then the woman came and scooped her right up. She bundled her close, so close and tight, and pushed through people and right out the door. No one paid any attention. Everyone was busy. She told Karen to be very quiet because she was taking her to see Santa Claus, and she walked very fast, down the avenue very fast, and there was a car waiting. A white Chevrolet with a dented right fender and New York plates.'

She let out a sigh, shook her head. 'I even had the plate number. God, it was all so clear. I could feel the bite of the wind as it whipped down the street. I told them all that, told them what the woman looked like after she took off the black wig. She had light brown hair and pale blue eyes and she was slim. She'd worn a big, bulky coat with padding under it.'

Tory glanced over her shoulder. Cade sat on the bed, watching, listening. 'She'd planned this for weeks. She wanted a little girl, a pretty little girl, and she'd picked Karen out when she'd seen her mama walk her to day care. So she took her, that's all. And she and her husband drove straight through to Florida. They cut her hair and dyed it, and didn't let her go outside. They said she was a little boy named Robbie.'

She blinked, turned back. 'They found her. It took a while because I couldn't see just where. But they worked with the police in Florida, and within a couple of weeks, they found her in a trailer park in Fort Lauderdale. The people who had her didn't hurt her. They bought her toys and fed her. They were sure she'd just forget. People think children forget, but they don't.'

She sighed. Outside an owl began to hoot in long bass notes that echoed through the marsh and into the room where she stood.

'So Karen was the first for me. Her parents came to see me after to thank me. They cried. Both of them. I thought, maybe this is a gift. Maybe I'm meant to help people like this. I began to open myself to it, to explore it, even celebrate it. I read everything I could, I submitted to tests. And I began to see Jack – Detective Jack Krentz, the younger of the two cops who'd investigated the kidnapping. I fell in love with him.'

She came back for the water, drained the glass. 'There were others after Karen. I thought I'd found the reason I was what I was. I thought I had everything. I was wildly in love with a man I believed loved me, and considered me a kind of partner. Now and again he'd bring something home, ask me to hold it. I was thrilled to be able to help in his work. We did it quietly. I didn't want any credit or any notoriety. But my work with missing children leaked, so I began to get both in that area. And with it, the letters, the calls, the pleas that haunt you night and day. Still I wanted so much to help.'

She set the empty glass aside, wandered away toward the window. 'I didn't notice the way Jack was starting to watch me. That cool-eyed stare of his. I thought it was just his way. He was the first man I'd been with, and we were together – we were lovers – for over a year when it started to fall apart.

'He was seeing someone else. She was there in his mind, her smell in his senses when he came to me. I was betrayed and furious and I confronted him. Well, he was more betrayed, more furious, and much better at it. I had spied on his thoughts. I was worse than a freak. How could he have a relationship with a woman who couldn't respect his privacy, who invaded his mind?'

'He managed to turn that one around on you. He cheats, and you're wrong.' Cade shook his head. 'You didn't buy that?'

'I wasn't quite twenty-two years old. He was my first and only lover. More, I loved him. And I had, however unintentionally, spied on his thoughts. So I took the blame, but it wasn't enough. He began to berate me, to accuse me of trying to take the credit for the good, hard work he put into cases. Whatever he'd felt for me in the beginning had turned into something else and it hurt both of us. And as things were falling apart between us, there was Jonah. Jonah Mansfield.'

She pressed a hand to her chest, squeezed her eyes shut a minute. 'Oh, it still breaks my heart. He was eight and had been kidnapped by his parents' former housekeeper. The police knew that, there was a ransom demand of two million dollars. Jack was assigned to the team working the case. He didn't bring it to me. The Mansfields did. They asked me for help, I told them what I could. The boy was being held in some sort of basement. I didn't know if it was a home or a building, but it was across the river. Jack was furious I'd gone around him, behind his back. He wouldn't listen to me. They hadn't hurt the boy, and they were prepared to give him back if the ransom was paid, and if it was delivered exactly as they'd outlined. Was I willing to risk a child's life so I could prove what a wonder I was? That's what he asked me, and he had so eroded my confidence that I wasn't sure.'

She let out a shaky breath. 'I'm still not really sure what the answer to that question is. But I could see the boy, and I could see the woman. She was going to let him go. It was only money to her, and petty revenge against the Mansfields for firing her. I told them he was being treated well. He was scared, but he was all right. I told them to pay the ransom, to do what she said and get their son back safe. Really, no more or less than what the police wanted them to do. But what I didn't see, what I didn't see because I was so devastated by Jack, was that the men working with her weren't as coolheaded as she.'

Her voice cracked. Oh yes, she thought. It still breaks the heart. 'I told Jack there were two men, but the investigation indicated there was only one. The woman, and one accomplice. I was muddying the waters, getting in the way. When the money was paid, they did what they'd planned to do, what I hadn't seen, all along. They killed Jonah, and the woman.'

She took a deep breath. 'I didn't know about it till I heard it on the news, until the reporters started calling me. I'd pulled back, curled up in my own little ball of misery because Jack had turned away from me.

'I don't know how they expected to get away. They had a van, and it seemed they planned to just drive off. But they hadn't really

299

planned anything. It was the woman who'd laid it all out, who'd calculated the steps. But in the end, they didn't want to share the money with her. They figured they'd just drive west, but the police had trailed the money and were waiting for them.

'Two police officers were shot, and one of the kidnappers was fatally wounded. I hadn't seen any of that. What I'd persuaded the parents to do resulted in the death of their child.'

'No, the kidnapping resulted in the death of their child. Circumstances, greed, fear.'

'I couldn't have saved him. I've learned to live with that. The same way I've learned to live with not saving Hope. But it left me broken. I spent weeks in the hospital, years in therapy, but I never really got it all back. Not all. Some of the blame was mine, Cade, because I was so distracted, so distraught about Jack that I didn't focus, I didn't pay enough attention. My life was falling apart and I was desperate to keep him part of it. Part of me. Even when he denounced me, helped smear me in the press, I didn't blame him. For a long, long time, I didn't blame him. Part of me still doesn't.'

'He was more concerned about his ego than you. More concerned about his ego than that child.'

'I don't know that. It was a difficult time. He was unhappy in our relationship and wary of me.'

'So he left you twisting in the wind on a rope he helped make. Is that what you expect from me, Tory?'

'It's what I expected,' she said calmly. 'At this point, I don't know what to expect from you. I just want you to know I understand what it's like for you.'

'No, I don't think you understand anything. He wasn't in love with you. I am.'

She made a sound, part gasp, part sob, but stayed exactly where she was.

'So.' He got to his feet. 'What are you going to do about it?'

'I—' Her throat closed. Not fear, she realized as she stared at him. It wasn't fear filling her. It was hope. Flying on it, she leaped into his arms.

Chapter Twenty-Three

As horrible as murder was, it was still interesting. A night's distance from it made it more like a movie than real life. Faith wasn't about to stay cooped up at Beaux Reves, when she could poke around in town and be in the center of the reel.

Lilah had seen through her, of course, and loaded her down with errands. If she was going to gossip, Lilah told her when she'd handed over her list, she might as well be productive, too.

And she shouldn't forget to report all the details when she got home again.

There was plenty of gossip to be found.

At the drugstore, odds were in favor of an old boyfriend who'd come to town to convince Sherry to mend things and then had gone crazy when she'd refused. After all, she'd only been in town a few weeks. A young, pretty girl like that was bound to have left a boyfriend or two back home.

At the post office there was little doubt the killer had been Sherry's secret lover, and the sex had gotten out of hand. No one named any likely candidates for the secret lover position, but it was a consensus over the stamp buying and certified-letter sending that she'd had one. A woman who looked like that was bound to have a lover. And it was a sure bet he was married, else why had nobody known about him?

This led to the theory that Sherry had threatened to go to his wife, and the ensuing argument had led to violence.

The smart money picked up this theory and ran with it, putting every married man in the area between twenty and sixty on the list of suspects, with the odds favoring a teacher or administrator from Progress High.

But Faith remembered what Tory had said while they'd sat on the grass outside Sherry's apartment. And she remembered Hope.
. It wouldn't hurt to stop by Southern Comfort and see what Tory had to say about things today.

She stopped by the market first and soberly contemplated the bananas. A few feet away Maxine loaded a bag with apples and sniffled. Faith edged a little closer and picked a bunch of bananas at random.

'Well, hi there, Maxine. You all right, honey?'

Maxine shook her head, blinked back fresh tears that swam into her eyes. 'I just can't seem to function. Wade gave me the day off because I was feeling so sad, but I couldn't stay home.'

'Maxine, sweetie.'

Faith cursed her faulty internal radar when Boots Mooney guided her shopping cart into produce. She wasn't in the mood to tangle with Wade's mother again.

The three carts bumped each other, face-to-face. Boots made cooing noises and handed Maxine a hankie.

'It just keeps hitting me, over and over.' Maxine dabbed at her eyes. 'I told Ma I'd do the grocery shopping, and now I can't think.'

Boots nodded. 'I guess we're all upset about poor Sherry Bellows.'

'I just don't know how it could happen. I don't understand it. It's not supposed to happen *here*.'

'I know. You shouldn't be scared.' Sympathetic, Faith rubbed Maxine's shoulder. 'Most people think it was a boyfriend who went crazy.'

'She didn't have a boyfriend.' Maxine fumbled in her pocket, pulled out a tattered tissue. 'She wasn't seeing anybody at all, but she had a little thing for Wade.'

'Wade?' Faith's hand froze, as did the expression of compassion on her face. Over Maxine's bent head her eyes locked with Boots's.

'She liked to come in and flirt with him. Started out pumping me for information about him. Not obnoxious like,' Maxine added with another sniffle. 'But friendly. Interested. You know, was he married, was he seeing someone, that kind of thing.'

Faith dropped her comforting hand. 'I see.'

'He's so good-looking, you know. I had a crush on him myself

302

a while back, so I couldn't blame her.' Remembering herself, Maxine flushed and peeked above the hankie toward Boots. 'Beg your pardon, Miss Boots. Wade, he never—'

'Of course not.' Boots gave Maxine's back a quick pat. 'Why, I'd think there was something wrong with a young woman if she didn't get herself a crush on my Wade.' Her gaze drifted to Faith again, narrowed. 'He's a wonderful man.'

'Yes'm, he is, so you couldn't blame Sherry for having an eye for him.'

Really, Faith thought. Couldn't you really?

'And we got to be friends, Sherry and me,' Maxine went on, comforted by the two sympathetic pairs of ears. 'She helped me study sometimes, and we were going to go out and celebrate when the semester was over. Drive down to Charleston, we thought, and go to some clubs. Said she was man-deprived just now. Didn't mind so much while she'd been getting her degree and starting her career, but she was looking to start dating again.' Maxine wiped her eyes again. 'She wanted to get married one day, have a family. We talked about it.'

'I'm sorry,' Boots answered. 'I didn't know you were close.'

'She was just so *nice*. And she was smart and we had a lot of things in common. She'd worked through college, just like I am. We could talk about clothes and guys and just anything. We both loved dogs. I don't know what's going to happen to her poor dog now. I'd take him, but I just can't.'

She began to weep then, as much for the dog as for her lost friend. 'Don't take on so, Maxine.' Faith's radar was working now, well enough for her to sense the other shoppers nudging closer to try to catch a few words. 'Wade'll find him a good home. And the chief'll figure all this out.'

'I feel so sick inside. Just yesterday she was laughing and excited. We had lunch together in the park. She was going to work for Tory Bodeen at the new shop. Least she hoped to. She was making all these plans. It's just that she was so alive one minute, and the next . . . I'm just so sad and confused about it.'

'I understand.' Faith knew very well what it was like to be left behind after death. 'Honey, you should just go on home. Want me to take you?'

'No, thanks, no. I think I'll just walk. I keep expecting to see her, coming down the street with Mongo. I just keep expecting that,' Maxine murmured, and scrubbing at tears, walked toward the exit.

'I know,' Faith said quietly, and turned blindly away. She couldn't explain how much worse it was when you did see the dead, every time you looked in the mirror.

'Here.' Boots held out a second hankie.

'You're prepared.' Annoyed with herself, Faith took it long enough to stop any damage to her mascara.

'I'm heartsick about that girl, and I barely knew her.' To give Faith a moment to recover, Boots began to select apples. 'I came out myself today because I couldn't think about anything else at home. Poor little Maxine. How much harder is it on her? It was kind of you to offer to take her home.'

'It would've gotten me out of marketing duty.'

Boots laid a hand on Faith's arm until Faith looked at her. 'It was kind of you,' she repeated. 'It's a comfort to me to see kindness in the woman my son is in love with. Just as it was to see that little flash of jealousy. All in all, I'm glad I decided to give myself and J.R. a break from our diet and make apple cobbler tonight. You give my best to your mother, and Lilah, won't you?'

Boots glided away with her apples, leaving Faith frowning after her. 'Pretty sharp, aren't you, Miss Boots, for all your fluttering?' Faith mumbled. 'Pretty goddamn sharp.'

Irritated, Faith pushed her cart through produce, plucking up Lilah's items and wishing she'd skipped the damn market altogether.

She had been jealous. Damn it. Had Wade flirted back? She scowled at the boxes of butter in dairy. Of course he had. He was a man. Very likely he'd considered doing more than flirting. The bastard. How many times had he imagined Sherry naked, fantasized about getting her that way, and then . . .

Good Christ, what was she doing? Working herself up into a mad on Wade over a dead woman? How petty, how shallow, how horrible could she be?

'Faith?'

'What?' She snapped it out, whirled with a box of Land O Lakes in her hand and a killing glare on her face.

Dwight held up a hand for peace. 'Whoa. Sorry.'

'No, I'm sorry. My mind was on something.' Making the effort, she put a bright smile on her face and bent down to the toddler riding in the basket seat. 'And aren't you the handsomest thing? You and Daddy doing the marketing today?'

Luke held up an open box of Oreos. 'Got cookies,' he announced, and as his face was already smeared with black, he'd been enjoying them.

'So I see.'

'His mama's going to scalp me if I don't clean him up before she sees him.'

'Faces wash.' But Faith moved strategically out of the reach of chocolate-gunked fingers. 'Lissy got you doing the shopping today?'

'She's not feeling well. Got herself in a state about what happened yesterday. She says she's afraid to set foot outside the house, and had me checking locks six times last night.'

And wasn't it just like Lissy Frazier to make it all about her, Faith thought, but nodded sympathetically. 'I guess it makes us all a little edgy.'

'She's a bundle of nerves right now. I'm that worried about her, Faith, seeing as she's got another month or so before the baby comes. Her mother's over there, staying with her awhile. I figure the Champ and me—' He paused to ruffle Luke's hair. 'We'd take ourselves off for a while. Give her some peace and quiet.'

'Aren't you the good daddy? Have you heard any more about where things stand?'

'Carl D.'s investigating, and he isn't sharing a lot. I guess it's too soon for that. I guess they'll get the autopsy results soon. Carl D.'s a good man, don't mean to say otherwise. But this sort of thing . . .' He trailed off, shook his head. 'It's not what he's used to dealing with. None of us is.'

'It's not the first time it's happened.'

He glanced back, looking blank for a minute, then his eyes clouded. 'I'm sorry, Faith, I wasn't thinking. This must bring back bad memories for you.'

'The memories are always there. I just hope they catch this one, catch him and hang him by his toes and cut off his—'

'Ah—' Lips twisted into a pained smile, Dwight squeezed her arm and rolled his eyes toward his son. 'Little ears.'

'Sorry,' she said, as Luke decorated his dandelion puff hair with the best part of an Oreo. 'Honey, Lissy's going to stomp you into the ground till your ears bleed if you bring her boy home in that shape.'

'I oughta get points for bringing home groceries.'

'You get minor points for that, we're talking major here. For major, try jewelry.'

'Well, you'd know.' Dwight scratched his head. 'Actually, I was thinking of hunting her up a present, take her mind off her worries. Thought I'd stop by the drugstore and find some perfume.'

'They haven't got anything special in there. Old-lady scents mostly. You go by Tory's place, and you'll find what you're looking for. Put a smile back on Lissy's face.'

Dwight took a good look at Luke, who was now happily coating the red plastic handle of the cart with black Oreo goo. 'You think I'm taking this bull calf in that china shop?'

'You got a point there.' The plan that formulated in her mind pleased her very much. 'I'll tell you what we'll do, Dwight. You give me the money, and I'll go on in and find something that'll make you a hero. When you're done marketing, and scrape a few layers of cookie off your Luke, you just come by, and I'll run it out to you.'

'Really? You wouldn't mind?'

'I was going by anyway. Besides, what are friends for?' She held out her hand, palm up.

'Good thing I just went to the bank. I got cash.' Delighted, he took out his wallet, counted bills into her hand. When he stopped, she simply stared balefully at him.

'Cough it up, Dwight. You can't be a hero for under two hundred.'

'Two hundred? Jesus, Faith, you'll take all but my last dollar here.'

'Looks like you'll have to go by the bank again.' She snatched the bills out of his wallet while he winced. 'That'll give me more time to find just the right thing.'

'What about your groceries here?' he called after her.

'Oh.' She waved dismissively. 'I'll come back later on.'

Dwight blew out a breath, put his nearly empty wallet back in his pocket. 'I think,' he told his son, 'we've just been hosed.'

It was perfect, Faith decided. She could go in, pick Tory's brain, and do a good deed. Then it was only a hop and skip down to

306

Wade's office. She'd have time to decide whether to punish him for making her imagine him imagining sex with Sherry Bellows.

It couldn't have worked out better.

This time she took Bee out of the car, snuggling, cooing. 'Now, you're going to be a good girl, aren't you, so mean old Tory won't complain. You sit like a sweetheart and I'll give you a nice chewy bone. That's Mama's baby.'

'Don't you bring that dog in here again.' Instantly Tory was out from behind the counter, ready to block Faith as she came in.

'Oh, stop being so pissy. She's going to sit right here like a doll baby, aren't you, Bee honey.' She lifted one of the puppy's paws, waved it, while they both stared at Faith with equally innocent expressions.

'Damn it, Faith.'

'She's just good as gold. You watch.' She dug out the bone first, as insurance, then set Bee down, pressing her rump until it hit the floor. 'Besides, what kind of welcome is that when I have a mission, and cash,' she said, pulling out the wad of bills.

'If that dog pees on my floor—'

'She's got too much dignity for that. I'm doing Dwight a little favor. Lissy's feeling poorly and he wants to cheer her up with a nice present.'

Tory blew out a breath, but she calculated the number of bills Faith was cheerfully waving. 'House or body decoration?'

'Body.'

'Let's have a look.'

'Good thing Dwight ran into me. Men don't have a clue about such things most of the time, and Lissy's taste is all in her mouth. And it's not so keen there.' Faith paused at the display case, lifted her eyebrows. 'Was that a snicker?'

'I have too much dignity for that.'

'You ask me, you've got too much dignity for your own good. Let's see that necklace there, the one with the pink topaz and moonstones.'

'You know your rocks.'

'You bet your ass. A woman wants to know if some man's trying to pass off a peridot as an emerald. This is nice.' She held it up, let the light play over it. 'But I think it's too much metal for her. Really more my style.'

'Is this how you accomplish a mission?'

'I can do more than one thing at a time. Let's just put this aside here so I can think about it.' She wandered down the case. 'You doing all right?'

'Yes.'

'Well, don't actually try to have a conversation and spoil your record.'

Tory opened her mouth, shut it again, blew out a breath. 'I'm all right, a little shaky inside, I guess, but all right. How about you?'

Faith glanced up, smiled thinly. 'See, your tongue didn't turn black and fall out or anything. I'm well enough. Been gathering the gossip as I go. And don't bother to look down your nose. You're as interested in what people are saying as I am.'

'I've heard what they're saying. I've had considerable traffic in here today. People love to come in and get a look at me, then flap about it all. It's different for you, Faith, you're one of them. I'm not. I don't know why I thought I ever could be.'

'I can't understand why you'd want to be, but if you do, you just have to stick with it. People get used to you around here. They'd get used to a one-eyed midget with a limp if he lived here long enough.'

'That's comforting.'

'Let's see this bracelet. Cade seems to have gotten used to you mighty fast.'

'Pink and blue topaz in silver. Lobster-claw clasp.'

'Very nice, very Lissy. Those earrings there. She'd want them to match. She doesn't have the imagination for otherwise.'

'Seems odd you taking the time to pick out gifts for her when you don't appear to like her.'

'Oh, I don't dislike her.' Faith pursed her lips and considered the earrings. 'She's too silly for me to work up the energy to dislike. Always was. She makes Dwight happy, and I like him. Box these up, and wrap them up pretty. Dwight'll owe me big. I think I'll take this necklace for myself. Cheer up my mood.'

'You're turning into my best customer.' Tory carried the jewelry to her counter. 'Hard to figure.'

'You have things I admire in here.' Bee had fallen asleep with the bone in her mouth. Faith stopped long enough to beam at her in adoration. 'Plus you seem to be making Cade happy, and I like him even more than I like Dwight.' She leaned on the counter while Tory boxed Lissy's gifts. 'Fact is, you're sleeping with my brother. I'm sleeping with your cousin.'

'That practically makes us lovers.'

Faith blinked, snorted, then threw back her head and laughed. 'Christ, that's a frightening thought. And here I was wondering if I should consider us being friends.'

'Another frightening thought.'

'Isn't it? Still, it occurred to me yesterday when we were sitting out there that you and I were probably feeling the same thing, thinking the same thing. Remembering the same thing. That's a powerful connection.'

Tory tied the cord very carefully, very precisely. 'It was very considerate of you to stay with me. I tell myself, often, that it's better to be alone. But it's difficult. Sometimes it's very difficult.'

'I hate to be alone. More than anything else in the world. I am, so often, irritated by my own company.' She caught herself, laughed. 'Well, listen to us, having almost an intimate conversation. I'm going to give you Dwight's nice fresh cash for Lissy's, but I'll charge mine.'

Before she could reach into her purse, Tory reached out, laid a hand on hers. Odd, how it had become easier to touch, to be touched, since she'd come back to Progress. 'In my life I never had another friend like Hope. I don't know as any of us ever have friends the way we do as children. But I could use a friend.'

Flustered, Faith stared at her. 'I don't know that I make a particularly good one.'

'I know I haven't, not since Hope, so that starts us on level ground. I think I'm in love with your brother.' She let out a long, shaky breath, moved her hand to keep it busy. 'If it turns out I am, I think it would be nice, for everyone, if you and I could be friends.'

'I know I love my brother, though he is a regular pain in my ass. Life has some awfully screwy angles.' Faith laid Dwight's money down, took out her credit card. 'You close up at six, don't you?'

'That's right.'

'Why don't you meet me after work? We'll have us a drink.'

'All right. Where?'

Faith's eyes glittered. 'Oh, I think Hope Memorial would be appropriate.'

'I'm sorry?'

'In the swamp, you know where.'

'For God's sake, Faith.'

'Haven't been there yet, have you? Well, it's time, I'd say, and it strikes me as a good spot to see if you and I turn a corner. Got the belly for it?'

Tory snapped up the credit card. 'I do if you do.'

She hauled groceries home, and met Lilah's complaint about her late arrival with just enough bitchiness at being given the chore in the first place to satisfy them both.

'And don't start yapping that the tomatoes are too soft or the bananas too green, or next time I won't be your errand girl.'

'You eat, don't you? Don't do another damn thing around here I can see, so you can haul the food in once in a blue moon.'

'The moon turns blue around here more than it used to.' Faith got out the iced tea, two glasses, then settled down to relay the gossip.

'So.' Lilah sat down, shifted comfortably. 'What are they saying?'

'All manner of things, most of which are as far-fetched as a liberal Republican. Lot of people are saying it must've been an old boyfriend or a lover. A new, married lover. But I ran into Maxine in produce, and it turns out she was friends with Sherry, and she says Sherry didn't have a boyfriend just now.'

'Don't mean some idiot man didn't think he should be.' Lilah took out her lipstick, twirling the tube up and down. 'I heard she let him in though, 'cause her dog didn't send up a racket and there wasn't no breaking like people thought at first.'

'Letting a man into your house doesn't mean you want him to rape you.'

'Didn't say so.' Lilah colored her lips, rubbed them together. 'Just saying a woman's got to be careful. You open a door for a man, you better be ready to boot his ass right back out again.'

'You're such a romantic, Lilah.'

'I got plenty of romance in me, Miss Faith. I just balance it with good hard sense. Something you're missing when it comes to men. Maybe that poor girl was missing it, too.'

'I've been sensible enough to kick plenty of them out on their ass.'

'Had to go and marry two of them first, though, didn't you?'

Faith took out a cigarette, smiled blandly. 'I could have married more than two. Least I'm not a spinster.'

Lilah met the smile equably. 'Marriage was all it's cracked up to be, it'd last longer. That girl, she didn't have an ex-husband, did she?'

'No, I don't think so.'

'Faith?' Margaret stood in the doorway, her face rigid. 'I need to speak with you. In the parlor.'

'All right.' Faith rolled her eyes at Lilah, crushed out her cigarette. 'I should've found more to do in town.'

'You show your mama some respect.'

'It would certainly be a shock to the system if she did the same for me.'

She took her time wandering to the parlor. Stopped once to check her manicure, another to smooth her hair in the hall mirror. When she walked in, her mother was sitting, stiff as dry plaster.

'I don't approve of you gossiping with the servants.'

'I wasn't. I was gossiping with Lilah.'

'Don't take that tone with me. Lilah may be a valued member of this household, but it's inappropriate for you to sit in the kitchen and gossip.'

'Is it appropriate for you to eavesdrop?' Faith slumped into a chair. 'I'm twenty-six years old, Mama. It's a long time since it would do you a lick of good to lecture me on behavior.'

'It never did any good. I'm told that you were with Victoria Bodeen yesterday. That you were together and were responsible for contacting the police.'

'That's right.'

'It's distressing enough that you have any connection with a situation as unseemly as this, but it's intolerable that you are now linked with that woman.'

'That woman being Tory rather than the one who was raped and murdered?' Faith's spine stiffened, but she remained lazily slumped.

'I will not have it. I will not have you associating with Victoria Bodeen.'

'Or?' Faith waited a beat. 'You see, there aren't any *or*'s at this point in our lives, Mama. I come and go when I please and with whom. I always did, but now you really have nothing to say about it.'

'I would think out of respect for your sister you would sever any connection, however tenuous it is, with the person I hold responsible for her death.'

'Maybe it's out of respect for my sister that I've made this connection. You never could stand her,' Faith said conversationally. 'I took your lead there, I suppose. You would have forbidden Hope to associate with her, but you could never really bring yourself to forbid Hope in anything. And if you did, she got around you. She was infinitely more clever than I in that area.'

'Don't speak of my daughter in that manner.'

'Yes, your daughter.' Now the brittle tone reflected in her eyes. 'Something I never quite managed to be. Here's something you may never have considered. Tory isn't responsible for what happened to Hope, but she may very well be the key to it. It might bring you comfort to remember Hope as a bright light, as a life cut off before it really lived. It would bring me more comfort to finally know why. And know who.'

'You won't find your comfort, or your answers, with that woman. You'll only find lies. Her whole life is a lie.'

'Well then.' With a bright smile, Faith got to her feet. 'Just gives us one more thing in common, doesn't it?'

She walked away, putting a swagger in her step.

Margaret got immediately to her feet, walked quickly out and into the library with its towers of books and ornately plastered ceiling. She made the call first, tugging on the strings of friendship to request that Gerald Purcell come to her as soon as possible.

Assured he would make the trip within the hour, she walked to the safe secreted behind an oil painting of Beaux Reves and took out two folders.

She would use the hour to study the paperwork and prepare.

Shortly, she ordered tea to be served on the south terrace, along with scones and the frosted cakes she knew Gerald had a weakness for. She enjoyed the ritual in the afternoons when she was at home, the china, the silver, the precisely cut wedges of lemon, the mix of brown and white sugar cubes in the bowl.

As long as she was mistress of this house, she thought, it was a ritual that would be preserved. Beaux Reves, and all it stood for, would be preserved.

It was warm for tea alfresco, but the white umbrella offered shade, and the gardens provided what Margaret considered the appropriate backdrop. The tree roses that flanked the brick in their giant white pots were heavy with bloom, and her hibiscus added an exotic touch with their crimson trumpets.

She sat at the rippled glass table, hands folded, and looked out over what was hers. She had worked for it, nurtured it, and now, as always, she would protect it.

She glanced over as Gerald came through the terrace doors. He'd roast in the suit and tie, she thought idly, as she lifted a hand to his.

'I appreciate your coming so quickly. You'll have some tea?'

'That would be lovely. You sounded troubled, Margaret.'

'I am troubled.' But her hand was rock steady as she lifted the Wedgwood teapot and poured. 'It concerns my children, and Beaux Reves itself. You were Jasper's attorney, so you understand the disposition of the farm, the properties, the interests of this family, as well as any of us. Better perhaps.'

'Of course.' He sat beside her, pleased that she remembered he preferred lemon to milk.

'Controlling interest in the farm was passed to Kincade. Seventy percent. That holds true for the factories, the mill as well. I hold twenty percent, and Faith ten.'

'That's correct. The profits are divided and dispersed annually.'

'I'm aware of that. The properties, such as our interest in the apartment buildings, the houses that are rented, including the Marsh House, are in all three names, equally. Is that also correct?'

'Yes.'

'And, in your opinion, what impact would it have on Cade's changes to the farm, his new operating system, if I withdrew my support, used my twenty percent and my influence with the board to sway them back toward more traditional methods.'

'It would cause him considerable difficulty, Margaret. But his weight is heavier than yours, and the profits add to his end of the scale. The board has no say in the farm in any case, just the mill and the factories.'

She nodded. 'And the mill, the factories, help keep the farm running. If I were able to persuade Faith to add her interest to mine?'

'That would give you more ammunition, certainly.' He sipped his tea, pondered. 'Might I ask, as your friend and your lawyer, if you're dissatisfied with Cade's performance at Beaux Reves?'

'I am dissatisfied with my son, and I believe he needs to put his mind and energies back into his inheritance without having it diverted into less worthy channels. Simply,' she said, as she buttered a scone, 'I want Victoria Bodeen out of the Marsh House, out of Progress. At the moment Faith is being difficult, but she will come around. She's always been a creature of the moment. I believe I can persuade her to sell me her interest in the properties. That would give me a two-thirds control. I would assume that the Bodeen girl has a year's lease on the house, and on the building on Market. I want those leases broken.'

'Margaret.' He patted her hand. 'You would be wise to let this lay.'

'I will not tolerate her association with my son. I will do whatever is necessary to end it. I want you to draw up a new will for me, cutting both Cade and Faith off.'

He thought of the scandal, the legal tangles, the vicious amount of work. 'Margaret, please don't be rash.'

'I won't implement the will unless I have no choice, but I will use it to show Faith just how serious I am.' Margaret's mouth thinned. 'I have no doubt that when she realizes she stands to lose such a large sum of money, she will become very cooperative. I want my house back in order, Gerald. It would be a great favor to me if you looked over those leases and found the simplest way to break them.'

'You risk turning your son against you.'

'Better that than watching him drag down the family name.'

Chapter Twenty-Four

I have not, since childhood, kept a diary or a journal, or written down my secret thoughts. It seems appropriate, since my childhood is so on my mind, to do so now. And to do so here, where Hope lost her life. Her childhood.

My papa, our papa, made this place for her with its pretty statue and its sweet-smelling flowers. It is more hers than the grave where he buried her on that steamy and sick-skied summer morning. I never shared this place with her. I chose not to, out of spite, certainly, but it gave me great satisfaction at the time.

What did I want with her silly games and her odd and unkempt friend?

I wanted them so desperately I refused to take them when they were offered. I am a difficult person. Sometimes I like myself that way. In any case, it is my nature to be contrary, so I of all people must live with it.

It might have been different for me, for all of us, if that night had never happened. If when I'd woken in the morning, Hope had been in the next room. I would still have been sulking over my disgrace the night before. That had been a minor combat over peas, which I despised then and despise now.

I would have sulked because I found some pleasure in that activity, particularly when someone put in the effort to win me out of my pouts. I enjoyed the attention. Most any kind of attention I could manage.

I knew, even then, that in the pecking order of siblings, I came in a lowly third out of three. Cade was the heir apparent. He, after all, possessed a penis, and I did not. This, I suppose, was no fault of his, but I did indeed envy him that member for a short time in my youth. Until, of course, I learned that it was more than possible for a woman to possess as many of those interesting appendages as she liked, and in such a pleasant variety of ways.

I discovered sex early, and have enjoyed it without apology.

In any case, at eight, the sexual connotations of men and women were still a foggy area for me. I only knew that Cade was the master-in-training of Beaux Reves because he was a boy, and this did not sit well with me. He was afforded privileges I was denied, again because of his gender. And, I suppose to be fair, the four-year difference in our ages.

My father looked on him with such pride. Certainly he demanded quite a bit from Cade, but the look in Papa's eyes, the tone of his voice, the very posture of his body, was a study in pride. Father for son. I could never be his son.

Nor could I be, as Hope was, his angel. He adored her. He had love for me, and he was a fair man. But it was painfully obvious that it was Hope who held his heart even as Cade held, well, his hopes. I was a kind of bonus, I imagine, the twin who came in tow with his angel.

With my mother Cade was also, I think, a source of pride. She had produced the son, as was expected of her. The Lavelle name would carry on because she had conceived and birthed a male. She was happy enough to give the dealing with him over to my father for the most part. What did she know of boys, after all? I wonder if Cade felt this smooth and easy distance. I imagine he did, but somehow he became a whole and admirable man despite it.

Because of it?

Naturally, Mama schooled him in manners, saw to his cleanliness, but his education, his time, his lot in life were my father's bailiwick. I don't remember ever hearing her question Papa about Cade.

Hope was her reward for a job well done. The daughter she could polish and mold, the child she would see from babyhood through to a proper marriage. She loved Hope for her sweetness and her quiet acquiescence. And she never saw, never, the rebel inside. Had Hope lived, I believe she would have done precisely what she pleased, and somehow have convinced Mama it was Mama's own idea.

She got around her with Tory. She could get around her with anything.

God, I miss her. I miss that half of me that was bright and fun and eager. I miss her outrageously.

Myself, I was a trial to Mama. How often I have heard her say so, therefore it must be true. I had none of Hope's sweetness, nor her quiet acquiescence. I questioned, and I fought bitterly over things I didn't even care about.

Notice me. Damn you all. Notice me.

How sad and pitiful.

Hope became friends with Tory a year before that summer. They were simply drawn together as some souls are. Even I could see the recognition between them, that click of connection. And they were, almost from the first, inseparable. More twins than my sister and I had ever been.

For that reason alone I disliked Victoria Bodeen intensely. I turned my nose up at her and her dirty feet and poor grammar, at her big watchful eyes and white-trash parents. But it was her closeness with Hope that was at the root of it.

I made fun of her as often as I possibly could, and ignored her the rest of the time. Pretended to ignore her. In fact, I watched her and Hope with hawklike concentration. Looking for a fissure, for some crack in their bond that I could pry wider so that their affection for each other shattered.

They played together on the day she died, at our house, as Hope was strictly forbidden to go to Tory's. She did so, of course, in secret, but they spent most of their time together in and around Beaux Reves, or in the swamp.

Mama didn't know about the swamp. She would not have approved. But we all wandered there, played there. Papa knew it, and only asked that we not go in after dark.

Before supper Hope played jacks on the veranda. I was punishing her by not playing with her. When this didn't appear to spoil her pleasure in the game, I went to my room to sulk and didn't come down until I was called to supper.

I wasn't hungry, and I was still in a vile mood over Hope's blithe acceptance of my anger with her. I took it out on myself by making an issue of the peas — though I continue to contend I had a right there — then ended up sassing my mother and being sent from the table.

I hated being sent from the table. Not that I cared over-much about the food, but it was banishment. I imagine a therapist would say that this tactic proved to me that I was not a part of the family as my brother and sister were. I was the outsider who on one hand reveled in my independence of them, and on the other wanted desperately to be part of the picture.

I went to my room, as if that's where I wanted to be in the first place. I was determined they would think so and not suspect that I was as mortified as I was angry.

A small hill of peas was more important than I was.

I laid on the bed, stared at the ceiling, and surrounded myself with resentment. One day, I thought, one day I would be free to do as I liked, when I liked. No one would stop me, least of all the family who so easily dismissed me. I would be rich and famous and beautiful. I had no clear idea how I would accomplish these things, but they were my goal. I saw money and glory and beauty as a kind of prize I would win while the rest of them stayed steeped in the traditions and the restrictions of Beaux Reves.

I considered running away, perhaps landing on my aunt Rosie's doorstep. That, I knew, would hit my mother where she lived as she considered her sister Rosie nothing more than an embarrassment. Somewhat like me.

But I didn't want to leave. I wanted them to love me, and that urgent and frustrated desire was my prison.

Later on I heard my mother's music. She would have been in her sitting room, writing letters, answering invitations, planning the next day's menus, schedules, and whatever else she did as mistress of the house. My father would have been in his tower office, seeing to the business of the farm, and having a quiet glass of bourbon.

Lilah snuck me in some supper, minus the peas. She didn't coax and cuddle, but simply by that one small act stroked me. Bless her, she has always been there, steady as a rock and warm as toast.

I ate because she'd brought it to me, and because it was a rebellion both of us shared, in secret. After, I lay there as the room grew dark. I imagined Mama brushing Hope's hair as she did every night after bath time. She would have brushed mine as well, to be fair, but I wouldn't sit still for it. She would have gone up to Papa after, Hope would, to say good night. And all the while she was doing what was expected of her, she was planning her own secret rebellion.

I heard her walk down the hallway, and pause at my room. I wish – it does no good to wish, but I wish I had gotten up, opened the door, and browbeat her into coming in to keep me company. It might have made a difference. She would have felt sorry for me, and she might have told me what she was going to do. In my state of mind, I might have gone along with her, just to thumb my nose at Mama. She wouldn't have been alone.

But I stayed grimly stubborn in my bed and listened to her walk away.

I didn't know she left the house. I might have looked out my window any time and seen her. But I didn't. Instead I scowled into the dark until I slept.

And while I slept, she died.

I didn't feel, as it's often said twins do, a break in the thread between us. I didn't experience a premonition or dream of disaster. I didn't feel her pain or her fear. I slept on as I expect most children do, deeply and carelessly while the person who shared womb and birth with me died alone.

It was Tory who felt that break, that pain and fear. I didn't believe it then, didn't choose to. Hope was my sister, not hers, and how dare she claim to have been such an intimate part of what was mine? I preferred to believe, as many others did, that Tory had indeed been in the swamp that night, and had run away and left Hope to face terror.

I believed this even though I saw her the next morning. She came limping down our lane, early in the morning. She walked like an old woman, as if each step was an effort of courage. It was Cade who opened the door for her, but I had tiptoed out to the top of the stairs. Her face was pale as death itself, her eyes huge.

She said: Hope's in the swamp. She couldn't get away, and he hurt her. You have to help.

I think he asked her in, politely, but she wouldn't come

across the threshold. So he left her there, and as I raced back to my own room, he went to look into Hope's. It all happened quickly then. Cade running back down, calling for Papa. Mama ran down. Everyone was talking at once, and paid no mind to me. Mama took Tory's shoulder, shook her, shouted at her. All the while, Tory just stood, a rag doll well used to, I supposed, being kicked.

It was Papa who pulled Mama off, who told her to call the police right away. It was he who questioned Tory in a voice that wasn't quite steady. She told him of their plans the night before, and how she hadn't gone because she'd fallen and hurt herself. But Hope had gone and someone had come after her. She said all this in a dull and calm voice, an adult's voice. And she kept her eyes on Papa's face the whole time, and told him she could take him to Hope.

I learned later that's exactly what she did, led Papa and Cade, then the police who followed, through the swamp to Hope.

Life was forever altered, for all of us.

Faith lowered the pad, leaned back on the bench. She could hear the twitter of birds now, and smell the perfume of dark earth and ripe flowers. Slivers of sunlight shimmered through the tangled canopy of branches and moss to dapple on the ground in pretty patterns and turn the green light into something that just hinted of gold.

The marble statue stayed silent, forever smiling, forever young.

It was so like Papa, she thought, to cover the hideous with the lovely. A pretense, perhaps, but a statement as well. Hope had lived, she imagined him thinking. And she was mine.

Had he brought his woman here? she wondered. Had the woman he'd turned to when he'd turned from his family sat here with him while he reminisced and remembered and grieved?

Why her, instead of me? Why had it never been me?

Faith set the notepad aside, took out a cigarette.

The tears came as a complete surprise. She had no idea they were in there, burning to be shed. Shed for Hope, for her father, for herself. For the waste of lives and dreams. For the waste of love.

Tory stopped at the edge of a bank of impatiens. The quiet,

flower-strewn park was enough of a shock. Her mind slid the image of how it had been, green and wild and dark, over the one in front of her eyes. They tangled, refused to merge, so she blinked the memory away.

There was Hope, trapped forever in stone.

And there was Faith, weeping.

Her stomach muscles danced uneasily, but she made herself walk forward, shivering as images of what had happened there eighteen years before fought to take over. She sat, she waited.

'I don't come here.' Faith dug a tissue out of her purse, blew her nose. 'I suppose this is why. I don't know if this is a horrible place or a beautiful one. I can never make up my mind.'

'It takes courage to take something ugly and make it peaceful.'

'Courage?' Faith stuffed the tissue back in her purse, then lighted her cigarette in one sharp motion. 'You think this was brave?'

'I do. Braver than I could be. Your father was a good man. He was always very kind to me. Even after . . .' She pressed her lips together. 'Even after, he was nothing but kind to me. It couldn't have been easy to be kind.'

'He deserted us, emotionally, the psychologists would say, I expect. He abandoned us for his dead daughter.'

'I don't know what to say to you. Neither of us has ever dealt with the loss of a child. We can't know how we would cope with it, or what we would do to survive that loss.'

'I lost a sister.'

'So did I,' Tory said quietly.

'I resent your saying that. I resent more knowing it's true.'

'Do you expect me to blame you for that?'

'I don't know what I expect from you.' On a sigh, she reached down for the cooler she'd set beside the bench. 'What I have here is a nice big jug of margaritas. A good drink on a warm evening.'

She poured the lime-green liquid into two plastic cups, offered one. 'I did say we'd have a drink.'

'So you did.'

'To Hope, then.' Faith touched her glass to Tory's. 'It seems appropriate.'

'It has more bite than the lemonade we'd usually drink here. She liked her lemonade.'

'Lilah would make it for her fresh. Plenty of pulp and sugar.'

'She had a bottle of Coke that night, gone warm in her adventure kit, and she . . .' Tory trailed off, shivered again.

'Do you see it, that clear, still?'

'Yes. I'd appreciate it if you didn't ask me. I didn't come here, in all the weeks I've been back, I haven't come. I haven't had the courage for it. As much as I dislike being a coward, I have to survive, too.'

'People put too much emphasis, too many demands, on courage, and they all put their own standards on it anyway. I wouldn't call you a coward, but I do keep my personal standards low.'

Tory let out a half laugh, drank again. 'Why?'

'Well, then I can meet them, can't I, without undo effort. Take my marriages, though God knows I wish I hadn't.' She gestured grandly with her cup. 'Some would say I'd failed in them, but I say I triumphed by getting out of them as unscathed as I did.'

'Were you in love?'

'Which time?'

'Either. Both.'

'Neither. I was in heavy lust the first time around. God almighty, that boy could fuck like a rabbit. As sex has been, for some time, a priority pleasure for me, he certainly fulfilled that part of the bargain. He was dangerously handsome, full of charm and fast talk. And a complete asshole.' She toasted him absently, almost affectionately. 'However, he fit the bill of being exactly what my mother despised. How could I not marry him?'

'You could've just had sex.'

'I did, but then marriage was a real slap in her face. Take this, Mama.' Faith tipped her head back and laughed. 'Christ, what an idiot. Now, the second time, it was more impulse. Well, and there was that sex angle again. It was still perfectly inappropriate, as he was much too old for me, and married when we began our affair. I suppose that one was a little shot at my father. You enjoyed adultery, well, so can I. Now, an illicit affair is one thing, but marriage to a philanderer is another. I believe he was faithful enough for the first little while, but my God, I was bored. And then, I suppose, he was just as bored and thought he'd follow his song lyrics by cheating on me, drinking himself blind. He had made a bit of a mark in the music scene. The first time he decided to take a swing

322

at me, I swung harder, then I walked. I got a nice chunk of money out of the divorce, and earned every penny.'

She and Hope had sat here, Tory thought, and talked about things they'd done, wanted to do. Simpler things, childhood things. But no less vital, no less intimate than what Faith spoke of now.

'Why Wade?'

'I don't know.' Faith let out a breath, sipped from her plastic glass. 'That's the puzzle, and the worry. It's not for gain or spite. He's pretty to look at and we do have amazing sex. But the town vet? That was never in my plans. Now he has to complicate everything by being in love with me. I'll ruin his life.' She chugged the margarita, poured a second. 'I'm bound to.'

'That would be his problem.'

Struck, Faith turned her head and stared. 'Now, that is the last thing I expected you to say.'

'He's a grown man who knows his own mind and his own heart. It appears to me he's always done what he wanted, and gotten what he wanted. Could be he knows you better than you think. Then again, I don't understand men.'

'Oh, that's easy.' She topped off Tory's glass. 'Half the time they think with their dicks, and the other half they're thinking of their toys.'

'That's not very kind from a woman with a brother, and a lover.'

'Nothing unkind about it. I love men. Some would say I've loved entirely too many.' There was a wicked gleam of humor in her eyes, and no apology whatsoever. Tory found herself enjoying it, envying it.

'I've always preferred men for company,' Faith added. 'Women are so much more sly than men, and tend to view other women as rivals. Men look at other men as competitors, which is entirely different. You, however, are not sly. It's taken too much effort, I realize, to dislike and resent you.'

'And that's the basis for this moratorium?'

'You have a better one?' Faith lifted a shoulder, then picked up the notepad. 'I had an urge to write somethings down, and I rarely ignore my urges. Why don't you read this?'

'All right.'

Faith pushed to her feet, wandered with her drink and her

323

smoke. She imagined she'd done more serious thinking that day than she had in a very long time. Honest and serious thinking. She hadn't solved anything, but she felt stronger for it.

Wouldn't it be odd if Tory's coming back to Progress had started her on the road to finding contentment in her own life? She paused by the statue of her sister, looked at the face they had once shared. Wouldn't it be, she mused, the ultimate irony if she found herself now, just when she realized she'd been looking all along?

She glanced back at Tory – so cool, she thought. So calm on the surface with all those violent ripples and jolts underneath. It was admirable, really, the way Tory maintained that shield and didn't turn brittle behind it.

Spooky, Faith thought with a little smile, but not brittle.

Brittle, she thought, was what her own mother had become. And brittle was what she herself had been on the edge of becoming. How strange, and somehow apt, that it was Tory who'd given her just enough of a jolt to break her stride before she'd rushed headlong into being what she'd fought against all her life.

A warped mirror image of her own mother.

She crushed her cigarette out, toed it under pine needles.

'Maybe I should take up writing,' Faith said lightly, as she strolled back. 'You appear to be riveted.'

She'd been caught up, sliding into the rhythm of Faith's words and the images they had running through her mind. She'd been both amused and sad. Then the pressure had come, the weight on her chest that caused her heart to beat too fast and hard.

The place, she'd thought, the memories that pounded fists on the white wall of her defense. She wouldn't answer them. Wouldn't heed them. She would stay in the here and the now.

But the cold skinned over her, and the dark crept toward the edges of her vision.

The notebook slipped from her fingers, fell on the ground at her feet, where a tiny breeze toyed with the pages. She was going under, being dragged under.

'Someone's watching.'

'Hmm? Honey, you've only had two glasses of this stuff, haven't you? That's a mighty cheap drunk.'

'Someone's watching.' She took Faith's hand, and her grip was like iron. 'Run. You have to run.'

'Oh shit.' Out of her depth, Faith bent over, tapped her hand on Tory's cheek. 'Come on back now. Get ahold of yourself.'

'He's watching. In the trees. He's waiting for you. You have to run.'

'There's nobody here but us.' But a chill worked through her. 'I'm Faith. I'm not Hope.'

'Faith.' Tory struggled to keep the pictures clear, to hold yesterday and today separate. 'He's back in the trees. I can feel him. He's watching. Run.'

Alarm rushed into her eyes, turning them big and bright. She could hear it now, just the faintest rustle from the brush beyond the clearing. Panic wanted to seize her, the cold fingertips of it scraped her skin.

'There are two of us, goddamn it.' She hissed it out as she snatched up her purse. 'And we're not eight years old and helpless. Run my ass.'

She pulled her pretty pearl-handled .22 out of her bag, and hauled Tory to her feet.

'Oh my God.'

'You snap out of it,' Faith ordered. 'We're going after him.'

'Are you crazy?'

'Now, that's the pot calling the kettle. Come on out, you limp-dicked son of a bitch.'

She heard the snap of a twig, the swish of leaves, and charged forward. 'He's running. Bastard.'

'Faith! Don't.' But she was already racing into the trees. Left with no choice, Tory rushed after her.

The path narrowed, all but died out in a tangle of underbrush. Birds shot toward the sky like bullets, screaming in protest. Moss dripped down, caught in Tory's hair. She batted at it as she sprinted to catch up to Faith.

'I think he went toward the river. We might not catch him, but we'll scare his sorry ass.' She pointed the gun toward the sky and pulled the trigger.

Gunshots blasted, echoed, and seemed to vibrate through Tory down to the toes. Birds exploded out of trees and rushed the clouds. At the sound of splashing, Faith grinned like a lunatic.

'Maybe he'll end up gator bait. Come on.'

Tory could smell the river, the warm ripeness of it. The ground went soggy under her feet, had Faith sliding like a skater. 'For God's sake, be careful. You'll shoot yourself.'

'I can handle a damn pissant gun like this.' But her breath was heaving, as much from the flood of emotion as the run. 'You know the swamp better than I do. You take the lead.'

'Put the safety on that thing. I don't care to get shot in the back.' Tory caught her own breath, pushed the tangled hair out of her face. 'We can cut this way toward the river, save time. Watch for snakes.'

'God, I knew there was a reason I hated this place.' The first rush of adrenaline was gone, and in its place was an innate disgust for anything that crawled or skittered. But Tory was pushing ahead, and pride left her no choice but to follow through.

'What was it about this place that appealed to you and Hope?'

'It's beautiful. And wild.' She heard footsteps, heavy, deliberate, and threw up a hand. 'Someone's coming. From the river.'

'Doubled back, did he?' Faith planted her feet, lifted the gun. 'I'm ready for him. Show yourself, you son of a bitch. I've got a gun and I'll use it.'

There was a thump as if something had fallen or been dropped. 'Christ Jesus, don't shoot!'

'You step out, and you show yourself. Right now.'

'Don't go taking potshots. Holy God, Miss Faith, is that you? Miss Faith, it's just Piney. Piney Cobb.'

He eased out from the trees with his back to the curve of the river where cypress knees speared the surface. His hands shook as he held them high.

'What the hell were you doing, sneaking around in here, watching us?'

'I wasn't. Swear to God. Didn't know you were hereabouts till I heard the shots. Scared me down to the skin. Didn't know whether to run or hide. I've just been frogging, that's all. Been frogging the last hour or so. The boss, he don't mind if I do some frogging in here.'

'Then where are the frogs?'

'Got the bag right over there. Dropped it when you called out. You scared ten years off me, Miss Faith.'

Tory saw nothing in his face but fear, felt nothing from him but panic. He smelled of sweat and whiskey. 'Let's see the bag.'

'Okay. All right. It's right back here.' Licking his lips, he pointed with one finger.

'You be real careful how you step, Piney. I'm awful nervous right now and my finger's liable to shake.'

She kept the gun aimed while Tory moved forward.

'See here? See? Been frogging with this old burlap sack.'

Tory crouched down, looked inside. Perhaps half a dozen unhappy frogs looked back at her. 'This is a pretty pitiful haul for an hour's work.'

'Lost most of 'em when I dropped the bag. Dropped it twice,' he added, as a flush worked up his neck. 'Tell you true, I damn near shit a brick when that gun went off. Thought I heard somebody running off thataway, barely had time to wonder on it when the gunfire started. I figured I'd best get myself out of harm's way, nice and quiet. Maybe somebody's target shooting like Mr. Cade and his friends used to, and I could catch a stray bullet if I wasn't careful. I do some frogging every couple weeks. You can ask Mr. Cade if that ain't so.'

'What do you think?' Faith asked Tory.

'I don't know. He has frogs, such as they are.'

He wasn't a young man, she thought, but he knew the swamp and his muscles were tough from fieldwork. Still, nothing could be proved.

'I'm sorry we frightened you, but someone was sneaking around near the clearing.'

'Wasn't me.' His eyes jumped from Tory to the gun, then back. 'I heard somebody running, like I said. Lotsa ways in and out of here.'

She nodded, stepped back. Piney cleared his throat, reached down for the bag. 'I guess I'll go on then.'

'Yeah, you go on,' Faith told him. 'If I were you, I'd make sure Cade knows when you plan to do some frogging.'

'I'll see to that for sure. You bet your life. I'm just gonna go on now.' He backed up, watching Faith's face until he could slide into the shadows of the trees.

Chapter Twenty-Five

For close on to thirty-five years J.R. and Carl D. fished on Sunday afternoons. It hadn't started as a tradition, and even now both men would have been annoyed and embarrassed to have called it one. It was simply a way to relax and pass the time.

After J.R.'s father died and his mother went to work, it had been Carl D.'s mother Iris had paid to watch Sarabeth after school and on Saturdays. And it had been an unspoken agreement between the women that she would run herd on J.R as well.

Fanny Russ cooked like an angel and had a will of steel. Both were a matter of pride. J.R. learned to call her ma'am in a quick hurry. And during his growing-up years in the fifties when the Klan still burned their hate throughout the South in shapes of crosses, and no coloreds were allowed to sit at the counter in the diner on Market Street, the young white boy and young black boy quietly became friends.

Neither made an issue out of it, and Sunday after Sunday, with a rare miss for holidays or illness, both men sat side by side with rod and reel on the bank of the river, just as they had as boys. They each had less hair and more girth than they'd had when they'd started, but the rhythm of the afternoon stayed essentially true.

For a time during J.R.'s courtship and through the early months of his marriage to Boots, she'd prepared fancy little lunches in a wicker basket for them. It had taken J.R. some little doing to discourage this without hurting her feelings. Picnic baskets filled with chicken salad sandwiches and neatly sliced vegetables made it all too female. All the men needed was a cooler of beer and a fistful of night crawlers.

And if they were lucky, a couple of wedges of Ma Russ's sweet potato or pecan pie.

All that had remained constant for years. There were little changes by the river. The old peach tree had died three winters before, but it had sent out a half dozen volunteers that had grown like weeds until the town council had elected to nurture the best pair of them, and cut down the rest.

Now the fruit, still underripe, hung on the branches and waited for children to come along to devour those hard green orbs and give themselves bellyaches.

The water flowed slow and quiet, as always, with the grand old willow bent over it to dip its lacy green fronds.

And now and again, if you were patient enough, fish stirred themselves to bite.

If they didn't, a man was no worse off than he'd been when he dropped his line.

Years had forged the men into solid citizens, pillars of responsibility. Family men with mortgages and paperwork. The few hours a week they spent drowning worms was a statement that each of them was still as much his own man as he'd always been.

Sometimes they argued politics, and as J.R. was a staunch Republican and Carl D. an equally hidebound Democrat, these debates tended toward the explosive and effusive. Both of them enjoyed the conflict enormously. On other Sundays, and depending on the season, it was sports. A high school football game could keep them both entertained and passionate for two hours.

But more often than not as their lives intersected, it was family, friends, and the town itself that dominated their meandering discussions as the water lapped the bank and the sun filtered through the trees.

What each knew was that he could depend on the other for a sounding board, and that what was said between them by the river stayed by the river. Still there were times when loyalties had to blur. Knowing this, Carl D. chose his words and approach carefully.

'Ida-Mae's birthday's coming up here shortly.' Carl D. spoke of his wife while he popped the top on his second beer and studied the calm surface of the water. 'That electric fry pan I bought her last year's still somewhat of a sore point between us.'

'Told ya.' J.R. took a fistful of the barbecue potato chips from the bag ripped open between them.

'Yeah, yeah.'

'You buy a woman something that plugs in, you're asking for grief.'

'She wanted a new one. Complained every time I turned around about how the old one had hot spots.'

'Don't matter. A woman doesn't want a kitchen appliance all wrapped up in a bow. What she wants is something useless.'

'I'm having a hell of a time thinking what's useless enough to suit her. Thought I might go by your niece's place, have her figure it for me.'

'Can't go wrong there. Tory's got a good sense of things.'

'Done her shop up nice. Lot of work there.'

'She's always been a good worker. Serious girl with a good head on her shoulders. Hard to believe she came out of what she did.'

It was the opening Carl D. had wanted, and still he maneuvered carefully. He got out a fresh stick of gum, went through his little ritual of unwrapping and folding. 'She had it hard growing up. I remember her hardly having a word to say for herself. Just looking, just watching things with those big eyes. Your brother-in-law had a heavy hand.'

'I know it.' J.R.'s mouth tightened. 'I wish I'd known more back then. Don't know as it would've made much difference, but I wish I'd known how it was.'

'You know now. We're looking for him, J.R., on that business back in Hartsville.'

'Like to see you find him, too, give him some of what he's got coming. My sister, well, her life's gone to hell either way. But putting him behind bars might give Tory a better night's sleep.'

'I'm some relieved to hear you say so, J.R. And the fact is, I got worse than that going on here. The kind of worse that might spill over on you some.'

'What are you talking about?'

'What happened to Sherry Bellows.'

'Christ, that was bad business. Bad business,' J.R. repeated with a solemn shake of his head. 'City business, not what we get here in town. Pretty young woman like that . . .' He trailed off, his shoulders straightening, stiffening as he turned his head to stare

330

into Carl D.'s face. 'God almighty, you don't think Hannibal had part in that?'

'I shouldn't be talking to you about it. Fact is I spent most of the night worrying it over in my head. Officially I should keep this to myself, but I'm not going to. Can't. Right now, J.R., your brother-in-law isn't just top of the list of suspects on this. He's the only suspect.'

J.R. pushed to his feet. He paced along the edge of the river, looked across its narrow curve. It was quiet, with just the absent chattering of a few busy birds. He had to listen hard to catch even the murmur of traffic from town. He had to want to hear it to make the connection between this solitary spot with its tall, wet grass and lazy water and the lives and business of Progress.

'I can't get my mind around that, Carl D. Hannibal, he's a bully and a bastard. I can't think of one good thing to say about him, but killing that girl . . . For God's sake, killing her . . . No, I can't get my mind around that.'

'He's got a history of roughing up women.'

'I know that. I know it. I'm not making excuses here. But there's a wide road between rough handling and murder.'

'The road narrows after a while, especially if there's cause.'

'What cause would he have had?' J.R. strode back, crouched down until their eyes were level. 'He didn't even know that girl.'

'Met her in your niece's shop the day she was killed. Met her, spoke with her, and as far as he knew, she and Tory were the only ones knew he was around. There's more,' he said, when J.R. shook his head. 'You're not going to like it. I'm sorrier than I can say your family's brought into this, but I got a duty and I can't let being sorry stop me.'

'I wouldn't ask you. But I think you're looking in the wrong direction, that's all.' He sat again. 'I have to think that.'

'I can't say I wasn't glancing that way to start, but it was Tory who turned me straight onto him.'

'Tory?'

'I took her back to the scene with me.'

'The scene?' J.R.'s eyes went blank, then filled with shock. 'The murder scene. Jesus, Carl D. Jesus Christ, why'd you do that? Why would you put her through something like that?'

'I got a girl about the same age as my own Ella who went

through something a hell of a lot worse. I got a duty to her, J.R., and I'll use whatever I can to see that through.'

'Tory's not part of this.'

'You're wrong. She's hitched into it tight. Now, you just listen a damn minute before you go kicking at me. I took her back there, and I'm sorry for how it was hard on her, but I'd do it again. She knew things she couldn't have known. Saw how it had been like she'd been right there while it was going on. I've heard about things like that, wondered on them, but never seen it before. Not something I'll ever forget.'

'She ought to be left alone. You had no business using her that way.'

'You didn't see that girl, J.R. I hope to God you never see anything like what was done to her. But if you did, you wouldn't tell me I had no business using anything that put that right again. It's the second time I've seen that kind of thing done. If we'd paid attention to Tory the first time, it might not have happened again.'

'What the hell are you talking about? We've never had a woman raped and murdered in Progress.'

'No, the first time it was a child.' He saw J.R.'s eyes widen, and the blood drain from his face. 'The first time it wasn't in town. But Tory was there. Just like she was here now. And when she tells me the same person killed Sherry Bellows who killed little Hope Lavelle, I'm going to believe her.'

The spit dried up in J.R.'s mouth. 'Some vagrant killed Hope Lavelle.'

'That's what the report said. That's what everyone wanted to believe. That's what Chief Tate believed and I can't say he was wrong to. But I'm not going to say the same, and I can't believe the same anymore. I'm not going to try to hang this one on some passerby. There've been other, too. Tory knows about them. The FBI knows about them, and they're coming here. They'll go after him, J.R., and they're going to talk to Tory, to her mama, to your sister. And to you.'

'Hannibal Bodeen.' J.R. laid his head in his hands. 'This'll kill Sarabeth. It'll kill her.' He dropped his hands. 'He'll go back there. That's where he'll go. Holy God, Carl D., he'll go to Sari and—'

'I've talked to the sheriff up there. He's got a man watching the place, keeping an eye on your sister.'

'I got to go up there myself. Make her come back here.'

'I expect if it was my sister I'd do the same. I'll go along with you, help smooth it out with the cops there.'

'I can handle it.'

'I reckon you can.' Carl D. nodded as he began packing up. He heard the anger, the resentment. He'd expected both. Just as he expected what he'd done, and what he would do, was bound to do some damage to a lifelong friendship.

There was nothing to do but wait and see how much could be mended again.

'I reckon you can, J.R.,' he said again. 'But I'm going just the same. I need to talk to your sister, and I'd like to do it before the federal boys get here and snatch the whole goddamn business away from me.'

'Are you going as a cop or as a friend of mine?'

'I'm both. Been your friend a lot longer, but I'm both.' He shouldered his rod and met J.R.'s eyes. 'Plan to keep being both. If it's all the same to you we'll take my car. Make better time.'

It was a struggle, but J.R. bit back words he knew would hang ugly between them. He managed a thin, humorless smile. 'We'll make better yet if you put on the siren and drive like a man instead of an old lady.'

Relief eased some of the weight from Carl D.'s heart. 'I might could do that, part of the way.'

Cade was working hard to control his own temper, to watch his own words. Every time he thought about what a foolish, reckless risk his sister and Tory had taken the evening before, fury stormed inside him.

Lectures, threats, recriminations would have released some of his tension, and would have gotten him nowhere. He wasn't a man who indulged himself in idle directions. He knew exactly where he wanted to go, and simply had to choose the best route for getting there.

Speed wasn't a priority, so he bided his time.

He hadn't indulged in a lazy Sunday morning for quite a while. The best way to begin one, in his opinion, was to keep Tory in bed as long as possible. That was a simple matter of pinning her down and nibbling however, wherever he liked until she got into the spirit of the thing. And had the added benefit of smoothing out some of his own raw edges.

He fixed breakfast because he was hungry and he'd come to the conclusion Tory considered the morning meal well met if she had a second cup of coffee. He steered conversation into casual lines. Books, movies, art. They were fortunate to share tastes. It wasn't something Cade deemed essential, but rather a nice, comfortable bonus.

He imagined she didn't think he noticed how often her eyes skimmed over to a window, and searched.

There was nothing he didn't notice. The nervous hands she tried to keep busy, the way she would stop, go still, as if straining to hear some change in the rhythm of sound outside. The way she jumped when he let the screen door bang when he came out to join her as she tended her flowers.

How many times in his life had he come across his mother working in her garden? he wondered. He was just as unable to judge the direction of her thoughts as she weeded and plucked.

How tidy, he mused, how precise both women were about the chore. Kneeling, wearing hat and gloves as they worked the bed, filling a basket with ruthlessly pulled weeds and spent blossoms.

And how furious both would be if he voiced the comparison.

Throughout the morning, Tory's voice, her face, stayed utterly calm. And that alone infuriated him. She wouldn't share her nerves with him. Still kept part of herself closed off and separate.

His mother, he thought again, as he loitered on the porch and studied Tory's bent head, had kept part of herself closed off and separate. He could do nothing, had never been able to do anything, to reach his mother.

He would damn well reach Tory.

'Come on, take a ride with me.'

'A ride?'

He pulled her to her feet. 'I've got some things I need to see to. Come along with me.'

Her first reaction was quiet relief. She would be alone. She could lie down, shut her eyes, and try to sort through the turmoil swirling inside her head. A few hours of solitude to shore up the wall and chase away the shakes.

'I have a dozen things to do, too. You just go ahead.'

'It's Sunday.'

'I'm aware of the day of the week. And tomorrow, oddly

334

enough, is Monday. I'm expecting some new shipments, including one from Lavelle Cotton. I have paperwork—'

'Which can wait till Monday.' He stripped off her garden gloves as he spoke. 'There's something I want to show you.'

'Cade, I'm not fit to go anywhere. I don't have my purse.'

'You won't need it,' he said, as he pulled her to the car.

'That's a statement only a man could make.' She snarled as he all but dumped her in the car. 'Well, let me go brush my hair, at least.'

He plucked off her hat, tossed it in the backseat. 'It looks fine.' He slid behind the wheel before she could make another excuse. 'Gets a little windblown, it'll just be sexier.'

He picked up his sunglasses from the dash, put them on, then shoved the car in reverse. 'And yeah, that's another statement only a man could make.' He turned onto the road, punched the gas. 'You look pretty when you're annoyed.'

'Then I must be gorgeous right now.'

'That you are, darling. But then I like the look of you no matter what your mood. That's handy, isn't it? How long have we known each other, Tory?'

She held her hair back with one hand. 'Altogether? About twenty years, I suppose.'

'No. We've known each other about two and a half months. Before that we knew of each other, we walked around the edges of each other. Maybe we occasionally thought about or wondered about each other. But for 'round about two months, we've known each other. Do you want to know what I've learned about you in that space of time?'

She couldn't quite judge this mood. His tone was light, his face relaxed, but there was something. 'I'm not sure I do.'

'That's one of the things I've learned right there. Victoria Bodeen's a cautious woman. She rarely leaps before she looks, and then she'll do a comprehensive study. She doesn't trust easily. Not even herself.'

'If you leap before you look, you lower your chances of landing on the other side in one piece.'

'There's another thing. Logic. A cautious and logical woman. Now, that might seem like a fairly ordinary, even uninteresting combination to some people. But those wouldn't have taken the entire package into account. They wouldn't have added in the determination, the brain, the wit, or the kindness. Most of all they would have missed the warmth that's all the more precious for being so rarely shared. And all of this is wrapped, sometimes too tightly, in a very appealing package.'

He turned onto a narrow dirt road, slowed.

'That's quite an analysis.'

'It barely scratches the surface. You're a complex and fascinating woman. Complicated and difficult. Demanding simply because you refuse to demand. Hard on a man's ego because you never ask for a damn thing.'

She said nothing, but her hands had linked together, a sure sign of tension. She'd heard the anger now, just the rougher edge of it, in his voice.

'We'll walk from here.'

He stopped the car and climbed out. On either side the fields spread with row after row of cotton marching like soldiers. She could smell earth and manure and heat, all ripe and sweet and strong. They must have cultivated recently, she mused, turned the weeds into the earth.

Puzzled, unsure what needed to be done here or why they had come, she followed him down the rows while the young plants brushed her legs and reminded her of childhood.

'We haven't had a lot of rain,' Cade said . . . 'Enough, but not a lot. We don't need as much irrigation as the other farms. The soil holds more water when it isn't full of chemicals. Treat it like a natural thing and it thrives like one. Insist on changing it, force it to live up to your expectations, and it needs more and more just to get by. Couple of months, the bolls'll open.'

He crouched down, removing his sunglasses and hooking them on his shirt before he lifted a tightly closed boll with a fingertip. 'My father would've used a regulator to slow the growth, a defoliant to kill the leaves. That's what he knew. That's how it was done. You do things different, people don't like it much. You have to prove yourself to them. You have to want to.' He straightened, met her eyes. 'How much do I have to prove to you, Tory?'

'I don't know what you mean.'

'The way I figure, most people treated you a certain way. That's what you knew. That's how it was done. I'd say I've done things different.'

'You're angry with me.'

336

'Oh yeah. I'm angry with you. We'll get to that. But right now I'm asking what you want from me. Just exactly what you want.'

'I don't want anything, Cade.'

'Goddamn it. That's the wrong answer.' When he strode away, she hurried after him.

'Why is it wrong? Why should I have to want things from you, or want you to be something, do something, when I've been happier with you, just as you are, than I've ever been.'

He stopped, turned back to her. The sun beat mercilessly down on the fields. He felt the heat roll over him, roll inside him. 'That's a first. You telling me I make you happy. But I'll tell you what's wrong with it. I want things from you, and it's not going to work between us if it's all one-sided. Neither one of us is going to stay happy for long that way.'

The ache punched into her stomach and up toward her heart. 'You want to end it. I don't—' Her breath caught, breaking her voice. Tears swam into her eyes, burned there. 'You can't—' Fumbling for words, she backed away. 'I'm sorry.'

'You should be, for thinking that.' He didn't fuss with her tears but narrowed his own eyes. Calculated. 'I told you I loved you. Do you think I can just switch that off because you're a lot of work? I brought you here to show you I finish what I start, that what belongs to me gets everything I've got. You belong to me.' He gripped her arms, brought her up to her toes. 'I'm getting tired of waiting for you to figure that out. I care for what's mine, Tory, but I expect something back. I told you I love you. Give me something back.'

'I'm afraid of what I feel for you. Can you understand?'

'I might, if you tell me what you feel for me.'

'Too much.' She shut her eyes. 'So much I can't imagine my life without you in it. I don't want to need you.'

'And of course it's easy for everyone else to need. For me to need you.' He gave her a little shake that had her eyes snapping open. 'I love you, Victoria, and it's given me some very bad moments.' He pressed his lips to her brow. 'I wouldn't change it even if I could.'

'I want to be calm about it.' She laid her cheek against his chest, smiling a little when he pulled the sunglasses free and tossed them on the ground. 'I just want to be normal about it.'

'Why would you think it's normal to be calm about love? I

don't feel calm.' He stroked a hand down her hair. 'Do you love me, Tory?'

She tightened her grip, anchoring herself. 'Yes. I think—'

'Just yes.' He tugged her hair until her face lifted. 'Let's leave it at yes,' he murmured, and covered her mouth with his. 'Say it a few times so we both get used to it. Do you love me?'

'Yes.' She let out a shaky breath, wrapped her arms around his neck.

'Better already. Do you love me, Tory?'

This time she laughed. 'Yes.'

'Nearly perfect.' He rubbed his lips over hers, felt hers soften. 'Will you marry me, Tory?'

'Yes.' Her eyes fluttered open, she jerked back. 'What?'

'I'll take the first response.' He swung her off her feet, kept her mouth busy with his until she was breathless and dizzy.

'No. Put me down. Let me think.'

'Sorry, I'm afraid you leaped before you looked. Now you have to live with it.'

'You know very well that was a trick.'

'A maneuver,' he corrected, as he carried her back toward the car. 'And a damn good one, if I do say so myself.'

'Cade, marriage is nothing to joke about, and it's something I haven't begun to think of.'

'You'll have to think fast then. If you want a big wedding we can wait till fall, after harvest.' He dropped her into the car. 'But if you'd like small and intimate, my preference, next weekend suits me.'

'Stop it. Just stop. I haven't agreed to marriage.'

'Yes, you did.' He hopped in beside her. 'You can backtrack, bluster, circle around, but the fact is, I love you. You love me. Marriage is where we're heading. That's the kind of people we are, Tory. I want a life with you. I want a family with you.'

'Family.' The thought of it ran cold in her blood. 'Don't you see that's why . . . Oh God, Cade.'

He took her face in his hands. 'Our family, Tory. The one we'll make together will be ours.'

'You know nothing's that simple.'

'There's nothing simple about it. Right doesn't always mean simple.'

'This isn't the time, Cade. There's too much happening around us.'

'That's why it's the perfect time.'

'We'll talk rationally about this,' she told him when he drove down the dirt road. 'When my head's not spinning.'

'Fine, we'll talk all you want.' When the work road split, he took the left fork. Instantly, Tory shot up in the seat, her stomach pitching.

'Where are you going?'

'Beaux Reves. There's something I need to get.'

'I'm not going there. I can't go there.'

'Of course you can.' He laid a hand on hers. 'It's a house, Tory. Just a house. And it's mine.'

Her chest hurt, and her palms went damp. 'I'm not ready. And your mother won't like it. It's your mother's home, Cade.'

'It's my home,' he corrected coolly. 'And it'll be our home. My mother will have to deal with that.'

And so, he thought, would Tory.

Chapter Twenty-Six

It was, Tory thought, the most wonderful house. Not grand and elegant like the lovely old homes in Charleston with their fluidity and feminine grace. But vibrant and unique and powerful. As a child she'd thought of it as a castle. A place of dreams and beauty and great strength.

On the few occasions she had dared to step inside, she had gawked and spoken in whispers like a pagan entering a cathedral.

She had gone in rarely, too shy and afraid to risk the tight-lipped disapproval of Margaret Lavelle. And as yet too young to protect herself against the sharp arrows of Margaret's thoughts.

But she had seen and smelled and touched every room through Hope.

She knew the view out of each window, the feel of the tile and wood floors. Under her feet she smelled the scent that hung in the tower office, the mix of leather and bourbon and tobacco that meant man.

Papa.

She couldn't allow herself to see it through Hope's eyes now, to be drawn to it, into it, that way. She had to see it through her own. Through the now.

It was as stunning as it had been the first time she'd seen it, she realized. Stunning and proud against the sky, with towers defiantly rising. Beaux Reves. Yes, it was exactly that. Beautiful dreams with flowers spread at its feet like an offering and grand old trees guarding its flanks.

For a few precious moments, Tory forgot that the last time she'd seen it, she'd limped up the lane with horror in her eyes and death in her heart.

'It doesn't change,' she murmured.

'Hmm?'

'No matter what goes on around it, even inside it, it stays. There's wonder in that.'

It meant something to him to hear the pleasure in her voice when she spoke of his home. 'My ancestors had ego and humor. Both are strong traits for building.' He stopped the car, turned off the engine. 'Come inside, Victoria.'

Her smile, one she hadn't known curved her lips, vanished. 'You're asking for trouble.'

He got out of the car, walked around to her door, opened it. 'I'm asking the woman I love into my home.' He took her hand and drew her out. She was reminded that however *genteel* he might be, he was equally stubborn. 'If there's trouble, we'll deal with it.'

'It's easier for you. You stand on a foundation, like the house. I've always teetered on boggy ground, so I have to watch my step.' She looked up at him. 'Is it so important to you that I take this one?'

'Yes, it is.'

'Well, remember that if I end up sinking.'

They walked up the steps onto the veranda. She remembered sitting there with Hope, playing jacks or studying one of their pirate maps. Long, tall glasses of lemonade beaded with damp. Frosted cookies. The scents of roses and lavender.

The image of it slipped in and out of her mind. Two young girls, arms and legs browned from the sun, their heads bent close. Whispering secrets though there was no one to hear.

'Adventure,' Tory said quietly. 'That was our password. We were going to have so many adventures.'

'Now we will.' He lifted her hand to kiss it. 'She'd like that, wouldn't she?'

'Yes, I suppose she would. Though she didn't care much for boys.' Tory managed a smile as he opened the door. 'You're so tedious and silly.' Her heart beat too fast, and the grand foyer with its lovely green tiles stretched in front of her like a pit. 'Cade.'

'Trust me,' he said and drew her inside.

The air was cool. It was always cool and fresh and fragrant. She remembered the magic of that, of how sharply it contrasted with the stuffy heat of her house, how the smells of last night's dinner never smeared the air here.

341

And she remembered standing there with Cade before, nearly there. 'You were tall for a boy.' She fought to keep her voice steady. 'It seemed to me you were tall, and so pretty. The prince of the castle. You still are. So little has changed here.'

'Tradition is a religion to the Lavelles. We're schooled in it from birth. It's both comfort and trap. Come into the parlor. I'll get you something cool to drink.'

She wasn't allowed in the parlor, nearly said so before she caught herself. She could sit in the kitchen if she went in the back. Lilah would give her iced tea or Coca-Cola, a cookie or some small treat. And if she helped with the sweeping, a quarter to tuck in her mason jar under the bed.

But she wasn't allowed in the family rooms.

With an effort, she blocked out the old images that wanted to intrude and concentrated on the now. The early lilies were in bloom, and there was a vase bright with them on a gorgeous table spread beneath the curve of the stairs.

The scent of them was utterly female. Beside them were tall white tapers in bold blue stands. No one had lighted them, so they stood pure, untouched and perfect.

Like a photograph, she thought. Every piece, every placement absolute as if it had remained, just exactly so, for decades.

And now she was walking into the picture.

Even as she stepped toward the doorway, Margaret appeared at the top of the sweep of stairs.

'Kincade.' Her voice was sharp, stinging. Her hand wanted to tremble as it held the banister, but she wouldn't permit it. Head lifted, she came halfway down. 'I would like to speak with you.'

'Of course.' He knew the tone, the stance, and didn't bother to mask his response with a polite smile. 'I'm about to show Tory into the parlor. Why don't you join us?'

'I prefer to speak with you privately. Please come upstairs.' She started to turn, assured he would follow.

'I'm afraid that'll have to wait,' he said pleasantly. 'I have a guest.'

She jerked to a halt, her head whipping around just as Cade led Tory into the parlor.

'Cade, don't do this.' Already the tension, the stabs of animosity were pricking her. 'There's no point.'

'There's an essential point. What would you like? I'm sure

Lilah has iced tea in the kitchen, or there's sparkling water behind the bar.'

'I don't need anything. Don't use me as a weapon. It's not fair.'

'Darling.' He bent down to kiss her forehead. 'I'm not.'

'How dare you?' Margaret stood in the doorway, her face pale and set, her eyes swirling with temper. 'How dare you defy me in this way, and with this woman? I made my wishes perfectly clear. I will not have her in this house.'

'Perhaps I didn't make my wishes perfectly clear.' Cade shifted, laid his hand on Tory's shoulder. 'Tory is with me, and welcome here. And I expect anyone I bring into my home to be treated with courtesy.'

'Since you insist on having this conversation with her present, I see no reason to bother with a pretense of courtesy or manners.'

The picture changed again as Margaret entered. The stage, Tory thought, was perfectly dressed. Only the characters revolved.

'You are free to sleep with whomever you choose. I can't stop you from spending your time with that woman or generating gossip about yourself and this family. But you will not bring your slut under my roof.'

'Be careful, Mother.' Cade's voice had gone soft, dangerously soft. 'You're speaking about the woman I'm going to marry.'

As if he'd struck her, Margaret took a staggering step back. Color flooded her face now, staining her cheeks. 'Have you lost your mind?'

Where are my lines? Tory wondered. Surely I must have some in this odd little play. Why can't I remember them?

'I'm not asking you to approve. While I regret this upsets you, you'll have to adjust.'

'Cade.' Tory found her voice, already rusty with disuse. 'I'm sure your mother would prefer to speak to you in private.'

'Don't put words in my mouth.' Margaret snapped at her. 'I see I might have waited too long. If you persist on this path, with this woman, you risk Beaux Reves. I'll use my influence to persuade the board of Lavelle Cotton to remove you as chairman.'

'You can try,' he said equably. 'You won't succeed. I'll fight you every step of the way, and I have the advantage. And even if you could undermine my position at the plant, which I doubt, you'll never touch the farm.'

'This is your gratitude? It's her doing.' Margaret's heels clicked on the hardwood as she rushed forward. Cade merely stepped to the side, putting himself between Tory and his mother.

'No, it's my doing. Deal with me.'

'Oh good, a party.' With Bee racing at her heels, Faith strolled in. Her eyes were bright with anticipation, her smile wicked. 'Hello, Tory, don't you look pretty. How about some wine?'

'That's an excellent idea, Faith. Pour Tory some wine. Deal with me,' he repeated to Margaret.

'You're disgracing your family, and your sister's memory.'

'No, but you are. It's a disgrace to blame one child for the death of another. A disgrace to treat a blameless woman with such contempt and viciousness out of your own guilt and grief. I'm sorry you could never see beyond them to the children you had left, to the life you might have made outside of that bubble you surrounded yourself with.'

'You would speak to me this way?'

'I've tried every other way. If you did what you had to do for yourself, I won't blame you for it. If you continue to live as you have these last eighteen years, it's your choice. But Faith and I have lives of our own. And mine is going to be with Tory.'

'Well, congratulations.' Faith lifted the glass of wine she'd just poured, then drank it herself. 'I suppose this should be champagne. Tory, let me be the first to welcome you into our happy family.'

'Be quiet,' Margaret hissed, and got no more than a shrug from her daughter. 'Do you think I don't know why you're doing this?' she said to Cade. 'To spite me. To punish me for some imagined wrongs. I'm your mother, and as such I've done my best by you since the day you were born.'

'I know that.'

'Depressing, isn't it?' Faith murmured. Cade merely glanced at her, shook his head.

'I've nothing to spite or to punish you for. I'm not doing this to you, Mama. I'm doing it for me. I've had a miracle in my life. Tory came back into it.'

He took her hand again, found it icy, drew her up beside him. 'And I found out I'm capable of more than I imagined. I'm capable of loving someone, and of wanting to do my best by her. I'm getting the best of the bargain here. She doesn't think so, won't even after this. But I know it. And I intend to treasure it.'

'By tomorrow, Judge Purcell will have my new will drawn up. I will cut you both off without a penny.' She aimed her furious gaze at Faith. 'Not a cent, do you understand, unless you stand with me now. You have no personal stake in this woman,' she said to Faith. 'I will see to it that you receive your share, and Cade's, beginning with the fair market value of your interest in the Marsh House and the Market Street property.'

Faith contemplated her wine. 'Hmmm. Now, what would that fair market value be?'

'In the vicinity of a hundred thousand,' Cade told her. 'I can't speak for what my share of our mother's estate might be, but I would assume it edges quite a bit closer to seven figures.'

'Oooh.' Faith pursed her lips. 'Imagine that. So all that will be mine if I just toss Cade to the wolves, so to speak, and do what you want me to do.' She waited a beat. 'Now, when, I wonder, have I ever done what you wanted, Mama?'

'You would be wise to think this through.'

'Second question. When have I ever been wise? Do you want wine, Cade, or would you rather a beer?'

'I will not make this offer a second time,' Margaret said coldly. 'If you insist on going through with this farce, I will leave this house, and you and I will have nothing more to say to each other.'

'I'll be sorry for that.' Cade's voice remained calm. 'I hope you'll change your mind given time.'

'You would choose her over your own family? Your own blood.'

'Without a minute's hesitation. I'm sorry you've never felt that way about anyone. If you had, you wouldn't question it.'

'She'll ruin you.' Gathering herself, Margaret looked at Tory. 'You think you were clever to hold out. You believe you've won. But you're wrong. In the end he'll see you for what you are, and you'll have nothing.'

The words were there, just there, making her understand she'd only been waiting to say them. 'He sees me for what I am. That's my miracle, Mrs. Lavelle. Please don't make him choose between us. Don't make all of us live with that.'

'I had another child who chose you, and she paid a high price for it. Now you'll take a second. I'll make arrangements to leave immediately,' she said to Cade. 'Have the decency to keep her away from me until they're complete.'

'Well, well.' Faith poured a second glass as her mother walked away. 'That was pleasant.'

'Faith.'

'Oh, don't give me that look,' she said, brushing Cade off. 'I don't imagine either of you were particularly entertained, but I was. Enormously. God knows she had it coming. Here.' She pushed the wine into Tory's hand. 'You look like you could use this.'

'Go talk to her, Cade. You can't leave it like this.'

'If he tries, I'll lose all this new respect and admiration I have for him.' Rising to her toes, Faith kissed his cheek. 'Looks like she didn't ruin both of us after all.'

He took her hand, held it. 'Thank you.'

'Oh, darling, it was my pleasure.' Holding her glass aloft, she dropped into a chair, grinning when Bee leaped into her lap. 'I, for one, plan to celebrate.'

'What? Cade's announcement that he intends to marry me, or your mother's unhappiness?'

Faith tilted her head as she studied Tory. 'I can do both, but apparently you can't. You have too much sensibility. And kindness. Oh, she'd hate that. One more thing to celebrate,' she decided, and sipped her wine.

'That's unattractive, Faith,' Cade murmured.

'Oh, let me crow for a minute, will you? Not everyone's as high-minded as the two of you. Good Lord, you really suit each other. Who'd have thought it? I'm happy for you. Imagine that. I'm sincerely happy for you. I believe I feel a little mushy inside.'

'Try to control this embarrassing display of sentiment.' Impatient with her, Cade turned to Tory, ran his hands up her arms, down again to her wrists. 'I need to get something out of my office, then we'll go. Will you be all right?'

'Cade, talk to your mother.'

'No.' He kissed her lightly. 'I won't be long.'

'Drink your wine,' Faith suggested, when they were alone. 'It'll put some color back in your cheeks.'

'I don't want any wine.' Tory set the glass aside, then walked to the window. She wanted to be outside again, where she could breathe.

'If you insist on looking unhappy, you'll only spoil this for Cade. He did this because he loves you.'

'And why did you?'

'Interesting question. A year ago, oh hell, likely a month ago, I might have taken her up on it. That's a powerful chunk of money, and I do like what money can buy.'

'No, you wouldn't have done it, not ever, and I'll tell you why.' Tory glanced back. 'First, it would have been to throw it back in her face, but second and more than the first, it would have been for Cade. Because you love him.'

'Yes, I do, and love doesn't come easy to either of us. My mother saw to that.'

'Will you blame her for everything?'

'No, just what she's entitled to. I screwed up my life plenty all on my own. But he didn't. He never did damage to himself, or anyone else. I love him tremendously.'

Surprised, Tory glanced over. Faith's eyes were still bright, but there were tears in them.

'He didn't say what he did to her to hurt her, but because it was truth. I would have said it to hurt her. Feel sorry for her if you must, but don't expect it of me. He has a chance with you, and I want to see him take it.'

'Why didn't you tell him that?'

'I'm telling you. I see what he feels for you, and I wish I could feel it for someone. Not to make myself a better person. I like myself the way I am. Still if someone matters that much . . .' Contemplatively she studied the wine in her glass, the light that shined through it from the window. 'If someone matters that much it's bound to take something out of you.' She shifted her gaze to Tory. 'Isn't it?'

'Yes. But I'm beginning to think it's something you don't need anymore. Not if someone loves you back.'

'Interesting. That's a nut to chew on.' She looked over as Cade came in. 'I suppose you want to be alone now.'

'Yes.'

'Then Bee and I will just take ourselves off, won't we?' She nuzzled the dog, then nudged her onto the floor. 'In fact, I think we'll go out and stay out until the air clears.' She touched Cade's cheek as she walked by. 'I'd suggest you do the same.'

'Not quite yet.' He waited until he heard the door close behind

347

his sister, then held out a hand for Tory. 'I want to do this here. We can consider it closing a circle.'

'Cade, that was difficult for you, for all of you. I—'

'No, it wasn't. And it's done. You and I, we're just beginning.' He took a box from his pocket, opened it. The diamond caught the sunlight, exploded with it. 'This was my grandmother's, and it came to me.'

Panic choked her. 'Don't.' She tugged at her hand, but he held her fingers firm in his.

'It came to me,' he repeated, 'with the hope that one day I'd give it to the woman I wanted to marry. I didn't give it to Deborah. It never occurred to me to give it to her. I suppose I knew I was keeping it for someone else. That I was waiting for someone else. Look at me, Tory.'

'It's all so fast. You should take more time.'

'Twenty years or two months. Time's never been the point for us. If you can't believe and trust what I say, if it isn't enough to steady you, look at what I feel.' He lifted her hand to his heart. 'Look in me, Tory.'

She couldn't refuse or resist. And the heat of it slid into her. Warmth and strength. And hope. His heart beat steady under her palm, his eyes never wavered from hers. Trust, she thought. He was trusting her with all that he was. The next step was hers.

'I wish you could look in me, because I don't know how to tell you what I feel. Scared, because there's so much of it. I never wanted to be in love with anyone again. But I didn't know it could be different. I didn't know it could be you. You're so steady, Cade.' Smiling now, she lifted a hand to toy with his hair. 'You steady me.'

'Marry me.'

'Oh God.' She took a deep breath, had to take a second. 'Yes.' She looked down as he slipped the ring on her finger. 'It's beautiful. I get dizzy looking at it.'

'It's a little big.' He ran a thumb around the gold band. 'You have delicate hands. We'll have it sized.'

'Not right away. I want to get used to it first.' She closed her hand into a fist, then let out a sigh. 'She loved him.' Her eyes swam as she lifted them again. 'Your grandmother. She loved him. Her name was Laura, and she was happy.'

'So will we be,' he promised.

She let herself believe him.

Carl D. kept the siren on and the speedometer at eighty straight up I-95. It wasn't called for, of course, but it did give him a nice little kick. And God knew it entertained J.R.

He shut it down as they approached their turnoff.

'Maybe we oughta be doing this on Sundays instead of fishing.'

'Gets the blood moving,' J.R. agreed. 'Hard to feel like an old fart when you're highballing down the road.'

'Who you calling an old fart? Tell you what I'll do, J.R., if you think it'll make it smoother for you. I'll drop you off at your sister's place, then I'll go on and check in with Sheriff. Give you time to talk to her and for her to get her things together.'

'I appreciate that.' J.R.'s mood plummeted, but he did his best to bolster it. 'She's not going to want to budge, so it'll take a little doing. I figure I'll tell her we're pretty sure Han's still around Progress, so she'll be closer to him if she comes on along with me.'

'It may just be the truth. And that being the case, I'm going to put extra patrols on your street. I want you to start using that fancy alarm system Boots talked you into a couple years back.'

'Been using it since you found the Bellows girl. Boots says she doesn't get a minute's rest unless we got it on.' He thought of his town, the streets he could walk with his eyes shut, the people he knew by name. And all who knew him. 'That's not the way it's supposed to be.'

'No, but sometimes that's the way it is. You and me, J.R., we grew up one way. We've seen the changes come into Progress, and most of them's good. We bend to them, maybe lose a little something when they plant houses in a field where we used to play ball, or put up another Jiffy Mart and talk about goddamn strip malls outside of town. But we bend. Some changes you have to meet another way altogether.'

J.R. smiled a little. 'What the hell does that mean?'

'Damned if I know. This the turn for her place?'

'Yeah. Road's rough. You're going to want to mind your oil pan. I'm ashamed for you to see how she's living, Carl D.'

'Put that aside. We've been friends too long for that kind of shit.' The cruiser bumped, scraped. Wincing, Carl D. slowed to a crawl. Then peering ahead, his eyes narrowed. 'What the hell's this? Goddamn it. There's trouble. Goddamn it,' he repeated, and hit the gas so they took the rest of the rutted road in wild bumps.

Two cruisers sat nose-to-nose outside the house. Yellow police tape was stretched around the scruffy yard. Even as he hit the brakes, the uniform standing on the sagging porch stepped down.

'Chief Russ outta Progress.' He fumbled out his ID, held it up for the uniform to scan. 'What happened here?'

'We had an incident, Chief Russ.' The officer's face was pale and coldly set, his eyes concealed behind dark glasses. 'I'll have to ask you to stay here. The sheriff's inside. He'll need to clear you.'

'This is my sister's place.' J.R. snatched at the cop's sleeve. 'My sister lives here. Where's my sister?'

'You'll have to speak with the sheriff. Please stay behind the line,' he ordered, and strode into the house.

'Something's happened to Sarabeth. I have to—'

'Hold on.' Carl D. grabbed his arm before J.R. could rush forward. 'Just hold on. Nothing you can do. Let's just hold on.'

He'd already spotted the dark stain on the dirt outside the chicken coop, and a second smearing near the overgrown grass.

Sheriff Bridger was a hefty man with a face seamed by years and weather. His eyes were faded blue and set in by lines that looked burned into the skin by the sun. He scanned the area as he stepped out, took a moment to wipe beads of sweat from his brow, then walked toward the waiting men.

'Chief Russ.'

'That's right. Sheriff, I brought Mr. Mooney here up to fetch his sister. Sarabeth Bodeen. What happened here?'

Bridger shifted his pale eyes to J.R. 'You brother to Sarabeth Bodeen?'

'Yes. Where's my sister?'

'I'm sorry to tell you, Mr. Mooney. We had trouble here, sometime early this morning. Your sister's dead.'

'Dead? What are you talking about? That can't be. I talked to her not two days ago. Not two days back. Carl D., you said they had police here, right here, looking out for her.'

'That's right, we did. And I lost a man this morning, too. A good man with a family. I'm sorry for your loss, Mr. Mooney, and I'm sorry for theirs.'

'J.R., you sit down now. I want you to sit until you get your legs under you.' Carl D. opened the car door, nudged his friend down on the seat. J.R.'s face was alarmingly red, and his big frame had started to shake.

'You mind having somebody bring him some water, Sheriff?'

With a nod, Bridger turned to signal the uniform. 'Purty, bring Mr. Mooney here a glass of water.'

'You sit here, now.' Carl D.'s knees popped like firecrackers when he crouched down. 'Just sit here and catch your breath. Let me do what I can do.'

'I just talked to her,' J.R. repeated. 'Friday evening. I talked to her.'

'I know it. Just you sit here until I get back.' He stepped away from the car, moving until he was out of J.R.'s hearing. 'Can you tell me what happened here?'

'We've been putting it together last few hours. Flint, he caught the two-to-ten shift. We didn't know there was trouble until his relief showed up, and found him. Over there.' Bridger gestured toward the coop.

They'd taken his man off to the morgue, zipped into a black bag. He was not going to forget it.

'He caught a round in the back. Took him down. He was young, strong. He tried getting back to his unit here, crawled over fifteen feet with that round in him. Had his weapon out. Had his weapon in his hand. Somebody put a gun in his ear and pulled the trigger.

'He was thirty-three years old, Chief Russ. Got a ten-year-old boy and an eight-year-old girl at home. I take responsibility they're without a father now. I sent him out here. We knew Bodeen was dangerous, but we didn't know he was armed. Never used a firearm in any of his other doings. The motherfucker shot my man in the back.'

Carl D. wiped the back of his hand over his mouth. 'And Miz Bodeen?'

Sarabeth. Sari Mooney, who'd sat on his ma's front porch, ate at her table.

'My guess is she knew he was coming. Had a suitcase packed. There's an empty coffee can in the bedroom, and looks to me like she might've kept her house cash in it. Gone now. Door was open, unforced. She let him in or he walked in. He shot her twice. Once in the chest, once in the back of the head.'

Carl D. shoved the sorrow aside, eyed the situation of the house, the land. 'Guess you've done a canvas.'

'Yeah. Talked to the neighbors. Finally got somebody to say they heard what maybe was gunshots about five, five-thirty this morning. People mind their own around here. Nobody paid any attention to it.'

The heat was merciless. Carl D. dragged out a handkerchief and rubbed it over his face as sweat soaked through his fishing shirt. 'How the hell'd he get here?'

'Can't say. Hitched a ride, maybe. Stole a car. We're looking into it.'

'For the money in a coffee can? Don't sit right. She had a suit-case packed?'

'That's right. Her clothes in it, and some of his. She knew he was coming. We're checking the phone records. Gotta figure he called her, and she gave him the lay of the land. She wasn't what you'd call cooperative with the police round these parts.'

And he blamed her, though she was dead as Eve, for the murder of his man.

'Mr. Mooney going to be up to doing a next-of-kin ID on her?'

'Yeah.' Carl D. rubbed his mouth again. 'He'll do it. You inform the deceased's mother yet?'

'No. I was going to handle that back at the office.'

'I'd appreciate it if you'd let me do that, Sheriff Bridger. Not wanting to step on your ground here, but she knows me.'

'You're welcome to that part of the job. It ain't one I relish.'

'Fine then. I'll take J.R. on by his mama's. It'll be easier for them that way.'

'All right. He's a cop killer now, Chief Russ. If it gives your friend there any comfort, you let him know that bastard won't be able to run far enough or fast enough.'

'You keep me up-to-date, Sheriff, and I'll do the same. I got the federals coming tomorrow or the day after. They'll want to pay you a call.'

'Welcome to. But this is my turf, and that was my man they carried away in a bag this morning.' Bridger spat on the ground. 'Bodeen better pray to his almighty God the feds get to him before I do.'

Miles away, Hannibal Bodeen tore into a pork chop. He'd gotten it, along with bread and cheese and a bottle of Jim Beam, from a

352

house he'd broken into. It had been simple enough, with the family gone off to church. He'd watched them stroll out of the house in their fancy Sunday clothes and pile into a shiny minivan. Hypocrites. Going to church to show off their material goods. Into the house of the Lord to flaunt themselves.

God would punish them, just like he punished all the proud and pompous. And God had provided, he thought, as he gnawed the pork bone clean.

He'd found plenty of food in that big house. Meat wrapped up from last night's dinner. Enough to restore his body. And drink to sustain him in his hour of need. This was his trial, his test, this wandering in the wilderness.

He tossed the bone aside and took a long drink from the bottle.

For a time he'd despaired. Why was he being punished, a right-eous man? Then it all came clear. He was to be tested, he was to prove his worthiness. God had shouldered him with temptation, time and time again. There had been times he'd been weak, times he'd succumbed. But now he was given this chance.

Satan had lived in his house, under his roof, for eighteen years. He had done his best to drive the devil out, but he had failed. He would not fail again.

He lifted the bottle, let the heat of the whiskey strengthen him. Soon, very soon, he would complete the task that had been given him. He would rest, he would pray. Then the way would be shown to him.

He closed his eyes and curled up to sleep. The Lord provided, he thought, and laid his hand over the gun tucked beside him.

Chapter Twenty-Seven

Tory watched Chief Russ's car drive slowly down her lane, make the turn onto the road to Progress. She sat where she had since her uncle had told her about her mother, where she'd lowered herself inch by inch into the old rocker on the front porch.

It was her stillness that worried Cade. Her stillness, and her silence.

'Tory, come on inside and lie down awhile.'

'I don't want to lie down. I'm all right. I wish I weren't so all right. I wish I felt more than I do. There's blankness inside me where there should be grief. I'm trying to write something on it, and I can't. What am I that I can't feel grief for my own mother?'

'Don't push yourself.'

'I felt more grief and pity for Sherry Bellows. A woman I met once. I felt more shock and horror for a stranger than I do for my own blood. I looked in my uncle's eyes and I could see the pain there, the sadness. But it's not in me. I've got no tears for her.'

'Maybe you've shed enough of them already.'

'Something's missing inside me.'

'No, it's not.' He came around now, knelt in front of her. 'She stopped being part of your life. It's easier to mourn a stranger than it is someone who should have been part of you, and wasn't.'

'My mother is dead. They believe my father killed her. And the question in my mind, most prominently in my mind at this moment, is why do you want to take on someone who comes from that?'

'You know the answer. And if love isn't enough, we'll add sense. You aren't your parents any more than I'm mine. The life we'll begin and build together is ours.'

'I should walk away from you. That's sensible, and I suppose loving, too. But I won't. I need you. I want so much what we might have together. So I won't do the courageous thing and walk away.'

'Darling, you wouldn't get two feet.'

She let out her breath in a shaky laugh. 'Maybe I know it. Cade.' It was so easy to touch him, to brush her fingertips over the gilt edges of his hair. 'Would we have come together, do you think, if Hope had lived? If nothing that happened had happened and we'd just grown up here like normal people?'

'Yes.'

'Sometimes your confidence is a comfort.' She walked to the end of the porch to look at the trees that tucked the marsh into shadows. 'This is the second time since I've come home someone has died. The second time I thought it would be me he came for. He'll come yet.'

'He won't get near you.'

Yes, she thought, his confidence could be a comfort. 'He'll have to come. He'll have to try.' She steadied herself, turned back. 'Can you get me a gun?'

'Tory—'

'Don't say you'll protect me, or that the police will find him, stop him. I believe all those things as far as they go. But he will come back for me, Cade. I know it as truly as I know anything. I must be able to defend myself if I have to. And I will defend myself. I won't hesitate to take his life to save my own. I might have once. But I have too much at stake now. I have you now.'

There was a sick dread in his stomach, but he nodded. Saying nothing, he walked to his car, opened the glove compartment. He'd started carrying the revolver with him since Sherry Bellow's murder.

He brought it back to Tory. 'This is a revolver, a thirty-eight.'

'It's smaller than I imagined.'

'It was my father's.' Cade turned the old Smith & Wesson over in his hand. 'What you call a hideout gun, I suppose, because it's compact. Do you know how to fire it?'

She pressed her lips together. It looked sinister and efficient in Cade's hand. The elegant farmer's hand. 'Pull the trigger?'

'Well, there's a little more to it than that. Are you sure about this, Tory?'

'Yes.' She let out a breath. 'Yes, I'm sure.'

'Come on then. We'll go out in the yard and I'll give you a lesson.'

Faith sang in a voice surprisingly light and sweet as she carried groceries up the stairs into Wade's apartment. Bee scrambled after her, sniffing the air that held memories of countless dogs, cats, and pet rodents. Delighted with herself, Faith shifted bags, managed the knob, and bumped the door open with her hip.

On a ragged pad in the living room, Mongo was lying with his head on his paws. His tail thumped, and his head lifted as Faith walked in.

'Why, hello there. You're looking lots better, you big old thing. Bee, Mongo's recuperating. Don't chew on his ears. He'll swallow you in one bite.' But Bee was already sniffing, nibbling, and nudging.

'Well, I guess the two of you better get acquainted. Where's the doctor?'

She found him in the kitchen, staring into a cup of coffee. 'There he is now.' She dumped her bags on the counter, then turned to wrap her arms around his neck from behind and kiss the top of his head. 'I've got a big surprise for you, Doc Wade. You're going to get yourself a home-cooked supper. And, if you play your cards right, a romantic interlude will follow dessert.'

There was a machine-gun burst of barking from the living room that sent her scurrying out. 'Now, isn't that the cutest thing? Wade, you ought to come out and see this. They're playing together. Well, this big dog here's pretty much squashing Bee with one paw, but they're having such a time.'

She was still laughing when she came back, then stopped when she saw Wade's face. 'Honey, what's the matter? Did something go wrong with the horse out at the Hill place last night?'

'No. No. The mare's fine. My aunt – my father's sister – she's dead. She was murdered early this morning.'

'Oh my God. Oh, Wade, that's awful. What is going *on* around here?' She sat down across from him, wishing she knew what to do. 'Your daddy's sister? Tory's mama?'

'Yes. I haven't seen her in, Christ, I don't even remember the last time. I can't even get a picture of her face in my head.'

'That's all right now.'

'It's not all right. My family's ripping itself apart. For God's sake, Faith, they think my uncle killed her.'

It was the horror in his eyes that had her pushing back her own. 'He's a bad man, Wade. A bad and dangerous man, and nothing to do with you. I'm sorry for Tory, I swear I am. And for your aunt and your family. But . . . well, I'm going to say it even if it makes you mad at me. She chose him, Wade, and she stayed with him. Maybe that's a kind of love, but it's a bad kind. It's a sorry kind.'

'We don't know what goes on in other people's lives.'

'Oh, hell we don't. We're always saying that, but we do know. I know what went on in my parents' lives. I know that if either of them had any gumption they'd have made their marriage work, or they'd have ended it. Instead my mother clung to the Lavelle name like it was some sort of prize, and Papa took up with another woman. And whose fault was that? I spent a long time letting myself believe it was the other woman's, but it wasn't. It was Papa's for not honoring his marriage vows, and Mama's for tolerating it. Maybe it's easier to say this is all Hannibal Bodeen's fault. But it's not. And it sure as hell isn't yours, or Tory's, or your daddy's.'

She pushed back from the table. 'I wish I could think of nice things to say. Of soft and comforting things to say, but I'm no good at it. I guess you want to go on over to your daddy's.'

'No.' He kept his eyes on her face as he had since she'd begun to speak. 'He's better off with my mother. She'll know what to do for him. Who the hell would've thought you'd know what to do for me?' He held out a hand. When she took it, he pulled her close, turned his face into her belly. 'Stay, will you?'

' 'Course I will.' She stroked a hand down his hair. Her insides were a little shaky, an odd feeling. 'We'll just be quiet awhile.'

He held on, as surprised as she that she would be an anchor for him. 'I've been sitting here since my father called. I don't know how long. Half an hour, an hour. Frozen inside. I don't know what to do for my family.'

'You will, when the time comes to do it. You always do. You want me to fix you some fresh coffee?'

'No. Thanks. No. I have to call my grandmother, and Tory. I have to figure out what to say first.' With his eyes closed and his face pressed against her, he listened to the dogs barking in the next room. 'I'm going to keep Mongo.'

'I know it, honey.'

'His leg's doing all right. It'll take a while to heal yet, but he'll be fine. A little gimpy maybe. I was going to find him a good home, but . . . I can't.' He looked up, puzzled. 'What do you mean you know it? I never keep dogs.'

'You hadn't found the right one yet, is all.'

His eyes narrowed on her face, but his dimples deepened as they did when he was amused. 'You're getting a little too wise for comfort.'

'It's the new me. I kind of like it.'

'And this new you cooks supper?'

'On rare occasions. I got us a couple of steaks in there, and the trimmings.' She walked to the counter, dug in the bag, and pulled out two white candles. 'Lucy down at the market asked me what kind of evening I had planned buying red meat and white candles and a fancy cheesecake in a box.'

He smiled a little, rose from his chair. 'And what did you tell Lucy down at the market?'

'I told her I was fixing a romantic dinner for two, for myself and Dr. Wade Mooney. A number of interested ears pricked at that tidbit of information.' She set the candles down. 'I hope you don't mind that I was indiscreet, and that we will now find ourselves the subject of considerable talk and speculation.'

'No.' He slid his arms around her, laid his cheek on her hair. 'I don't mind.'

'Lissy, honey, I don't feel right about this.'

'Now, Dwight, we're paying a grievance call on friends and neighbors.' Trying to find comfort, Lissy shifted on the seat of the car, hauling her belly up with one arm. 'Tory's just lost her mother, and she'll appreciate some sympathy.'

'Tomorrow maybe.' Dwight gave the road ahead a pained look. 'The next day.'

'Why, she won't feel up to making herself a decent meal, now, will she? So I'm taking her a nice chicken casserole. Help keep her strength up. Lord, it will be trying for her.'

Despite her pious sigh, there was a lively fascination dancing inside her. Tory's own mother shot dead by her own father. Why, it was just like something out of the tabloid papers, or out of Hollywood. And since she'd dragged Dwight out of the house hardly an hour after the news hit, she'd likely be the first to get a look at Tory.

Not that she wasn't sympathetic to Tory. Naturally she was. Hadn't she taken that casserole her mother had made for her to heat up after the baby came and brought it along? Food was for death, everyone knew that.

'She's not going to feel up to company,' Dwight insisted.

'We're not company. Why, I went to school with Tory. The both of us have known her since we were children. I couldn't bear the idea of her being alone at such a time.' Or of someone else getting there first. 'Besides all that, Dwight Frazier, you're mayor. It's your duty to call on the bereaved. Goodness, watch these bumps, honey. I have to pee again.'

'I don't want you getting too excited or upset.' He reached over to pat her hand. 'No going into labor out here, Lissy.'

'Don't you worry.' But it pleased her that he did. 'I've got three weeks left, at least. Goodness, how do I look?' Anxious, she flipped down the vanity mirror. 'I must look a fright, rushing out the way I did. A big, fat frightful cow.'

'You're beautiful. Still the prettiest girl in Progress. And all mine.'

'Oh, Dwight.' She flushed rosily and fluffed her hair. 'You're so sweet. I just feel so fat and ugly these days. And Tory's so slim.'

'Skin and bones. My woman's got curves.' He reached over to rub her breast and made her squeal.

'Stop that.' Giggling, she gave his hand a swat. 'Shame on you. 'Shame on you. Now look, we're almost there and you've got me all flustered.' She snuck her hand between his legs. 'Got yourself flustered, too. Remember how we used to park out this way when we were young and foolish?'

'And I talked you into the backseat of my daddy's car.'

'Didn't take much talking. I was just crazy about you. The first time we made love it was out here. It was so dark, so sexy. Dwight.' She walked her fingers up his leg. 'After the baby comes, and I get my figure back, let's have Mama come over and baby-sit. You and I'll drive on out here and see if you can still talk me into the backseat.'

He blew out a breath. 'Keep talking like that, Lissy, and I'm not going to be able to get out of this car without embarrassing myself.'

359

'Slow down a little. I want to put some lipstick on anyway.' She dug a tube out of her purse.

'Mama said she'd keep Luke overnight. We should go by and see Boots and J.R. after we leave Tory's. I guess they'll have the funeral up around Florence. We'll have to go, of course, represent the town, and so on. I don't have any black maternity dresses. I suppose I'll have to make do with the navy, even though it has that pretty white collar. People'll understand, don't you think, if I wear navy blue? And we'll have to send flowers.'

She chattered until they turned into the lane. Dwight was no longer aroused, but he was getting a vague headache.

Fifteen minutes, he promised himself. He'd give Lissy fifteen minutes to fuss over Tory, then he was taking her home and making her put her feet up. That way, he could get himself a beer, kick back, and watch whatever was on ESPN.

Nobody in Progress was going to do any grieving over Sarabeth Bodeen except her immediate family. He didn't see why a death so far removed from him, and his town, need occupy more than the minimum amount of his time, personal or official.

He'd pay his duty calls, then forget it.

'I don't know why anybody would want to live way out here without a single soul for company,' Lissy said, as Dwight hauled her out of the car. 'Then again, Tory always was an odd one. Rare as a two-headed duck, my mama would say. Then again . . .' She trailed off and gave Cade's car a significant look. 'I guess she doesn't lack for company after all. I swear, I can't see those two together, Dwight, not for a New York minute. They can't have a thing in common, and as far as I can see, Tory's not the kind to keep a man very warm, if you know what I mean. She's good-looking enough if you like that type, but she's nothing compared to Deborah Purcell. I can't for the life of me figure what Cade sees in her. A man in his position could have his pick of women. God knows I've tried to steer him toward plenty of them.'

Dwight said 'Hmmm' and 'Uh-huh' and 'Yes, honey' a couple of times as he got the casserole dish out of the car. It wasn't necessary to actually listen to his wife when she started on one of her ramblings. After several years of marriage he had her rhythm down so that he managed to punctuate her statements at the appropriate times without having a clue what she was talking about.

The system served them both well.

360

'I imagine he'll get tired of her before much longer and they'll drift apart the way people do when they don't have a real bond like we do.'

She fluttered at him, gave his arm a little pat, and he read the signal correctly. He glanced down and gave her a warm and loving look.

'Once he's shaken loose again, we'll have him over for dinner with, oh, maybe Crystal Bean. I might even be able to find some nice man for Tory, more her kind. That'll take some doing as I don't think there're many men who'll be willing to take on such a strange one. I swear, sometimes she'll just look at me and give me the shivers, if you know what I mean. Tory!'

She exclaimed it when Tory opened the door, and immediately opened her arms. 'Oh honey, I'm just so sorry about your mother. Dwight and I came the minute we heard. You poor thing. Now, why aren't you resting? I was sure Cade would have you lying down at a time like this.'

The embrace was smothering and hot. 'I'm all right.'

'Of course you're not all right, and you don't have to pretend with us. Old friends.' She flapped her hand against Tory's back. 'Now, I want you to sit down, and I'm going to make you a nice cup of tea. I brought you a casserole here. I want you to have a hot meal, keep your strength up during this painful time. Cade.'

She released Tory to turn her attention on Cade as he came in from the kitchen. 'I'm glad you're here, seeing to Tory. A time like this she needs all her friends. Now, you come on with me, honey.' She slipped an arm around Tory's waist as if to support her. 'Dwight, you bring that dish on back to the kitchen so I can warm it up for Tory.'

'Lissy, that's very kind of you,' Tory began.

'Nothing kind about it, not between friends. I know you must be half out of your mind right now, but we're here for you. Whatever's said or done, you count on us, isn't that right, Dwight, honey?'

'Sure it is.' He gave Cade a pained look as Lissy pulled Tory toward the kitchen. 'I couldn't stop her,' he murmured. 'She means it for the best.'

'I'm sure she does.'

'It's a terrible thing. Terrible. How's Tory holding up?'

'She's coping.' Cade glanced back toward the kitchen where

Lissy's voice ran on and on. 'I'm worried about her, but she's coping.'

'They're saying it was Hannibal Bodeen who did it. Word's spreading fast. I figured you'd want to know that's what's being said. It's going to get worse, I expect, before it gets better.'

'I don't think it gets any worse. Chief Russ give you any updates on the manhunt?'

'He's playing it close. I guess he's got to. Haven't had anything like this around here since you lost your sister, Cade.' He hesitated, then shifted, the dish still in his hands. 'It can't be easy on you, either, bringing all that back again.'

'No, it's not. But I'll tell you the way it's starting to look, and that might close this off once and for all. It's starting to look like it might have been Bodeen who killed Hope.'

'Killed—' He took a long breath, blew it out again as he, too, glanced toward the kitchen. 'God almighty, Cade. I don't know what to say. What to think.'

'Neither do I. Yet.'

'Dwight, come on and bring me that casserole, will you?'

'On the way,' he called back. 'I'll move Lissy along, soon as I can. I know you don't want company.'

'Appreciate it. And I'd appreciate it if you wouldn't mention Tory's father's connection to Hope. To Lissy or anyone just yet. Things are hard enough on Tory right now.'

'You can count on me. I mean that, Cade. You let me know what you want done and when, and I'll see to it.' He managed a smile. 'You and me and Wade, we go back. All the way back.'

'I will count on you. I do. I—'

There was a sudden squeal from the kitchen that had Dwight bolting across the room in alarm. He burst in to see Lissy, eyes wide, mouth open, with Tory's hand clutched in hers.

'Engaged! Why, I just can't believe it! Dwight, look here what Tory's wearing on her finger, and neither of them saying a word about it.' She jerked Tory's hand forward, her own face alive with the bliss of being, she was sure, the first to know. 'Isn't this something?'

Dwight studied the ring, then looked into Tory's eyes. He saw the fatigue, the embarrassment, the faint irritation. 'It sure is. I hope you'll be very happy.'

'Of course she'll be happy.' Lissy dropped Tory's hand so she

362

could waddle around the table and hug Cade. 'Aren't you the sly one, never letting on. Then snapping Tory up so fast. Why, her head must still be spinning. We have to celebrate, drink a toast to the happy couple. Oh.'

She stopped, had the grace to flush even if her eyes continued to dance. 'What am I thinking? I'm just a scatterbrain, that's all. Oh honey, you must be so torn.' She scurried back to Tory as quickly as she could manage. 'Getting engaged and losing your mama this way so close together. Life goes on, you remember that. Life does go on.'

Tory didn't bother to sigh, but she did manage to get her hand in her lap before Lissy could grab it again. 'Thank you, Lissy. I'm sorry, I hope you understand, but I need to call my grandmother. We have to see about arrangements.'

'Of course we understand. Now, I want you to let me know if there's anything I can do. Anything at all. Nothing's too big or too small. Dwight and I are more than happy to help. Aren't we, Dwight?'

'That's right.' He put his arm firmly around Lissy. 'We'll go on now, but you can call us if there's anything you need. No, don't you get up.' He steered Lissy toward the doorway. 'We'll let ourselves out. You call now, you hear?'

'Thank you.'

'Imagine that. Imagine it!' Lissy could hardly wait until they'd gotten to the front door. 'Wearing a diamond big enough to blind you, and on the day she finds out her daddy killed her mama. I swear, Dwight, I don't know what to think. She'll be planning a wedding and a funeral at the same time. I told you, didn't I tell you, she was a strange one.'

'You told me, honey.' He nudged her into the car, shut the door. 'You surely told me,' he murmured.

Inside, Cade sat at the table. For a moment he and Tory studied each other in silence. 'Sorry,' he said at length.

'For?'

'Dwight's my friend, and she comes along with him.'

'She's a silly woman. Not particularly crafty, not particularly mean. She thrives on other people's business, good and bad. Right now, she doesn't know which to highlight. Here's Victoria Bodeen, in the middle of a tragedy and scandal. And here she is again, engaged to one of the most prominent men in the county.'

Tory paused, glanced down at the ring on her finger. It was a jolt to see it there, she thought. Not a bad sensation, just an odd one.

'Such bulletins,' she continued. 'It all must be rattling around in her head like marbles. Clinking together as there isn't much else in there to get in the way.'

His mouth twitched. 'Is that speculation, or did you take a look?'

'There's no need to. And I don't do that, anyway, when everything she's thinking runs riot over her face. Dwight would never have gotten her out so quickly if she hadn't been jumping to get to a phone and start spreading the word.'

'And that bothers you.'

'Yes.' She pushed back from the table, wandered to the window. Odd that it comforted somehow to look out into the dark shadows of the marsh. 'I knew when I came back here I'd be under the microscope. I understood that. And I'll deal with it. My mother . . . I'll deal with that, too. There's nothing else I can do.'

'You don't have to deal with it alone.'

'I know. I came back here to face myself, I suppose. To resolve or at least accept what had happened to Hope, and my part in that. I expected the talk, the looks, the speculation and curiosity. I planned to use them to build my business. I have, and I'll keep on using them. That's cold.'

'No, it's good sense. Tough maybe, but not cold.'

'I came back for me,' she said quietly. 'To prove I could. I expected to pay for it. To quiet the restlessness inside me, but to pay for it. I never expected you.'

She turned back. 'I never expected you, Cade. And I don't know quite what to do with all of this feeling I have inside me for you.'

He got to his feet, crossed to her to brush her hair back from her face. 'You'll figure it out.'

'This is so easy for you.'

'I guess I've been waiting for you.'

'Cade, my father . . . What he is. Part of that's in me. You have to consider that. You have to weigh it in.'

'Do I?' He gave her a considering look as he turned her to walk

364

toward the bedroom. 'You're probably right. I suppose I should give you the same opportunity to weigh in my great-grandfather Horace who engaged in a long, lascivious affair with his wife's brother. When she discovered it, and in what you can imagine was her shocked distress, threatened to expose him, Horace, along with his lover, displeased by this reaction, dismembered her and kept the alligators fat and happy for several days.'

'You're making that up.'

'No indeed.' He drew her down on the bed. 'Well, the business about the alligators is family legend. There are some who say she simply fled to Savannah and lived to the age of ninety-six in mortified solitude. Either way, it isn't a proud footnote in the Lavelle family history.'

She turned to him, found the curve of his shoulder, and rested her head there. 'I suppose it's a good thing I don't have any brothers.'

'There you go. Sleep awhile, Tory. It's just you and me here. That's what matters now.'

While she slept, he lay wakeful, listening to the sounds of the night.

Chapter Twenty-Eight

I'm asking you to indulge me.'

Tory looked up at the peaks and lines of Beaux Reves. 'You're putting me between yourself and your mother again, Cade. That's not fair to any of us.'

'No. But I need to speak with her, and I don't want you driving into town by yourself. I don't want you alone until this is over, Tory.'

'Well, that makes two of us, so you can rest easy there. But I'd as soon wait in the car while you do what you have to do inside.'

'Let's compromise.'

'Oh, when did that word enter your vocabulary?'

He slanted her a slow and very bland smile. 'We'll go around back. You can wait in the kitchen. My mother doesn't spend a lot of time there.'

She started to object again, subsided. He would, she knew, simply roll over her excuses and she was too worn out to fight about it. Too many dreams in the night, too many images sliding into her head in the day.

When it was over, he said. As if it would be. As if it could.

She got out of the car, walked with him around the garden path, through the wildly blooming roses, past the glossy-leafed camellia where a young girl had once secreted her pretty pink bike, wound through the hills of azaleas with their blooms long since spent, and fragrant spires of lavender that would scent the air all the way into winter.

The world was lush here, full of color and shape and perfume. A lazily elegant place of bricked paths and lovely benches set just so among the beds and shrubs with overflowing pots of mixed

366

blooms tucked artistically among the stream. The result was like a painting, meticulously executed.

Margaret's world again, Tory realized, just like the studied perfection of the rooms inside. Nothing to mar it, nothing to change it. How wrenching it would be to have some invader burst in and skew the balance of it all.

'You don't understand her.'

'Excuse me?'

'Your mother. You don't understand her at all.'

Intrigued, Cade laced his fingers with Tory's. 'Did I give you the impression I thought I did?'

'This is her world, Cade. This is her life. The house, the gardens, the view she sees out the windows. Even before Hope died, it was the center for her. What she tended and preserved. And continued to after she lost her child. She could keep this,' she said, turning to him. 'Touch it, see it, make certain it didn't change. Don't take this from her.'

'I'm not.' He cupped Tory's face in his hands now, holding it up to his. 'But neither will I tolerate her using it, or the farm, as a threat to hold me under her thumb. I can't give her more than I've already offered, not even for you.'

'There has to be a compromise. Just as you said.'

'One would think.' He laid his lips on her brow. 'But sometimes, with some people, there's only yes or no. Don't take this on.' He drew her back, and his eyes were troubled. 'Don't ask me to, Victoria.' The sound he made wasn't so much a sigh as a rush of air. 'Don't ask me to bargain our happiness against her approval. I've never had her approval to begin with.'

It was so strange to realize it, and all at once. He'd grown up in a castle and had been just as starved for kind words as she. 'It hurts you. I'm sorry I didn't see that it hurts you.'

'Old wounds.' He ran his hands down her arms, laced fingers again. 'They don't bleed like they used to.'

But they would seep and trickle from time to time, she thought, as they began to walk again. No one had ever used a belt on him, or fists. There were other ways to pummel a child.

Even here, in all this beauty, so far removed from the barren and stifling rooms of her childhood. Beautiful, yes, Tory thought, as they walked under an arbor buried in morning glories, but lonely. That was just another word for barren.

There should be someone sitting on the bench or clipping the gerberas for a basket. A child stretched belly-down over the path studying a lizard or toad.

The painting needed life, and sound and movement.

'I want children.'

Cade stopped in his tracks. 'Excuse me?'

Where had that come from, and why had it popped out of her mind as if it had always been there? 'I want children,' she repeated. 'I'm tired of empty yards and quiet gardens and tidy rooms. If we live here, I want noise and crumbs on the floor and dishes in the sink. I couldn't survive in all those perfect, untouched rooms, and that's something you can't ask me to do. I don't want this house without life inside it.'

The words rushed out of her mouth, and the panic riding in them made him smile. He remembered a young boy who'd wanted to build a fort. Scrap wood and tar paper.

'This is such an interesting coincidence. I was thinking two children, with an option for three.'

'Okay.' She blew out a breath. 'All right. I should've known you'd already figured it out.'

'I am a farmer. We plan. Then we hope fate cooperates.' He bent to pluck a sprig of rosemary from the kitchen garden. 'For remembrance,' he said, as he gave it to her. 'While you're waiting for me, remember we have a life to plan, as messy and noisy as we like.'

She went inside with him, and there was Lilah, as she was so often, working at the sink. The air smelled of coffee and biscuits and the sweet rose scent Lilah sprayed on every morning.

'You come in late for breakfast,' she said. 'Lucky for you I'm in a good mood.' She'd been watching them the last few minutes with a lightness of heart. They looked right together. She'd been waiting to see her boy look right with someone.

'Well, sit down, coffee's fresh enough. I made up some flapjack batter nobody's bothered to eat.'

'Is my mother upstairs?'

'She is, and the judge is cooling his heels in the front parlor.' Lilah was already getting down mugs. 'Don't have much to say to me today. Been on the phone considerable, and got her door shut. That sister of yours, she don't even bother coming home last night.'

Cade's stomach clutched. 'Faith's not home?'

'Nothing to worry on. She's with Doc Wade. Breezed out of here yesterday saying that's where she'd be and I'd see her when I see her. Seems nobody sleeps in their own bed around here these days but me. Too damn hot for all these carryings-on. Sit down and eat.'

'I need to speak to my mother. Feed her,' he ordered, pointing at Tory.

'I'm not a puppy,' Tory muttered as he strode away. 'Don't go to any trouble, Lilah.'

'Sit down, and take that martyr look off your face. It's his place to settle things with his mama, and not yours to fuss your head over it.' She got out the griddle to heat. 'And you'll eat what I put in front of you.'

'I'm beginning to think he takes after you.'

'Why shouldn't he? I did most of the raising of him. I'm not speaking against Miss Margaret. Some women aren't built to be mothers, is all. Don't make them less, just makes them what they are.'

She got a bowl out of the refrigerator, peeled back the cover. 'I was sorry to hear about your mother.'

'Thank you.'

Lilah stood a moment, bowl in the crook of her arm, her eyes dark and warm on Tory's face. 'Some women,' she said again, 'aren't built for mothering. That's why, just like the song says, God blesses the child who's got his own. You got your own, honey. You always did.'

For the first time since she'd heard the news of her mother's death, Tory wept.

Cade stopped at the parlor first. Manners would never have permitted him to walk by an old family friend.

'Judge.'

Gerald turned, and the stern, contemplative lines of his face relaxed fractionally when he saw Cade. 'I was hoping I'd have a chance to speak with you this morning. I hope you can spare me a minute.'

'Of course.' Cade stepped in, gestured to a chair. 'I hope you're well.'

'A little arthritis, acts up now and again. Old age.' Gerald gestured it aside as he sat. 'Never think it's going to happen to you, then you wake up one day and wonder who the hell that old man is in your shaving mirror. Well.' Gerald laid his palms on the knees of his trousers. 'I've known you since you were born.'

'So there's no need to pick your words,' Cade finished. 'I'm aware my mother has spoken to you about some legalities and changes in her will.'

'She's a proud woman, and she's concerned for you.'

'Is she?' Cade lifted his eyebrows as if fascinated by that information. 'She needn't be. I'm fine. More than fine. If her concern is for Beaux Reves,' he continued, 'it's also misplaced. We're having a very good year. Better, I think, even than last.'

Gerald cleared his throat. 'Cade, I knew your father most of my life, was his friend. I hope you'll take what I have to say in that spirit. If you would postpone your personal plans, take a bit more time to consider. I'm fully aware of a man's needs and desires, but when those desires are put ahead of duty, of practicality, and most of all ahead of family, it can never come to good.'

'I've asked Tory to marry me. I don't need my mother's blessing, or yours, for that matter. I can only regret those blessings aren't forthcoming.'

'Cade, you're a young man, with your life in front of you. I'm only asking, as a friend of both your parents, for you to take time to consider, time you can well spare at your age. To look at the entire picture. Particularly now that this tragedy has come into Tory Bodeen's life. A tragedy,' Gerald added, 'that speaks volumes of who and what she comes from. You were just a boy yourself when she lived here, and were sheltered from the harder facts of life.'

'What facts would they be?'

Gerald sighed. 'Hannibal Bodeen is a dangerous man, undoubtedly ill in his mind. Such things come down in the blood. Now, I have every sympathy for the child, make no mistake, but there's no changing what is.'

'Is this "The apple doesn't fall far from the tree"? Or is it "As a twig is bent so it grows"?'

Irritation flickered over Gerald's face. 'Either is apt. Victoria Bodeen lived in that house, under his hand, too long not to be bent by it.'

'Under his hand,' Cade said carefully.

'Figuratively, and I'm afraid, literally. Many years ago, Iris Mooney, Victoria's maternal grandmother, came to see me. She wanted to sue the Bodeens for custody of the girl. She said Bodeen beat the child.'

'She wanted to hire you?'

'She did. However, she had no proof of this abuse, no substantiation. I have no doubt, had none then, that she was telling the truth, but—'

'You knew,' Cade said very quietly. 'You knew that he was beating her, putting welts and bruises on her, and you did nothing?'

'The law—'

'Fuck the law.' He spoke in that same deadly cool voice as he got to his feet. 'She came to you for help, because she wanted to take a child out of a nightmare. And you did nothing.'

'It was not my place to interfere with the blood family. She had no proof. The case was weak.' Flustered, Gerald rose as well. He was unused to being questioned or looked at with such disgust. 'There were no police reports, none from social services. Just the word of a grandmother. If I had taken the case, nothing would have come of it.'

'We'll never know, will we? Because you didn't take the case. You didn't try to help.'

'It was not my place,' Gerald said again.

'It was your place. It's everyone's place. But she got through it without you, without anyone. Now, if you'll excuse me, I have personal business.'

He walked out quickly. Upstairs, Cade knocked on his mother's door. It occurred to him that there had often been closed doors in this house, barriers that required a polite request before they were removed. Manners forever took precedence here over intimacy.

That would change. He could promise himself that. The doors of Beaux Reves would be open. His children wouldn't have to wait like company for an invitation to enter.

'Come in.' Margaret continued to pack. She'd seen Cade drive up with that woman and had been expecting him to knock. She assumed he would ask her to change her mind about leaving, would attempt to reach a compromise. He was a deal maker, she mused, as she laid tissue paper between precisely folded blouses, as his father had been.

It would give her enormous satisfaction to listen to his requests and offers. And refuse them all.

'I'm sorry to disturb you.' The prologue came automatically. He'd said the same thing countless times when admitted to her rooms. 'And I'm sorry you and I find ourselves at odds.'

She didn't bother to look over. 'I've made arrangements to have my luggage picked up this afternoon. I will, naturally, expect the rest of my belongings to be shipped to me. I have a partial list of what is mine. It will take a bit more time to complete. I have acquired a number of possessions in my years in this house.'

'Of course. Have you decided where you'll be staying?'

The smooth tone of the question had her hands fumbling, her gaze darting toward him. 'I've made no permanent arrangements. Such things require careful consideration.'

'Yes. I thought you might be more comfortable in a house of your own, and somewhere nearby, as you have ties to the community. We own the property at the corner of Magnolia and Main. It's an attractive brick house, two stories, with a well-established yard and garden. It's tenanted at the moment, but the lease runs out in just over two months. If you're interested, I'll give the tenants notice.'

Staggered, she stared at him. 'How easily you put me out.'

'I'm not putting you out. The choice is yours. You're welcome to stay here. It's your home, and can continue to be. But it will also be Tory's home.'

'You'll see what she is eventually, but she'll have ruined you by then. Her mother was trash. Her father is a murderer. And she herself is nothing but an opportunist, a calculating sneak who never knew her place.'

'Her place is here with me. If you can't accept that, and her, then you'll have to make your place elsewhere.'

Sometimes, for some people, the answer was yes or no. It occurred to him that this time it applied to him as much as his mother.

'The house on Magnolia is yours if you want it. If, however, you prefer to go elsewhere, Beaux Reves will acquire the property of your choice.'

'Out of guilt?'

'No, Mama. I have no guilt for taking my happiness or loving a woman I also admire and respect.'

'Respect?' Margaret spat out. 'You can speak of respect?'

'Yes. I've never known anyone I respect more. So guilt plays no part here. But I will see to it you have a comfortable home.'

'I need nothing from you. I have money of my own.'

'I know that. Take whatever time you need to decide. Whatever that decision is, I hope you'll be happy with it. Or at least content. I wish . . .' He closed his eyes a moment, weary from maintaining the facade of manners. 'I wish there was more between us than this. I wish I knew why there can't be. We disappoint each other, Mama. I'm sorry for that.'

She had to press her lips together to stop their trembling. 'When I leave this house, you'll be dead to me.'

Grief swam into his eyes, swirled there, then cleared away. 'Yes, I know.'

He stepped back, then quietly shut the door between them.

Alone, Margaret sank onto the bed and listened to the silence.

Cade gathered what paperwork he thought he'd need over the next day or two, and listened to his phone messages while he loaded his briefcase. He needed to check in with Piney, return calls from the factory, and run by a couple of the rental units. There was a board meeting the next day, but that could be rescheduled.

His quarterly meeting with his bookkeeper couldn't. He'd just have to find a safe place to plant Tory for a few hours.

He glanced at his watch, picked up the phone. Faith answered, her voice slurred with sleep.

'Where's Wade?'

'Hmmm? Down with a cocker spaniel or something. What time is it?'

'It's after nine.'

'Go away. I'm sleeping.'

'I'm coming into town. Tory's with me. She's making noises about going into the shop. She doesn't plan to open today, but I expect she wants to find something to keep her busy. I want you to keep an eye out, then go over and stay with her.'

'Maybe you didn't hear me. I'm sleeping.'

'Get up. We'll be there within a half hour.'

'You're awful damn bossy this morning.'

'I don't want either of you alone until Bodeen's in custody. You stick with her, you hear? I'll be back around as soon as I can.'

'What the hell am I supposed to do with her?'

'You'll think of something. Get up,' he repeated, then broke the connection. Satisfied, he carried his briefcase downstairs.

The first thing he noticed was that Tory's plate was nearly cleared. The second was that she'd been crying.

'What's wrong? What did you say to her?'

'Oh, stop fussing.' Lilah swatted him off like a fly. 'She's had herself a nice weep and she's the better for it. Isn't that so, little girl?'

'Yes. Thanks. I can't eat any more, Lilah. I really can't.'

Lips pursed, Lilah studied the plate, then nodded. 'You did all right.' She glanced over at Cade. 'Will Miss Margaret or the judge be wanting breakfast?'

'I don't think so. My mother's made arrangements to leave this afternoon.'

'She going through with it?'

'Apparently. I don't want you staying here alone, Lilah. I thought you might like to visit your sister for a couple of days.'

'I could do that.' She picked up Tory's plate to carry it to the sink. 'I'll wait and see, if it's all the same to you Cade.'

'I'll check in later.'

'Best thing, her going. She breaks free of this house, she'll be the happier for it in the long run.'

'I hope you're right. You call your sister,' he said and held out a hand for Tory.

Tory got to her feet, and after a moment's hesitation stepped over to press her cheek to Lilah's. 'Thank you.'

'You're a good girl. Just remember to hold on to your own.'

'I'm going to.'

She waited until they were outside, in the car and driving down the tree-lined lane away from the house. 'I don't want a big wedding.'

Cade arched his brows. 'Okay.'

'I'd like to do it as quietly as possible and as . . .'

'And?'

He made the turn onto the road. Tory glanced out the window toward the edges of the swamp. 'And as soon as possible.'

'Why?'

How like him to ask, she thought, and turned to him again. 'Because I want to start our life. I want to begin.'

374

'We'll arrange for the license tomorrow. Will that suit you?'

'Yes.' She laid a hand over his. 'That suits me fine.'

Smiling at him, she saw nothing, felt nothing from the marsh. Or what waited in it.

Faith strolled across to Southern Comfort when she saw Cade's car pull up. She put on a big smile and hooked her arm companionably through Cade's. 'There you are. I thought you'd forgotten.'

'Forgotten?'

'Remember, honey, you said I could borrow your car today. Here you go.' She dropped her own keys in his hand and fluttered her lashes. 'So sweet of you, too. Isn't he just the best brother, Tory? He knows I have a partiality for his little convertible, and he's always letting me borrow it.'

She nipped the keys out of Cade's fingers, then gave him a big, noisy kiss. 'Tory, I'm just bored silly with Wade so busy today. I'm just going to keep you company awhile, all right? I'm thinking of buying Wade one of those fat candlesticks you've got in here.'

Smoothly, she transferred her grip from Cade to Tory. 'His place could sure use some fixing up. Well, you've seen it yourself, so you know. Looks like I'm going to be spending more time there, and I just can't abide that primitive male decor of his. Car's around the back of Wade's building,' she called out to Cade, as she steered Tory toward the door. 'It's low on gas.'

With a last glance at Cade's annoyed face, Tory unlocked the shop. 'Was the car a bribe?'

'No, he didn't trouble to offer a bribe. He woke me up this morning, so he's got to pay a price. He wants us looking out for each other.'

'Where's your dog?'

'Oh, she's having a fine time at Wade's.' Faith turned to the window and waved cheerfully to Cade. 'Oh, he's steaming. He just hates for me to drive this toy of his.'

'So naturally you drive it as often as possible.'

'Naturally. Got anything cold to drink? It's hot enough to steal your breath out there today.'

'In the back. Help yourself.'

'Are you opening today?'

'No. I don't want people today. So don't be offended if I ignore you.'

'Same goes.'

Faith slipped into the back room and came back with two bottles of Coke. Tory had the music on low and was busy with glass cleaner and a cloth. 'You might as well give me something to do before I do die of boredom.'

Tory held out the cloth. 'You ought to be able to manage this. I have plenty of work in the back. Please don't let anyone in. If someone comes to the door just tell them we're closed today.'

'Fine by me.'

She shrugged as Tory went into the back, then entertained herself by rearranging stock to her liking, imagining what it would be like to run a shop.

Entirely too much work, she decided, too much trouble. Though it was fun to be around so many nice things and speculate who would buy what.

She found the keys for the jewelry case behind the counter and tried on several pairs of earrings, admired a bracelet fashioned out of a coil of silver and tried that on as well.

When someone knocked on the door, she jumped guiltily, and closed the display.

She didn't recognize the faces. The man and woman stood outside the door studying her as she studied them. It was a shame, Faith thought, that Tory wasn't open. At least customers would be a diversion.

Faith smiled brightly and tapped the closed sign. The woman held up a badge.

'Oops.' The FBI, she thought. An even better diversion. She unlocked the door.

'Miss Bodeen?'

'No, she's in the back.' Faith took a moment to size them up. The woman was tall and tough, with short black hair and cool dark eyes. She wore what Faith considered a very unflattering gray suit and dead-ugly shoes.

The man had more potential, with curling brown hair and a square jaw with a sexy little dent in it. She tried the smile on him and got the faintest glimmer of response. 'I've never met an FBI agent before. I guess I'm a little flustered.'

'Would you ask Miss Bodeen to come out?' the woman requested.

'Of course. Just excuse me for one minute. Y'all wait right here.' She hurried to the stockroom, closed the door behind her. 'It's the FBI.'

Tory's head snapped up. 'Here?'

'Right out there. A man and a woman, and nothing like those two on the TV show. He's not half bad, but she's wearing a suit I wouldn't be buried in. She's a Yankee, too. I don't know about him. He hasn't opened his mouth. Ask me, she runs the show.'

'For God's sake, what do I care about that?' Tory got to her feet, but her knees were shaking.

Before she could steady herself, there was a brisk knock on the door, and it opened. 'Miss Bodeen?'

'Yes, I – yes.'

'I'm Special Agent Tatia Lynn Williams.' The woman showed her badge again. 'And this is Special Agent Marks. We need to speak with you.'

'Have you found my father?'

'Not at this time. Has he contacted you?'

'No. I haven't seen him, or heard from him. He'd know I wouldn't help him.'

'We'd like to ask you some questions.' Williams gave Faith a pointed look.

Instantly Faith scooted behind the desk to wrap an arm around Tory's shoulder. 'This is my brother's fiancée. I promised him I'd stay with her. I won't break my word to my brother.'

Marks took out his notebook, flipped pages. 'And you would be?'

'Faith Lavelle. Tory's going through a very distressing time. I'm staying with her.'

'You're acquainted with Hannibal Bodeen?'

'I know him. And I believe he killed my sister eighteen years ago.'

'We have no evidence of that,' Williams said flatly. 'Miss Bodeen, when did you last see your mother?'

'In April. My uncle and I went to see her. I've been estranged from my parents for a number of years. I hadn't seen her since I was twenty, or my father, either. Until he came here, to my shop.'

'And at that time you were aware he was a fugitive.'

'Yes.'

'Yet you gave him money.'

'He took money,' Tory corrected. 'But I'd have given it to him to keep him away from me.'

'Your father was physically violent with you.'

'All of my life.' Giving in, Tory sat.

'And with your mother?'

'No, not really. He didn't have to be. I believe he battered her in more recent years, when I wasn't there. But that would be speculation.'

'I'm told you don't have to speculate.' Williams glanced up, fixed her eyes on Tory's face. 'You claim to be psychic.'

'I don't claim anything.'

'You were involved in several cases of abducted children a few years ago.'

'What would that have to do with my mother's murder?'

'You were friends with Hope Lavelle.' Marks picked up the pattern smoothly, slid into a chair himself while his partner remained standing.

'Yes, very good friends.'

'And you led her family and the authorities to her body.'

'Yes. I'm sure you have the reports. There's nothing I can add to them.'

'You claimed to have seen her murder.' When Tory didn't respond, Marks leaned forward. 'Recently, you enlisted the aid of Abigail Lawrence, an attorney in Charleston. You were interested in a series of sexual homicides. Why?'

'Because they were all killed by the same person, the same person who murdered Hope. Because each of them was Hope to him, at a different age.'

'You . . . sense this,' Williams commented, and drew Tory's gaze.

'I know this. I don't expect you to believe me.'

'If you know this,' Williams continued, 'why didn't you come forward?'

'To what purpose? To amuse someone like you? To have what happened to Jonah Mansfield dragged up again and my part in it thrown in my face? You know all there is to know about me, Agent Williams.'

Marks took a plastic bag from his pocket, tossed it on the desk. Inside was a single earring, a simple gold hoop. 'What can you tell us about that?'

Tory kept her hands in her lap. 'It's an earring.'

'One of the things we know is you're very cool under fire.' Williams stepped forward. 'You were interested enough in the murders to gather information on them. Aren't you interested enough to see what you can pick up, let's say, from that?'

'I've told you all I can about my father. I'll do whatever I can to help you find him.'

Marks picked up the bag. 'Start with this.'

'Was it my mother's?' Without thinking, Tory snatched it out of his hand, broke the seal, then closed her fingers over the earring.

She opened herself, wanting this last connection more than she'd realized. She shivered once, then dropped the earring onto the desk. 'The mate's in your pocket,' she said to Williams. 'You took them off as you were driving into town, put this one in here.' Her eyes tracked up, stayed level. 'I'm not required to put myself on display for you.'

'I apologize.' Williams stepped forward to pick up the earring. 'I do know quite a bit about you, Miss Bodeen. I was interested in the work you did in New York. I've studied the Mansfield case.' She slipped the earring back into her pocket. 'They should have listened to you.' She gave her partner a quiet look. 'I intend to.'

'There's nothing more I can tell you.' She got to her feet. 'Faith, would you show them out please?'

'Sure.'

Williams took out a card, laid it on the desk, then followed Faith out of the storeroom. Minutes later Faith came back in, took out a fresh Coke, and settled down in the chair Marks had vacated.

'You could tell that just by touching that earring. You knew it was hers and all that just by touching it?'

'I have work to do.'

'Oh, get over yourself.' Faith took a long swig from the bottle. 'I swear, I've never known anybody takes every damn thing so serious. What we ought to do is go buy ourselves some lottery tickets or run on up to the racetrack. Can you tell with horses? I don't see why you couldn't.'

'For God's sake.'

'Well, why not? Why can't you have some fun with it? It doesn't have to be some dark, depressing weight. No, I've got it.

Better than horses. We'll go to Vegas and play blackjack. Jesus Christ, Tory, we'd break the bank in every casino.'

'It's not something to profit from.'

'Why not? Oh, of course, I forgot. This is you. You'd rather mope about it. Poor little me.' Faith dabbed an invisible hankie under her eyes. 'I'm psychic, so I must suffer.'

The insult was so huge, Tory couldn't imagine why her lips wanted to twitch into a ridiculous grin. 'I'm not moping.'

'You would, given half a chance. I'm an expert on moping.' She edged a hip onto the desk. 'Come on over to Wade's with me. You can, like, brush up against him or whatever, and find out what's going on in his head about me.'

'I will not.'

'Oh, be a pal.'

'No.'

'You're such a bitch.'

'That's right, now go away. And put that bracelet back where you got it.'

'Fine. It's not my style anyway.' She leaned over the desk. 'What am I thinking right now?'

Tory glanced up, and her mouth quivered. 'It's inventive, but anatomically impossible.' She swiveled back to her keyboard. 'Faith, thanks.'

With a sniff, Faith pulled open the door. 'For what?'

'For deliberately annoying me so I wouldn't mope.'

'Oh, that. My pleasure. It's so easy, after all.'

Chapter Twenty-Nine

'Wade, honey?' Faith cocked the phone on her shoulder and peered over the counter toward the storeroom, where it seemed to her Tory had been holed up for ten days. 'You busy?'

'Me? Of course not. I just finished neutering a dachshund. Another day in paradise.'

'Oh. What exactly do you – no, never mind, I don't think I want to know. How's my baby?'

'I'm just fine, and how are you?'

'I meant Bee. Is she all right?'

'Usurped by puppy breath.' He let out a weighty sigh for form. 'She's enjoying herself. I'm sure she'll tell you all about her first day at work later.'

'I'm having a first day at work, too. Sort of.' Faith studied, with a surprising sense of satisfaction, the glass displays she'd polished to a sparkle. 'What time do you think you're going to be done over there?'

'I should be wrapped up by five-thirty. What did you have in mind?'

'I have Cade's convertible, and I was thinking how it would be if we took us a long drive. It's so hot and sticky. I'm not wearing a thing but that red dress.' With a sly smile on her face, she twirled a lock of hair around her finger. 'You remember my red dress, don't you, honey?'

There was a long, long pause. 'You're trying to kill me.'

Her laugh was low and satisfied. 'I'm just trying to be sure, since we've been spending a lot of time lately having conversations and so forth, that a certain part of our relationship isn't neglected.'

'I can get behind that.'

'Then why don't we take that drive. We could find us a cheap motel and play traveling salesman.'

'What are you selling?'

This time her laugh was long and robust. 'Oh honey, just trust me. The price is going to be right.'

'Then I'm buying. We'd have to drive back late tonight or early tomorrow morning. I have appointments.'

'That'll be fine.' She was getting used to this making-plans business. 'Wade?'

'Yeah?'

'You remember how you said you were in love with me?'

'I seem to recollect something of the sort.'

'Well, I think I love you back. And you know what? It doesn't feel half bad.'

There was another long pause. 'I think I can get out of here by five-fifteen.'

'I'll pick you up.' She hung up and danced around the counter. 'Tory, come on out of there. Might as well be in jail,' she stated, as she pulled open the door.

Tory merely looked up from her inventory list. 'You've never actually had a job, have you?'

'What would I want one of those for? I have an inheritance.'

'Fulfillment, self-satisfaction, the pleasure of completing a task.'

'All right, I'll work with you.'

'Have they built a ski lift in hell?'

'No, really, it might be fun. But we'll talk about that later. Now, you have to come along with me. I've got to run home and get some things together.'

'Go ahead.'

'Where I go, you go. I promised Cade. And we've played here, your way for . . .' She checked her watch, rolled her eyes. 'Almost four hours.'

'I haven't finished here.'

'Well, I have. And if we stay here the rest of the day, those FBI people might come back.'

'All right.' Tory tossed down her pencil. 'But I promised my grandmother I'd be at my uncle's by five.'

'That's perfect. I'll drop you off there before I pick up Wade.

382

Grab us a couple of Cokes, honey. I'm just parched.' Faith breezed out to freshen her lipstick in one of Tory's decorative mirrors.

'Since when do you have a reflection?' Tory asked, sweetly, as she brought out the bottles.

Unoffended, Faith slipped the top on the lipstick tube and dropped it in her purse. 'You're just cross because you've been holed up in your cave all day. You're going to thank me when we get out on the road and I open up that beauty of Cade's. Get some wind in your hair, it might actually have a little style.'

'There's nothing wrong with my hair.'

'Not a thing. If you want to look like an old-maid librarian.'

'That's a ridiculous cliché, and an insult to an entire profession.'

Faith stood another moment at the mirror, fluffed her own sleek blond mane. 'Have you seen Miss Matilda down at Progress Library lately?'

Despite her best intentions, Tory's lips quivered. 'Oh, shut up,' she suggested, and shoved the Coke bottle into Faith's hands.

'That's what I like about you. Always the snappy comeback.' She gave her hair a toss, then started to leave. 'Well, come on.'

'You changed things.' Tory scanned the shelves, the cases, noted the small shifts in stock.

Snappy comebacks, Faith thought. And an eye like a damn hawk. 'So?'

She wanted to complain, nearly did on principle. But honesty got the better of her. 'It's not bad.'

'Excuse me. I'm so overwhelmed with flattery I feel a little faint.'

'In that case, I'll drive.'

'The hell you will.' Laughing, Faith danced out the door.

As she followed, locked up, Tory realized she was enjoying herself. Dealing with Faith made it impossible to brood. The idea of a fast ride in an open car held a great deal of appeal. She'd focus on that, just that, and worry about the rest later.

'Fasten your seat belt,' she ordered, as she slid into the passenger seat.

'Oh, right. The air's so thick you could chew it.'

Faith clicked her belt on, took out her sunglasses, then turned the key. Gunning the engine, she gave Tory a mischievous grin.

'Now for some mood music.' She punched the CD button, flipping through until Pete Seeger wailed out about rock-and-roll. 'Ah, classical. Perfect. We're about to see what you're made of, Victoria.'

Deliberately Tory took out her own sunglasses, slipped them on. 'Stern stuff.'

'Good.' Faith waited for a break in traffic, then shot away from the curb in a screaming U-turn. She nipped through the light at the square seconds before it turned red.

'You're going to get a ticket before you get out of town.'

'Oh, I bet the FBI's keeping our locals plenty busy. Jesus! Don't you just *love* this car?'

'Why don't you buy one of your own?'

'Then I'd miss the fun of nagging Cade to death about borrowing it.'

She crossed the town limits, and poured it on.

The wind whipped over Tory's face, tore at her hair, and thrilled her blood. An adventure, she thought as they streamed around turns. Foolishness. It had been a long, long time since she indulged in simple idiocy.

Speed. Hope had loved going fast, riding her bike like it was a stallion, or a rocket ship. Daring the devil as she threw her arms high in the air and gave herself to the moment.

Tory did the same now, throwing her head back and letting the speed and the music pour over her.

The smells were summer, and summer was childhood. Hot tar melting under the searing sun, still water going ripe in the heat.

She could race through the fields when the cotton had burst from its bolls and pretend she was an explorer on an alien planet. Do cartwheels across the road and feel the tar go soft under her palms. Into the marsh that was any world she wanted it to be. Running there, running with the ground spongy under her feet, with the moss tumbling down and mosquitoes singing for blood.

Running. Running away with her heart pounding and a scream trapped in her throat. Running—

'There's Cade.'

'What?' Tory jerked back, light-headed, clammy, her eyes wide and nearly blind as she swiveled her head.

'There.' Carelessly Faith gestured toward the field where two men stood in a sea of green cotton. She gave the horn a cheerful toot, waved, and laughed. 'Oh, he's cursing us now, giving Piney an earful about his crazy, irresponsible sister. Don't you worry,' she added smugly. 'He'll just figure I'm trying to corrupt you.'

'I'm all right.' Tory forced herself to breathe in, breathe out. 'I'm fine.'

Faith gave her a longer, more considering look. 'Sure you are. You sure go pale though. Why don't you – oh shit.'

The rabbit darted across the road, a brown streak of confusion. Instinctively Faith hit the brakes, swerved. The car fishtailed, squealed, and under her firm hands found its balance again.

'I just can't stand hitting anything. Though God knows why they run out like that. Seems they wait for a car to come along, and . . .' She trailed off as she looked at Tory again. The snicker escaped before she cleared her throat and slowed down. 'Uh oh.'

Saying nothing, Tory looked down. Most of the Coke that had been in the bottle was now splattered all over her shirt. With two fingertips she pulled it away from her skin and slanted her gaze to Faith.

'Well, gee whiz, I couldn't run down the little bunny, could I?'

'Just do me a favor and get me home so I can change, okay?'

Tapping her fingers on the wheel, Faith swung into Tory's lane, kicking dust and gravel into the air as she braked.

Laughing, but cautious, Faith hopped out of the car. 'I'll run some cold water over that shirt while you clean up. Shame to ruin it, even if it is deadly ordinary.'

'Classic.'

'You keep believing that.' Pleased with the diversion, Faith strolled up the steps. 'You take your time straightening yourself up,' she said, as Tory pulled open the door. 'You need it more than I do.'

'I don't suppose it takes long to look ready to hop in the next available bed.'

Grinning, Faith followed her into the bedroom, then making herself at home, she opened Tory's closet and poked through. 'Hey, some of this stuff's not half bad.'

'Get your fingers out of my clothes.'

'This is a good color for me.' She pulled out a silk blouse in a deep, dusky blue, then turned to the mirror. 'Brings out my eyes.'

385

Stripped down to her bra, Tory snatched the blouse and shoved the damp shirt at Faith. 'Go make yourself useful.'

Faith rolled her eyes, but headed out to rinse the shirt in the bathroom sink. 'If you're not wearing it in the next few days, you could lend it to me. I was thinking Wade and I could have an evening at home tomorrow night. If things go as they're supposed to, I wouldn't have it on that long anyhow.'

'Then it doesn't matter what you wear.'

'A statement like that just proves you need me.' Faith splashed the shirt around in the bowl. 'What a woman wears is directly related to how she wants a man to respond.'

Tory reached in her closet for a white camp shirt, frowned, then eyed the silk blouse. Well, why not?

Tory buttoned the blouse and walked to the mirror to brush out her hair. It needed to be tamed and tied back, she told herself. She was going to comfort her grandmother, to do what she could to help hold what was left of her family together. It wasn't the time for the frivolous or the selfish now. Though God, she'd needed just that, and wouldn't forget that Faith had provided it.

Lifting her arms, she began to work her hair into a braid. The repetitive motion, the hum of the ceiling fan lulled her until her eyes were half closed and she was smiling dreamily into the mirror.

She saw the rabbit dart out into the road. A panicked brown streak. Running. Fleeing from the scent of man.

Someone was coming. Someone was watching.

Her arms froze over her head, and the panic tripped her heart. The air went thick, heavy, edged with the faintest taste of stale whiskey.

She scented him, prey to hunter.

In one leap she was at the nightstand, and the gun Cade had given her was in her hand. There was a whimper in the back of her throat, but she closed it off. All that came out was the ragged panting of fear. She rushed from the room just as Faith wandered out of the bathroom.

'I left it soaking. You can wring it out when—' She saw the gun first, then Tory's face. 'Oh God,' was all she managed before Tory grabbed her arm.

'Listen to me, don't ask questions. There isn't much time. Go out the front, hurry. Get in the car and go for help. Get help. I'll stop him if I can.'

'Come on with me. Come on now.'

'No.' Tory broke away, swung toward the kitchen. 'He's coming. Go!'

She ran toward the back of the house to give Faith time to escape. And to face her father.

He kicked in the back door, lurched through. His clothes were filthy, his face and arms raw with scratches and the swollen bites of greedy insects. He swayed a little, but his eyes stayed steady on his daughter's face. He had an empty bottle in one hand, and a gun in the other.

'I've been waiting for you.'

Tory tightened her grip on the revolver. 'I know.'

'Where's that Lavelle bitch?'

Gone. Safe. 'There's no one here but me.'

'Lying little whore. You don't take two steps without that rich man's brat. I wanna talk to her.' He grinned. 'I wanna talk to both of you.'

'Hope's dead. There's just me now.'

'That's right, that's right.' He lifted the bottle, then realizing it was empty, heaved it against the wall where it shattered like gunshots. 'Got herself killed. Asked for it. Both of you asked for everything you got. Lying and sneaking. Touching each other in unholy ways.'

'There was nothing but innocence between me and Hope.' Tory strained her ears for the panther roar of Cade's engine, but heard nothing.

'You think I didn't *know?*' He gestured wildly with the gun, but she didn't flinch. 'You think I didn't see you, swimming naked, floating in the water, splashing in it so it ran down your bodies.'

It sickened her that he could twist a simple childhood memory into the profane. 'We were eight years old. But you weren't. The sin was in you. It always was. No, you stay back.' She lifted the gun now, and the trembling ran from her shoulder to her finger-tips. 'You won't lay a hand on me again. Or anyone else. Didn't Mama give you enough money this time? Didn't she move fast enough? Is that why you did it?'

'I never raised my hand to your mother unless she needed it. God made man head of the house. Put that down and get me a drink.'

'The police are on their way by now. They've been looking for you. For Hope, for Mama, for all the others.' The gun jerked in her hand as he came forward. In her mind there was the hiss and snap of a Sam Browne belt.

'You come near me, and we won't wait for them. I'll end it now.'

'You think you worry me. You never had a lick of gumption.'

'Nobody's ever said that about me.' Faith stepped up behind Tory. The little gun gleamed in her hand. 'If she won't shoot you, I promise I will.'

'You said she was dead. You said she was dead.' He was a big man with a long reach. In panic as much as fury he lunged, knocking Tory hard against the wall. A gunshot rang out, and the smell of blood drenched her senses.

She stumbled back against Faith as her father howled and stormed out the broken doorway.

'I told you to go.' Teeth chattering, Tory went down to her knees.

'Well, I didn't listen, did I?' Because her vision was going gray, Faith braced against the wall and shook her head fiercely. 'I used Cade's car phone to call the police.'

'You came back.'

'Yeah.' Blowing little panting breaths, Faith bent over from the waist to try to get some blood back in her head. 'You wouldn't have left me.'

'There was blood. I smelled blood.' Instantly Tory was on her feet, jerking Faith upright again. 'Are you shot? Did he shoot you?'

'No. It was you. You shot him. Tory, snap out of it.'

Tory stared down at her own hand. The gun was still in it, shaking as if it were alive. With a little gasp of shock she dropped it clattering to the floor. 'I shot him?'

'Your gun went off when he shoved you. I think. God, it happened fast. There was blood on his shirt, I'm sure of that much, and I didn't fire. I think I'm going to be sick. I hate being sick. Sirens.' Hearing them, Faith rested her back against the wall. 'Oh, thank God.'

Then she heard the roar of an engine, and shoved away from the wall. 'Oh no. Oh Jesus. Cade's car. I left the keys in the car.'

Before Tory could stop her, she was darting toward the front door. They burst out together in time to see the car squeal onto the road.

'Cade's going to kill me.'

Tory drew in a breath like a sob, but when it came out it was laughter. Edging toward hysteria, but laughter. 'We just chased off a madman, and you're worried about your big brother. Only you.'

'Well, Cade can be pretty fierce.' As much to comfort as to support herself, Faith draped an arm around Tory's shoulder. Tory let her head droop, closed her eyes.

The scream of sirens battered her ears. She saw hands on the wheel of the car. Her father's hands, scored deep with scratches. She felt the speed, the dance of the tires as the car was whipped around.

Coming back, pushing for speed. The radio blaring hot rock. Lights whirling. You see them in the rearview mirror as your eyes dart up. Panic, outrage, hate. They're getting closer.

Your arm burns from the bullet and the blood drips.

But you'll get away. God's on your side. He left the car for you. Fast. Faster.

A test. It's just another test. You'll get away. Have to get away. But you'll come back for her. Oh, you'll come back and you'll make her pay.

Hands slicked with blood. The wheel spins out of your grip. The world rushes at you, shapes tumbling.

Screaming. Is that you screaming?

'Tory! For God's sake, Tory. Stop it. Wake up.'

She came back facedown on the shoulder of the road, her body jerking, screams ripping through her head.

'Don't do this. I don't know what I'm supposed to do.'

'I'm all right.' Painfully, Tory rolled over, shielded her eyes with her arm. 'I just need a minute.'

'All right? You went tearing out to the road when they drove by. I was afraid you were going to run right out in front of them. Then your eyes rolled back in your head and you went down.' Faith dropped her head in her hands. 'This is too much for me. This is just more than enough.'

'It's all right. It's over. He's dead.'

'I think I figured that part out. Look.' She pointed down the road. The flames and smoke pillared up, and the sun bounced off the chrome and glass of the police cars circled in the distance.

'I heard the crash, then a kind of explosion.'

'A fiery death,' Tory murmured. 'I wished it on him.'

'He wished it on himself. I want Wade. Oh my God, I want Wade.'

'We'll get someone to call him.' Steadier, Tory got to her feet, held out a hand for Faith. 'We'll go down and ask someone to call him.'

'Okay. I feel a little drunk.'

'Me too. We'll just hold on to each other.'

Arms wrapped around each other's waists, they started down the road. The heat bounced off the asphalt, shimmered on the air. Through the waves of it, Tory saw the fire, the spin of lights, the dull beige of the government car with the FBI agents beside it.

'Do you see where he crashed?' Tory murmured. 'Just across from where Hope . . . just on the bend of the road across from Hope.'

She heard the car coming behind them, stopped, turned.

Cade leaped out, raced forward to wrap his arms around both of them. 'You're all right. You're all right. I heard the sirens, then saw the fire. Oh God, I thought . . .'

'He didn't hurt us.' Cade's scent was there, sweat and man. Hers. Tory let it fill her. 'He's dead. I felt him die.'

'Ssh. Don't. I'm going to get you home, both of you.'

'I want Wade.'

He pressed his lips to the top of Faith's head. 'We'll get him, honey. Come on with me. Hold on to me for now.'

'He took your car, Cade.' Faith kept her eyes shut, her face pressed against her brother's chest. 'I'm sorry.'

Cade only shook his head, held her tighter. 'Don't think about it. Everything's going to be all right.'

Clinging to control by a thread, he helped them into the car. As he drove forward, Agent Williams stepped out in the road, signaled.

'Miss Bodeen. Can you verify that's your father?' She gestured toward the wreck. 'That Hannibal Bodeen was driving that vehicle?'

'Yes. He's dead.'

'I need to ask you a few questions.'

'Not here, not now.' Cade shoved the truck back in first gear. 'You come to Beaux Reves when you're done out here. I'm taking them home.'

'All right.' Williams looked past him, toward Tory. 'Are you injured?'

'Not anymore.'

Her mind went dull for a while. She was aware, in a secondary way, of Cade taking her into the house, leading her up the stairs. She drifted a little further away when he laid her on a bed.

After a while, there was something cool on her face. She opened her eyes, looked into his.

'I'm all right. Just a little tired.'

'I got one of Faith's nightgowns. You'll feel better once we get it on you.'

'No.' She sat up, put her arms around him. 'Now I feel better.'

He stroked her hair gently. Then his grip vised around her, and he buried his face in her hair. 'I need a minute.'

'Me too. Probably a lot of minutes. Don't let go.'

'I won't. I can't. I saw y'all go by. Faith driving like a maniac. I was going to blister her good for it.'

'She did it on purpose. She loves to agitate you.'

'She did, plenty. I stalked back over the fields, vowing to pay her back for it, with Piney walking along with me grinning like an idiot. Then I heard the shot. Liked to stop my heart. I started running, but I was still a good piece from the road and the car when the police went by. I saw the explosion. I thought I'd lost you.' He began to rock her. 'I thought I'd lost you, Tory.'

'I was in the car with him, in my mind. I think I wanted to be so I'd know the exact moment it was over.'

'He can't ever touch you again.'

'No. He can't touch any of us again.' She rested her head on the strong curve of his shoulder. 'Where's Faith?'

'She's downstairs. Wade's here. She can't keep still.' He leaned back, let his gaze roam her face. 'She'll rev until she falls down, and he'll be there for her.'

'She stayed with me. Just like you asked her to.' She let out a sigh. 'I have to go to my grandmother.'

'She's coming here. I called her. This is your home now, Tory. We'll get your things from the Marsh House later.'

'That sounds like a very good idea.'

Dusk had fallen when she walked the gardens with her grand-mother. 'I wish you'd stay here with us, Gran, you and Cecil.'

'J.R. needs me. He lost a sister, one he wasn't able to save from herself. I lost a child.' Her voice cracked. 'I lost her long ago. Still, no matter how you deny it, there's always that stubborn hope that you'll get it all back, put it right. Now that's gone.'

'I don't know what to do for you.'

'You're doing it. You're alive, and you're happy.' She clung to Tory's hand. She couldn't seem to stop holding, stop touching.

'We all have to make our peace with this, in our own way.' Iris drew in a steadying breath. 'I'm going to bury her here, in Progress. I think that's the way it should be. She had some happy years here, and, well, J.R. wants it. I don't want a church service. I'm holding against him on that. We'll bury her day after tomorrow, in the morning. If J.R. wants it, his minister can say a few words at the gravesite. I won't blame you, Tory, if you choose not to come.'

'Of course I'll come.'

'I'm glad.' Iris lowered to a bench. The fireflies were out, bumping their lights against the dark. 'Funerals are for the living, to help close a gap. You'll be better for it.' She drew Tory down beside her. 'I'm feeling my age, honey-pot.'

'Don't say that.'

'Oh, it'll pass. I won't tolerate otherwise. But tonight, I'm feeling old and tired. They say a parent isn't meant to outlive the child, but nature, and fate, they decide what's meant. We just live with it. We'll all live with this, Tory. I want to know you're going to take what's in front of you with both hands and hold it tight.'

'I am. I will. Hope's sister knows how to do that. I'm taking lessons.'

'I always liked that girl. She mean to marry my Wade?'

'I think he means to marry her, and he's going to let her think it was her idea.'

'Clever boy. And a steady one. He'll keep her in line without bruising her wings. I'm going to see both my grandchildren happy. That's what I'm holding on to tight, Tory.'

392

Chapter Thirty

Wade fought with the knot of his tie. He hated the damned things. Every time he put one on, it brought a flashback of his mother, wearing an Easter hat that looked like an overturned bowl of flowers, strangling him into a bright blue tie to match his much hated bright blue suit.

He'd been six, and figured it had traumatized him for life.

You wore ties for weddings, and you wore ties for funerals. There was no getting around it, even if you were lucky enough to have a profession that didn't require a goddamn noose around your neck every day of the week.

They were burying his aunt in an hour. There was no getting around that, either.

It was raining, a thundering bitch of a storm. Funerals demanded lousy weather, he figured, just like they demanded ties and black crepe and overly sweet-scented flowers.

He'd have given a year of his life to have crawled back in bed, pulled the covers over his head, and let the entire mess happen without him.

'Maxine said she'll be glad to look after the dogs,' Faith announced. She walked in, dressed in the most dignified black dress she could find in her closet. 'Wade, what have you done to that tie?'

'I tied it. That's what you do with ties.'

'Mauled it's more like. Here, let me see what I can do.' She plucked at it, tugged, twisted.

'Don't fuss. It doesn't matter.'

'Not if you want to go out looking like you've got a black goiter under your chin. My great-aunt Harriet had goiters, and they were not attractive. Just hold still a minute, I've nearly got it.'

'Just let it be, Faith.' He turned away from her to pick up his suit jacket. 'I want you to stay here. There's no point in your going out in this, or in both of us being wet and miserable for the next couple of hours. You've been through enough as it is.'

She set down the purse she'd just picked up. 'You don't want me with you?'

'You should go on home.'

She glanced at him, then around the room. Her perfume was on his dresser, her robe on the hook behind the door. 'Funny, here I was thinking that's just where I was. Is that my mistake?'

He took his wallet off the dresser, stuffed it in his back pocket, scooped up the loose change. 'My aunt's funeral is the last place you should be.'

'That doesn't answer my question, but I'll pose another. Why is your aunt's funeral the last place I should be?'

'For Christ's sake, Faith, put it together. My aunt was married to the man who killed your sister, and who might have killed you just two days ago. If you've forgotten that, I haven't.'

'No, I haven't forgotten it.' She turned to the mirror and to keep her hands busy picked up her brush. With every appearance of calm, she ran it over her hair. 'You know, a lot of people, probably most, believe I don't have much more sense than a turnip green. That I'm flighty and foolish and too shallow to stick to anything for longer than it takes to file my nails. That's all right.'

She set the brush down, picked up her bottle of perfume and dabbed scent on her collarbone. 'That's all right,' she repeated. 'For most people. But the funny thing is, I expect you to think better of me. I expect you to think better of me than I do myself.'

'I think considerable of you.'

'Do you, Wade?' Her eyes shifted and met his in the mirror. 'Do you really? And at the same time you think you can put on that irritable attitude and buzz me off today. Maybe I should just go get my hair done while you're at your aunt's funeral. Then the next time you have to deal with something difficult or uncomfortable, I'll go shopping. And the time after that,' she continued, her voice rising, hardening, 'I'll just have moved on anyway so it won't be an issue.'

'This is different, Faith.'

'I thought it was.' She set the bottle down, turned. 'I hoped it

394

was. But if you don't want me with you today, if you don't think I want to be with you today, or have the belly for it, then this is no different than what I've already done. I'm not interested in repeating myself.'

Emotion stormed into his eyes, raged through him until his hands were fists. 'I hate this. I hate seeing my father torn to pieces this way. I hate knowing your family's been ripped again, and that mine had a part in it. I hate knowing you were in the same room with Bodeen, imagining what could have happened.'

'That's good, because I hate all those things, too. And I'll tell you something maybe you don't know. As soon as it was over that day, as soon as I started thinking again, I wanted you. You were the one person I needed with me. I knew you'd take care of me, and hold on to me, and everything would be all right. If you don't need the same from me, then I won't let myself need you, either. I'm selfish enough to stop. I'll go with you today, and stand with you and try to be some comfort to you. Or I'll go back to Beaux Reves and start working on getting over you.'

'You could do it, too,' he said quietly. 'Why is it I admire that? Flighty? Foolish?' He shook his head as he walked to her. 'You're the strongest woman I know. Stay with me.' He lowered his forehead to hers. 'Stay with me.'

'That's my plan.' She slipped her arms around him, ran her hands up and down his back. 'I want to be there for you. That's new for me. It's your own fault. You just kept at me till I was in love with you. First time I haven't aimed and shot first. I kinda like it.'

She held him, felt him lean on her. She liked that, too, she realized. No one had ever leaned on her before. 'Now, come on.' She spoke briskly, kissed his cheek. 'We'll be late, and funerals aren't the kind of occasions where you make grand entrances.'

He had to laugh. 'Right. Got an umbrella?'

'Of course not.'

'Of course not. Let me get one.'

When he went to the closet to root around, she angled her head and studied him with a faint smile. 'Wade, when we get engaged, will you buy me a sapphire instead of a diamond?'

His hand closed over the handle of the umbrella, then simply froze there. 'Are we getting engaged?'

'A nice one, not too big or gaudy, mind. Square cut. That first

395

moron I was married to didn't even get me a ring, and the second got me the tackiest diamond.'

She picked up the black straw hat she'd tossed on the bed and walked to the mirror to set it on her head at an appropriately dignified angle. 'Might as well have been a big hunk of glass for all the style it had. I sold it after the divorce and had a lovely two weeks at a fancy spa on the proceeds. So what I'd like is a square-cut sapphire.'

He took the umbrella down, stepped back out of the closet. 'Are you proposing, Faith?'

'Certainly not.' She tipped back her head to look down her nose. 'And don't think because I'm giving you some inclination of my response it gets you out of asking. I expect you to follow tradition, all the way down on one knee. With,' she added, 'a square-cut sapphire in your hand.'

'I'll make a note of it.'

'Fine, you do that little thing.' She held out a hand. 'Ready?'

'I used to think I was.' He took her hand, laced his fingers firmly with hers. 'No one's ever ready for you.'

They buried her mother in rain that pelted the ground like bullets while lightning ripped and clawed at the eastern sky. Violence, Tory thought. Her mother had lived with it, died from it, and even now, it seemed, drew it to her.

She didn't listen to the minister, though she was sure his words were meant to comfort. She felt too detached to need it, and couldn't be sorry for it. She'd never known the woman inside the flower-draped box. Never understood her, never depended on her. If Tory had grief, it was for the lack she'd lived with all her life.

She watched the rain beat against the casket, listened to it hammer on the umbrellas. And waited for it to be over.

More had come than she'd expected, and stood in a small dark circle in the gloom. She and her uncle flanked her grandmother, with the sturdy Cecil just behind them. And Cade stood beside her.

Boots, bless her easy heart, wept quietly between her husband and son.

Heads were bowed as prayers were read, but Faith's lifted, and her eyes met Tory's. And there was comfort, so unexpected, from someone who understood.

Dwight had come, as mayor, Tory supposed. And as Wade's friend. He stood a little apart, looking solemn and respectful. She imagined he'd be glad to be done with this duty and get back to Lissy.

There was Lilah, steady as a rock, eyes dry as she silently mouthed the prayers with the minister.

And oddly, Cade's aunt Rosie, in full black, complete with hat and veil. It had caught everyone off guard when she'd arrived, with a trunk, the night before.

Margaret was staying temporarily at her place, she'd announced. Which meant Rosie had immediately packed to stay temporarily elsewhere.

She'd offered Tory her mother's wedding dress, gone yellow as butter with age and smelling strongly of mothballs. Then had put it on herself and worn it the rest of the evening.

When the casket was lowered into the fresh grave, and the minister closed his book, J.R. stepped forward. 'She had a harder life than she needed to.' He cleared his throat. 'And a harder death than she deserved. She's at peace now. When she was a little girl, she liked yellow daisies best.' He kissed the one he held in his hand, then dropped it into the grave.

And turned away, to his wife.

'He'd have done more for her,' Iris said, 'If she'd let him. I'm going to visit Jimmy awhile,' she told Tory. 'Then we'll be going home.' She took Tory's shoulders, kissed her cheeks. 'I'm happy for you, Tory. And proud. Kincade, you take care of my little girl.'

'Yes, ma'am. I hope you'll come and stay with us, both of you, when you come back to Progress.'

Cecil bent down to touch his lips to Tory's cheek. 'I'll look after her,' he whispered. 'Don't you worry.'

'I won't.' She turned, knowing she was expected to receive condolences. Rosie was right there, her eyes bird-bright behind her veil. 'It was a proper service. Dignified and brief. It reflects well on you.'

'Thank you, Miss Rosie.'

'We can't choose our blood, but we can choose what to do with it, what to do about it.' She tipped up her face, looked at her nephew. 'You've chosen well. Margaret will come around, or she won't, but that's not for you to worry about. I'm going to talk to Iris, find out who that big, strapping man is she's got with her.'

She plowed through the wet in a two-thousand-dollar Chanel suit, and Birkenstocks.

Struggling against twin urges to laugh and weep, Tory laid a hand on Cade's arm. 'Go take her your umbrella. I'll be fine.'

'I'll be right back.'

'Tory, I'm very sorry.' Dwight held out a hand, and clasping hers, kissed her cheek even as he shifted his umbrella to shield her from the rain. 'Lissy wanted to come, but I made her stay home.'

'I'm glad you did. It wouldn't be good for her to be out in this weather today. It was kind of you to come, Dwight.'

'We've known each other a long time. And Wade, he's one of my two closest friends. Tory, is there anything I can do for you?'

'No, but thank you. I'm going to walk over and visit Hope's grave before I leave. You should go on back to Lissy.'

'I will. Take this.' He brought her hand up to the handle of the umbrella.

'No, I'll be fine.'

'Take it,' he insisted. 'And don't stay out in the wet too long.'

He left her to walk back to Wade.

Grateful for the shelter, Tory turned away from her mother's grave to walk through the grass, through the stones, to Hope's.

Rain ran down the angel's face like tears and beat at the fairy roses. Inside the globe, the winged horse flew.

'It's all over now. It doesn't feel settled yet,' Tory said with a sigh. 'I have this heaviness inside me. Well, it's so much to take in at once. I wish I could . . . there are too many things to wish for.'

'I never bring flowers here,' Faith said from behind her. 'I don't know why.'

'She has the roses.'

'That's not it. They're not my roses, not mine to bring her.'

Tory looked behind her, then shifted so they were standing together. 'I can't feel her here. Maybe you can't, either.'

'I don't want to go in the ground when my time comes. I want my ashes spread somewhere. The sea, I think, as that's where I plan to have Wade ask me to marry him. By the sea. She might have felt the same, only hers would have been for the river, or near it in the marsh. That was her place.'

'Yes, it was. It is.' It seemed important, and natural, to reach out a hand and clasp Faith's. 'There are flowers at Beaux Reves, that was her place, too. I could cut some when the storm passes,

398

take them to the marsh. To the river. Put them there for Hope. Maybe it would be the right way, laying flowers on the water instead of letting them die on the ground. Would you do that with me?'

'I hated sharing her with you.' Faith paused, closed her eyes. 'Now I don't. It'll be clear this afternoon. I'll tell Wade.' She started to walk away, stopped. 'Tory, if you get there first—'

'I'll wait for you.'

Tory watched her go, looked back over the gentle slope, the curtaining rain, the gathering ground fog. There was her grandmother with Cecil strong at her back, Rosie in her veil and Lilah holding an umbrella over her.

J.R. and Boots still by the grave of the sister he had loved more than he might have realized.

And there was Cade, with his friends, waiting.

As she walked to him, the rain began to thin and the first hint of sun shimmered watery light through the gloom.

'You understand why I want to do this?'

'I understand you want to.'

Tory smiled a little as she shook rain from the spears of lavender she'd cut. 'And you're annoyed, just a little, that I'm not asking you to come with me.'

'A little. It's counterbalanced by the fact that you and Faith are becoming friends. And all of that is overpowered by the sheer terror of knowing I'm going to be at Aunt Rosie's mercy until you return. She has a gift for me, and I've seen it. It's a moldy top hat, which she expects I will wear for our wedding.'

'It'll go well with the moth-eaten dress she's giving me. I tell you what. You wear the hat, I'll wear the dress, and we'll have Lilah take our picture. We'll put it in a nice frame for Miss Rosie, then we'll pack them away someplace dark and safe before the wedding.'

'That's brilliant. I'm marrying a very wise woman. But we'll have to take the picture tonight. We're getting married tomorrow.'

'Tomorrow? But—'

'Here,' he said, as he turned her into his arm. 'Quietly, in the garden. I've taken care of most of the details, and will get to the rest this afternoon.'

'But my grandmother—'

'I spoke with her. She and Cecil will be staying another night. They'll be here.'

'I haven't had time to buy a dress or—'

'Your grandmother mentioned that, and hoped you'd be receptive to wearing the one she wore when she married your grandfather. She's running up to Florence to get it this afternoon. She said it would mean a lot to her.'

'Thought of everything, didn't you?'

'Yes. Do you have a problem with that?'

'We're going to have lots of problems with that over the next fifty or sixty years, but just now? No.'

'Good. Lilah's baking a cake. J.R.'s bringing a case of champagne. The idea brightened him considerably.'

'Thank you.'

'Since you're grateful, I'll just add, Aunt Rosie plans to sing.'

'Don't tell me.' She drew back. 'Let's not spoil the moment. Well, since everyone has approved the schedule and the details, who am I to object? Have you arranged for the honeymoon, too?' She saw him wince and rolled her eyes. 'Cade, really.'

'You're not going to argue about a trip to Paris, are you? Of course not.' He gave her a quick kiss before she could. 'You might want to close the shop for a few days, but Boots really liked the idea of running it for you, and Faith had some ideas.'

'Oh God.'

'But that's up to you.'

'Thank you very much.' She pushed a hand through her hair. 'My head's spinning. We'll discuss all this when I get back.'

'Sure. I'm flexible.'

'The hell you are,' she muttered. 'You just pretend to be.' She shifted the basket of flowers, handed him the shears. 'Don't start naming the children while I'm gone.'

Exasperating man, she thought, as she slid into her car and set the basket of flowers on the seat. Planning their wedding behind her back. Planning exactly the sort of wedding she wanted, too.

How irritating, and how lovely, to be known that well.

So why wasn't she relaxed? As she turned onto the road, she shifted her shoulders. She just couldn't quite break through the tension. Understandable, she reminded herself. She'd been through a hideous ordeal. She couldn't imagine getting married within twenty-four hours with so much still tied up inside her.

But she wanted to begin. She wanted to close this door and open the next. She glanced at the flowers beside her. Maybe she was about to.

She pulled off onto the side of the road, where Hope had once parked her bike. And climbing out, she crossed the little bridge where tiger lilies burst into storybook bloom, then took the path she knew her friend had taken that night.

Hope Lavelle, girl spy.

The rain had turned to steam, and the steam rose out of the ground in curling fingers that broke apart, then twined together again around her ankles. The air was thick with wet, with green, with rot. Mysteries waiting to be solved.

As she approached the clearing, she wished she'd thought to bring some wood. Everything would be too damp to start a fire, and perhaps it was foolish to want to in all the heat. But she wished she'd thought of it, and could have laid one, the way Hope had.

Just thinking of it, remembering it, she caught a drift of smoke.

There was the fire, small and carefully built to burn low, a little circle of flame with long, sharpened sticks beside it waiting for marshmallows.

She blinked once, to clear the vision. But the fire simmered, and the smoke puffed sluggishly in the mist. Dazed, Tory stepped into the clearing, the basket tipping to spill out flowers at her feet.

'Hope?' She pressed a hand to her heart, almost to make sure it continued to beat. But the marble child who'd been her friend stood in her pool of flowers and said nothing.

With a trembling hand, she picked up one of the sticks and saw that the cuts to sharpen it were fresh.

Not a dream, not a flashback. But here and now. Real.

Not Hope. Never again Hope.

The pressure rose up in her, a hot gush of fear, and of knowledge.

In the brush came a rustling, wet and sly.

She whirled toward it. *Password.* She thought it, heard it sound in her head. But she wasn't Hope. She wasn't eight. And dear God, it wasn't over after all.

Cade was in the garden deciding where they should set up tables for the wedding reception when Chief Russ pulled in.

'Glad you're here. I just got news I thought you should know.'

'Come on inside where it's cool.'

'No, I gotta get back, but I wanted to tell you in person. We got ballistic reports on Sarabeth Bodeen. The gun she was killed with wasn't the same one Bodeen had with him. Not even the same caliber.'

Cade felt one quick knock of dread. 'I'm not sure I understand.'

'Turns out the one Bodeen had when he broke in on Tory and your sister was stolen from a house about fifteen miles south of here, on the morning Tory's mother was killed. House was broken into between nine and ten A.M. that same day.'

'How can that be?'

'Only way it could be is if Bodeen spouted wings and flew down here from Darlington County or if somebody else put those bullets in Miz Bodeen.'

Carl D. cupped a hand over his chin, rubbed it hard. His eyes burned with fatigue. 'I've been in touch with those federals, and I'm piecing it together. The phone records show Miz Bodeen got a call just after two that morning, from the pay phone outside the Winn-Dixie north of town here. Now, we were figuring that would've been Bodeen calling her from here, telling her he was coming for her. That's fine as far as it goes. But it don't fit when you add the rest.'

'It had to be Bodeen calling her. Why else would she have packed up?'

'I can't say. But you've got him calling from here at round about two in the morning, getting up there, doing the shooting between five and five-thirty, then heading back here and moving south another fifteen miles, breaking into a house and stealing a gun, a bottle, and some leftover supper. Now, why would the man be zigzagging back and forth that away?'

'He was crazy.'

'I won't argue with that, but being crazy doesn't make him able to all but break land and speed records in one morning. 'Specially since it doesn't look like he had any kind of vehicle. Now, I'm not saying it couldn't be done. I'm saying it don't make sense.'

'What kind of sense does it make otherwise? Who else would have killed Tory's mother?'

'I can't answer that. I gotta work with facts here. He had the wrong gun, we got nothing to show the man had a car. Now, could be we'll find one yet, and the gun that he used on his wife. That could be.'

He took his handkerchief out of his pocket, wiped the back of his neck. 'But it appears to me, if Bodeen didn't do those murders up in Darlington County, maybe he didn't kill anyone. That means whoever did is still walking free. I was hoping to have a talk with Tory.'

'She's not here. She's—' White hot fear burned through his belly. 'She's gone to Hope.'

Tory opened herself, tried to feel him, gauge him. But all she saw was dark. Cold, blank dark. The rustling moved in a circle, a taunting. She turned with it, even as the saliva dried up in her mouth, she turned to face it head-on.

'Which of us did you want that night? Or did it matter?'

'It was never you. Why would I want you? She was beautiful.'

'She was a child.'

'True.' Dwight stepped out in the clearing. 'But so was I.'

It broke her heart. One quick snap. 'You were Cade's friend.'

'Sure. Cade and Wade, like twins themselves. Rich and privileged and handsome. And I was their chubby little token. Dwight the Dweeb. Well, I fooled them all, didn't I?'

He'd have been twelve, she thought, staring at the easy smile on his face. No more than twelve years old. 'Why?'

'Call it a rite of passage. They were always first. One or the other of them, always first in everything. I was going to be the first one to have a girl.'

Amusement – it couldn't be anything but amusement – danced in his eyes. 'Not that I could brag on it. Kinda like being Batman.'

'Oh God, Dwight.'

'Hard for you to see that, you being a female. We'll call it a guy thing. I had a bad itch. Why shouldn't it have been my good friend Cade's precious sister I used to scratch it?'

He spoke so calmly, so casually, that the birds continued to sing, liquid notes that ran like tears.

'I didn't know I was going to kill her. That just . . . happened. I'd snuck some of my daddy's whiskey. Drink like a man, you know? My mind was a little fuzzy.'

'You were only twelve. How could you want such a thing?'

403

He circled the clearing, not really coming closer, just stalking, a patient, anticipatory cat and mouse. 'I used to watch the two of you, skinny-dipping, or sprawled out here on your bellies telling secrets. So'd your old man,' he said with a grin. 'You might say I was inspired by him. He wanted you. Your old man wanted to fuck you, all right, but he didn't have the guts. I was better than him, better than any of them. I proved it that night. I was a man that night.'

Town mayor, proud father, devoted husband, loyal friend. What kind of madness could hide so well? 'You raped and murdered a child. That made you a man?'

'All my life I heard, "Be a man, Dwight." ' The amusement died out of his eyes so they turned cold and blank. 'For Christ's sake, be a man. Can't be a man if you're a virgin, can you? And no girl would look twice at me. I fixed that. That night changed my life. Look at me now.'

He spread his arms, stepped closer, watching her. 'I got confidence, got myself in shape, and didn't I end up with the prettiest girl in Progress? I got respect. A beautiful wife, a son. I got position. It all started that night.'

'All those other girls.'

'Why not? You can't imagine what it's like – or maybe you can. Yeah, maybe you can. You know how to feel it, don't you? Their fear. While it's happening I'm the most important person in the world to them. I *am* the world to them. There's a hell of a kick to that.'

She thought of running. The idea whipped in and out of her mind. And she saw the gleam in his eyes, saw he was waiting for her to do just that. Deliberately she slowed her breathing, opened herself. There was the blankness again, like a pit, but around the edges was a kind of ugly hunger.

Recognizing it, anticipating it, was the only weapon she had. 'You didn't even know them. Dwight, they were strangers to you.'

'I just imagine they're Hope, and it's that first night all over again. They're nothing but tramps and losers until I make them into her.'

'It wasn't the same with Sherry.'

'I didn't want to wait.' He shrugged. 'Lissy isn't much on sex these days. Can't blame her. And that sexy little teacher, she

404

wanted it. Wanted it from Wade though, stupid bitch. Well, she got it from me. She wasn't quite right though. Not quite. Faith's perfect.'

He saw Tory jolt. 'Yeah, you've gotten pretty tight with Faith, haven't you? I plan to be pretty tight with her myself. I was going to wait till August for her, got my little ritual, you know. But I'll have to move things up. Oh, she'll be late, by the way. I talked Lissy into going over to see her, and I know my girl. She'll keep Faith occupied just long enough.'

'They'll know this time, Dwight. You won't be able to pass it off on someone else.'

'Your father sure did cooperate, didn't he? Did I mention I was the one who killed your mother? Gave her a call, told her I was a friend and her loving husband was on his way to get her. It just seemed like a nice touch, one that kept the cops on his ass and let me sit back and watch with my concerned-mayor attitude.'

'She was nothing to you.'

'None of them was. Except Hope. And don't you worry about me. Nobody'll look to me. I'm an upstanding citizen, and right now I'm out at the mall buying a teddy bear for my unborn child. A big yellow bear. Lissy's just going to love it.'

'I could never really feel you,' she murmured. 'Because there's nothing there to feel. You're almost blank inside.'

'I wondered about that. Gave me some bad moments. I took your hand today, a kind of test, just to see. You got nothing from me. But you're going to feel me, before we're done. Why don't you run, the way she did? You know how she ran, and called out. I'll give you a chance.'

'No. I'll give myself one.' Without an instant's hesitation, she stabbed out with the stick, aiming for his eye.

When he screamed, she ran as Hope had done.

The moss tangled in her hair, slithering spider legs, and the ground sucked greedily at her feet. Her shoes slithered, tearing through soaked ferns as she batted viciously at branches.

She saw as Hope had seen, the two images blending into one. Hot summer night merging with steamy afternoon. And felt as Hope had felt, with her own fear and rage leaping just ahead of the childhood terror.

She heard as Hope had heard, the footsteps pounding behind her, the thrashing through the brush.

It was the rage that stopped her, that made her turn before the intent was clear in her mind. It seared through her, black as pitch, as she charged him with teeth and claws.

Stunned by the sudden attack, half blind from the blood, he went down beneath her, howling as she sank her teeth into his shoulder. He struck out, felt the blow connect, but she clung like a burr, raking her nails down his face.

None of the others had been able to fight him, but she would. God, she would.

I am Tory. The words were a battle cry ringing in her ears. She was Tory, and she would fight.

Even when his hands closed around her throat, she tore at him. When her vision grayed, when she was gasping for air, she used her fists.

Someone was shouting her name, wild, desperate calls that echoed inside the roar of blood in her head. She clawed at the hands around her throat, choking when the grip loosened. 'I feel you now. Fear and pain. Now you know. Now you know, you bastard.'

She was being lifted away, and she fought mindlessly, her gaze locked on Dwight's face. Blood ran from his eye, and his cheeks were ripped from her hands.

'Now you know. Now you know.'

'Tory. Stop. Stop. Look at me.'

His face white and running with sweat, Cade held hers until her eyes cleared.

'He killed her. It was always him. I never saw it. He's hated you his whole life. He's hated all of you.'

'You're hurt.'

'No, I'm not. It's his blood.'

'Cade. My God, she went crazy.' Coughing, Dwight rolled to his side, struggled up to hands and knees. It felt as if he were bleeding from a thousand wounds. His right eye was a burning coal. But his mind worked, and worked fast and cool. 'She thought I was her father.'

'Liar!' Rage bloomed again and had her struggling wildly against Cade. 'He killed Hope. He was waiting here for me.'

'Killed Hope?' Blood dripped from his torn mouth as Dwight sank back on his knees. 'That was almost twenty years ago. She's sick, Cade. Anybody could see she's sick. Jesus, my eye. You have to help me.'

He tried to get to his feet and was genuinely shocked when his legs wouldn't hold him. 'For God's sake, Cade, call an ambulance. I'm going to lose my fucking eye.'

'You knew they came here.' Cade kept Tory's arms pinned as he studied the ravaged face of his old friend. 'You knew they snuck out at night to come in here. I told you myself. We laughed about it.'

'What does that have to do with anything?' Dwight's good eye wheeled as he heard the slash of wet branches. Carl D., panting with the effort, pushed through the brush. 'Thank Christ. Chief, call an ambulance. Tory had some kind of breakdown. Look what she did to me.'

'Sweet Jesus Christ,' Carl D. muttered, as he hurried forward to Dwight's side.

'He wanted me to run. But I've stopped running.' Tory stopped struggling and lay a hand over Cade's as Carl D. crouched to tie his handkerchief over Dwight's ruined eye. 'He killed Hope, and the others. He killed my mother.'

'I tell you, she's crazy,' Dwight shouted. He couldn't see. Goddamn it, he couldn't see. His teeth began to chatter. 'She can't face what her father did.'

'We'll get you to the hospital, Dwight, then we'll sort this all out.' Carl D. looked over at Tory. 'Are you hurt?'

'No, I'm not hurt. You don't want to believe me. You don't want to believe what he is has been living side by side with you all these years. But it has. It found a way.'

She shifted, met Cade's eyes. 'I'm sorry.'

'I don't want to believe you, either. But I do.'

'I know it.' And drawing on that, she got to her feet. 'The gun he killed my mother with is in the attic of his house, up in the rafters on the south side.' Gently, she rubbed a hand over her throat where the violence of his fingers left their mark. 'You made a mistake, Dwight, letting me in that far, getting that close. Should've been more careful with your thoughts.'

'She's lying. She planted it there herself. She's crazy.' He stumbled as Carl D. pulled him to his feet. 'Cade, we've been friends all our lives. You have to believe me.'

'There's something you have to believe,' Cade told him. 'If I'd gotten here sooner, you'd be dead now. You believe that. And you remember it.'

'You gotta come on with me now, Dwight.' Carl D. snapped cuffs over his wrists.

'What're you doing? What the hell are you doing? You're taking the word of a crazy woman over mine?'

'That gun isn't where she said, or it doesn't match what was used to kill a young police officer and a helpless woman, I'll give you a big apology. Come on with me. Miss Tory, you best go on to the hospital yourself.'

'No.' She wiped the blood off her mouth with the back of her hand. 'I haven't done what I came to do.'

'You go ahead,' Carl D. told them. 'I'll take care of this. Miss Tory, I'll be by later to see you.'

'She's crazy.' Dwight screamed it, kept screaming it as Carl D. pulled him away.

'He's insulted.' With a shaky laugh, Tory pressed her fingers to her eyes. 'That's the primary emotion running through him right now. Insult, that he would be treated like a criminal. It's even bigger than the hate and the hunger.'

'Step back from him,' Cade demanded. 'Don't look at him.'

'You're right, Cade. You're right.'

'Second time I almost lost you. I'll be damned if it'll ever happen again.'

'You believed me,' Tory murmured. 'I could feel how it hurt you, but you believed me. I can't tell you what that means.' She put her arms around him, held tight. 'You loved him. I'm so sorry.'

'I didn't even know him.' And still, Cade grieved. 'If I could go back—'

'We can't. I've spent a lot of time learning that.'

'Your face is bruised.' He turned his lips to it.

'His is worse.' She leaned her head against his shoulder as they began to walk. 'I was running, and I was going to keep on running, then, all at once there was this life inside me. This rage of life. He wasn't going to win, he wasn't going to chase me like a fox after a rabbit. For once, he was going to know what it was like. He was going to know.'

He would never get the picture completely out of his head, Cade knew. Of Tory, her face bruised and bloody, tearing like a cat at Dwight. And his hands around her throat.

'He'll keep denying,' Cade said. 'He'll hire lawyers. But it won't matter. In the end, it won't matter what he does.'

'No. I think you can depend on Agent Williams to tie it all up. Poor Lissy.' She sighed. 'What will she do?'

Tory stopped in the clearing to gather the fallen flowers. The fire had burned down to sputters, and the light, watery streams of it, slanted through the trees. 'I'll come back and do this another time with Faith. This time is for you and me.' Together they walked to the banks of the river.

'We loved her, and we'll always remember her.' Tory tossed flowers on the water. 'But it's over now. Finally. I've waited so long to say goodbye.'

She had tears in her yet, but they were quiet, and they were healing. They glimmered on her cheeks as she turned to Cade. 'I'd like to marry you in the garden tomorrow, and wear my grandmother's dress.'

He took her hand, kissed it. 'Would you?'

'Yes, I would. Yes, I very much would. And I'd like to go to Paris with you, and sit at a table in the sunlight and drink wine, make love with you when the sun's coming up. Then I want to come back here and build a life with you.'

'We're already building one.'

He drew her close. The sun shimmered in thin beams, and moss dripped with rain.

Flowers, bright blossoms, floated silently down the river.

Other bestselling titles available by mail: